MW01400731

TITAN IV SABOTAGE

TITAN IV SABOTAGE

Douglas Keith Swift

To Bill
Douglas Keith Swift

NPI

Northwest Publishing, Inc.
Salt Lake City, Utah

Titan IV Sabotage

This is a work of fiction.
All characters and events portrayed in this book are fictional, and any resemblance to real people or incidents is purely coincidental.

For information address: Northwest Publishing, Inc.
6906 South 300 West, Salt Lake City, Utah 84047

JC 08 16 94

PRINTING HISTORY
First Printing 1994

ISBN: 1-56901-328-4

NPI books are published by Northwest Publishing, Incorporated, 6906 South 300 West, Salt Lake City, Utah 84047.
The name "NPI" and the "NPI" logo are trademarks belonging to Northwest Publishing, Incorporated.

PRINTED IN THE UNITED STATES OF AMERICA.
10 9 8 7 6 5 4 3 2 1

1

Tuesday, January 23, a small but intricately complex satellite circles high above the geodetic surface of the Earth. In a highly elliptical orbit, the billion dollar American space vehicle has an apogee altitude of over 39,000 kilometers. Designated as SIGS-1, this deep space satellite is one in a constellation of three, helping provide a vital link in the coverage of a troubled area on the surface of the planet, the Russian subcontinent.

Ironically, these specialized orbits, used by the American military for espionage purposes, were initially discovered by Russian orbital astrodynamicists. With a majority of the Soviet Union lying at northern latitudes the typical geosynchronous orbit, which favored near equatorial latitudes, was proving insufficient for their peculiar needs. An extremely elliptical orbit was the ideal solution. With perigee passing close to the Earth along the southern hemispheres, the apogee would be conversely far out in space. When oriented with apogee over the northern Soviet landmass, a satellite in these orbits could obtain long dwell times above the Russian Empire.

These unique orbits were initially used exclusively by the

Soviet Union for communication satellites; however, they soon attracted the attention of another type of satellite user, the American spy masters.

Used to keep watch on the activities of fellow nations, America has three types of satellites in its space-based arsenal. The first category is the ultra-sensitive infrared detection systems, valuable primarily for early warning and tracking of Russian nuclear attacks. These are capable of detecting heat signatures from a multitude of targets, such as jet aircraft or ICBM missiles. Another type is the well-publicized super-sensitive optical photographic satellite. The third type, less well-known, but of infinitely greater worth, is the electronic signal gathering satellite.

SIGS-1 was a Signal Intelligence Gathering System (SIGS*) spy satellite. Built for the Department of Defense under government contract, it was deployed in orbit under a cloak of secrecy. SIGS-1's mission in life was to spy on Russia and her allies for the cause of democracy, the American way of life, and to enhance the political and military careers of America's current leaders.

Unfortunately, all was not well with SIGS-1. After five unblemished years of faultless total devotion, SIGS-1 was sick. The satellite's combined earth sensors, the CES, used to maintain attitude and critical pointing with respect to the center of the Earth, had become suddenly dysfunctional. Losing earth-lock, the billion dollar satellite had commenced a sporadic tumble.

SIGS-1 was out of control, spinning at a rate that exceeded the capability of its reaction wheel control loops. SIGS-1 needed help, but all was not lost, her human creators were not totally unmindful of their precious child in space.

Situated in the heart of California's fabulous Silicon Valley, buried within the confines of an air force installation called CSTC, the Consolidated Space Test Center, was a specialized but obscure MCC, a Mission Control Center, dedicated to the monitoring and control of the SIGS constellation.

Technical Sergeant Andres Rameriz stifled the urge to yawn and quietly took up his position behind a telemetry monitoring console. He wondered if a person ever became truly accustomed to the graveyard shift. Regardless of how much he slept, hitting the sack seemed always on his mind.

SIGS-1 was scheduled for a 600 minute pass with the rise time at 1117 hours GMT, which was 0317 hours local PST. Bored with

* Refer to acronym key beginning on page 455.

the dull paceless monotony of his job, baby-sitting flying hunks of temperamental metal in space, monitoring CRT (cathode ray tube) terminals at all hours of the day and night, Rameriz strained to focus his weary eyes on the screen. He waited, watching for the arrays of numerical data to appear as SIGS-1 crested the horizon.

"Siggie's running late today," Rameriz called to Rob Burns, his contractor support representative, a civilian.

Three-seventeen, three-eighteen, three-nineteen, the minutes passed by with no acquisition. Nothing to worry about though, perturbations in the Earth's atmosphere often caused delays in tracking station acquisitions. The satellite was a long ways up there.

"Here she is," Rameriz breathed a heavy sigh of relief as a flood of numbers suddenly filled the screen before his anxious eyes.

But no, all was not well, something was wrong, dangerously wrong. The majority of digits on his screen were flashing and most had a warning asterisk to the side. Why, almost every single telemetry parameter was out of tolerance!

"Look at this, Burns," Andres Rameriz called with alarm to his civilian colleague, but before the Lockheed engineer could reach Rameriz's side, the telemetry data froze.

"We've lost acquisition," Rameriz lamented, pointing to the columns of unchanging numbers on his console. "And just look at the last values of those parameters, Siggie's gone crazy."

Without warning the data stream commenced again, causing the static values on Rameriz's monitor to begin updating once more. "What in tarnation?" Rameriz stared with bewilderment at his CRT.

"The satellite is tumbling," Rod Burns spoke from experience, the calm level tone of his voice contrasting sharply against the excited pitch of the sergeant's words. A tumbling satellite was nothing new to Rod Burns. Now in his fifties, he had lived the past two decades monitoring these sometimes unpredictable orbital machines.

"No, it cannot be!" Andres Rameriz expressed his concern with unabated alarm. New to CSTC, this was Rameriz's first on-orbit anomalous condition.

"Believe it," Burns commented sternly. He had seen worse anomalies, a tumbling satellite could be recovered.

"But, what can we do?" Rameriz questioned.

"Read your OOH (orbital operations handbook). We simply monitor the satellite through this pass to collect data, and then command the appropriate recovery sequence on the next pass. It's easy, we'll spin up the SV (satellite vehicle) about the Z-axis to effect a spin stabilized vehicle, and then execute the normal de-spin, earth acquisition, and finally sun acquisition procedures. With the proper RCS (reaction control system) thruster firings, we should be able to stabilize Siggie, no problem."

Rod Burns noticed his blue-suiter friend's fears were not to be so easily placated. "Better call the colonel," Burns recommended.

Andres Rameriz grimaced at the thought. Rising stiffly, he moved to another console and reached for the red phone. "Call the colonel," he anguished, imagining what Colonel Glaser would think. Shoot, the general would have to hear about this one. With SIGS-3 operating in a degraded state, they could hardly afford to lose SIGS-1.

Why did Siggie have to act up now? Why on his shift? Gulping audibly, Andres Rameriz lifted the receiver to Colonel Glaser's direct-line red phone.

2

"This heat makes me crazy," John Hughes muttered audibly, swerving his old commuter Escort into the front driveway of his home. John lived in a ranchstyle suburban house of common tract design at 7338 74th East Avenue in the south part of beautiful cosmopolitan Tulsa. Switching off the ignition to his car's economy-class engine, he sat motionless for a few minutes, tired of the routine.

As the stagnant heat began to build within the now motionless car, John's lethargic feelings were soon overcome and he was driven out into the burning Oklahoma sun. He stood surveying his front lawn with disdain. The grass begged to be mowed. He would not get to it that day though, not with such heavy humidity in the air. Besides, there were clouds on the horizon and it might rain later that evening. It really wasn't a good day for yard work anyway.

John felt tired. Not that his day had been that busy at the office, just the opposite in fact. If anything there was too little work, certainly not enough to justify his pay. Lately he had found himself feeling worn-out and tired more and more frequently. Life had become a boring routine and he felt neither the strength nor the energy to cope with everyday aggravations.

With a sigh John pushed through the unlocked front door to his home. At least now he could loose his tie and change into something more comfortable, perhaps a sweat suit. The mail was littered across a small hall-table just inside the doorway. John checked to see if Eleanor had left him anything of interest. No, she had taken all the letters and bills, leaving only junk mail.

Before John could move on, a small perky child rounded the corner, investigating the noise of John's entry with knowing curiosity. It was Chrissy, John's oldest, a shy seven-year-old little girl. Small for her age, Chrissy was lovable, but not very outgoing. She was the stay-at-home type, preferring the company of family and the TV over playing outside with friends.

"Daddy, Daddy," Chrissy shrieked loudly and ran toward her father with outstretched arms. It was Chrissy's typical reaction when her daddy arrived home from a day at work. John knew the show of affection wasn't spontaneous, but was done out of habit to derive attention. Regardless, he loved playing the role of hero for his little girl. Placing his briefcase on the floor, John lifted Chrissy up into the air and hugged her affectionately.

At the sound of more small footsteps padding down the hallway, Chrissy possessively squeezed her daddy all the tighter. Around the corner came Billy, Chrissy's younger brother. When Billy spotted the two of them, he too called out "Daddy, Daddy," mimicking his older sister with precision, and then ran toward them with outstretched arms.

John returned Chrissy gently to the floor and picked up Billy instead. Billy was John's little toddler and the youngest always had priority rights on being held. After all, dear Chrissy had received two years of being the only child. As John brought Billy to his chest, the little fellow hugged him affectionately. Chrissy stood by her father's side smiling contentedly, she knew the routine. Placing a hand on daddy's forearm, she was rewarded as he shifted Billy's weight to his opposite arm and took her hand into his large palm.

John leaned back to distribute the boy's weight more onto his chest. Billy was getting heavy fast. Funny how stocky and heavyset the lad was, his older sister was all gangly arms and legs. Although two years younger, Billy already weighed nearly as much as Chrissy and lifting him was like taking hold of a solid mass.

John hesitated, wondering if Eleanor would come to greet him also, but no; she seldom did these days. Eleanor never had been one to show a lot of outward affection.

Lumbering down the short hallway to the master bedroom, John took joy in the adoring attention of his little ones. He entered the familiar bedroom and rounded a corner into the walk-in closet. Chrissy halted just out of view, circumspectly respecting her father's privacy.

"I get to come in while you change because I'm a boy, right, Daddy?" Billy chirped proudly, as John placed him on the floor. John saw his sweats were dirty. Instead he selected a pair of jeans and a striped pullover shirt with a tiny dolphin sewn on the chest.

"Whatever you say, Billy," John tousled his son's hair and smiled at him with amusement.

"No, Billy," Chrissy huffily corrected her little brother from around the corner. "It's just that I know enough to wait out here. Daddy likes to dress in private, right, Daddy?"

"That's right, Chrissy," John called to her. He saw nothing wrong in agreeing with them both.

"Come out of the closet, Billy!" Chrissy demanded righteously. John thought it funny how older children, sometimes even when misbehaving themselves, wanted their younger siblings to act with perfect conformity to the rules.

"No!" Billy resisted his sister obstinately, the volume of his voice rising. He suddenly wrapped his arms around John's leg as if to hang on for dear life.

"It's okay, Billy, you can stay," John pried the tot's arms away. "Chrissy, don't worry about what Billy does, he's only five."

"He should know better," Chrissy pouted, but at least she relinquished her demands.

"I'm hungry, let's go see what's for dinner," John spoke with exaggerated enthusiasm, for his children's amusement. He pulled on a comfortable pair of moccasin slippers as he stepped out of the closet and patted Chrissy on her stomach, causing her to giggle. "How's that tummy of yours, feels pretty empty to me?"

The three of them marched as a troop toward the kitchen. As they passed the family room with its continuously playing TV, they lost Billy, distracted by cartoons. Eleanor stood in the kitchen with her back toward them, working on a meatloaf.

"Hi, dear, I'm home," John called to his wife. Dinner was going to be late, he thought; she hadn't even put the meatloaf in to cook yet. He felt a sudden pang of hunger in his stomach.

"I know, I heard you come in," Eleanor answered, without turning to face her husband.

Knowing Eleanor could not see him, John stared openly at his wife's slender figure. He liked the way she looked. Eleanor wore a light chartreuse blouse, through which he could see the strap of a white bra across her inclined back. She also wore a tight pair of faded jeans, probably shrunken by too many washings, or else she had put on a few extra pounds since their purchase. Approaching from behind, John circled her, thinking to give his wife a kiss. She disappointed him though, tilting her head in a manner that only offered a cheek.

Upon receiving the traditional spousely peck, Eleanor returned her attention to the meatloaf. "You forgot to take the trash cans out to the curb this morning," Eleanor chastened her husband in a weary voice. "You know Tuesday is pick-up day."

"I was rushed," John rationalized, stepping back to recover a full view of Eleanor's curvy figure.

"Well, Chrissy and Billy had a hard time dragging the bulky trash cans out to the curb," Eleanor continued. "They complained it was extra heavy this time."

"Why didn't you do it?" John sulked, feeling defensive. He turned to exit the kitchen.

"It's not my responsibility," Eleanor countered, matter-of-factly.

"And I suppose you told them it was my fault they had to take the trash out," John groused, irritation rising in his voice.

"It was your fault!" Eleanor retorted. "You need to fulfill your family responsibilities, dear."

John could just imagine how it went, "Chrissy, take the trash out, Daddy forgot again!"

Suddenly Eleanor turned, looking her husband in the face for the first time. "John, you have got to do something about Billy. Today he took all his clothes off, outside, in the front yard, and was playing with the garden hose stark naked."

"Nobody cares, he's only five."

"Nobody cares…one of the neighbors came to our house and told me, Mrs. Riggs. You need to talk with Billy, it is a father's responsibility!"

The hunger pang in John's stomach was turning into a dull ache. Silently escorting Chrissy out of the kitchen, John sank into their large, well-used, family room couch. Chrissy climbed contentedly onto his lap.

The TV dominated the room. A frustrated wolf was trying to catch his nemesis, a desert road runner, with sticks of dynamite. Every time, the wolf invariably blew up himself instead.

Billy, totally delighted with the show, moved from the floor to the couch without taking his eyes off the screen. He ran into trouble trying to evict Chrissy from her daddy's lap though. John diplomatically slid Chrissy over to his side, snuggling her close against him, and then lifted little Billy onto his lap.

"Well?" Eleanor had followed them into the family room. She held her hands out to the side at an odd angle, they were caked with raw sticky hamburger grease. "I don't think you are teaching Billy about modesty, John."

"I have to go out tonight," John changed the subject. He wished Eleanor would not be so critical in front of the children.

"Out, what do you mean go out?"

"I have a meeting."

"What kind of meeting?" Eleanor was suspicious that John was just speaking out of anger, he never went out at night.

"A work meeting," John answered, puzzling Eleanor all the more. That would be a first, he never had work meetings in the evening. If he had to stay late at the office, he typically remained after hours. He never came home first and then left after supper.

Eleanor knew very little about her husband's job, just that he was employed as an aerospace engineer at Krang Enterprises, and that he worked on one of the space programs, with rockets and satellites and things. He called himself a professional Integrator, whatever that was, and he had an advanced degree in astronautical engineering, orbital mechanics, from Oklahoma State University.

Eleanor never asked John about his work. He had always been kind of secretive about it anyway, ever since graduating from OSU and accepting employment in Tulsa at Krang Enterprises, good old KE. He told her once that he wasn't supposed to talk about work, company proprietary or secret or something. She wasn't that interested anyway.

"What time is your meeting?" Eleanor asked. "You know Chrissy has a T-ball game this evening."

John groaned, he hated going to those T-ball games. Chrissy was the smallest one on the team and they always put her way out in right field, or else she sat on the bench. When she got her turn at bat, she usually struck out, even though the ball was stationary on a rubber T. Eleanor insisted that Chrissy play though, it didn't matter if Chrissy was not the least bit interested in sports. Eleanor wanted her to be more outgoing, more involved in physical activities.

"Guess I'll have to miss this one," John mumbled.

Eleanor was upset. She did not think it right for John to miss T-ball games, not without an extremely good reason. "What time is your meeting?" she repeated her question, suspicious he didn't really have one.

"Whenever I get around to going, we are meeting at the apartment of another engineer from my office and will start whenever I get there."

"Why don't you go right now? If you get done early, perhaps you can catch up with us at the game."

"I haven't had supper yet," John complained.

"Sacrifice a little for the family, John, skip supper. You don't want to take up family time do you?"

"Eating dinner together is family time."

"You know what I mean!"

"All right," John rose from the couch in exasperation. "I'll go now if you want."

Eleanor nodded her head in the affirmative, at least she could have that concession.

John retrieved his car keys from the bedroom and left for his meeting. He didn't bother leaving Eleanor a good-bye kiss, they had long since gotten out of the habit.

It was still sweltering outside, hot and muggy. Situated in the northeast corner of Oklahoma, near the foothills of the Ozark Mountains, summer days in Tulsa were sometimes unbearable. John noticed the grass on his frontyard turning brown in some spots. So why fuss over mowing it anyway. In Phoenix, where his parents now lived, a lot of the yards were composed of colored rock and gravel. That would be nice.

Driving to a nearby Wendy's fast-food restaurant, John ordered a chicken sandwich, french fries, and a Frosty to go. He wasn't going to skip supper just because Eleanor was being unreasonable. Putting a little food on his stomach, especially the chocolate Frosty, helped to calm his frustration.

A short distance down Sheridan he drove onto the entrance

ramp of the Broken Arrow Expressway heading downtown. Once his speed settled at sixty mph, John pulled a crumpled note from his pocket to confirm the address in his mind. His destination had to be close to the center of town, maybe near the river, 1147 South Quaker, #6, the Achen Apartments. John was curious why any KE employee would want to live in downtown Tulsa when their factory was located out in the suburbs near Broken Arrow.

Everything about this whole affair was strange indeed. He played the events over again in his mind. It had started earlier that day, when he had received a mysterious phone call at lunchtime.

"Hello," John had answered. Because of security rules they weren't allowed to answer in a typical office manner, one that announced the company or division which the caller had reached.

"John Hughes, is that you?" a familiar older man's voice queried.

"Who is this?" John asked in amazement, recognizing the voice but not believing it.

"It's me, Goldsmith."

"Bernie Goldsmith," John almost dropped the sandwich grasped lightly in one hand. The office had not seen or heard from Bernie Goldsmith in months.

"Shhh," the voice cautioned. "John, are you alone?"

"Yes," John answered, looking around the room. John realized that Goldsmith would have expected him to be alone at that hour. John's normal habit was to eat a sack lunch at his desk during the noon break, a lunch he had to prepare for himself each morning. Eleanor would not make John's lunches for him. 'I'm not your slave!' she would say.

Most everyone else in the office went out to eat, either to the cafeteria or off-plant, and some took the opportunity to exercise, either going jogging or for long walks. John however would sit quietly at his desk and read from a good novel, science fiction was his favorite, while eating his lunch. It was always the same, a sandwich and piece of fruit. He used to lift Nautilus weights at the company gym during lunchtime, but he had tired of that.

Bernie Goldsmith knew John's habits because they had worked in the same group on the same project ever since John had hired on with Krang Enterprises. For the past two years they had shared a cubicle with adjoining desks. Goldsmith probably knew more about John's work patterns than anyone else.

"Where have you been?" John questioned incredulously.

Goldsmith's sudden disappearance had been a topic of much discussion at the office, a great mystery. Goldsmith had left work two hours early one day, approximately four months ago, and never returned. There was no letter of resignation, no request for vacation, no phone call, nothing; he had simply disappeared. When the secretary had called his home a day later, there was no answer; his wife had vanished with him.

"Never mind," Goldsmith sounded extremely agitated, like he was under a tremendous strain. "John, don't tell anyone I've called, okay?" Then, after a silence, with desperation in his voice, "John, promise me you won't tell anyone I called."

"I promise, I promise!" John consoled him. Bernie Goldsmith was a peculiar man, an elderly Jewish engineer in his late fifties. For the past year his health had been failing and John feared to upset him. If Goldsmith wanted him to keep the call confidential, then he would do so, they got plenty of practice in keeping secrets at KE.

"Good," Goldsmith sounded relieved; even so, his breathing was still strained and heavy.

"What is going on, Bernie?"

"We have to talk."

"Go ahead, I'm listening."

"No, in person."

"Why?"

"Please, John, can you come to my apartment? You must come tonight."

"I suppose. What's this all about?"

"Thanks John, I knew you would help. My address is 1147 South Quaker, the Achen Apartments, #6. Come alone!" Goldsmith was suddenly having a hard time speaking, a coughing spell making him sound almost incoherent.

"Okay, Bernie, I'll be there, but can't you tell me what's going on?"

"I will, come as soon as you can," Goldsmith hung up the receiver without saying good-bye.

As John parked alongside the curb in front of an old decaying apartment building, rechecking the address against the one given by Bernie Goldsmith, he became all the more curious. It definitely was not the type of apartment complex he had expected to find, nor was the neighborhood as anticipated. Standing before John, in a depressed sector of Tulsa, was an old, decaying, painted brick building, two stories, with only eight units.

John had expected a modern upscale condo development rather than the type of housing where welfare families or social security elderly might live. A man of Bernie Goldsmith's station in life could surely afford much better. Goldsmith was an aerospace engineer, a "Grade 20" at Krang Enterprises with over thirty years of seniority. Why was Goldsmith living in the low-income slums?

John stepped out of his car, making double sure the doors were all locked, even though it was unlikely even the most hard-up thief would look twice at the old Escort.

Entering the front doorway of Achen Apartments, John climbed a set of creaking stairs to the second level. The hallways were well kept, had recently-painted walls and frequently-swept linoleum flooring. Even so, cleanliness could not mask the depression of age and previous years of neglect.

John checked his note again to make sure before knocking, unit number six. Through the peephole in the door he could see light. Someone had to be home. There were no TV sounds coming from inside though.

Rapping loudly upon the door, John nervously glanced about the dark hallway, worried that his noise might attract unwanted attention. The environment made John apprehensive of muggers. Fortunately there was no one else about.

When the door creaked open, there stood Bernie Goldsmith, beckoning John to enter. After coaxing John inside, Goldsmith hastily shut the door, threw the deadbolt, and fastened a door chain. His actions added to John's misgivings.

Astonished at the old man's appearance, John involuntarily stepped back. Goldsmith was obviously sick and had not been keeping himself up. His clothes were dirty and wrinkled, with stains all along the front of his shirt, he hadn't shaved in days, and his normally well-groomed stock of silver hair was uncombed and scraggly. On Goldsmith's head was a small black Jewish cap. John had never seen the man wear one of those before.

Worse than his clothes or grooming, was Goldsmith's haggard face; his features were thin and drawn, bloodshot eyes, even an odd yellowish tint to the old fellow's skin. Goldsmith would have fit right in with the street bums and winos one might find lying in the gutter. Was this the highly paid, Grade 20, professional engineer John had once known?

Glancing around the stark meagerly furnished apartment, John was disturbed to see an environment that matched the man. The furniture was secondhand, run-down, and broken. A scene of total neglect, there were dishes in the sink, leftover food on a dirty unbalanced table in the kitchen, an open bottle of wine and one glass on a cluttered coffee table. There were no pictures on the walls, only some posters with Hebrew script.

"For heavens sake Bernie, what's happened to you?" John exclaimed, overcoming his shock enough to speak.

Goldsmith shuffled over to the coffee table, hardly lifting his feet enough to step. Pouring himself a glass of cheap wine, he gulped it down. John shook his head negatively when Goldsmith raised his glass in an offer. He couldn't help but notice the shaking in Goldsmith's hands.

The wine seemed to steady him somewhat. "I have been sick," Goldsmith spoke.

"I can tell."

Goldsmith's eyes narrowed, "Did anyone follow you?"

"What?" John frowned. "Why would anyone follow me?"

"Did you see anyone following you?" Goldsmith said again, more loudly. He seemed serious.

"How would I know? No, I didn't see anyone."

Goldsmith tried to manage a smile, his teeth were stained from coffee. "Thanks for coming, John. I need your help."

"Sure, Bernie, what can I do?" John wondered how much money Goldsmith needed. How had a professional aerospace engineer come to live in such an impoverished condition? Where was his wife? Why weren't his children helping out?

"Where to begin," Goldsmith moaned. "I cannot go on alone. I need help, I'm just an old man."

"Calm down, it's okay," John spoke reassuringly. Goldsmith had always been high-strung, the nervously worried type.

Back when he worked at KE, Goldsmith had never been very good at stress, never able to relax. Whenever behind schedule with an assignment, or faced with difficulties, whenever under pressure, Goldsmith was sure to overreact. During such times he would often spend excessive, usually wasteful, hours at the office, as if his mere presence could solve his problems. As Goldsmith's age advanced in years, his assignments become more mundane, more predictable, the high-pressure jobs having been relegated to others.

Bernie Goldsmith fixed John with an intense stare, his eyes glazed from alcohol, "When is the next launch scheduled?" he asked suddenly.

Taken back with surprise, John could scarcely believe his ears. "We cannot talk of such matters outside a secure environment," he whispered. To do so would be a breach of security. They worked on a military satellite project that was cloaked with an elaborate, highly secretive, classification system. One important fact that was always protected, was the launch date.

"Come on, John," Goldsmith pressed. "You know I'm cleared. Is it still set for the spring of next year?"

"You know the rules," John answered resolutely, now really worried about his former office friend. Had Goldsmith become so lax he was no longer reliable? Was the wine affecting his judgment to the point he could not be trusted with national secrets?

Goldsmith didn't know about the recent acceleration to their launch schedule. He was still thinking of the old manifest date in the spring, a year away. The current ILC (Initial Launch Capability) for their next launch had actually moved forward to August 31, barely two and a half months away, but John was not about to disclose that fact. Typically launch dates could be expected to slide several times to the right before the big day actually arrived, but an on-orbit failure had left their constellation in jeopardy and their schedule had been accelerated. August 31 was now the start date for the opening of their first launch window.

"You are in enough trouble with security already," John cautioned the old man. "Let's not compound matters by talking about classified information outside the office."

"Ahhh," Goldsmith responded and coughed. "Security doesn't know anything. Those people are a bunch of fools. It's ludicrous, they have no idea what they are really protecting."

"Security has been asking questions about you," John cautioned.

"What?"

"Investigating your disappearance, Bernie. You can't just walk away without any explanations and not cause concern. Why didn't you tell anyone you weren't coming back? Why didn't you tell us you were quitting, and also moving?"

"I couldn't," Goldsmith responded and shuffled toward an overworn couch. He slumped into the cushions like a sack of heavy groceries.

John felt a surge of compassion, "I came to help you, Bernie. What's the cause of all this?"

Reaching for a small gilded box next to a lamp on the end table, Goldsmith produced a short fat cigar. Lighting up, he drew a few short puffs, hardly inhaling. A sweet sickly smell filled the air of that poorly ventilated room, offending John's nose.

"For the past couple of years, one of my main functions has been integration of potential add-on payloads, piggybacks," Goldsmith began. He looked toward a framed travel poster of the Wailing Wall in Jerusalem, as if talking to the picture instead of his guest.

"Secondary payloads," John prodded. "We do have excess weight margin." Whenever satellites weighed less than the capacity of the booster rocket they became candidates for small secondary payloads, sometimes attached permanently to the main satellite bus, sometimes ejectable during ascent to final orbit.

"That's the problem," Goldsmith inhaled too rapidly and began coughing again.

"What, a piggyback? How is that a problem?"

"Just wait and I'll explain. Let me give you the background first."

"Whatever you say, Bernie."

"Do you remember...around the first of the year...I made a trip to Los Angeles, to attend the CDR (Critical Design Review) for a new piggyback?"

"Sure," John remembered, it was about the time that Goldsmith's erratic behavior had first begun. On the following Monday Goldsmith had called in for a week's vacation. When he finally did return to work, he had not seemed well, more nervous than usual, tired. Over the next few weeks Goldsmith had seemed to deteriorate very rapidly, aging right before their eyes, till that one fateful day when he disappeared from work. People had commented how they had seen it coming.

"Well, this piggyback is slated for our next satellite," Goldsmith continued. "On the last day of the design review, after all the integration items had been summarized very neatly, everything looked well, hardly any action items had been written, and then they called a special topics meeting."

"Special topics?" John started getting nervous again. "You mean restricted attendance?" These were things one just did not talk about, not outside a secure office area.

"Exactly, I was talking to an associate and didn't hear the announcement."

Probably dozed off, John thought, knowing Goldsmith.

"I saw people leaving the conference room, but thought I would stay and see what this carryover meeting was about. When they shut the doors and started the closed session, I was still inside, but no one seemed to notice, or else they assumed I had the proper clearance."

"Wow!" John exclaimed. "A compartment you weren't briefed for." It was typical on top-secret missions to have separate compartments for various aspects of the project. Only those people directly needed to work in a particular compartment were briefed to handle or see compartment information.

"Didn't they state the clearance level at the start of the meeting?" John asked.

"They did," Goldsmith shook his head sadly. "But by then I was too embarrassed to leave. Just hearing the code words was already a violation."

"So you stayed!" John exclaimed. Amazing as the event was, John understood Goldsmith's fear. Two or three violations and a person would lose his job. People like Goldsmith, nearing retirement after twenty or thirty years with a company, often became paranoid about security violations.

"I stayed for the entire confounded briefing," Goldsmith closed his eyes, as if trying to shut out the memory of what he had seen.

"You compromised that compartment."

"Yes, and I wish the God of my fathers had struck me dead on the spot."

"Did you report it later?"

"No, that would have been a big error, possibly fatal."

"Come on, keeping it secret is not doing wonders for your health." John did not realize Goldsmith was serious.

"Would I lie, John? You know me, Abraham forbid."

"So you feel bad about what happened. Bernie, there is no sense ruining your health and your career because you made a mistake."

"No...there is more."

"What?" John pitied the old fellow. Working on secret government projects was beyond the capability of some people, the stress, the deception, it preyed on their minds.

"It's what they are building, John. What they, no WE, are putting up into space. It's an abomination, and we are ALL responsible. To think we are building the mother satellite to carry those things."

"What things?"

"The piggybacks, SPL-551 (secondary payload), one of them is going on our next flight."

"What are they for?" John asked, then hesitated. "No wait, don't tell me. If you tell me then I will be in violation too."

"You have to know, John, this thing is bigger than you or me. Personal concerns are trivial in comparison. You have to know."

"Go ahead," John said, his curiosity level now too high to contain. Besides, what further harm could be done. If it came down to it, how could he be blamed for listening to the rambling of a deranged old man.

"It's called DWARS, a DWARS virus," Bernie pronounced the acronym as if it was a distasteful word.

"DWARS virus?" John was unfamiliar with the term.

"Yes, DWARS, Dormant Womb Activated Reproductive Sterilization. It's a virus, John, the most horrible virus ever conceived. To think, Moses forbid, it is man-made."

"Bernie, you are crazy. No one puts viruses on satellites. What would be the purpose? How would they live?"

"It's true, John. I wish upon the Holy Land it wasn't."

"But why?"

"Biological warfare, it's the only explanation I can think of, and don't kid yourself into thinking these viruses would not survive in space." Goldsmith stood up for a moment, but then sat back down, the exertion tiring him.

"I've seen the design, not just the interface, but the interior subsystems of an SPL-551," he continued. "They are hermetically sealed from all outside environments and frozen in a state of virtual hibernation. The piggyback has its own hydrazine propulsion system and an S-band antenna to receive ground station targeting commands."

"Orbiting space-based biological weapons," John said slowly, shaking his head, refusing to believe.

"Exactly."

"But, would they survive reentry?"

"The Space Shuttle does. From orbit, with the proper coordinates, they could hit any target on Earth."

"But why space-based? We have biological weapons here on Earth that could be loaded into missiles also capable of reaching anywhere on the planet."

"I don't know," Goldsmith was starting to sweat profusely. "I can only speculate that it's because of the unpardonable evil of the DWARS virus and its repulsive effects on humans. You could never store the abominations on Earth, too risky. What if they fell into the wrong hands? What if their existence was exposed to the public or the press? Perhaps from space they hope to control their deranged weapons with absolute obscurity. Only a few people would need know they existed and terrorists could never get their hands on them. No, space is the perfect location for this abominable doomsday horror."

"I don't understand."

"Look, once they have deployed enough of these DWARS piggybacks—"

"The SPL-551s?"

"Yes! Once enough are deployed, they could destroy all Earth-based production labs and stockpiles. No one could prove anything then, you must have proof to go to the press. That's why I have not gone to the press, I have no proof. I don't know where the DWARS viruses are grown, where the labs are, anything. Once they have them up in space, it will be too late, they'll destroy all evidence."

"But what does the DWARS virus do?" This talk of going to the press with information about a classified project added a new dimension to John's worries.

"DWARS virus, Dormant Womb Activated Reproductive Sterilization virus! They attack the reproductive capability of an infected carrier's offspring. Once a person is infected with the DWARS virus, their children will all be born sterile!"

"Genocide?" John questioned.

"Yes, the perfect genocide weapon. The target would not even know she was infected until her children reached the age of puberty, or even later, till they tried and failed to have children of their own."

"A genocide weapon," John sat down next to Goldsmith, his senses reeling. He didn't even care about the dirt and filth accumulated on the cushions.

"It wipes out the third generation," Goldsmith went on. "DWARS bugs don't hurt the infected carrier generation, and the second generation appears normal at birth, but there is NO third generation. It could mean the death of whole races or nations," Goldsmith's face looked pale and ashen.

"By the time you realize the danger, it's too late," John said, feeling uncomfortably hot. The smoke, the stuffiness, he felt an urgent desire to get out of that room.

"Now you know," Goldsmith rasped, noticeably relieved. The secret had been too terrible a burden to carry alone.

"I don't believe you!" John stood up suddenly, angry at the thought.

"You must!" Goldsmith cried. "Think of our interface requirements for the piggyback, keep it out of the sun during ascent, the added thermal and vibration constraints."

"I never worked that system," John responded.

"Wait, I've got the ICD (Interface Control Document)." Goldsmith struggled to his feet and scurried into his bedroom. He returned shortly with the classified document.

John was aghast, "You can't take these documents home." "Secret" markings were plastered all over the document, front, back, and every page.

"No one knows I have it," Goldsmith brushed John's objections aside. "My last month at work, I copied lots of material. Had to, we've got to prove our case."

"We?..."

Suddenly there was a knock at the door. Startled, Goldsmith dropped the classified document.

"They're here!" Goldsmith groaned.

"Who's here?" John snatched up the classified ICD. He glanced about the room for a place to hide it.

"I am too old," Goldsmith cried. "I couldn't do it alone. I needed help."

There was another louder rap at the door, conveying a distinct message of impatience.

Goldsmith rushed up close to John's ear, whispering in a rush of alcohol reeking breath. John could barely hear the words, "Rocky Mountain National Park, at campsite Desolation, on the north side of a boulder, azimuth thirty-nine degrees, that's where I buried the rest."

"What?!" John stepped away from Goldsmith in confusion. He watched in frozen horror as Goldsmith crossed the room and opened the creaky front door of the meager apartment.

In stepped two businessmen in dark suits with red ties. They had black hair and Slavic complexions. While one man begin a check of the apartment, the taller of the two confronted Goldsmith. "I thought you were told to be alone," he growled.

"This is my associate, John Hughes," Goldsmith spoke, his voice wavering with fear as he gestured toward John. Then Goldsmith introduced the strangers to John, "These men are from the Russian Embassy."

John groaned in dismay as his hands, still clutching the top-secret classified document, began to tremble.

3

Headquarters, Central Intelligence Agency, Langley, Virginia, Dan Newby sat in a small windowless office watching the orange phone on his desk with nervous anticipation. A major operation was underway back at the regional Southwest U.S. Special Support Office, Newby's section, and he had left strict instructions for hourly field reports.

Newby glanced at his watch and blinked nervously, 6:44 P.M. The last report had come in at six o'clock, exactly on time. The operation was underway and Newby was anxious for the vital intelligence this next call would bring. A lot could take place between reports, an awful lot.

At the six o'clock report, Newby had left instructions for the seven o'clock call to be made fifteen minutes early. They were supposed to call at 6:45 instead of 7:00 P.M., but what if they forgot? It would be an easy thing to do, out of habit they were used to calling on the hour. In the excitement it would be easy to forget.

At 6:50, Dan Newby had to leave, 6:55 at the latest. He had a seven o'clock appointment with his boss, Henry Maxwell, the head of the Western Hemisphere Division under the DDO, Deputy

Director of Operations, and Newby dared not be late. That was the reason for an early report at 6:45. It was at least a five minute journey to the scheduled conference room, down several long, mauve decorated corridors, up the second of five elevators to the seventh floor, through more corridors, past special access doors.

Dan Newby was a portly man, in his late forties. He had always been afflicted by weight problems, even as a child. Not that he was obese, or even fat, just comfortably chubby, a manageable twenty or thirty pounds over the norm. Even at his age, Newby still planned and halfway strived, as he had all his life, to lose the extra weight.

Being a perfectionist by nature, a very precise and meticulous man, Newby could not rationalize even physical deficiencies. His favorite subjects were intricate and complex mind teasers, crystal structures, chess, the detailed paintings of the realists, etc. He had never accepted the excess fat as a given part of his physique.

Newby ran a tight operations Section within the CIA, a highly successful special support group composed of skilled intelligence officers, available to support short term, time critical, foreign operations in the Western Hemisphere. Highly-skilled specialists were attracted to Newby, and they felt secure working in his division. Newby was a section chief that took care of his people.

It had been a long time since his group had last run a major operation as important as the one going down that night. They had spent years in seemingly fruitless research and minor investigations getting ready; now, after years of investigation, they had a chance. It had to bear fruit, it had to pay off.

Newby stared at his wristwatch, 6:46. Agonizing, he watched the minutes digit slowly increase...47...48...where was that call? He needed an update, he needed that call. The phone on his desk was orange, a secure line on which cleared personnel could carry out classified conversations. On the hook however, it was as useless as any ordinary phone.

"Whoa!" the sudden ring startled Newby, reverberating about the room with an unusual echo.

"Hello," Newby snatched up the phone. His voice showed no emotion, calm and businesslike.

"Dan Newby please," a younger high-pitched voice queried.

"Maconey," Newby recognized the voice of his deputy, who had been left in charge of the regional office during Newby's trip to headquarters. "You're late."

"Sorry, Ostermann just phoned in a field report. I thought it important enough to wait."

Newby glanced at his watch. "Go ahead, I've got three minutes. Make it short."

Andrew Maconey sighed, "To be brief, Randy Ostermann just informed us that the accomplice, identified as John Hughes, the one we were expecting, arrived at the old Jewish engineer's apartment at 5:05 P.M. He's still there now."

"Did Goldsmith talk?"

"Yes, he's confessed to espionage, the stealing of those classified government documents."

"Good," Dan Newby was delighted, "Now he's involved the Hughes fellow too, excellent. Everything is on tape I presume?"

"We have it all chief, enough for a definite conviction. Missed one thing though."

"Important?"

"Goldsmith mentioned the location of his stash, but we couldn't pick it up."

"That's not important," Newby mused. "What about the Russians?"

"On their way up, Chief. Our men are all in position and ready. The perimeter surveillance team was in place well before Hughes arrived."

"Okay, I want a call every twenty minutes now, although I may not be in the office for a while. Who knows how long this briefing with the DDO will last, but keep ringing this number every twenty minutes."

"Right. Oh…ah…Boss?"

"Yes."

"Good luck with the DDO."

Dan Newby was satisfied, the operation was going down as planned. This positive bit of news was sure to enhance his position with the head man. Straightening his tie, Newby grabbed his suit jacket and hurried out the office door.

He had an option of going either right or left, different corridors back to the elevators. To the left he saw one of the secretaries walking down the hallway, a pretty gal wearing a short skirt. It was a bit longer that way, but the view would be nicer. Newby glanced at his watch, he had five minutes and ten seconds. Why not? Newby turned left and hurried on his way.

4

John Hughes realized he was sweating profusely. There was no time to think, his mind was spinning. Things were moving too fast, his world was being violently transfigured and he felt powerless. Could the story about the DWARS virus be true? Would anyone ever use such an abominable weapon? Who could have conceived of such a thing? biological warfare and genocide combined in an unholy marriage of horror, two of the greatest evils known to mankind.

How could Bernie Goldsmith have afflicted him with such a grievous burden? Why him of all people? He had a wife and two small children to consider, he was no great crusader with a history of fighting social injustices. He was a family man, why him? Perhaps Goldsmith had no one else to turn to for help. Over the past few years John had been his closest work associate. Perhaps Goldsmith thought of him as someone who would understand. Still, to involve someone in espionage, there was no excuse. Did he actually think John would help him with treason?

If the unthinkable actually was true, he could understand Goldsmith's desperate motivation to somehow put a stop to the effort. Goldsmith said he had no proof though, at least not enough with which to go to the press. Yet he seemed convinced the evil was a reality. So he had turned to the Russians, our enemies, a government at one time actively bent on the destruction of America, atheistic oppressors of their own people, murderers of thousands under Stalin, enslavers of whole nations. Goldsmith was mad calling in the Russians.

Glaring down at the classified document still in his hands, John noticed he was trembling again. He recognized the familiar document all too well, it was the main ICD, the Interface Control Document between the satellite vehicle and the Titan IV Launch Vehicle. Should this ICD fall into the hands of the Russians, it would compromise the entire program, their cover and mask of secrecy would be blown. The enemy would know what type of satellite was being built by Krang Enterprises and would have several good indicators as to its mission.

As the two strangers entered the room, John realized, with despair, that the situation was beyond his control. One man, a tall, hulking, dark-featured man, angrily confronted Goldsmith, while the other, a medium sized, wiry man with a slight beard, searched the apartment. Both men wore dark-colored suits with red ties; either could pass as an average American accountant or salesman, and each carried a rather large briefcase. They moved with a smoothness that bespoke of athletic prowess and confident self-assurance.

"Where is Karl Helmick?" Goldsmith asked with alarm, frightened by the early arrival and rude treatment extended by these men.

"Helmick has been transferred," the tall man responded, frowning with a scowl. His accent, whether by training or by accident, sounded like a New Yorker from the Bronx.

"I only work with Helmick," Goldsmith stammered, his voice cracking with apprehension.

"Helmick has been found-out," the Russian spoke sharply, his eyes narrowing on Goldsmith, causing the old gentleman to retreat a few paces. "You'll be dealing with me now, and I want the list back."

"What list?" Goldsmith lied unconvincingly.

"The list Karl Helmick put into your hands. We know all about it you old fool. Karl Helmick has confessed and we want the list back."

"I don't care about the list," cried Goldsmith, almost pleading.

"Of course you can have the list back. I never wanted it in the first place."

"Get it," the Russian threatened menacingly.

"I don't have it, at least not here. I only took it because Helmick asked me too. I didn't want the list, we have other, more important matters to discuss. John give them the ICD."

John recoiled in alarm.

"Where is the list?" the Russian moved closer, taking hold of Goldsmith's shirt near the collar.

"It's with the documents from my office, all securely hidden away. I have a sample here, an ICD, to prove what type of project I work on. Helmick said you people would be very interested."

The Russian seemed unimpressed though. He motioned to his friend, who began a more detailed systematic search of the apartment, to confirm the absence of Helmick's list.

"Look here," Goldsmith again beckoned for John to come forward with the ICD, but John only backed away further. With surprising speed, Goldsmith shuffled over and snatched the ICD from John's grasp. He then thrust it into the hands of the Russian. The large stranger accepted the thick document and idly flipped through a few pages, as if leafing through a magazine.

John was aghast, that was it, the act of treason had been consummated. A top-secret classified document had been passed to the Russians. Bernie Goldsmith, regardless of his intentions, was now a traitor. John felt sick.

"Wait," the smaller Russian called from the far corner of the room, causing all eyes to turn. He pulled a small picture, a landscape of the Jordan River, off the wall. Taped to the back was a small round mechanical device, a listening bug.

For a moment the room was dead silent, then the larger Russian moved into action. He drew a black 9mm handgun from beneath his jacket, a large CZ-99 Yugoslavian automatic. Speaking in a non-chalant, unalarmed voice, for the sake of those listening, he said, "So, you and Mr. Hughes wish to offer this document as proof you work on a secret government project."

While he talked, the Russian quietly shoved Goldsmith away from the window and forced him spread-eagle against a wall. He searched Goldsmith thoroughly, looking for additional wires, and then approached John, who quickly raised his arms and submitted to a similar search.

John's mind raced, somebody was listening to their conversation, that meant it was probably also being taped. Who was it, the FBI, the CIA, the police? John just knew he was going to jail now. What would Eleanor think? What would the children think? Would they put him on trial as a spy? Could he prove his innocence?

"They're coming in," the shorter Russian, who was peering watchfully through the blinds of a front window, called out in alarm.

Both Russians dropped their briefcases to the floor and opened the attaches. The bigger of the two pulled out an Uzi mini-carbine submachine gun with a forward folding metal stock. The other carried an Ithaca Model 37 handgrip shotgun, with a five-shot magazine.

The larger Russian shoved Goldsmith across the room in sudden anger. "You set us up to die, you old Jew."

A sudden knock on the door caused them to take cover. The large Russian panicked, pulling the trigger on his Uzi mini-carbine, spraying the front door with automatic fire.

Noise filled the air from the rapid explosive crack of the 9mm automatic followed by dull consecutive whacks as each bullet slammed into wood and smacked through the door. Anyone standing directly outside the apartment would surely be pulverized.

Goldsmith screamed and raced toward the bathroom to hide. John stood witnessing the events like a ghostly spectator, not thinking to move for cover himself.

Canisters smashed through the bedroom and kitchen windows spraying broken glass upon the floor. One rolled into the living room, belching a spray of white smoke. With an angry oath, the larger Russian leaped to his feet and pursued Goldsmith. "You're not getting away, you Jew," he screamed.

Reaching the doorway to the bathroom, the Russian fired his CZ-99 handgun after Goldsmith, but then seemed shocked by what he had done. "You fool," he muttered.

John heard Goldsmith shrieking with pain. He saw the old man stumble from the bathroom and fall at the Russian's feet, blood flowing from an open chest wound. A sickening pool of red fluid began to collect around Goldsmith's crumpled body.

He was dead! John felt bile rise to his mouth and fought to keep from vomiting. Bernie Goldsmith was dead, murdered right before his eyes.

Then John's eyes noticed the Russian, the murderer, staring at him malevolently, and John knew he was next. At that moment of greatest peril, the killer was distracted when someone kicked open the front door and a hail of bullets sprayed into the room, thudding ineffectively against the back wall of the apartment near the ceiling.

The storming of the apartment caused Goldsmith's murderer to dive for cover, saving John's life for the moment. Spinning away to flee, John stumbled to his knees, but quickly regained his feet and raced into the kitchen, half-aware of more canisters being lobbed into the apartment. The smoke was filling the room, it hurt his eyes and he could hardly breathe.

In the kitchen, John was drawn to the shattered window. Flinging the frame open, he looked outside, searching for an avenue of escape. The old apartment building was square in shape and two stories high. Along the back was a row of parking carports against the building. Beyond that was an alley.

John hoisted himself onto the kitchen counter and, moving in a panicky haste, recklessly climbed out the window. It was a three foot drop to the carport roof, and John didn't know if the metal roof would hold or not, but he couldn't wait, he was scared beyond caution. Adrenaline sped John's movements as he squirmed out the window and hurled to the carport roof, sprawling on his hands and knees. Frantically John scrambled to the edge and rolled awkwardly off, dropping to the ground.

Scurrying back underneath the carport, John crouched between two cars, out of sight from the window above. His breathing was heavy, his lungs hurt, and his heart was pounding so hard he wondered if he was going to have a heart attack. John had never been so scared in all his life.

He waited a moment, vainly trying to catch his breath, knowing he had to move on, he wasn't safe yet. Bernie Goldsmith was dead. That Russian was responsible; no, ultimately it was the people developing that DWARS satellite who were responsible. They had killed Goldsmith.

Working up his courage, John sprinted across the parking lot to the alley. Surely they would not shoot him out in the open; nevertheless, at any moment John expected a bullet to smack into his exposed back.

Racing down the dirt alley, he reached a paved street, 12th Street. Feeling safer, he slowed to a jog. John regretted leaving his car, another indicator to the police he had been there, but he was not about to go back for it, those men had guns.

As John walked briskly away from the scene, he could feel his heartbeat slowing and his thoughts returning. Although he had developed a throbbing headache, the rush of adrenaline felt exhilarating, now that the danger was past. John felt an odd sense of pride. His successful escape from the Achen Apartments had been nothing less than miraculous, although quick wits and fast actions definitely played a role.

John wondered if either of the Russians had gotten out alive, probably not. They seemed prepared to make a fight of it. The night breeze felt cool against his sweat-soaked shirt. He felt like he was walking along in a dream. John became aware of the pain from nasty scrapes on both of his legs, from when he had climbed out the broken glass window. Funny he hadn't noticed it before. John could tell he was bleeding beneath his jeans. His left foot also felt sore, from when he had rolled off the carport and onto the ground. John started to limp now.

Up ahead, John noticed two men approaching along the sidewalk. They seemed out of place in the neighborhood, and for a moment he couldn't tell why? Then he realized it was the suits. They had on conservative business suits, at night, in a run-down section of town.

John knew danger was approaching but what could he do? Should he run, should he fight, what? Out of ignorance, he did nothing, continuing along the sidewalk toward the two strangers, hoping they would leave him alone.

Their paths intersected at the mouth of another alley, by design no doubt. The two men parted to pass on either side of John, but then turned and grabbed him by the arms. Efficiently and effectively they hustled him into the alley.

John found himself slammed against the back wall of a garage, the nozzle of a cold 9mm pistol rammed up against his throat. An odd cologne filled his nostrils, for some perverse reason disturbing him greatly. Again, for the second time that evening, the hands of strangers searched him, this time looking for more than weapons or listening wires.

The man conducting the body search handed his partner John's wallet.

"John Hughes," the second man rasped, viewing John's driver's license. "We saw you exit out the back window of the apartment." He placed John's wallet into his own pocket.

John groaned, a back-up team, he should have expected that, but whose side were they on, the Russians, the police, the FBI?

"What happened up there?" the first man shook John violently, causing John's head to bump against the hard brick behind him.

When John tried to speak, he coughed, the pistol at his throat still pressing against his Adam's apple.

The strangers both stepped back. "What happened?" the first repeated, louder and more menacingly.

"I just came because of a phone call," John begged. "I knew nothing before tonight."

"Shut up," the stranger growled, waving his pistol between John's eyes. "Was it a set up? What happened to our associates?"

So, these men were Russians, John thought with anguish. The first pair had proven to be ruthless. They had even murdered poor Goldsmith. John spoke with fear, pleading, "No, no, it was no set up. They found a wire in the apartment. The room was bugged."

"Go on!"

"Shortly after they found the bug, men rushed the apartment from outside. One of your…ah…associates, fired on the door."

"Enough of that. What about the list? Did Goldsmith return it to one of our comrades in the apartment?"

"List, I don't have any list!" John cried. Goldsmith hadn't mentioned any list to him.

"Didn't say you did, did I?" the Russian mocked. "Goldsmith had it, did he give it to our associates?"

"No."

"To you then?"

"No," John was feeling desperate.

"He told you where it was though?"

"No."

"Don't lie to me," the pistol moved closer.

"No, well yes, I mean no."

"You know where it is."

"Yes, well maybe. Goldsmith told me where he had stashed some stolen documents. It could be there."

"Where is that?" the Russian's voice grew louder with impatience.

"If I tell you, then you'll kill me," John resisted, amazing himself. He could not allow these Russians to have those secret documents.

The speaker spit in John's face and hissed, "I am going to kill you personally if I do not get the list back."

"He is lying anyway," the other Russian asserted. "We had better search him."

John thought they already had searched him, but the Russian's intentions soon became clear. After forcing John to strip, piece by piece they minutely examined each article of his clothes, finding nothing.

John feared what they might do next, when suddenly a spotlight illuminated the three of them. It was a police car trying to enter from the far end of the alley. Unfortunately they were blocked by an illegally parked flatbed truck.

"Let's go," one of the Russians called to his partner, and started to flee.

His friend was not in such a big hurry though. Thrusting his face in John's, he warned, "Don't go home, your house is being watched by the FBI. We shall be in touch, I must have that list. If we don't get the list back, then I'll get your wife and kids instead." He smiled cruelly and then turned and raced after his partner.

"Step out of the alley," an authoritative female voice called from the police car, as the doors popped open.

Grabbing his trousers from the dirt, John too fled down the alley away from the police. That list consumed his thoughts, he couldn't allow himself to be captured by the police, he had to escape, he had to get that list. Fortunately the police had been enroute to the nearby shoot-out at Achen Apartments. They had no time to give chase to a mugger victim.

After rounding the corner, John stopped to pull his pants back on. He needed to get home, but how? He had lost most of his clothes, he had no money, no billfold, and for all he knew, the Russians were right, perhaps it wasn't safe to return home.

5

Tuesday, January 23, the MCC for the SIGS satellite constellation was now swarming with people. It was three o'clock in the afternoon, fifteen hundred hours, almost twelve hours since SIGS-1's disastrous tumble had first been discovered by watchful air force technicians. On a twelve hour orbit, the satellite would soon be cresting the horizon again, circling the Earth twice each day.

SIGS-1, known as Siggie by the air force and Lockheed satellite controllers who cared for her daily upkeep and maintenance, was in jeopardy. Siggie was tumbling through space out of control and if lost, the nation's network of spy satellites would be severely crippled. Siggie, the first SIGS satellite, had been launched over five years ago. With a mean mission duration of only three years, Siggie had nevertheless functioned with only minor anomalies for five productive years, up until earlier that day.

A sister satellite, SIGS-2, known as Shelley, had been launched three years ago. The third satellite, SIGS-3, known as Sindy, had been launched barely a year ago to complete the constellation. Unfortunately Sindy had never operated properly from the start. Problems with her solar array deployment mechanisms had left

Sindy flying with one wing only and reduced power production. This would not, by itself, have put Sindy out of commission, but the undeployed solar array blocked a passive heat dissipation path, which cooled vital components prone to over-temps. As a result Sindy had been powered down, except for critical health and maintenance functions, and was only commanded to the active mode for short intervals during crises target over-passes.

Siggie and Shelley had been maneuvered into new orbital positions to compensate for the holes left by their partially functioning sister. This was easily accomplished with the large, five-pound, delta-velocity thrusters, effecting a LAN (Longitude of the Ascending Node) change while maintaining the same inclination and eccentricity. Together, Siggie and Shelley still overlooked all of the Soviet Union's land masses, even though roving blind spots prevented complete twenty-four-hour coverage. Now, with Siggie threatened also, it appeared to the air force as if fate stood poised to poke out the orbiting electronic ears of the nation's intelligence community.

Colonel Glaser glanced nervously at the universal time indicator. The presence of General Mauvus, one of the most influential generals within the DoD, made the colonel nervous. It was unfortunate that the general had been in the area on a routine tour of the CSTC facilities. Well, now he would see a real operation.

The tumble recovery procedures had been well rehearsed that morning. Expert Lockheed technicians, operating contractor for CSTC, and Rockwell engineers, the builders of the SIGS satellites, had pored over every aspect of the plan, under the watchful eye of air force overseers. All were in complete agreement, everything was ready, and they expected a fairly routine recovery.

There were three plausible theories that could explain the sudden loss of earth-lock by the CES, the satellite's Combined Earth Sensors. The most logical explanation was a series of random hits by cosmic particles. A more exotic theory was an electrostatic, high-voltage arc discharge between components, caused by the slow build-up of asymmetrical charge.

The least likely theory, albeit the one that received the most speculative attention, was the possibility of ground based laser illumination while over Russian territory. At the Tary Thagan Test Facility they were known to have three different types of laser devices and were suspected of occasionally directing such weapons at American satellites.

"Acquisition!" Rob Burns, a Lockheed technician called out. Seated next to him was an air force technical sergeant, Andres Rameriz, the man who had first discovered Siggie's distress. All eyes turned to the telemetry monitoring screens as the flood of numbers burst into activity. Displayed on a large overhead screen in the main control room were key parameters on view for the VIP spectators.

"Orbital degradation still within limits," Rob Burns announced, assessing the situation.

Colonel Graves questioningly glanced at the gentleman by his side, Mr. Edward Randall, managing supervisor of the Lockheed employees at the CSTC. Mr. Randall perceived the colonel's question and offered an explanation. "We had scheduled a station keeping burn for the previous pass-over, which of course did not take place. My people had a concern about the rate of orbital deterioration."

"ATO (Automatic Turn-On) completed," Rob Burns announced. "DCD (Dual Command Decoder) activated, the CEA (Control Electronics Assembly) is now ready to process a magnitude command via TT&C (Telemetry Tracking and Command) uplink."

"Initiate yaw thruster burn at one-five-thirty," an air force captain, the SVOD (Space Vehicle Operations Director) directed, marking the time on a freshly typed checklist. Their intent was to initiate a thruster firing to place the satellite in a controlled spin about the Z-axis, a nominal condition used during transfer orbit operations.

"Go," Sergeant Andres Rameriz, gave his approval, first on the checklist for operational go-ahead.

"Proceed," recommended Rob Burns for Lockheed.

"Go ahead," concurred the Rockwell engineering representative.

Out of courtesy the SVOD turned to the group of observing brass, "Sir, it appears we are ready to proceed." The clock was approaching the designated time at a steady rate.

"It's your call, captain," Colonel Glaser voiced confidence in his SVOD. Out of the corner of his eye, he noticed General Mauvus glance nervously toward Mr. Randall, who gave his customer a reassuring nod.

"All right, go," announced the SVOD, as he checked off the line by his own position on the checklist.

At exactly 15:30:00.00, they beamed the uplink fire command

along a two GHz narrow band command link to yaw thrusters ten and twelve. As the high gain, directional antenna caught the signal, the digital command decoder validated the decrypted bit stream and relayed the internal command to the CEA via the on-board computer. Within scant microseconds, two 0.1 pound hydrazine thrusters located on each RCS module began a precise controlled delta-velocity burn.

Sergeant Andres Rameriz was monitoring the spin rate of the space vehicle calculated by piper counts of the SSS, the Spin Sun Sensor. "Twenty-three, thirty-six, forty-eight, sixty-one," his heart seemed to speed with the accelerating angular velocity. It stabilized at sixty-one RPM, close enough to their goal of sixty RPM.

A sigh of relief could almost audibly be heard throughout the room as the SV fell into the spin stabilized mode and the passive nutation damper automatically eliminated any wobbling or coning effects. Now the SCE (Spin Control Electronics) and CEA would control accuracy within 0.5° in pitch and roll, and 1.0° in yaw.

In rapid succession they executed the nominal despin procedures. Using the opposite yaw thrusters, eleven and thirteen, three smaller delta-velocity firings were performed reducing the spin rate from sixty RPM to twenty-five RPM, then to six RPM, and finally to one RPM, the nominal acquisition rate.

"We have earth-lock," Andres Rameriz exclaimed spontaneously, as CES data appeared on his monitor. A round of applause erupted simultaneously about the room, the three axis stabilized mode had been recovered.

Commands were then sent to take the CEA out of JCL (jet control logic) and activate WCE (wheel control electronics). Nominal control of the satellite's attitude was being returned to the control reaction wheels which maintained pointing and orientation through axis torque produced by wheel acceleration.

"Something's wrong with the CEA!" Rod Burns exclaimed. "The WCE modules are toggling into the dormant mode."

"What about the back-up CEA?" the SVOD exclaimed.

"We haven't one, it's a single unit."

"But those CEA units are dual fault tolerant," Rameriz cried out in disbelieving alarm.

"Sure, CEA redundancy is achieved with duplicate interlocked functions on a multi-layered board, but if the WCE modules, 4A and 4B are not receiving acceptable commands, there is no other way for the reaction wheels to counter attitude errors. As old as this satellite is, we haven't the propellant to maintain attitude by JCL for long. We are dead in the sky!" Rob Burns proclaimed.

That was it, Siggie was finished. After five years of faithful service, the expensive billion-dollar showcase of human engineering genius was now a piece of worthless orbiting space debris. It would remain such for nineteen years (as calculated by numerical estimation), slowly decaying in orbit due to lunisolar perturbations until reentry through the Earth's lower atmosphere where it would vaporize in a glow of hot metal.

Colonel Glaser turned to General Mauvus with a forlorn expression. There was nothing anyone could do now.

"Pack your bags, colonel," General Mauvus commented sourly.

"What?" Colonel Glaser exclaimed, afraid the general meant to fire him on the spot for this catastrophe.

"We leave for the Pentagon on the next flight available," the general continued. "I'll need your help in explaining the details to the chief and the secretary."

Colonel Gloves turned red, "The chief of staff and the secretary of the air force?"

"Of course, we'll need immediate authorization to schedule a top-priority manifest date for the next launch."

"SIGS-4?" Sergeant Rameriz whispered under his breath. Everyone in the room had overheard the general's remarks.

"That's right, the first of our phase two birds. Our currently scheduled launch date is not till next year, but that will change. The LVIC (Launch Vehicle Integration Contractor) is on contract for a ninety-day launch-on-demand cycle."

Rameriz and Burns exchanged a skeptical glance. Off the record, the crew at CSTC had already nicknamed that satellite "Spooky", because of doubts about the aerospace firm that had been contracted to build it, Krang Enterprises.

6

"You may enter now," the uniformed female security guard stood before Dan Newby, nodding toward the entrance to an alarmed doorway.

Newby noticed her uniform shirt seemed particularly tight. He wondered if it was because the shirt had been designed for a man's chest, or if she simply wore a small size on purpose. Funny how the male security guards never wore tight shirts, well, around the middle maybe, but that was because of extended potbellies.

Reaching the door, Newby slid his ID card through the badge reader, punched in his IAN (Individual Access Number) and placed his face before the retina scanner. The computer first checked to see if Newby's card was on the access list, and then compared his retina pattern to ensure the right human had the card. Instantly an audible click could be heard at the door handle. The computer had decided to allow Newby entry and the door was now unlocked, the entire process taking less than a second.

Pushing the door open, Newby stepped into a narrow aisle. The first door on the left led to the main conference room where they would be expecting him.

As Newby entered the small conference room, his boss met him at the doorway. “Good to see you,” Henry Maxwell greeted Newby cordially with a vigorous hand shake. “Just in time, have a seat.”

Plush high-back leather chairs faced a large finely-polished mahogany conference table. Besides Newby’s boss, there were two other men present at the table. One Newby did not recognize, but the other was the DDO himself, the Deputy Director of Operations. Newby was impressed, although he felt a bit like a vassal coming before royalty.

Henry Maxwell commenced the briefing immediately, “The level of this meeting is 88, a compartment of the Albatross Control System.” Newby sucked his breath in, the Albatross Control System was reserved for tightly controlled programs involving counter-espionage. Although Newby was the section chief of a Special Support Office, Southwest U.S.A., he had only recently been cleared to the Albatross level.

“A few words on security might be appropriate for Mr. Newby’s sake,” Henry Maxwell continued, enjoying the floor and the chance to speak in front of the DDO. “As with all Albatross programs, the very strictest level of security must be maintained. Only those personnel absolutely required will be briefed to Program 88. If we indeed have a case of infiltration by hostile agents, the most stringent measures must be enforced. We do not currently know the full depth of the penetration, however it does appear to be extensive. Portions of Program 88 will be released from the Albatross Control System with an operational code name of Carrier Pigeon.”

“Currently, we four are the only ones briefed 88, myself; Dan Newby, our section chief; Mr. Boruchowitz, head of Counter Intelligence Staff; and yourself Mr. Deputy Director.”

Henry Maxwell turned to his subordinate, “Mr. Newby, the first item of discussion is to determine who on your team should be briefed 88. What are your thoughts on the matter?”

Newby appreciated his boss for asking his input. This was Maxwell’s way of giving Newby the floor, a little exposure in front of the DDO. Most people considered Henry Maxwell hard, uncompromising, almost cruel, but Newby liked the man. Maxwell had taken a personal interest in Newby some time ago and had been active in promoting Newby’s career. In return Newby worked for Maxwell with unwavering loyalty.

Since Henry Maxwell remained standing at the head of the

table, opposite from the DDO, Newby answered from his seat. "I believe my entire office should be briefed, most are already involved. The only exception would be Rachel Maris, who we suspect to be the double agent."

Newby realized he had made a mistake, he could tell by the immediate negative expressions on Mr. Boruchowitz's and the DDO's faces.

The DDO leaned forward and addressed Newby cordially. "Tell me, Dan, if your office contains one mole already, what guarantees do you have there aren't others?"

Newby was impressed to hear the DDO call him by his first name, but he was not sure how to answer. The Deputy Director had an excellent point.

"I think we must keep this in mind," Henry Maxwell came to Newby's rescue. "Although Dan's entire office may be involved in Operation Carrier Pigeon, to one extent or another, they need not all be briefed to the goals or reason for the operation. Remember, anyone briefed 88 must be cleared to Albatross."

"I don't understand how this operation could already be underway," Mr. Boruchowitz broke in curtly, changing the subject. "Has the Office of Security been notified, and how did you think to run a counter-espionage operation, against people within the agency, without my knowing about it?"

"That's why you're here now," Maxwell defended their position.

"But this comes under the jurisdiction of my division, conducting counter-intelligence operations." Suddenly Newby realized who Mr. Boruchowitz was, the head of the CIA group responsible for combating, finding, and discouraging all foreign activities directed at the agency itself, or any branch thereof.

"Because I ordered it," the DDO broke in, silencing Mr. Boruchowitz.

"Perhaps a little background—" Henry Maxwell started, but was interrupted by the DDO.

"Look, Alex, we don't know how deep this infiltration is, but Maxwell and his people think it might be extensive. No one else has been brought in yet, you are the first to know."

Henry Maxwell continued, "The next item on the agenda is a summary of our work thus far. Everything should become clear at that time, Mr. Boruchowitz. But first let us settle the issue of clearances."

Newby could tell Mr. Boruchowitz was not at all pleased. His territory had obviously been violated and he had lost face in front of the DDO. They needed to move on though. Newby restated his request along more acceptable lines, "In that case, I think two intelligence officers: Andrew Maconey, who is my deputy, and Randy Ostermann, my case officer over the field operation. At a minimum, those two must know the details." Newby hoped they would at least give approval for Andrew Maconey, who already knew the details of their plans.

The proposal was apparently acceptable, and Henry Maxwell moved on to the next agenda item. He outlined the results of an investigation by Dan Newby's office, gathering data over the past three years, and described how they had first become aware that there might be an alien network embedded within the agency; a society who owed their true allegiance elsewhere.

Although they had uncovered no clues as to what foreign government was sponsoring the network, the more they dug, the more extensive and deep they found the roots of this mysterious society, penetrating all facets and branches of the agency like an obscene cancer.

All was conjecture up to a point, mostly the work of substantiating computer analyses, but when backed up by field research from Newby's intelligence officers, it appeared most conclusive. It was Henry Maxwell that had first initiated the work three years ago, periodically providing vital information from other divisions for Newby's people to investigate.

Maxwell explained how the theories worked, how unexplainable circumstances seemed to substantiate the existence of an underground society. The statistics pointed to a group of self-supporting members who worked for their own mutual benefit and advancement. Convenient accidents, failed missions, lucky circumstances, chance vacations, miscellaneous rendezvous, unaccounted absences—there was a definite network in operation, of that they had no doubt. Still, all they had was theory, no proof.

Six months ago they had received their first break. A defecting East German intelligence officer had positively identified an intelligence officer within the network. Although he knew nothing more than her name, Rachel Maris, and code name, "Gyrfalcon," and that she was a courier between this sinister American network and a similar sister group in Europe, it was enough.

Shocked by the possibility that this covert network was linked to his own staff, and also foreign countries in the former Soviet block, Newby's group had quickly corroborated the report. Rachel Maris' field record supported such an accusation: frequent trips to Europe, overseas vacations, late returns from missions with plausible but suspicious explanations, it all made sense.

It then became a question of how to positively link Rachel Maris to the mysterious head of the covert organization. The computer pointed to one man in particular, the prime suspect, a man with whom all paths seemed to intersect at one point or another, the man whom their investigation had come to center upon, Ellis Hughes.

Ellis Hughes, otherwise known as the "Baron," held a position in the CIA of equivalent rank to Henry Maxwell, he was the head of the European Division under the DDO, in charge of covert operations in the European Theater. The influence he could exercise at that level of authority was beyond estimation.

Ellis Hughes had picked up the alias of the Baron when on assignment to Britain during the early days of the cold war. Hughes claimed his ancestors were early pre-revolutionary immigrants to America from Wales, literal descendants of Welsh nobility. The Baron was a man of great influence within the intelligence community, a well respected figure with powerful friends at high levels in both the CIA and the DIA.

As Maxwell finished up his summary, the floor was again offered to Dan Newby for an explanation and review of progress thus far on the current operation. The crucial moment now hung on Newby's shoulders. After years of work by his people, after becoming increasingly alarmed by the dire threat hanging over the agency, a decision here would either kill the operation, or else give the go-ahead and allow them to force the desired confrontation with the infamous Baron.

"The goal of Operation Carrier Pigeon," Newby began haltingly, "is to establish a link between Rachel Maris, whom we know to be a double agent, and Ellis Hughes, the suspected head of the network. This provocation would then induce the Baron into an incriminating response."

"Excuse me," Mr. Boruchowitz interrupted, "We've seen evidence that your intelligence officer, Rachel Maris, is a member of the alleged network." He was skeptical that such a network could exist without his division's knowledge. "What does she know of your operations thus far?"

"Nothing! Once she was identified, we compartmented our research. Nothing has been done in her presence and our studies have gone underground, except for times when she was out on assignment. We have been giving her extensive undercover work in Central America to keep her isolated from the main office."

"I'm sorry Mr. Deputy Director," Boruchowitz shook his head. "I am finding this whole story a little hard to swallow."

"Remember, Alex," the DDO commented. "The whole thrust of this alleged covert society, I believe, is one of mutual self advancement. It's my personal opinion that they don't owe allegiance to any foreign government, merely to themselves. Consequently they aren't involved in the type of activities that would alert or make themselves suspect to your organization. Otherwise, you surely would have been on to them long before now."

Mr. Boruchowitz seemed slightly mollified. Newby was encouraged by the fact that the DDO was already defending the operation. That was a good sign.

Newby continued, "Recently a case came to light with good possibilities, a matter of industrial espionage within an aerospace company in Tulsa, Oklahoma, where a man named John Hughes is employed. John Hughes is a nephew of the Baron."

Eyes opened around the table. "Tell them how you identified him," Henry Maxwell suggested.

"Right, fairly routine actually. In our background searches on the Baron's history, we checked on all relatives. We found this one of particular interest, possessing a top-level clearance at Krang Enterprises in Tulsa. We did a more extensive investigation on him, to see how he might be involved with the Baron's society, but he came up clean. Nevertheless, we maintained a periodic check on his activities. I personally think he must be associated with the network somehow."

"This is scandalous, how can they be allowed to conduct investigations on members within the agency?" Mr. Boruchowitz complained. "Only the Office of Security is authorized for that type of activity."

"I authorized it," Maxwell spoke gruffly, and the two men stared at each other. The DDO, their common superior, remained neutral, not taking sides or intervening.

Newby continued hastily, "It started with Bernie Goldsmith, an aerospace engineer from the same office as John Hughes. Goldsmith disappeared from work, an unaccountable absence. Plant security at Krang sent us the query instead of the FBI, perhaps because of our recent contacts, a lucky break. Wondering about Goldsmith's possible association with John Hughes, we took an active interest. Locating Bernie Goldsmith, we wired his apartment and put him under watch. It was discovered he had stolen top-secret government documents and was making clumsy attempts to contact the KGB. We kept him under extensive surveillance hoping to discover the connection with John Hughes."

"What has this got to do with the Baron and the alleged covert society?" Mr. Boruchowitz demanded.

"I'm getting to that. We supplied a phony East German contact named Karl Helmick. He gave Goldsmith some deception material, a list of names, a list which identifies Rachel Maris as a double agent."

"But why?"

"Helmick feigned an interest in defecting. This list was given to Goldsmith as bonafides, proof of intent, supposedly because of limited contact with Americans, outside of well monitored operations."

"How childish," Boruchowitz exclaimed.

"Yes, but plausible to a layman like Bernie Goldsmith. You see, on this list we placed the names of all identified suspects, and code names, associated with the Baron's covert organization, and also any other likely names, however remote the connection. That list also includes Rachel Maris and her code name, 'Gyrfalcon.'"

"Why?"

"The idea is to assign Rachel Maris to this industrial espionage case. When she retrieves the stolen documents, she'll also run across our provocation list, which exposes the Baron's entire organization as we presently understand it. If she runs it to the Baron we'll have established a link, we'll have our proof. We'll also monitor the Baron's reaction to having his society uncovered, flush him out and see if he runs."

"Why involve this John Hughes fellow? You said he was an innocent relative of the Baron?"

"Yes, but he gives Rachel Maris a convenient cover for running to the Baron. John Hughes will naturally try to contact his uncle for help. All Rachel need do is simply let him deliver the list for her, without thinking she is blowing her cover to us."

"I like it," the DDO declared abruptly, the complexity of the scheme pleased him. "Let's go with it," he said, and the meeting stood adjourned.

7

John Hughes was frightened, strangers were hunting for him, foreigners with guns, heartless killers. They had murdered Bernie Goldsmith. His friend was dead, actually dead! What would Goldsmith's wife think, or his children, or his grandchildren? Bernie Goldsmith was dead! John had seen his blood flowing from an open gunshot wound onto the cold dirty floor of that filthy apartment. John wondered if the poor old Jewish man had been welcomed by his God to the company of Abraham and the righteous. Goldsmith had seemed like a good decent man, one who loved and cared for his wife and children.

John knew Eleanor would be wondering where he was. He had to call home, she could be worried. The Russians had said his house was being watched. Besides that, if the police were not already there, they soon would be. There might even be a warrant out for his arrest by now, he dared not go home.

Where could he go? Where could he hide? The river, the Arkansas River? That was the place, somewhere along the banks like at Riverside Drive Park with miles of bushes and trees and bike paths. It would be the ideal place to hide for the night.

John slipped anxiously down Eleventh Street toward the river. He sought a place of refuge, a place of hiding where he would not be seen. He looked like a half-naked street bum, no shirt, no shoes, a dirty pair of blue jeans, but at least it was June and he was not cold. It might be uncomfortable having to sleep in the park with no shelter and light clothes, but it would not hurt him.

John grieved over the loss of his billfold and all his money. How was he going to call home? At least he still had his watch. It was eight o'clock already, where had the hours gone? John passed a small city park called Tracy Park. That would not do, he needed to make Riverside Drive Park, there would be places to hide there, he could sleep in safety there. Unfortunately, the Arkansas River was approximately two miles west. John felt self-conscious walking down Eleventh Street, a major inner-city road. People would think he was drunk or stoned or insane. If the police saw him he was sure to be stopped.

Passing a public phone booth, John stepped inside. He checked his pockets again, knowing they were empty. Perhaps he should return to the alley and search for his billfold or some change; no, too dangerous. Besides, the Russians had kept his wallet. He checked the coin return, nothing. Perusing the dialing instructions on the phone, John realized he could get the operator or call long distance without depositing a coin.

Nervously, John dialed zero.

"Operator," came the monotonic bureaucratic voice of a person accustomed to talking with strangers she never saw or met.

"Yes, can I have this call charged to my home address?"

"Is someone there to confirm the charge?"

"I believe so, please hurry." John recited his home phone number.

"And the number you wish to dial?" John could hear her dialing his home number.

"I want to call home, the same number."

The operator stopped dialing. With irritation she explained, "Then you want to call collect. You can't call your own number and charge it to the same number."

"Okay," John tried to remain patient. "Collect then, I need to hurry."

"Who shall I say is calling?"

"John, John Hughes! I live there!"

John's spirits rose expectantly as the phone rang. When the receiver was picked up, he felt a surge of hope. Then he heard Eleanor's sleepy voice answering with a mumbling hello. She must have already gone to bed.

"Eleanor, it's me—" John blurted out, but was interrupted by the operator.

"I have a collect call from John Hughes, will you accept the charge?"

"Yes," the sleepiness had left Eleanor's voice. "John, is that you?"

"Eleanor, thank goodness I reached you."

"It's past eight, where are you, you missed the entire T-ball game?"

"I've been mugged."

"Oh my goodness," Eleanor's voice was filled with alarm. "Are you hurt?"

"No, I'm okay, but I lost my billfold, and the car, I left the car."

"Where are you, John?"

"I saw a murder."

"What?"

"A murder. I saw a man killed."

"You're not serious? Where are you, John? I'll come and get you."

"Eleanor, I need you to do something. Are you listening?"

"Yes."

"Go to the window and see if anyone is watching the house."

"What do you mean, watching the house?"

"Just do it, Eleanor."

"John, you're scaring me."

"Don't be scared, but be careful, and don't let them see you looking."

The phone was silent for a while. John began to get very nervous, but Eleanor returned shortly. "I don't see anyone. Should I, John? What on earth is going on?"

"Honey, I cannot come home tonight, I have to hide. I'll call again tomorrow."

"John, you don't have to hide. I want you to come home now," Eleanor demanded.

"I have to hide. I just wanted to hear your voice."

"No, John, I'll come get you. I'll call the police for you."

"Sorry, honey, this is not the time to explain. Listen, you'll have to get the car tomorrow. It's at...ah...it's at...I can't remember. I'll tell you tomorrow."

"John!"

"I know, I love you, Eleanor."

John didn't feel any safer after talking to his wife, but just hearing her voice was a big comfort, to be able to talk with someone who loved him.

Moving on, John eventually reached the area where Eleventh Street intersects a bridge across the Arkansas River. Hastily he sought out a secluded area along the river bank. He did not have to look far, the sandy river bottom, nearly dry, was alive with bushes. It would not be the cleanest accommodations, but he would be safe there for the night.

As John lay in the sand under the bushes, he relived over and over again the events of the night. Now that he was safe, for the moment, he could sort things out in his mind and try to analyze events. John was an engineer, he liked to analyze things, break down the factors, make sense and order out of the world.

Bernie Goldsmith was dead, that was the most important fact, the controlling parameter in the equation. Goldsmith had given his life to resist deployment of the DWARS virus on board their satellite. Had he died in vain? No, perhaps not. John decided it was his duty to find the documents Goldsmith had hidden. The directions had been whispered in his ear. It was the only way to learn for sure about the DWARS virus. All information back at Krang Enterprises would be cloaked, in the name of national security. He had to learn the truth, and those documents were the only way.

Unfortunately, there was not much time. The launch was scheduled to take place August 31, barely two and a half months away. What could he do in two and a half months? Something had to be done though. Tomorrow he would head for campsite Desolation in the Rocky Mountains. Maybe there he could find the answers.

8

Dan Newby caught the first morning flight, 6:15 A.M. on American Airlines, direct from Washington D.C. to Dallas, Texas, arriving at Dallas/Fort Worth International at 8:45 A.M. It was already hot outside; the day was promising to develop blistering temperatures. He had originally planned to fly back tomorrow, till having been informed of a shocking tragedy during the initial phase of Operation Carrier Pigeon.

Their offices were located on the third floor of a modern highrise just off the beltway, Interstate 635. It was a newly constructed office building distinguished by its squat appearance and oddly opaque windows. American Airlines occupied the second floor, but the tenants of the first floor were unknown to Newby. He suspected the possibility of underground floors also, but couldn't say for sure. It was a tempest secure structure, with armed security guards controlling access through all entrances to the building.

Newby flashed a badge at the security guard and took the elevator to the third floor, where the people under his supervision were located, the CIA Southwest U.S. Special Support Office. On the third floor was a honeycomb of additional hallways leading to protected doorways with entrance-restricted doors. In addition to card readers, each individual bay of offices was guarded by cipher locks.

A second security guard greeted Newby as he stepped off the elevator, handing him a different badge and card for the reader. In return, Newby exchanged his common ID card.

"New IAN (Individual Access Numer) numbers," the guard announced.

"They always change when I'm out of town," Newby complained jokingly, although it did seem to be true.

A clerk was seated in an office facing the guard station, separated by a small sliding-glass customer window. She monitored the security computers which could tell where each individual was currently located by tracking their movements through the various doors. Punching Newby's name and social security number onto a computer keyboard, she revealed his new IAN, "Twenty-six one two," she announced.

"Thanks," Newby responded. Approaching the card reader, he slid his badge through and keyed in 2-6-1-2. Upon reexiting the door later that night, he would have to run his card through an exit reader also, or else the computer would think he was still inside and would not grant him access anywhere else. A click announced the door was unlocked and he pushed it open. Newby was now in the main hallway, a large corridor with nothing but secure doors all along each side.

Halfway down the corridor, he halted at another card reader alongside a blue door. Running his card through this reader and punching in his IAN number, Newby entered a lesser aisle. Past a cipher lock he arrived at his personal office bay, which contained a secretary's desk, a small conference room, and his own private office, which was the largest on the floor, he being the highest level supervisor of the group.

Annette, Newby's executive secretary, smiled at his approach. "Good morning, Mr. Newby, have a nice flight?"

"No, couldn't sleep at all." Newby noticed Annette's skirt was particularly short that day, probably because of the heat.

"I can tell," Annette smiled even more congenially. "You look terrible. You need a shave, Mr. Newby." Their relationship was semi-strained, strictly business; their personalities were not a good match. Annette was quite cute though, and Newby liked having her around. She was in her early twenties, unmarried, always sporting a nice tan, and seemed to love light summery clothes.

"Any messages?" Newby asked, lingering to the side of Annette's desk to catch a fuller glimpse of her legs. Those long, well-shaped legs, now crossed under her desk in a short skirt, were a familiar distraction for Newby.

"Just your better half," Annette responded.

"Okay, thanks. Could you get Maconey?" Newby proceeded on into his office and sat at his desk. "Dumb," he thought, he should have called Victoria last night and told her he was coming home early. With the press of trying to schedule a last-minute flight, he had forgotten his wife. Victoria must have called the Hilton and learned he had checked out. Now she would be wondering where he was or even if he had ever been in D.C. Oh well, she was probably used to it by now.

There was a knock on the door and Andrew Maconey strolled in, a questioning look on his face. He was a young man, according to Newby's standards, in his middle thirties, balding, glasses, a distance runner with a slender physique. Despite his meek appearance, he was an excellent intelligence officer and a top-notch deputy, a future leader for the agency.

"What happened?" Newby slapped his arm on the desk, making an unintentional noise.

Maconey was surprised by Newby's show of displeasure. The chief was usually unreadable as far as emotions. "It was an accident, sir, pure and simple."

"I figured it wasn't intentional," Newby took a deep breath.

"No sir, an unfortunate mishap."

"Who messed up?"

"No errors in procedure occurred, it just happened. One of those unforeseen things. It was Ostermann who shot him."

"You're kidding." Randy Ostermann was Newby's best field officer. It was not like Ostermann to make mistakes.

"Ostermann has been recalled to give an accounting. Basically, the way I understand it, Goldsmith fled into another room away from the target. Ostermann pursued, and then fired a shot to his side, intending to scare the old man into better cooperation. Unfortunately, Goldsmith ducked to the side just as Ostermann pulled the trigger. He took the shot in the chest."

"He died quick?"

"Yes sir, killed him dead on the spot."

"How do we explain that one, Maconey?" Newby stood and paced over to the picture of an ancient sea galley in stormy waters. There were no windows in his office. "What will the reports say? Think of the flap. This operation is already in jeopardy, and we just now got authorization to proceed. We have executed a civilian."

"Sir, perhaps we can keep it under wraps for a while, at least till the operation further develops. At a minimum we could delay the paperwork."

"Yes, let's do so. By the way, this operation has been compartmentalized further by Langley. Only you, Ostermann, and myself are to be fully briefed. All other personnel, including those involved on the field team, are only to have need-to-know information, nothing about the mission or who we are really after."

"The Baron?"

"Right, but that's not to get out." Newby's mind narrowed as he considered Ellis Hughes, the Baron as he was called. What a misnomer, a title of nobility bestowed upon a self-serving dangerous traitor. To think, that man had been a recipient of the Distinguished Intelligence Cross.

"All else is proceeding according to plan. John Hughes escaped from the mock assault and seems convinced he was meeting with real Russian intelligence officers.

"Good, anyone else hurt?"

"No, although the apartment was torn up pretty good. Our people barely got away before the police arrived."

"What about clean-up?"

"Clean-up arrived shortly after the police."

"Good, and the target, where is he now?"

"He went into hiding. We scared the wits out of him I suspect. Two of our men relieved him of his wallet and warned him not to return home. Nevertheless, he did call his wife. We have it on tape if you should care to review the conversation. He spent the night hiding in bushes along the Arkansas River."

"Good, think he'll make a run for the list?"

"He has to, we have left him nowhere else to go, and plenty of pressure to produce it."

Newby returned to his seat, his face impassive and unreadable once more. "This afternoon, security personnel from Langley should arrive. After they brief you and Ostermann, we shall reconvene and discuss our plans to deploy Rachel Maris. Her mission will be to contact John Hughes and retrieve the stolen classified documents."

"She won't know the real object of her mission."

"Right, however, we do want the government documents back eventually. When Rachel Maris uncovers our provocation list, then we'll watch the mole fly to her real boss."

"The Baron, we'll have him at last, sir."

Newby felt a twinge of regret. He had always liked Rachel Maris, she was one of his favorites in fact, kind of a troubled child whom he had tried to take in under his wing. She was good too, very good, but often seemed to be operating under a cloud, unpredictable. Maybe it was the gypsy in her blood. Anyway, he had always liked her. It had hurt to learn she was a double agent, like being betrayed by one's own children.

"By the way, Maconey, the project name for this operation is Carrier Pigeon."

"How apt."

"Yes, considering Rachel's code name, Gyrfalcon."

"Well, we'll see if the little pigeon will fly home to her roost with our incriminating message."

9

Chrissy and Billy seemed to sense their mother's tension, her worries reflecting almost immediately in their behavior. Before the hour was over, Billy managed to dump an entire box of Captain Crunch cereal on the kitchen floor. Chrissy, instead of playing her normal role as tattletale, this time took delight in Billy's mischief and goaded him into further trouble, laughing with great enthusiasm at his antics and telling him what interesting noises the cereal made as he crunched the sugary chunks under his feet.

By the time Eleanor had the mess cleaned up, her ornery children fed, dressed, and teeth brushed, her tension had turned into frustration and parental irritation. "Turn off the TV, Billy, it's time for school," she yelled at her son. He was sitting in the family room ignoring her. It seemed as if he was purposely stalling to see how far he could push her. Eleanor was past frustration though. She did not like raising her voice, but if she didn't yell at the children, they would not obey.

"Let me finish this show," Billy hollered back.

"No, Billy, now get your shoes on and let's go," she spoke with barely-controlled firmness.

Billy still ignored her, this time causing Eleanor to stomp into the family room for dramatic effect and push the off button herself. Billy rolled onto his back and made a face. He thought to lie there stubbornly, till noticing the stern look on his mother's face and realizing she was about to cry.

Eleanor was worried about her husband, worried and mad. True to his word he had not come home last night. Was he really in trouble with the law? Had he really witnessed a murder? Why couldn't he come home?

"Are you walking us to school this morning?" Chrissy interrupted, noticing mommy had her shoes on. Usually Eleanor didn't get dressed for the day till after they were out the door.

"Yes, Mommy's coming too," Eleanor affirmed.

That caught Billy's attention, something different. Hurrying to find his shoes, he asked, "Can we play catch on the way?"

"Not this time," Eleanor, did not feel up to games.

"Please, Mommy, please?"

"Oh, okay, if you hurry and get ready."

As they walked the short distance to school, Eleanor and her small children tossed a tennis ball back and forth. Sometimes it amazed Eleanor, the things she did. Imagine a grown woman throwing a tennis ball about as she walked down the street at eight in the morning, not too elegant. Eleanor saw another mother, Mrs. Riggs, walking her child to school, the two of them strolling sedately hand in hand. That would never do with Billy, he was too hard to control. Life could not be that easy for her.

Eleanor didn't catch too many throws that morning, she had other matters on her mind. It did not matter to the children though, any she missed they scurried to retrieve for her. They were happy just to have her along.

Normally the children walked to school alone, it was only two blocks, but that morning Eleanor had been alarmed to discover a suspicious looking van parked across the street and down the block from their home. It looked like an average van, but had been there since early that morning. Consequently Eleanor had decided not to let the children out of her sight until safely escorted behind school doors.

On any other day she would not have noticed or cared about a van, but this one was parked in front of the McCormick's house and they had been gone on vacation for two weeks. There was plenty of parking all along the block, so why was the van there? Normally people parked in front of the house they were visiting, why add walking distance? The only advantage for parking at that location was the fact that it commanded an unobstructed view of Eleanor's home. That van made Eleanor feel nervously ill. Were sinister men lurking out of sight in that closed vehicle? Spying on Eleanor's every move? Watching her children? Waiting for her husband to come home?

After having successfully chaperoned her children to their classes, Eleanor returned home via the opposite side of the street, daring a closer inspection of the mysterious van. As she approached, she noticed fatigue in her hand from squeezing the tennis ball, nervous tension. Wanting to appear nonchalant, she started to stroll by, but then noticed the sliding door on the van, facing the curb, facing her. What if strangers jumped out and attempted to abduct her? She could throw the tennis ball at them. A lot of good that would do, some weapon. It was too late to turn back, that would look foolish. Eleanor could see the driver and passenger seats were vacant. She tried to glance in as she passed, and then hurried on to the safety of her house.

How dare those people make her frightened in her own neighborhood, Eleanor fumed, as she bolted the front door and shut all the windows. The back door worried her, it had a lock, but was flimsy and a good shove could easily force it open. John had been asked to fix it many times. The house was feeling hot already and it would get worse with all the windows shut. Air conditioning would be a necessity that day, despite the exorbitant cost of utilities.

Pondering what to do with herself, Eleanor decided a soothing bubble bath was in order. The housework could wait and she certainly did not want to go out shopping. As it always happened, just as Eleanor settled down to her hot steamy bath, the phone rang.

Afraid not to answer, Eleanor stumbled into the bedroom, tracking and dripping a trail of water on the carpet. The house was already getting hot and humid, but the coolness of wet skin felt invigorating.

"Hello," Eleanor answered softly, hoping it was John.

"Eleanor," responded the familiar voice.

"John, it's you. Where are you John? What is happening?

"Did you get Billy and Chrissy off to school? I figured they would be gone by now."

"Yes, John, you know school starts at eight-thirty. Now tell me what is going on."

"I can't talk over this line."

"And why not, may I ask!" Eleanor exploded.

"It might be bugged."

"JOHN HUGHES!" Eleanor spoke sternly. "You stop this nonsense right now! You are making a nervous wreck out of me and if you ask me something foolish again, like if the house is being watched, I'll scream."

"Is it?"

"No, of course not!" Eleanor fumed.

"Okay, okay, I don't mean to alarm you," John knew he was doing just that, but what could he say.

"Just a minute," Eleanor put down the phone, none too gently, and stalked angrily out of the bedroom to peer out a front window. To her vast relief she saw the blue van was gone; but then, to her extreme consternation, she discovered a plumber's service truck parked directly across the street.

Eleanor hurried back to the phone. "John, are you still there?"

"Yes."

"What do they want?"

"You saw something?"

"Well...no."

"Exactly what did you see? Tell me exactly."

"A truck, across the street, but it could be a coincidence."

"I don't think so."

"Stop it, John, or I shall call the police." Eleanor clutched at the phone in mounting frustration. Why couldn't John listen to her?

"Don't bother, they are probably the ones in that truck. Listen, Eleanor, there is no danger to you or the children."

"John Hughes, you stop this foolishness! I want you home right this minute!!"

"I just called to see if you were okay."

"Stop it! It's not fair of you to cut me out of your problem. Come home, we'll work this out together. Please come home?"

John wondered if he could ever go home now, with the police after him, and also the Russians. Involving Eleanor was out of the question. What would become of Billy and Chrissy with both of their parents in jail?

"Eleanor, I need a phone number. Could you get my parents

number?" John asked, not sure she would respond.

Eleanor's mind felt terrible. In a daze she set the phone down and retrieved her purse. Procuring a small address book, she muttered the number into the phone.

"Thanks," John replied wearily. He figured his parents would have the number for Uncle Ellis, the one person in the world who might be able to help him.

"John, what should I do?" Eleanor asked, shivering, the wetness on her bare skin making her feel cold now, cold and vulnerable.

"Nothing, Eleanor, there is nothing you can do. I will call again if I get the chance."

Reluctantly John Hughes turned toward the Chrysler 300 parked at the curb behind him. It was not his car, unless possession made him the owner. He had stolen the vehicle.

That morning, alongside the Arkansas River, John Hughes had risen with the first rays of morning, shivering from the cold. The sun was up, and so were a multitude of small bothersome insects, bugs, and flying creatures. Suddenly John's refuge in the river bushes was not so comfortable. Besides the pesky insects, branches were scratching the skin on his bare back.

Climbing out from under cover, John stood in a quandary, perplexed as to what he should do next. He had a goal in mind, but what was the first step? He needed to reach Colorado and find a campsite called Desolation in Rocky Mountains National Park. There, he could retrieve the documents Bernie Goldsmith had stolen from Krang Enterprises, and then he would be able to ascertain if Goldsmith was telling the truth.

John shuddered, thinking about a weapon of biological warfare that was so diabolical it was perverse, a virus that would destroy the children of a nation, an inhumane weapon of genocide. If this did turn out to be true, it would have to be stopped. There was not much time though, Goldsmith had said the piggyback was scheduled for their next launch.

How was he to proceed? He had no money, no identification, no car, how could he get to Colorado? John did not dare go home first. Perhaps it was better that way, the last thing he wanted was to involve his family.

He would start this mission armed with nothing but his wits. For some strange reason the challengc appealed to John's sense of adventure. He would do it for Bernie Goldsmith, nay, for all mankind. John felt like a knight of King Arthur's court, about to commence a quest. The dragon called DWARS would have to be slain.

Money, that was the first challenge. In order to reach Colorado, John needed money. He would have to steal it, there was no other rational option. John considered the ethics of robbery. Compared to the evil of a virus that threatened the safety of all mankind, he considered it justified. Although if caught, John knew the police might not see it that way, neither would Eleanor.

John moved on, working his way along the sandbars of the river for over a mile, before climbing the bank and crossing Riverside Road into a residential area. Traveling down 26th Street he found himself in an older blue-collar neighborhood with small, one-story, wood-frame houses and large, plushly-leaved trees overshadowing the road. It was a crowded neighborhood, but most of the homes were neat and tidy.

John was painfully aware of his appearance. He looked like a crazy man. Something had to be done, and that meant stealing some clothes, too.

John nervously surveyed a row of small houses along one of the blocks down a side street. How could he know which one to break into? The perfect house would have no dog, no alarm system, and the owners would have to be away. How could he tell? It was still early in the morning, people inside the homes were starting to stir, getting ready for another average day of work and school. This would not be an average day for John; he might never have an average day again for the rest of his life.

Suddenly a paperboy rounded the corner and turned down the sidewalk ahead of John. He was working his way down that side of the block. John froze. As he considered running, his heart beat furiously within his chest. "Great," John thought, just planning a robbery had made him a guilty wreck. Trying to act nonchalant, John continued walking till the boy had passed. The small child gave him an odd glance and then continued on about his business.

As he proceeded down the street, John noticed some people starting to leave for work. He watched for an opportunity. When he saw an entire family leaving through the side door to their home, he knew they were the ones. The husband had on jeans, tennis shoes, and a sleeveless shirt. He wore a loaded carpenter's belt around his waist. The wife was better attired, with a nice office dress. She had on makeup and had even styled her hair. They had two small children, one with a lunch pail, the other with a stuffed bear.

It was a typical scene being enacted all across the country. Out of economic necessity both mother and father worked. The children would go to a daycare center early in the morning and not see their parents till evening, an unfortunate thing, but necessary for many.

John watched the mother struggling to load her children into an older four-door Reliant parked in the driveway under a carport. Her husband went straight to a small Ford pickup, parked alongside the curb, and left first. There was a third car parked on the grass, an old 1968 Chrysler 300.

Mentally marking the house, John continued walking for two more blocks before crossing the street to head back. It was important not to draw attention. As he drew closer though, his heart began to beat faster and faster again, even though all looked deserted inside the small house. John turned up the driveway, he could not wait any longer or people would see him loitering about.

Ducking under the carport, John located a small side door that opened onto the driveway. He tried to force the door open, but the lock held firm. Seeing no other way, John picked up a shovel to break out a pane of glass. His hands were shaking so badly, he could hardly hold the shovel. With a quick short thrust, John smashed to pieces the tiny rectangular pane. Startled by the noise he had created, especially loud to his guilt-laden ears, John ducked out of sight behind a trash can. Glancing around the neighborhood, he was relieved to see no one had heard the break-in.

Hastily John reached inside, unlocked the door, and entered the violated house. Now he had done it, he had actually forced entry into a house for the purpose of robbery.

Too nervous to pause and catch his breath, John hurried forward, crouching like the thief he was. The kitchen was tiny, there were dirty dishes piled up in the sink, a countertop crowded with small appliances, and a card table for meals. Aware of glass underfoot, John stepped carefully across the kitchen floor. The thought of fingerprints worried him, but he dismissed the thought, he was in worse trouble already, an accomplice to treason.

The living room had an old TV and modest worn-out furniture. For a two-income family this couple did not seem too well-off, perhaps most of their disposable income went to clothes and entertainment, or more likely, into servicing debts. John felt guilty about stealing from them, they might not even have insurance.

Making his way into the larger of two bedrooms, John first searched the dresser. He found a green pullover shirt, which fit loosely, and some socks. From the closet he selected a pair of worn gym shoes. They were large, but workable when laced tightly. Hurrying, he grabbed a light jacket, anxious to get away as soon as possible.

A sudden movement in the living room scared him half to death, but it was just a frightened cat. John was amazed at how much his arms were shaking. He could never make a living as a thief. In the kitchen John selected a long stainless steel carving knife, in case he needed a weapon. Tucking the knife into the back of his pants, with the jacket and shirt obscuring the protruding handle, John started to exit the victimized house, glad to be away.

Then he saw it, a set of keys. Grasping them in his hands as if he had just found a pot of gold, he hurried out front to the old Chrysler. Hoping beyond hope, he tried them in the ignition, and they fit. He turned them once and the engine sputtered, but then died. He tried again, but it would not turn over. The engine was close to flooding. Once more he tried, and the old engine roared to life.

John took it to be a sign. Fate was on his side. He had clothes now, and a car, and there was even change in the ash tray to call Eleanor with. All he really needed now was some money.

A mile east and he found a busy street, Peoria Avenue. Then south, past 31st Street, he began to see business establishments and started searching for a phone booth from which to call his wife.

After checking in with Eleanor, John headed straight for the freeways. He circled town as a precaution, going east and north on Skelly Bypass, then back west on the Crosstown Freeway, and east again on the Broken Arrow Expressway. Exiting on 21st Street, he drove toward a large shopping area.

Utica Square was a forerunner to modern-day malls, a conglomeration of a large number of stores, each opening onto small, private streets within Utica Square. As of late Utica Square had developed into a fashionable center for chic expensive shops and fancy boutiques.

John cruised the streets of Utica Square. He needed some money, but how was he to get it? He did not want to hurt or scare anyone, but he had to have money for gas. He had to get to Colorado and time was slipping by.

10

Wednesday, February 14 at Cape Canaveral Air Force Station in Florida, a directive from the Pentagon reached the desk of Colonel Roe, commander of the 6454th Space Launch and Test Group. It was a highly-classified launch notification, the go-ahead to implement a launch processing cycle to put a covert intelligence satellite, SIGS-4, into deep space. The liftoff was to take place from Colonel Roe's launch base at ETR (Eastern Test Range) on a covert Titan IV.

Similar top-secret messages would be arriving simultaneously at the home locations of key defense contractors and their associated air force SPOs (System Program Offices). The directive came from the highest of government offices, it was signed by the chief of staff and carried the concurrence signature of the secretary of the air force. Manifest dates for the launch of other space missions would be delayed to accommodate the rapid deployment of the SIGS satellite. It was a nice little valentine to receive from the big boys in Washington.

For Colonel Roe the challenge would be significant, a ninety-day turnaround on LP-55, Launch Pad number 55. After a DSP launch scheduled for June 1, the commencement of the ninety-day SIGS countdown would begin. The SIGS missions were known in the launch community by number only, as AFP-775 (Air Force Program-775), with the actual mission of the military satellite a highly-classified, well-protected secret.

The manifest date for AFP-775 was set at August 31. There were four major defense contractors on the line with hundreds of associated subcontractors, and all would have to do their parts if this was to succeed. Armies of people had been involved in the development and building of the satellite and its booster rocket, but it all came down to that one fatal day, August 31. It was all or nothing with launch vehicles, either a glowing success or an abject total failure. If Colonel Roe's people failed the launch, then the entire development and manufacturing effort for that satellite would all be for naught.

A magnificent Titan IV had been selected as the launch vehicle to place this expensive toy into space. Titan IV rockets were built in the foothills of the Rocky Mountains by MMC, the Martin Marietta Corporation of Denver, Colorado. These were the newest and most powerful of the nation's space launchers, the latest descendants from a long family of Titan rockets. Initially used to carry ICBMs into space, Titans were now built for the sole purpose of boosting satellites from the surface of the Earth, past the grips of gravity, and into the depths of deep space.

The Titan IV, deemed necessary after the Challenger disaster in January of 1986, was developed as an unmanned alternative to the Space Shuttle. It was composed of a core vehicle with two internal liquid stages and twin solid rockets attached to the exterior. Titan IVs stood anywhere from 170 feet high up to 200 feet high, depending on the length of its payload. Stage One of the core vehicle could deliver 547.6 thousand pounds of thrust, Stage Two was capable of 103.5 thousand pounds of thrust, and each solid rocket an additional 1.4 million pounds of thrust. In a scant 543.1 seconds, this monstrous rocket could place an average satellite into near-earth orbit.

However, even this behemoth of rocket power was not strong enough to do the total job. For those satellites requiring high-earth orbits, a powerful upper-stage vehicle was also required. The strongest of these was the Centaur G, built by GDSS, General Dynamics Space Systems in San Diego, California. This mighty, liquid-rocket stage vehicle could produce an additional 33,000 pounds of thrust, in space, to maneuver the prized satellite into the proper orbit.

Housing the upper-stage and the satellite, high atop the Titan core, was a massive payload fairing. This protective structure, weighing up to 14,000 pounds, was designed to protect the fragile satellite from the harshness of the launch environment. They were built by MDAC, the McDonnell Douglas Astronautics Corporation of Huntington Beach, California.

As grand and awe inspiring as the Titan IV launch vehicle was, it was not an end unto itself. The purpose of this marvel of American engineering rocketry genius was to service the priceless satellite.

The new block of SIGS satellites were being built by KE, Krang Enterprises, at a top-secret space facility located in the heartland of what was once Indian Territory, at oil-rich Tulsa, Oklahoma. Few suspected, outside of those employed on the project, that the Krang Tulsa factory had satellite manufacturing and testing capabilities. Those involved were committed to stringent levels of secrecy; the mere identity of the defense contractor chosen to build the SIGS satellite was a highly protected fact.

Colonel Roe gently laid his launch notification orders upon one corner of his desk and stared for a moment at a picture of Robert Hutchings Goddard. All right, if the boys in Washington wanted a SIGS satellite placed in orbit, then come August 31, he would see to it they got one.

11

"Will that be all?" Annette stamped her foot with displeasure, making no attempt to mask her frustration. Annette had not expected her boss to insist she work tomorrow, not on Friday, not when she had scheduled vacation to make a three day weekend. Her boyfriend had promised a water-skiing trip and she did not like office work interfering.

"I am sorry," Dan Newby apologized. "However, you know we cannot spare anyone just now, not with this operation outgoing." Newby was perturbed by his secretary's behavior and starting to get a bit angry himself. Why was she acting so selfishly anyway, giving him a hard time because they needed her at the office?

It was his own fault, he should have known better than to hire overqualified personnel for positions with limited growth potential. How could one expect a secretary with Annette's looks and intelligence to have her heart in the job? Why she was probably smarter than half the college-trained intelligence officers in his office, and yet she didn't make half the salary. He should have known she would be bored with the job, but she had no other skills or training, and she had applied.

"Office trouble?" Andrew Maconey smiled knowingly as he and Annette crossed paths in Newby's doorway.

Annette glared at him indignantly, then spun away in a huff, his attempt at levity irritating the situation even more. "Don't antagonize her any further," Newby begged, only half-jokingly. "If we make Annette any madder, we'll all be lost."

Maconey chuckled and drew up a chair facing the corner of his boss' well polished mahogany desk. "I just received a field report from Ostermann."

"Must be good news," Newby surmised, judging from his deputy's demeanor.

"Yes, Operation Carrier Pigeon is going quite well. Our target has proven himself quite predictable, although Ostermann is having the devil of a time covering the man's tracks."

"Ostermann nearly lost the target, a layman?" Newby was surprised.

"No, no, not that. John Hughes decided to turn amateur thief and put Ostermann through some unbelievable gyrations preventing his arrest." Maconey told his story with relish, periodically waving his hands in short choppy motions for emphasis. "First the idiot broke into a home, burglarized it, and then stole their car, in broad daylight no less. The owner reported it to the police within hours, and Hughes was still in town, making no efforts at concealment. With an APB out for the stolen vehicle, the Tulsa metropolitan police would have picked him up for sure. Ostermann had to go right to the top to get that APB off the airwaves."

"That was just the beginning," Maconey continued with growing amusement. "Next Hughes appeared on the verge of mugging a civilian to obtain some funds, at knife point, in a crowded shopping area. Half the police in Tulsa would have been on his tail if not for our man," Maconey was grinning uncontrollably. "Boy was Ostermann livid. Hughes would not do us much good cooling his heels in a jail cell though," Maconey's sense of humor was almost getting the better of him.

"So what became of Hughes?" Newby couldn't help chuckling.

"Well, in order to halt the amateur crime spree, it seems Ostermann had to send one of his field team in to be mugged, Sally I believe. She ever so innocently asked Hughes the time, and then allowed him to steal her purse, with several thousand dollars conveniently on hand, cash of course."

"Good, that should satisfy him," Newby was pleased. Although headstrong, Ostermann could always be counted on to handle a difficult situation.

"Yes," Maconey concurred. "Now our target is enroute to Colorado. In his last phone call to his wife, he indicated he would not be back for several days."

"Everything is going according to plan, ah...what about the dead engineer?" Newby corrected his initial statement.

"The corpse is down at the mortuary, a John Doe on the city's unidentified transients list. They will hold the body for three days, then we'll have to release his name or else the poor fellow will receive a city burial."

"Well, we cannot allow that," Newby felt bad enough about the death. "His family will need to be informed eventually. Perhaps within three days we'll have some solid evidence on the case. Regardless, we cannot allow the man to be buried without releasing his name and notifying his family." Mention of Goldsmith's death had effectively doused Maconey and Newby's lighthearted jocosity. It was a bad situation when a life was lost, and civilian casualties always hurt. True, Goldsmith was trying to engage in espionage, with men he thought to be Russian agents, but still, they had been manipulating him.

Annette stuck her head back inside the office. "Rachel Maris is here, Sir." The irritation in her voice was not totally submerged and she had never called Newby "sir" before.

Newby glanced at his watch, "Ten o'clock already."

Rachel Maris brushed past Annette and entered Dan Newby's office. Annette was such an irritant, purposely making her wait to see the boss, trying to announce her arrival as if he might be too busy to see her. Annette didn't treat any of the male intelligence officers in such a manner, just her.

Annette was not alone in her dislike of Rachel Maris though, none of the female administrative staff cared much for the tall dark Romanian. Rachel assumed it was because she was a female intelligence officer and they were all jealous of her position, but in reality it was to a large degree Rachel's own fault. She insisted on being treated like one of the men, intelligence officers like unto herself, rather than associating with the women in the office. Rachel felt she had to be a little more class conscious than her male peers, otherwise her standing in the office would be diminished by association.

"Shut the door please," Newby stood courteously, as Rachel strolled up to his desk. She smiled sweetly as she closed the office door and selected a seat next to Maconey.

Newby couldn't help but feel guilty about the task before him, setting Rachel up to take a fall. Even though Newby was sure the lady was betraying the agency, he still felt somewhat responsible for her well being. He liked Rachel, more than that, he felt instinctively protective of her.

Wearing a stylish burgundy colored dress, the hem just higher than knee length when standing, Rachel was adorned like a fashion model from *Vogue*, with color coordinated belts, gold necklaces, bracelets, earrings, and a brass hair clip. The front of Rachel's dress parted down the middle like a coat, with large golden buttons engraved with animals and a satin sash for a belt. Rachel's luxurious coal-black hair and Eastern-European complexion were complemented by her gypsy style of apparel in a most beguiling and enticing manner.

Facing Dan Newby, she sat with her legs crossed, one hand holding the hem of her dress at the knee to keep it from parting. Rachel wore dark nylons and her sleek shapely legs had not gone unnoticed by Newby, who had to struggle keeping his eyes focused upwards. With Rachel looking him square in the face, he could not very well be caught staring.

"Umpht," Andrew Maconey cleared his throat, impatient with the silence. He felt uncomfortable sitting next to Rachel Maris, thinking she was a double agent, that she had betrayed their trust.

Maconey was not surprised though, he had never trusted Rachel Maris, not from the beginning. She was a loner. She had no friends among the office staff. It was because the lady did not seem to care much or show any interest in the lives of her fellow intelligence officers. She never attended any of the office socials and didn't even bother coming to Eddie Sanders' wedding last year. Once Maconey had overheard his boss' wife, Victoria, at a mandatory promotion ceremony, remark that Rachel Maris looked like a communist. Maconey thought the remark so appropriate now, in light of recent revelations.

"Oh," Newby spoke up loudly, as if jarred by a sudden though. "Thank you for coming, Rachel. We have a new assignment for you."

"I see." Rachel did not look pleased.

"Is something the matter?" Newby asked, worrying that he had upset her.

"I just got back to the States yesterday, from six months undercover you know. I was expecting some time off, comp time, or at the very least some slack between assignments to catch up on my office work. Also, I'm due for an advancement test and never seem to have any time lately to prepare." Rachel spoke with a deep husky voice, almost like a man's, although definitely feminine. She was of Romanian ancestry; her parents had immigrated to the United States from Germany at the beginning of Nazi persecutions.

"Would you like a few days off?" Newby asked, and then regretted it. He felt like kicking himself. Why did he ask her that? If she said yes, he would have to backtrack and find an excuse to take back his words.

"No, it's okay," Rachel unfolded her legs and gazed past Newby at a picture on the wall. With hands now on her lap, her dress parted, sliding down each side of her knees.

Newby glanced down and then quickly away, his eyes had been drawn to Rachel's legs like a magnet, the slightest motion catching his vision. He hoped Rachel had not noticed.

"Good," Newby exclaimed nervously. "You might find this somewhat of a challenge, although you'll be happy to know there is no foreign travel involved. You'll be placed in Colorado." Then Newby chuckled and said with a smile, "May even get to do some backpacking."

Rachel was not amused by Newby's attempt at a joke, he knew good and well how she disliked camping and such, anything that might involve getting dirty. Rachel was more at home on the social circuit than sitting around a campfire with bugs and smoke and grubby clothes.

"Where is the folder?" Rachel asked. She would take the assignment of course, Rachel Maris was a good trooper and she would go where she was told. Besides, Dan Newby had been good to her, she liked him and felt a sense of loyalty.

"Still in typing," Maconey broke in, "should be ready within the hour. We need to deploy you immediately though, that is the reason for this early pre-briefing."

Rachel looked at Maconey critically. He was always business, always disdaining small talk. She sensed tension in his voice. He didn't like her much.

"It involves some undercover work," Newby continued where Maconey left off. "Nothing difficult, no danger involved. We've had a case of industrial espionage. A couple of engineers out at Krang Enterprises in Tulsa have copied a set of classified government documents. It's important to recover those documents intact, they have to do with one of the Pentagon's top-secret spy satellites."

"I see," Rachel looked bored, "and why isn't the FBI handling this difficulty?"

"Ah...well, it involves the relative of a high-ranking officer within the company. We'd like to keep this all within the family."

"Strictly CIA business then, I understand. Do you know where the documents are?"

"Not exactly," Newby lied. "But we know they are hidden in the mountains of Colorado, and one of the engineers is heading there now. We would like to place you with the man. Accompany him in recovering the documents and, when you have them secure, alert your field support crew and make the arrest."

"Sounds easy enough."

"Yes, and it should look nice in your personnel files." Newby wondered if he was trying too hard to sell the assignment.

"One question though," Rachel leaned forward and recrossed her legs.

Newby struggled to keep his gaze at eye level. "Yes," he said uncomfortably.

"Why do we need someone undercover?"

Andrew Maconey answered for his boss, "The documents are extremely sensitive, Rachel." As Rachel turned toward the man next to her, Newby's eyes began to wander.

Maconey continued, "It would be fairly easy for us to follow the man, we think. We even have a homing device planted in his car, but the documents reveal high technology. We simply cannot afford to take chances."

"We think it best," Newby confirmed. "That is where you come in, Rachel. We want to make absolutely sure we get those classified documents back. We are taking no chances, not after the slip up yesterday. You see...ah...it is all in the file...but...ah...we killed the other engineer."

Rachel was astonished.

"All a big mistake," Maconey muttered. "We were conducting a scenario to frighten them into running for the stash, and Ostermann shot him by accident."

Rachel could scarcely believe it, "Randy Ostermann? Randy Ostermann shot him?"

Newby stood and discretely turned to face the back wall, it was the only way he could keep his eyes off Rachel's legs. Since there were no windows in the office, he studied the pastoral scene on one of his office pictures. Then he spoke, "We cannot afford any more slip-ups. No more mistakes."

Rachel, recovering from her amazement, was inwardly pleased. Although she was not friends with any of her fellow intelligence officers, except for maybe the boss, there was one in particular that she disliked, no, more than disliked, that she hated—Randy Ostermann. What had started out as mutually negative feelings, a spontaneous personality conflict, had grown through the past years into an intense rivalry. Ostermann was openly critical of Rachel, especially among their peers, and at times, although she had no proof, contrived to make her look bad. There was no lost love between the two of them.

Randy Ostermann was one of those large, athletic, ruggedly handsome men that seemed to think they were God's gift to women. He was self-confident and proud to the point of being arrogant, a real jerk. When Rachel showed no interest in his machoism, the man reacted as if personally threatened. A beautiful woman that did not fall at his feet, how could it be? There must be something wrong with her? From that point on Ostermann had become her critic, her rival, and eventually, even her enemy.

"You can understand the predicament we are in," Newby continued, turning to face her once more.

Rachel wondered why Newby was staring above her head. "Of course, sir," she responded, "I can understand your wanting someone else to take over the field operation."

"Ostermann is still in," Andrew Maconey corrected Rachel.

"Still in?"

"Yes, Ostermann will remain in command of your backup team."

"But, Dan," Rachel protested, raising her arms into the air. "You know I cannot work with Ostermann."

"I am sorry, Rachel, we cannot pull him off this one."

Rachel was visibly frustrated. "If you say so."

"That's the right attitude," Maconey said. He meant to be

encouraging, but instead sounded patronizing. "Review your folder while Annette schedules an airline flight for later this afternoon. You can catch up with Ostermann's team in Wichita."

"Ostermann's team?"

"Ostermann is senior on this one," Newby said. "He will continue as the case officer in charge."

"I see, anything else?" Rachel had trouble masking her discontent.

"Good luck, Rachel."

As Rachel stood to leave, Newby felt much better. It had been an awkward meeting, but apparently successful. Rachel was taking the mission and they would soon see how she reacted to the bait. He had intentionally put Ostermann in charge of her backup team just to tempt her to turn elsewhere for help when things started to go sour. Ostermann being in charge was an added incentive to coax her into running for her other network when trouble arose, especially when she discovered the incriminating provocation list.

As Rachel departed, Maconey extended a hand to his boss. "Congratulations, sir, we have worked many years to reach this point. The operation has finally begun."

'Yes,' Newby thought, 'Operation Carrier Pigeon is under way.'

12

The big Chrysler 300 roared along Interstate 35 at a steady hum, the engine not too good on gas mileage, but hardly straining even at high speeds. John Hughes kept the speedometer pegged at a steady sixty-five, a sense of urgency dominating his thoughts. The DWARS piggyback, that immoral launch, was hardly more than two months away. Much as he wanted to go faster, he could hardly afford to be stopped for speeding, possessing no drivers license or identification of any type.

John missed Eleanor, although scarcely more than a day had passed since he had skipped out on Chrissy's T-ball game to meet with Goldsmith. How John wished his wife could be at his side. The fact that he might never see her again heightened his homesickness. John was a realist, he understood all too well the gravity of the mission he had undertaken. Penalties for treason were quite severe. A lifetime in some forsaken federal penitentiary was not that far-fetched.

The struggle against that DWARS abomination had cost Bernie Goldsmith his life. The concept was pure evil, surely emanating straight from the devil, for no decent human mind could contemplate such horrible maliciousness without shrinking away with trembling shame. If it weren't for the involvement of Russians, John would have had a difficult time believing it possible. When this whole sick mess was over, John figured he would either be hailed as a national hero, or else incarcerated as a vile traitor. If he did not lose his life along the way.

John had risen early that morning, after a fitful night's sleep in a cheap Oklahoma City motel near an old amusement park called Frontier City. Yesterday he had thought it important to put some distance between himself and metropolitan Tulsa, where undoubtedly he was now a wanted man. He would feel even more secure once across the border into Kansas.

At ten o'clock John entered the heartland of America's wheat belt, a state of fertile rich farmlands and good decent people. Oklahoma, his beloved home state, was behind him now, ahead lay long flat expanses of plotted farm fields. John was already feeling sleepy from the drive, and he had hardly begun. He had wanted to reach the Rockies that day.

The sun had risen enough to make life uncomfortable, heating the black interior of John's new vehicle beyond the limited capability of the car's ancient air conditioner. The problem seemed to be the fans. Although the unit put out cold air, the knob for fan settings seemed ineffectual and the fan speed would not go higher than the low setting. John tried opening the windows, but the outside air was so hot that the cooling effect was no better, and the road noise from the big engine was another irritant.

In spite of the scorching Midwest summer heat, John remained undaunted, perhaps even excited. He had embarked upon an important quest and, excepting yesterday's gun battle, nothing so exciting as this had ever happened to him before. Now it was John against the world, and so far he had been quite successful. Starting out with nothing but a pair of pants, he now had money, a car, and was well on his way to Colorado.

If not for the anger occasionally clouding his thoughts, he could be enjoying this adventure. At least his anger was focused though, he hated those who had designed and built the DWARS virus, using him and his fellow engineers at Krang Enterprises without their knowledge. To think, he and his peers were being used as unwitting accomplices in the evil deployment of that weapon.

Noticing the exit sign for a small town called Derby, John

pulled off the interstate to buy some gasoline. He still had half a tank, but drowsiness from driving in the sun was tiring him fast and he needed a break. Signs directed John to state highway K-15 heading south a short distance into the Derby city limits. The road soon merged into the main street of Derby, entering the small town from the north through a series of stoplights.

Driving through the main business district, John bypassed several high-priced gas stations hoping to find a cheap one. It was stolen money he would spend, but John would still be frugal, out of habit. Unfortunately there were no stations with cheaper gas and he almost exited the southern limits of Derby before he realized it. John ended up stopping at a Phillips 66, wondering why the prices in Tulsa were lower.

After paying for fifteen gallons of regular, John parked next to a phone booth to make an important set of calls. Eleanor had thought it odd he needed to ask for his parent's phone number, but he could not remember it, they had moved twice since he had lived with them as a child.

"Hello," a comforting voice answered, after two short rings.

"Mom, it's me."

"John."

"Yes, how are you and Dad?"

"We are fine, but what about you? What kind of trouble are you in?" Her voice sounded strained.

"You have been talking to Eleanor?"

"Dad called Eleanor a few hours ago. A man from the FBI called early this morning, John. They are searching for you."

John was stunned! It seemed almost inconceivable that the FBI was digging after him already. It had not taken them long to trace out who John Hughes was.

"Sorry to worry you, Mom, but I am okay, really."

"Where are you, John?"

"Do you really want to know?"

"No, I guess not. What can we do to help?"

"I need Uncle Ellis' phone number, do you have it?"

"You think Uncle Ellis can help?"

"I don't know, but he might." Ellis Hughes, Uncle Ellis to John, had always been a mysterious but favorite relative.

Originally an air force officer, Ellis Hughes had served with distinction in Europe during the Berlin Airlift. John's early childhood was filled with memorable war tales from his exciting adventuresome uncle. He had retired at the rank of colonel and then taken a job at the Central Intelligence Agency, further adding to the glamour and mystique attributed him by an impressionable youth. Now he was retired from the CIA, divorced, and living in Washington D.C. where he ran a small consulting firm on international politics. Still, although no longer associated with the CIA, if anyone could help John, it was Uncle Ellis.

"Just a moment," John's mother let the phone drop. She returned shortly and gave him the phone number. "Good luck reaching him."

"Thanks, do you know the area code?"

"Let me check the phone book...2-0-2."

"Thanks again, Mom, don't worry, I will be in touch."

"We love you, Johnny."

"Love you, too. Say hi to Dad."

With intrepid hope and a handful of coins, John dialed the long distance D.C. number for his uncle. On the fourth ring an answering machine responded with the polished professional voice of Uncle Ellis. "Thank you for calling. I apologize for not being available at the moment. Please leave your name and phone number, and I shall return your call upon my return to Washington. In case of an emergency, please hold the line and my answering service will respond."

Clenching his fist, John waited impatiently for the beep and then through the long pause. It sounded like Uncle Ellis was not available. He had to reach him though, he had too.

"Good afternoon," a crisp woman's voice answered in a practiced secretarial manner. "This is the office of Hughes and Barclay, how may I be of assistance?"

"Is Ellis Hughes there?" John spoke in a loud voice, worried about the traffic sounds near his phone booth.

"I am sorry. Mr. Hughes is out of the country on business. Is there someone else who may be of service, or would you prefer to leave a message?"

"Out of the country," John moaned. Suddenly he felt very alone. "Look," he said, almost pleading, "this is his nephew, John Hughes. We have to talk, it is a family matter, an emergency. Do you have a number where he may be reached?"

"I am sorry. Mr. Hughes is not available."

"This is an emergency I said."

"On a regular basis Mr. Hughes calls his office for messages. Leave your name and phone number and perhaps he will get back to you."

Why did she insist on treating him like some pestering salesman? "I said I was his nephew," John complained.

"Quite, John Hughes I believe."

"That's right." It occurred to John that she did not believe him. Was it her job to screen Uncle Ellis' phone lines and turn away bothersome callers? In disgust John hung up.

Mother had said it would be hard to get hold of Uncle Ellis. John tried to think of who else might know his whereabouts? Perhaps his uncle's ex-wife, she still lived in Tulsa; no, she would not know anything. Besides, he could not call her, she was no longer family. Uncle Ellis had been divorced for many years now. He had left behind one child with his wife and marriage, a daughter, Gwen. Now she might know how to reach her father.

Gwen Hughes had grown up a real whiz kid, highly intelligent, athletic, socially involved. John had not seen his cousin Gwen since she was twelve years old, but he had heard all about her accomplishments. One could not talk to Uncle Ellis without hearing all about her latest. She was presently in college, a cadet at the United States Air Force Academy.

Gwen would surely know how to contact her dad. John considered calling her, but the cadets all lived in military dorms at the academy and it might be awkward and difficult to get through, especially long distance from a pay phone. The academy was located just outside of Colorado Springs, not too far away. It would just be a short detour from John's planned route to Denver and Rocky Mountains National Park. He entertained the idea of stopping by to speak with his cousin along the way. It seemed like a plausible thing to do.

John drove north through Derby feeling a bit discouraged, he had accomplished little more than obtaining a tank full of gas. The fun of this adventure was fading fast. He needed the help of his uncle.

Reaching the last stop before leaving the business district of Derby, John was startled by a sudden jolt and accompanying crash. His head whipped back against the headrest as the Chrysler lurched forward, rear-ended by another vehicle. John arrested his forward motion by stomping on the brakes.

In the rearview mirror was a battered old Nova, crowded behind John's big Chrysler. Semi-stunned, John watched an older country gentleman pull off to a parallel side road and exit his Nova to inspect the damage. Worried that someone might summon the police, John hastily pulled over too, parking his Chrysler next to the Nova in the parking lot to a row of small business shops, a bar, a cafe, a used clothing store, and a small grocery. At least they were no longer blocking traffic.

"Sorry about that, mister," the farmer apologized with embarrassment. "I just wasn't paying attention," his voice sounding odd, lacking any country accent.

Fortunately the Chrysler had sustained very little damage. The Nova hadn't fared so well though, the vehicle was smashed up pretty good on the front end: a damaged grill, bent hood, and broken headlights.

"Looks like I took all the damage," the worried offender remarked, looking hopefully toward John for some relief.

"No damage to my car," John responded. "Scratches don't bother me any, not with this old vehicle." The farmer seemed pleased that he was not going to be collared with any repairs. John was even more relieved.

"You want my phone number or insurance number?" the farmer asked. "I live just down the road in Mulvane."

"No, it's okay," John reassured him.

"Sorry to have troubled you."

"Don't let it bother you," John wanted to hurry, acutely conscious that the longer he delayed, the higher the risk of police showing up.

As John opened the door to his Chrysler, he was distracted by an angry woman storming out of the tavern across the parking lot. The distraught lady was wearing tight, form-fitting, blue jeans and a chartreuse colored cowgirl shirt, but it wasn't her looks, it was her vexed demeanor that was catching everyone's attention.

Bursting out of the bar in hot pursuit, emerged a large, red-faced man with a mustache. He sported an immense western hat and pointed cowboy boots.

"You pervert," the woman screamed at him, her voice loud and filled with hate. "I never want to see your sick face again."

"Get your tail back over here or I'll whip the tar out of you," the angry man cried, trotting to catch up with her.

As the cowboy reached the distraught woman, she swore at him, using words that curled John's ears. Stung by her insults, the man slapped her harshly across the face, hitting the helpless woman in the mouth. John was shocked at the sight, seeing the battered lady's head whipped forcefully to the side. He could clearly see the pain on her face.

Recovering her senses, she swung hack at her assailant, but the cowboy blocked the woman's slap and then punched her directly on the jaw with a closed fist. She fell sprawling to the asphalt, her face toward John, twisted with agony from the pain.

Her assailant was not through with her. Cursing at her now, the cowboy kicked the fallen lady hard in the side, eliciting a painful scream from her lips. John was immobilized with shock, he had never seen a man strike a woman before, and the force of that kick made him flinch just from watching.

A friend, who had followed the cowboy from the bar, rushed up to grab the berserk man from behind and pull him away from the shrieking woman. Given a respite, the injured lady struggled to her feet and attempted to flee.

"I am going to cut you, Rachel Maris!" the cowboy screamed. Breaking free from his friend, he drew a pocket knife from his pants.

John watched in silent amazement as the woman fled in a panic, running smack into the side of his Chrysler 300, which was directly in her path. With a look of desperate pleading in her eyes, she locked stares with John, and then opened the passenger door to his Chrysler and leaped inside.

The terrified lady locked both doors on her side as the angry cowboy ran up, afraid she might escape.

As John hastily got into the car also, the woman turned to him and cried, "Drive, please drive!" her terror starkly evident. A strong smell of beer assailed John's nose.

When the angry cowboy reached the Chrysler, he thumped the window alongside the woman's face with the butt of his knife handle. She shrieked in horror and ducked. John needed no further incentives to spur his actions. Stomping on the gas pedal he roared away with tires squealing.

13

Eleanor Hughes sighed nervously, yearning for her husband, confused about recent events, angry, depressed, tired. With misgivings she watched Chrissy and Billy playing innocently in the front yard. They were supposed to be working at chores, but without close supervision their diligence to the assigned tasks had waned. Billy had been asked to water the bushes and Chrissy had been given the job of sweeping the sidewalk. Just beyond them, Eleanor could see another of those ever present reprehensible vans.

Eleanor watched as the temptation for Billy to spray his sister with the hose, as might be expected for one his age, soon became too difficult to resist. He had barely kept to his chore for five whole minutes. Chrissy quickly got the upper hand though, and soon stood defiantly before her little brother, kinked hose in hand, berating him for not sticking to his job. Billy continued to threaten her, waving the non-functioning hose in his sister's direction. As long as Chrissy held the kink though, no water would come out. Eleanor studied the van out front. This one had no commercial markings on the side, it was the type one would expect a family to own. Eleanor had written down the license number. She was keeping a log.

The inevitable finally happened out on the front lawn. Billy, only five, turned the hose toward himself to stare down the nozzle. Chrissy, seeing her chance, gleefully released her kink and allowed the flow to continue. Eleanor pondered calling the police. She just didn't know what to do, John had said not to call the police, and she had never actually seen anyone inside one of the vans. She knew people were in there though, watching her, watching her children, watching, watching. It made Eleanor shiver, knowing strange eyes were upon them.

As Billy yelped in angry astonishment, Chrissy applied her protective kink again, just before he could redirect the spray in the direction of his gleeful older sister. Now Billy's astonishment turned to tears. Eleanor stepped out the front door to intervene, even though emerging from her house would put her in full view of the van. For all Eleanor knew, they might be taking pictures of her at that very moment. She felt self-conscious, exposed.

"Chrissy, you let go of that hose and get back to work right now," Eleanor scolded.

"Billy started it!" "Chrissy got me wet!" they complained simultaneously.

"I don't care! The next one to cause trouble will not be watching TV tonight."

Dropping the hose, Billy came running toward his mom, tears still running down his face and onto his soaking wet Spiderman shirt. "Mommy," he wailed.

Eleanor took him into her arms, even though it would get her own clothes wet too. Although Billy had initiated the trouble, he had obviously gotten the worst of the situation. Eleanor observed Chrissy obediently picking up her broom, but grumbling about it. Eleanor stared at the van again. It must be hot in there. The temperature outside was overbearing at 102 degrees and they had parked their vehicle in the sun.

"Say, Chrissy, why don't you and Billy set up a lemonade stand?" Eleanor suggested. "Put it in the shade, out in front of our house?" The idea of tormenting those people inside the van, regardless of how minor, pleased Eleanor immensely.

Chrissy's eyes lit up, "Can we keep the money?"

"Sure can. I will make up some nice cool lemonade. You find the big pitcher and fill it with lots of ice."

As Chrissy and Billy scurried about making preparations,

drawing a sign, finding a small table, Eleanor made plans of her own. She knew it was silly, but just in case, she dropped a fresh roll of film in her Kodak Instamatic and placed a chair by the front window in the living room. If someone came out, she would be ready to take some snapshots.

An hour later, one full hour of wasted time, although the children managed to attract a dozen passing motorists, no one from inside the van was enticed into the open. It was a stupid idea anyway, Eleanor fumed. Able to stand it no longer, she threw caution aside and angrily marched out of the house, stalking past her startled children, straight for the ominous van.

"Come out of there!" Eleanor screamed at them, as she banged her fist on the driver's window. There was no answer from inside though, and a curtain had been pulled behind the front seats blocking her view into the rear. Eleanor clutched at the door handle, but it was locked. Furious now, she marched around to the other side, but of course that door was locked also.

"Leave us alone," she screamed out of frustration, banging on the passenger window now.

Then Eleanor noticed the neighbor, Mrs. Riggs, the fussy lady who lived in the house in front of which the van was parked. Mrs. Riggs was watching out her living room window with a shocked expression on her face. Suddenly Eleanor became worried. Perhaps this was not a surveillance van, maybe this one belonged to some legitimate visitor who had come to see Mrs. Riggs.

Anger turning to embarrassment, Eleanor backed away, only to trip on the curb and fall flat on her back, right in front of the neighbor. Feeling an urgent need to hide, Eleanor hurried across the street and shuffled her children back indoors. The entire neighborhood would surely hear about her eccentric behavior before the week was out.

Still not feeling secure, Eleanor hurried about the house, shutting all the windows, pulling the blinds and curtains, and locking the doors tightly. After switching on the central air conditioning, Eleanor turned on the TV and found a dumb cartoon show for the children to watch.

Retiring to her bedroom, Eleanor lay flat on her back and tried to collect her thoughts. She could not go on like this. Where was John? What was he doing right now? How could he have brought this trouble upon her?

14

"What have I done now?" John Hughes thought to himself, as he glanced furtively toward the beautiful, dark-haired, beleaguered woman who had taken refuge inside his Chrysler. Still breathing heavily from her recent assault, the unfortunate woman's face was still strained with fear and pain. Slouched into the passenger seat next to John, she sat low, almost hiding it seemed.

The woman appeared to be at least thirty and John thought she might be part Indian. Her hairstyle and dress were urban western, and she had a dark complexion with deep richly-colored black hair and long striking eyelashes. She was very pretty.

After picking up the stranger, John had taken a right at the first intersection and was speeding east down a paved road, 63rd Street South, with barren fields of wheat stubble on the left and a modern suburban development going in to the right. The road was level, wide, and straight, and the trees were sparse, not obstructing his view, so John threw caution aside as his speed steadily climbed to seventy-five mph. John figured that cowboy would try to follow, and that was one dangerous character John wanted no part of.

"Turn left on Rock Road here!" the woman exclaimed, sitting

up, but then grimacing with pain. She could not suppress a moan, clutching at her side where she had been kicked.

John blasted through the intersection making a hard left as the traffic light turned a warning yellow. He had no intention of stopping though. Feeling a little safer now that they had turned twice and probably eluded pursuers, he slowed within the speed limit. As they passed an air force base, McConnell AFB, Rock Road brought them to the southeastern city limits of Wichita, a large metropolitan city of approximately 300,000.

"I must thank you for this kindness," the suffering woman attempted to speak.

John nodded, curious about the cause of the assault. He did not think it appropriate to bother her with questions at the moment though, she had been beaten badly and was obviously in pain. The woman in his car was wearing a new pair of still unfaded jeans, a pastel-colored cowgirl blouse, and fancy boots. The blue jeans looked expensive, definitely designer, although this pair hadn't held up too well, having ripped along the seam during her frantic scuffle with the cowboy. Her boots did not look very utilitarian either, designed for style rather than comfort, and her chartreuse shirt was definitely chic. She wore large oversized jewelry, too much for John's taste, expensive turquoise and silver, and her make-up was polished and refined, not what one would expect on a country girl.

"Are you hurt?" John asked cautiously, when she moaned again.

"I cannot believe he beat me," she muttered angrily between breaths.

John grimaced in sympathy, her accent causing him to wonder. Her speech had a distinctly New England sound, maybe Philadelphia, and her voice was deep and husky, low, almost like a man's, but very feminine.

"You took quite a hit," John spoke in agreement.

"How could he do this to me?" she exclaimed, raising a hand to her face. She felt her cheekbone where the swelling was already turning a deep reddish color. "Look at my clothes," she moaned. Her jeans were torn along the seam, the stitching pulled apart at the hip from the beltline to her knee, and her delicate blouse was smeared with dirt and grease from when the cowboy had knocked her to the asphalt.

"Are you going to be okay?" John asked again, wanting to express his concern.

"Is there any air conditioning?" she asked, brushing at her clothes.

Then John noticed her face and neck were covered with beads of sweat. It was hot in the car and she had been through a traumatic ordeal. John felt stuffy also, and the smell of beer on her breath was not helping.

"Sorry," he apologized. "It's broken, let me unroll my window some more."

John looked away when the woman next to him gingerly commenced pulling the tail of that chartreuse shirt out from her pants. At first he thought it was because the badgered woman was hot, but she was just wanting to examine her side where the cowboy had maliciously kicked her. Carefully raising her shirt, she exposed a nasty bruised area, already turning an ugly deep purple.

"Ouch," the woman exclaimed despairingly, running her fingers over the damaged skin. "I think he broke my ribs," she sniffled.

"We'll find a hospital!" John declared in alarm.

"No, no, just get me out of here," she smiled at his reaction. "My name is Rachel, Rachel Maris. Thanks for the help."

John was unconvinced though, questioning in his mind the wisdom of not seeking medical help. "Are you absolutely certain? We can turn around, the fire station back there could direct us to a medical facility."

"I am fine," she produced a small package of cigarettes and lit one up.

John winced, she had not even asked if he minded smoke in the car. John did not smoke himself and would never have allowed cigarettes in one of his cars back home. He tolerated it this time though, since she was hurt and maybe she really needed to smoke. This Rachel Maris lady had been through an ordeal.

John focused his attention on the road once more, ignoring the waifs of smoke that the wind swirled in his direction. "My name is John Hughes. Why did that man attack you?"

"Who, Randy? I don't know, he's a jerk." Rachel Maris straightened her shirt and surveyed her target critically. So this was her target, John Hughes. The contact had gone well, he was not the least bit suspicious.

Rachel could not believe Ostermann had struck her so violently.

She would get him back for that. There was no reason to punch and kick her so hard, it simply wasn't necessary. If he broke one of her ribs it would jeopardize her ability to complete this mission. Of course, Ostermann would be delighted, he would love to see her fail. She would get back at him though, the man was a woman beater, using their ploy as an excuse to violently assault her. He had picked the wrong person to bully this time though, Rachel wasn't one to forget a debt.

"Where can I take you, Rachel?" John asked, wondering what he was to do with this stranger beside him.

"Home, I guess," she replied as if it was a joke. Rachel Maris thought it odd to hear the target using her real name. Why had Ostermann called her by her real name? It was probably done just to irritate her. "Which way are we headed?" she asked.

"I just stopped for gas. Do you live in Derby or Wichita?"

"Neither, are you kidding."

"Then you don't need to return to that small town behind us, good!"

"No," Rachel closed her eyes, wishing the throbbing in her side would go away. She needed her wits, this was the moment to play on her target's pity. "I cannot deal with Randy anymore," Rachel whispered.

"Your husband?" the target asked innocently.

"No way!" Rachel put bitterness in her voice. "We were engaged, but no more. What did I ever see in that jerk?"

The target grew silent, Rachel could tell he was empathizing with her distress. "I don't know anyone in Kansas," she whispered softly. "We came down to meet his parents, some joke. He had the audacity to step out with an old girlfriend. At the bar I confronted him, I had no idea the beast would turn violent. You think you know a man, but he was like a different person. When I told him we were through, he became really angry. You know what I mean, out-of-control angry." Rachel thought maybe she was going too fast, slow down, slow down.

"Sure," John agreed, although he really didn't, he had never seen a man strike a woman before. It was hot in the car and the smoke was irritating. John felt uncomfortable, he could not relate to this woman's situation. Where did she want to go? "So where is home?" he asked.

"Colorado," came the response. Rachel opened her eyes and

glanced at the target. He wasn't smiling.

John frowned. Should he tell the woman he was going to Colorado? He was starting to develop a painful headache, it was too hot in the car, and he was sweating.

"Fort Collins," Rachel elaborated, wanting a response. What was wrong? Most men would jump to aid a beautiful damsel in distress. She was hoping to entice him into offering her a ride. Then, with more time during the drive, she could get him involved, perhaps even romantically if necessary. Eventually she hoped to manipulate him into taking her along to retrieve the stolen documents.

This was a critical decision step. He had to offer her a ride to Colorado. She had purposely chosen Fort Collins as a destination because it was in the far northern part of the state's population belt.

"I'm going to Colorado too," John responded eventually, realizing that he was being rude. "You can ride along as far as Denver if you like," John offered, but then regretted it. What was he thinking, he had spoken out of politeness.

"Thank you," Rachel responded, relaxing now. "I haven't any money for bus fare home, and didn't know how I was going to manage." Why was the man being so unreceptive? She had dressed to make herself attractive. The split in her jeans had been cut intentionally so as to come apart in her scuffle with Ostermann, and her blouse was open at the top with several buttons undone. Rachel sat up straighter, surely she was appealing to him.

Why worry, Rachel thought, settling back into her seat. He had offered her a ride, that was the first step. Rachel knew the target's age from the operation folder. She had expected him to be more bookwormish looking, the meek studious type. He was a rocket scientist of some kind. Instead she found the target to be an average looking guy, slender build, even slightly athletic looking. She would not mind getting to know him better. He would lighten up with a little effort.

Snubbing out her cigarette, Rachel laid her head back against the headrest. A small nap would feel so good right now. Her jaw hurt too. She needed to stay awake though, she had to work her target.

15

Thursday, February 15 on the eastern coast of Florida, at thirteen hundred hours, Colonel Roe entered room 1525, the main conference room of the 6454th STLG E&L (Building 1704, Cape Canaveral Air Force Station). Yesterday he had received official direction for the emergency launch processing of AFP-775, the SIGS mission, and Colonel Roe would waste no time implementing his orders.

Constructed on a once inhospitable cape along the Atlantic coast of central Florida were two American space launch facilities, each with its own set of unique launch pads. The one, operated by NASA, the National Aeronautics and Space Administration, operated under the constant, although sometimes unwanted, attention of the American public, a facility often frequented by tourists and the media. All Americans, from as far away as Death Valley Arizona to the snowy glaciers of arctic Alaska, were proudly familiar with NASA, the famous institution that had once placed Americans on the moon.

A lesser know fact, although not particularly shrouded in secrecy, was the existence of military launch bases, one along the west coast at Vandenberg AFB (VAFB) and the other on the east coast at Cape Canaveral AFS (CCAFS), next door to NASA's Kennedy Space Center (KSC). At CCAFS operations were run by the military under control of the 6454th STLG, the Space Launch and Test Group. Commander of the 6454th STLG was Colonel Roe, a brilliant but reserved former fighter pilot, a man who knew how to make things happen.

As Colonel Roe entered the conference room, junior officers, sergeants, and enlisted men snapped to attention out of respect for their commander. "At ease gentlemen," Colonel Roe spoke, as he assumed his customary position at the head of a large planning table. Behind him were twin projector screens for the display of vue-foil charts. Along the walls to each side hung the pictures of dramatic space and missile launches.

"Yesterday I received a launch notification for AFP-775, to follow DSP on a ninety-day cycle. Let's see how we are going to make it happen." Colonel Roe spoke with authority and self-confidence, dissipating any doubt as to who was in charge.

A nervous major arose and approached the head of the table. Standing to the side of his colonel, he laid a stack of hastily prepared schedule charts next to the vue-foil machines. The major was chief of planning and it had been a long night for him and his staff.

"The first chart explains our overall master schedule," the major lit up the screen and displayed a chart of horizontal schedule bars, punctuated with triangles marking key milestones. Picking up a three-foot pointer, the major pointed to the top bar, at a key milestone. "DSP is scheduled for a June 1 launch date. We were given August 31 for our ILC, ninety-one days actually, so we do have margin beyond our ninety-day advertised cycle, one day."

There was a nervous chuckle around the room. The task ahead of them was going to be challenging, if not impossible.

"What are the critical paths?" Colonel Roe questioned, not wanting to be bogged down with details. The major's stack of several dozen charts worried him.

"After launch, there is a scheduled two week turn around at LP-55, to prepare the launch pad for receival of the next booster. At that point, the Titan IV core vehicle, already mated with SRMs, Solid Rocket Motors, will be transported to LP-55. The Centaur upper-stage can then be mated four days later."

"What about the payload fairing?"

"The aft segments are critical. They are necessary early in the process for assembly around the Centaur. The forward segments are not on a critical path and won't be needed till after SV arrival."

"Okay," Colonel Roe leaned forward. "We all know the standard plans for a ninety-day cycle starting with pad availability. What needs to take place between now and the DSP launch, if we are to be ready once the launch pad is turned around?"

Anxious to show he knew his business, the major shuffled through his charts and selected a set halfway down the stack. "Five key deliveries are critical to commencing AFP-775 launch processing. First, we must have delivery of all seven segments for each SRM (Solid Rocket Motor). Ten have already been delivered and are currently in storage at the SRS (Segment Ready Storage) Building. The final two have an on-dock delivery date of March 9, by rail to the RIS (Receipt Inspection Shop) Building. We are in good shape there, on June 3 they will go to the SMAB (Solid Motor Assembly Building)."

"Good, this is the detail I want, go on," Colonel Roe was satisfied.

"At the VIB (Vertical Integration Building), we need delivery of the LREs (Liquid Rocket Engines), and the Titan IV booster core, for assembly and checkout. March 22 and April 1st are the on-dock delivery dates respectively, which does support the schedule. At the VIB they will undergo receiving and inspection, and then assembly and processing in the low bay. Core erection on the transporter will take place there, vehicle systems testing, and then vehicle acceptance. On June 12 we can then commence core and SRM mating procedures."

"Just a top-level overview right now, major."

"Yes sir, right. Moving along, the payload fairing is due on-dock in one week, February 22. I have verified that it was shipped from the factory at Huntington Beach early this morning and should be on the road as we speak. After undergoing receival, inspection, and flight preps at the MIS (Missile Inspection and Storage) Building, the aft segments will be taken immediately to the VIB for Centaur processing."

"Excellent! You mentioned five deliveries?"

"Yes sir, I have just reviewed the delivery status of the SRMs, the Titan core, the LREs, and the PLF (Payload Fairing)."

"That leaves the Centaur."

"Correct, the upper-stage delivery looks shaky. Typical processing at the VIB would normally require eight and a half weeks, giving us an on-dock date of April 19. With great optimism, the best we can hope for is April 27, one week later."

"That appears workable."

"The schedule is already marginally tight, sir. Two weeks after the DSP launch, we commence the Titan integration operations at LP-55. Five days later, we perform Centaur mate."

"One week's compression we can work. I want an early ship date from San Diego if possible; and if not, then we will simply accelerate the Centaur processing flow at the VIB."

"Yes sir."

"You look skeptical, major."

"No sir, I ah…"

Colonel Roe stood up, raising his hand for silence. Sternly facing the assembled group of air force and civilian launch integrators, he spoke. "I want to make this one point clear to everyone. Come August 31, we are going to launch AFP-775. I have firm commitments from General Mauvus, the satellite is going to be delivered on July 2. Now, gentlemen, this is war. Let's make it happen.

16

Driving into the parking lot of a mall called Towne East Square, John Hughes halted to collect his thoughts and struggle with his feelings. Now that he was no longer alone, with a strange lady sharing his car, fleeing her own set of problems, John wasn't so sure he wanted to continue onward. The woman reminded him of what he had left behind, Eleanor. Even if he should find out DWARS was true, could he really think to stop this virus from being deployed? He was just one lone man.

The female at his side possessed a dark elegant beauty that was quite enchanting, and at the same time, with her face relaxed in sleep, so innocent. Feeling a surge of compassion for the lady, John fought an urge to place an arm on her shoulder for comfort.

Who was he to offer comfort? Why had circumstances placed him in this role, a traitor to his country, a car thief, a mugger of women? He was no better than the brute who had assaulted this innocent woman. She was in more danger now, in his company, hunted by the authorities, than out on the streets of Derby, Kansas.

Why did they have to kill Goldsmith? That kind old gentleman was dead, murdered, a terrible ending to a ruined man. After thirty years of hard working, devoted, loyal service, they had broken and destroyed him. What had Goldsmith received for his service except a ruined career, an aborted marriage, a spoiled retirement, and a drunken bloody death.

Goldsmith was dead, but maybe not in vain, John would not forget. If it was true, if he and Goldsmith and all those thousands of other deluded employees at Krang Enterprises had indeed worked and sacrificed for years to build an orbiting genocide platform, then he would feel no qualms in exposing it. If true, the masterminds would have to be stopped, regardless of the government security systems behind which they hoped to hide their abominations.

John glanced at the sleeping form of the woman beside him. She seemed so relaxed and peaceful now, so quiet, so free of the worry that was distressing her earlier. She had needed help and, in a time of crisis, had reached out for someone, anyone. What unfortunate twist of circumstances had put his car, of all the vehicles on the road, directly in her path? How ironic that before her only difficulty was merely to escape a woman-beating fiancé. Now she was unknowingly riding in the car of a fugitive from the law, a man hunted by the police, the FBI, the CIA, even the KGB.

It was not fair to her. John clenched his right hand into a fist and punched the palm of his other hand. The noise caused the dozing woman to shift in her sleep. She had not done anything, why had fate plucked her from one problem and thrust her into a far worse one? She was innocent, what was he doing to her, offering her a ride to Colorado?

Hauntingly, John recalled the face of that other guiltless woman, a stranger in the parking lot of Utica Square, whom he had terrorized yesterday, threatening the horrified lady with a drawn knife, demanding her money. The shock and horror, the look of abject terror on her face, what had he done? The memory of that experience would forever be ingrained in his mind.

John closed his eyes, almost overcome with guilt. Wanting to rest, he laid his head back, but then Rachel Maris stirred and awoke.

"Where are we?" she asked huskily, sitting up to chase the sleep from her eyes. The wind from the open car windows had blown and tangled her hair in a wild conflagration.

"Just resting," John answered curtly, as he drew a handkerchief and wiped his face, hoping his moment of self-pity and doubt had not been evident. "You have to get out here," he exclaimed.

"What?" Rachel protested, fully awake now, alert to her crisis. She drew her legs up into the car seat and hugged her knees. Her target had a pained expression on his face. Why was he throwing her out?

"I...ah...it is for your own good," John said. "You do not know what you are getting into." John wished she would not sit with her legs bent at the knee like that, causing the split in her jeans to hang open.

"You cannot be serious," Rachel pleaded, trying a hurt scared voice. "You promised I could ride with you to Colorado."

"I know, but I have changed my mind." John stared out his window, not wanting to look into those dark beguiling eyes.

"Look," Rachel begged, sounding convincingly desperate. "I won't cause you any trouble. I promise not to be a bother. Why not? What harm is it to you? Let me ride along?"

"Well, ahh...what is your name again?" John turned to try and explain.

"Rachel."

"You see, Rachel," John noticed tears forming in her eyes. "It's not safe. You cannot stay with me."

"But what will I do? I have no money, no identification. You cannot desert me here. Look at my clothes, they are torn. Please help me."

The car was rapidly heating up, sitting motionless, parked in the scorching sun. John's thoughts were drawn to his wife, Eleanor. What was she doing right now? What did she think about his sudden flight from Tulsa?

The lady next to him was sitting with her head bowed, resting on her knees, her black wavy hair obscuring most of her face. She was breathing heavily. He could tell she was on the verge of sobbing. "What do you want me to do?" he asked softly.

"I don't feel well," she replied, barely audible between breaths, turning her deep dark eyes toward him. A sheen of glistening sweat had formed on her face and chest. "Have you any aspirin, or something to drink?"

"No, but we can buy some," John conceded. "Perhaps we could also get something to eat and find you some new clothes. There is a Target discount store across the street."

"Thank you," Rachel whispered, grateful that he was starting up the car again. The heat inside was intolerable. Why didn't he have a car with an air conditioner that worked? Rachel could tell she was going to have to work harder to get her way with this one. Apparently the helpless damsel in distress routine was not going to be enough.

She would manage him somehow, despite his reluctance, she was good at her work. Rachel knew his type, spineless, gullible, a bleeding heart. He was probably concerned about involving her in his troubles, what a weakling. Contrary to his athletic looks, John Hughes was, in reality, the bookwormish type she had expected. He probably spent a few minutes at the gym three times a week and the rest of the day sedentary behind a desk. His muscles looked handsome, but artificial. He could never hold his own in a fight, or in a survival situation, she could tell.

Personally Rachel did not care for his type, but she was a professional, she would come alive for him, show an interest in the man, make him feel like she adored him, although he meant nothing to her, simply another assignment. She wished Randy Ostermann had not exposed her real name to the target.

"How are we going to work this?" Rachel asked, as John found a parking spot at the Target discount store. "I can hardly be seen in public with these ripped pants." Rachel was not pleased with the store John had selected for shopping. She would wear discount clothes, if she had to, although the thought pained her. She was a professional.

"Do you want me to pick out some clothes for you?" John offered, glancing at the rip in her jeans.

Rachel put on an extremely skeptical expression, exaggerating her concern for modesty and causing John to laugh.

"I am married you know, I do have an idea of what women wear, and what does and does not match," John said.

"John," Rachel exclaimed with mocking bashfulness. "And does your wife let you pick out her clothes?"

"No," John chuckled, "never."

"It's all right," Rachel squeezed his arm. "Maybe your wife won't, but I will. A pair of shorts and a blouse will do just fine, something cool please."

"What size do you wear?" John asked, a little embarrassed at the touch of her hand on his arm.

"Size six," Rachel lied without flinching. Her thought was to cause John to buy her something unacceptably small; then, if she could squeeze into it, she could go back into the store and exchange for something more to her own liking.

As John left to make the purchases, Rachel Maris sat sweltering in the hot sun, waiting. It was not a hard task to pick out a few clothes, yet it seemed to take him forever. Finally he reappeared.

Rachel smiled pleasingly and thanked John when he offered her the clothes. Climbing into the back seat to change, she examined the contents of the clothing sack. He had bought her a pair of tan square-cut shorts and a pink shortsleeve shirt. As Rachel removed her own soiled shirt to change, she glanced at the rear view mirror to see if John was trying to watch. Disappointed that he was not, Rachel dressed with haste, forcing the undersized shorts over her hips.

"Oh look," Rachel exclaimed, acting frustrated. "They are simply too small. I am sorry."

"Shall I exchange them for a larger size?" John offered.

"Could we?" Rachel asked. "I am going in too."

Together they made their way to the women's department at Target. The clothes there were reasonably priced, fashionable, and well-made, but still the labels were not to Rachel's liking. She could tell John enjoyed being out with her. He acted like it was a shot to his ego to be in the company of such a beautiful woman, which Rachel took to be flattering. In return she paid such obvious attention to John that he was pleasantly embarrassed, although bothered by twinges of guilt.

John didn't mind when Rachel asked to buy a few personal items in addition to the clothes. She promised to pay him back and had such a nice smile, how could he refuse her? Rachel tried on and selected a pair of form-fitting shorts, socks, a pullover tank top, and a breezy transparent blouse. Finding an oversized baggy purse, she also bought some cosmetics, a hair brush, hand mirror, and other personal items. To top it off, she also purchased a large, wide-rimmed, sun hat and a pair of sunglasses. Rachel also considered buying some matching jewelry, but couldn't imagine herself being seen with such trinkets.

John seemed to have no end of patience and she made it enjoyable for him. Rachel was in no hurry, it was important the target get to know her as a person.

"Hungry?" John asked, as they walked toward the car. "There are several fast food restaurants across Kellogg."

"I am famished," Rachel smiled. "And perhaps there will be a place for me to change inside the restaurant, rather than trying to dress in the back seat."

"Good," John agreed. "After we eat, maybe we can find a phone book and see where the bus station is."

Rachel was crestfallen, was she loosing her touch? She could not believe John was still entertaining the thought of going on without her? The fact that she was failing bothered Rachel a great deal, so much so that she became sullenly silent and remained so all the way to the restaurant.

Her disappointment did not go unnoticed by John. It was quite a contrast to her previously friendly chatter. Apparently he had hurt Rachel's feelings, but that was okay. It was better than allowing her to be hurt for real, or to be arrested and thrown in jail if the police caught up with him.

As they entered a Grandy's fried chicken restaurant, John found a small table while Rachel excused herself to change clothes in the bathroom. Once alone in the women's restroom, Rachel quickly checked about to ensure no one else was in one of the stalls, and then locked the door. She had brought her original jeans along. Removing the belt, Rachel spoke to the listening wire secreted inside the lining.

"Ostermann, do you hear me? I need some help, some type of confrontation to make him fear for my safety. Make it convincing, he wants to leave me at the bus station. Oh, in case you lost us, we are at the Grandy's on Kellogg, across from Towne East Mall." She had to throw in that last remark, to tell Ostermann what she thought of his capabilities. His helping her wasn't going to change that either, it was his job, not a personal favor.

It bothered Rachel to ask Ostermann for assistance, but she could not afford to let John ditch her. Quickly Rachel changed into her new clothes, dropping the jeans and her old purse which no longer matched, into the trash. She threaded her old belt into the loops of her new shorts and dropped a sturdy F-S British stiletto and a Blackjack concealment push knife into her new purse. Rachel also had two small Viper throwing blades, one secreted inside each shoe. She was partial to knives as weapons, they were more personal.

John was just starting to get impatient when Rachel Maris reappeared. She was stunning, not only having changed her clothes, but also taking time to brush her hair and apply make-up. John rose as she neared the table and held her chair out.

"Thank you," Rachel smiled coyly, as she took her seat. She enjoyed being treated with courtesy. "I feel much better now," Rachel said radiantly.

"Ah...we have to go through a line," John spoke, stumbling over his words.

"John, please get me something, I don't like lines," she smiled at him.

"What would you like?"

"Anything," she beamed at her target, pleased that he was reacting again.

In no time at all, John returned with some much needed food. He had purchased his companion a breast, mashed potatoes, and fried okra. Rachel would have preferred a shrimp cocktail followed with quiche and then topped off with cappuccino and a slice of cheesecake, but such were the hardships of field duty.

Sympathy and charm were starting to do the trick again, Rachel thought, considering that an even more frontal approach might be required. It was absolutely critical she win him over. Rachel would do whatever was necessary to gain his complete trust; he had to take her with him when he went to retrieve the stolen government documents.

As the meal wore on, Rachel was sure she had John eating out of her hand. It was too bad she had already called in Ostermann for help. If the jerk struck her again, like he had in Derby, she would kill him. Perhaps Ostermann was monitoring their conversation and was perceptive enough to realize she did not need his help after all. She doubted it though.

Rachel stood close to John as he paid for the meal. It came as quite a shock when he asked for a phone book. Directed to a pay phone inside the doorway, John begin searching the yellow pages for the address to the city bus station. Rachel stood nearby with arms folded, totally miffed. Didn't this fool want her company? What was the matter with him?

"Can I make a phone call?" she asked icily, as John dropped the phone book after having memorized the bus station address. Rachel had been watching out the doorway for Ostermann's arrival, but had not seen him yet. She needed to stall, things were not working out with this dummy. She knew John was married, but still, why was he being so cold to her?

"Sure," John replied, stepping aside.

"It's long distance. I want to call home."

"Okay."

"How can I pay for it?" Rachel was having difficulty controlling her displeasure toward John, and was showing her anger openly.

"Ah…charge it to my home phone," John offered, feeling slightly intimidated. He thought Eleanor had mood swings, but nothing so extreme as this woman.

What an idiot, Rachel thought, as he quoted her his home phone number. Surely he must know his home phone would be tapped, any long distance operator assisted calls would instantly be traced. She dialed zero, then a CIA safe number, direct to her home office in Dallas. The line was used for backstop calls when needing supporting cover for a legend.

"Hello," came the response, once past the operator and charging instructions. It was Annette who took the call, answering the phone as if the caller was interrupting her.

"Hi, Mother," Rachel Maris said, knowing it would bother Annette. "How is Daddy?"

Annette did not bother with a reply. She knew the game Rachel Maris was playing, obviously talking for the sake of someone listening. Annette would hold the line open, listening patiently in case someone else took the phone. If needed, she would become a real voice talking to Rachel. Annette did not know if she could make herself sound like Rachel's mother though, how ludicrous.

"Yes, Mother," Rachel continued her monologue.

"Not too good," Rachel said.

"No, Mom, I need some help."

"I left Randy and I don't have any money," Rachel glanced at John with convincing embarrassment.

"Yes, Mother, I know you said not to go."

"Yes, Mother. I'm sorry."

"No."

"No, I'm in Wichita."

"Please, Mother, don't hang up!"

"Mother—" Rachel put a dismal look on her face and slowly hung up the receiver.

Turning to John, she again feigned embarrassment. "I guess I cannot go home. She treats me like I am still a teenager."

"Then where will you go?" John asked.

"Oh, if I can get back to Fort Collins, I have friends there." Suddenly a look of shock crossed Rachel's features. "No," she exclaimed, looking over John's shoulders.

"What's the matter?" John questioned, turning to see the source of Rachel's discomfort.

"There, across the street. That's Randy's car."

"What!"

"He must have been following us. I don't believe it," Rachel groaned.

"Let's hurry and get to my car," John suggested anxiously. He knew this Randy fellow was dangerous, besides assaulting Rachel physically, he drew a knife on her.

No sooner had they stepped outside the door, when there he was, standing in the parking lot. John had not remembered the cowboy being so big, and he had the same angry look on his face.

"Get away from me, Randy," Rachel Maris shrieked, causing him to start toward them. Rachel felt the muscles in her stomach tightening. She clutched at John's arm. If Ostermann actually struck her again, she would slit his throat.

To both their surprise though, the cowboy's attention seemed centered on John, not Rachel. As the tall man approached, John stood his ground, for the moment.

"Beat it, twerp," Randy snarled, halting in front of John, his mustached face inches away from John's.

"Oh no," groaned Rachel to herself. "That's not the right approach for this bookworm, he'll turn and run for sure, leaving me behind." Ostermann was intentionally trying to sink this phase of the operation and make her look bad. He knew she was the one they would blame for the loss of contact.

Pressing closer against John, Rachel placed her arm around his, hoping to bolster his courage. "You beat it, Randy," she challenged Ostermann. "John here is twice the man you'll ever grow up to be."

Horrified, John watched as the already angry man's face contorted. He saw the clenched fist coming, but with Rachel hanging on his arm he could not dodge. Taking the blow on his chin, John staggered back, dazed with pain. Then he did a surprising thing, he rushed his attacker.

Rachel watched with disgust as John swung away futilely at Ostermann, who stood before him, blocking his blows with ease, laughing almost in his face. Ostermann was a trained killer, and

John Hughes was a sedentary paper pusher, a weakling. Rachel hated weakness. In a real fight, Ostermann could have killed John in a second.

When Ostermann decided to strike back, it was all over in an instant. Two hard left jabs to the jaw, and then a powerful thrust to the gut. John fell to the ground, doubling over, the breath forcibly expelled from his lungs.

Over the tumult, John could hear Rachel behind the cowboy, screaming, "No, no, stop it!" Lying on the ground, as his vision cleared, he saw her pick up a nearby piece of lumber and strike their assailant over the head.

Rachel swung with all her might at Ostermann's skull, not pulling any punches. Ostermann had done violence to her yesterday and now he was hurting her target. She had no qualms about striking back. Ostermann saw her coming though and raised a hand to deflect her blow, knocking it aside enough to render it ineffectual, but still make a good show of it.

Falling to the ground, Ostermann pretended unconsciousness. He had done his part. Rachel resisted the urge to kick Ostermann in the ribs, and instead rushed to John Hughes' side, cradling his head until his breathing recovered. Throwing one of his arms over her shoulder, she helped him stand and together they shuffled over to the car where she helped him into the passenger seat.

Hurrying around into the driver's side, Rachel started up the engine and sped onto Kellogg, past the intersection with Rock Road, and then turned the corner into a residential neighborhood on Heather Street. "Are you going to be okay?" Rachel questioned her target, as she parked and slid over next to John, concern registering on her face.

"I don't think so," John moaned.

"You don't look so good," Rachel commented, brushing the hair back from his forehead.

John flinched from pain at her touch, his face felt bruised and puffy. "Guess we showed him," John managed to speak, causing Rachel to smile.

"I guess so," she started laughing. "If you are up to it, we had best be going, I'll drive."

"Sure," he smiled back.

"Great," Rachel slid behind the driver's wheel. "Don't worry about a thing, with me driving, we'll be in Fort Collins by nightfall."

17

"Special delivery," Annette chirped, rousing Dan Newby from an unintended nap at his desk. It was sunny outside, air conditioned-cool inside, and Newby's system was still recovering from a big lunch at Braum's, a cheeseburger with french fries and a two-scoop hot fudge sundae. He was feeling justifiably sleepy.

Annette neatly dropped a set of papers onto the corner of Newby's desk. An orange coversheet was stapled to the front of the first page and the back of the last page, hiding the classified contents from casual observers. "Albatross Control" was stamped in bold print on the top and bottom of each coversheet, with the number "88" in bold letters directly in the center.

Newby's eyes widened at the recognition of that special control system. Already, since members of his group had been briefed and cleared to one of the Albatross compartments, new safes had arrived for Albatross only material. In addition, a new fax and new orange phones had been installed for secure communications and the control handbooks and classification security guides had been delivered. Every control system had its own set of unique rules and regulations. Often the rules for various compartments within a control system even varied. Program 88 was a newly created program with its own separate Albatross compartment.

Annette was amused at having caught her boss napping. "I have extra typing I could pass on, if you have nothing else to do? How many words a minute can you type, Chief?"

"Ha ha," Newby replied good naturedly. "We have to keep the typing in the hands of competent members of the division. How did this package come in, secure FAX?"

"Nope, special courier, triple wrapped even. The top wrapping was addressed to a sterile PO Box in Dallas, in case the courier lost his package, however unthinkable that might be." On a daily basis Annette made a run to the post office picking up incoming deliveries. "The second wrapping was addressed to my home address, and the third was marked, "DO NOT OPEN, Return to the FBI" with the corresponding address of a local branch office." If anyone went to the trouble of illegally opening the first two wrappings, perhaps the warning on the third would scare them off.

Security precautions were a burden to deal with, but necessary in their business. Annette had an administrative clearance which allowed her to handle all office paperwork, regardless of the compartment or classification. Upon receipt of this material, Annette filled out the proper control forms, entered it into accountability, opened the wrappings, selected the proper coversheets, and delivered it to her boss. Annette was proficient at her job, even if she was difficult at times.

Before turning the coversheet to see what Annette had delivered into his hands, Newby watched his secretary exit the office. Not that he found a nice pair of legs more interesting than his job, it was just a momentary distraction. He wondered why women put up with wearing such tight clothes for the sake of style, a dress like that would surely grow uncomfortable as the day wore on.

Sighing, Newby turned his attention to the courier-delivered material. It was a memo from his boss, Henry Maxwell, head of Western Hemisphere Division, CIA operations. The subject was the announcement and agenda for a special topics meeting next Wednesday, back at Langley, with Newby's name assigned to speak on two agenda items.

Shaking his head, Newby rapped his knuckles across the polished surface of his desktop in frustration. Why would they pull him away at a critical time like this, right in the middle of Operation

Carrier Pigeon? A trip to Langley would shoot at least two days out of his schedule. It was no wonder they couldn't get any work accomplished, not with all these meetings. Now he had to prepare charts for a presentation too.

Also attached to the package was a printout from the Office of Central Reference, the latest listing of all personnel, along with current and past responsibilities, who were presently serving in positions under the Baron's jurisdiction. That material had not been entered into accountability, a bootleg copy to be destroyed after use. It was amazing what security rules the bosses could ignore. This was information for their computer databases, continuing the monumental task of cross-correlating and identifying possible members of the Baron's covert organization.

Suddenly the intercom buzzed on Newby's desk, causing him to start and almost drop the illegal bootleg material. Newby pushed the transmit button and responded generically, "Hello."

It was Maconey, his deputy, "I have Ostermann on the line, do you want in on the field report?"

"Be right there," Newby responded. Gathering up the Albatross material, he hurried from the office. "File this would you?" Newby spoke as he passed Annette's desk, dropping the material next to her keyboard. Newby did not wait for a response, but did notice her exasperated frown. Annette always acted like he was dumping tons of work on her lap. That was her job though, what did she think the taxpayers paid her for?

Entering a smaller office, Newby found Maconey already set up for a conference call. "Okay, Ostermann," Maconey began. "Dan Newby is here, what have you got for us?"

"All according to plan," Randy Ostermann's confident voice boomed out of the speaker box. "We contacted the target without flaw. With my help Rachel Maris has her legend established and the target does not suspect a thing."

Maconey adjusted the volume down on the speaker box. "So Rachel Maris is currently with the engineer?"

"That's right, he stopped for gas and to make some phone calls in Derby, a small town south of Wichita, Kansas. That gave us time to set up a distraction. I have Rachel with him now, no problems."

"And you are monitoring current progress, real time?"

"Yes, sir, Rachel is carrying a listening wire in her belt and a homing device in her purse. We have also planted a second homing device on his vehicle. In addition, I secretly planted a third homer in the sheath of one of Rachel's knives, unbeknownst to her. She is following directions perfectly though, so far. I instructed her to try and win his confidence first, play helpless."

Somehow Newby could not imagine Rachel following Ostermann's directions, knowing the bad feelings between them. Most likely Ostermann was just trying to take credit.

"What about outside contact?" Newby asked his intelligence officer. He had to admit, the operation had been going smoothly thus far, except for the Goldsmith killing.

"John Hughes made one attempt to contact his uncle, but could not get through."

"Did he leave a message identifying himself?"

"Affirmative."

"Good," Newby mused upon the implications. Now that the Baron knows there is trouble, and that his own nephew is involved, he is sure to step in.

"What about other contacts?" Maconey asked.

He called his mother once, and also home to his wife several times. She is endeavoring to persuade the target to return home and turn the matter over to the police."

Newby glanced at Maconey to see if he caught the significance of that bit of information. They had just that morning held a lengthy discussion upon how John Hughes' wife might be a source of potential trouble. She was an unknown in their plans, a variable that might disrupt their carefully orchestrated operation.

After the close of Ostermann's telecommunications, Newby raised the subject again with his deputy. "I think the wife is developing into a definite problem."

"Indeed," Maconey concurred. "If Hughes is maintaining contact, she must be a source of influence. Right now he may be committed to pursuing those documents. But I agree, his wife is not helping our cause."

"Yes," Newby knew where their logic was leading, "and don't forget the disturbing report this afternoon. Mrs. Hughes knows she is being watched. What are the scenarios?" Newby asked rhetorically.

"She might remain at home and continue with life as normal, forgetting about her husband. That would be ideal for us, but I think unlikely."

"Go on," Newby had been over these scenarios many times himself. He was hoping Maconey would come up with something new though, something he had overlooked. Otherwise, their choice of action seemed set, an action Newby did not relish.

"She might take the children and seek refuge somewhere, like moving in with her parents or with a sister. That would be all right, if she left her husband alone."

"Yes."

"She also might seek help. The police would be awkward and the press might be difficult to contain, depending how much she knows."

"What else?"

"The worst case would be if she succeeded in talking her husband into returning home, and that seems a likely scenario. As she becomes more fearful, Hughes will become more and more concerned for the welfare and safety of his wife."

"So what do you conclude?"

"At best, she's not helping us. At worst, she spoils the entire operation. If we are to get a line on the Baron, then John Hughes must recover the documents and pass our provocation list to Rachel Maris."

"Yes," Newby agreed solemnly, "and we know just letting the list fall directly into Rachel Maris' hands would never work. She would smell a trap. We have waited two years for an opportunity like this."

"With the Baron's nephew involved, Rachel will have a convenient excuse. All she need do is convince us she has not yet recovered all the documents. Then she and John Hughes could fly to the Baron, like a carrier pigeon returning to its roost. Then, not only will we have established a link, but the Baron will surely expose himself further, adding to the proof."

"Let us hope," Dan Newby interrupted. "No, let's not hope, let's make it happen. We must cover all the bases."

"The wife, she is a weak link in the plan."

"So, let's sever the umbilical between John Hughes and his wife," Newby said, nevertheless disappointed at their seemingly unavoidable conclusion. If only there were some other way.

"You do not mean to kill her?" Andrew Maconey asked.

"Heavens no," Newby exclaimed. "You are letting that Goldsmith mess affect your reasoning, Andrew. We are the good guys, don't forget."

"Sorry, Chief."

"We'll simply have her arrested. Get a warrant out and have her picked up this evening. We'll bring Mrs. Hughes in for questioning, charge her, and then let her sit out the duration in the city jail."

"You know she is totally innocent in this whole affair," Maconey murmured on her behalf.

"I know," Newby shrugged, feeling sympathy for her also, "but what else can we do? We'll keep her safely behind bars, that would be best for all our sakes. No one must interfere with John Hughes reaching those hidden documents, not even his wife."

18

"Don't worry!" Eleanor Hughes shouted into the phone with frustration, seething at her husband's patronizing attempt to placate her fears.

"It is not going to help matters to let yourself get into a huff," John Hughes gently rebuked his wife. His voice sounded distant, and there was the noise of traffic in the background. He was using a phone next to the restrooms at a roadside rest area.

"How would you like to be kept in the dark?" Eleanor complained indignantly. "What would YOU do, if I took off suddenly, with no explanation, and then the police showed up watching YOU?" The phone receiver felt sweaty in Eleanor's hand. She realized that she had been pressing the handle hard against her ear, it hurt when she relaxed the pressure.

In the distance John could see Rachel Maris returning from the women's restroom. She paused, loitering by a large vertical map, waiting for her driver to finish his phone call. John spoke quickly, "I am sorry, honey. I never meant to involve you or cause any pain."

Eleanor was till fuming, "Well you have caused me pain. Now you must come home, no more delays."

It was just like Eleanor, John thought. She related everything to herself, her pain, her fear, her frustration. Never mind how he felt or what he was going through. John looked up and saw Rachel watching. She waved and smiled cheerfully.

"I'm sorry," John spoke to Eleanor in a quiet voice. "I guess I had better be going."

"Wait," Eleanor cried, feeling her anger turn to doubt and fear. "When will you call again?"

"When I get the chance," John sounded sad.

"I love you," Eleanor offered. "Please come home?"

"I love you too, honey," John started to hang up.

"Promise me you will at least reconsider coming back home, I think it would be best. We should trust the police to straighten out your difficulties."

"Okay, I'll think about it."

"Let me know tonight, John. I want an answer tonight. Oh, I almost forgot, your uncle called."

"Uncle Ellis?" John's voice rose.

"Yes."

"What did he say? I've been trying to reach him."

"Just that he had received a message you called. I told him you were unavailable, that I did not know when you would be back."

"Okay, thanks, that's fine."

"If you change your mind and decide to come home," Eleanor offered, "I will be waiting."

"I know."

"It really would be best to come home."

"Good-bye, sweetheart, I'll call again tonight."

Despondently Eleanor wandered out of the bedroom to check on her children. John's phone calls were depressing, she could not understand why he had to treat her so poorly. Eleanor found Chrissy at the kitchen table, drawing little figures with a pencil that needed sharpening. Billy was in the TV room, rolling on the carpet, halfway absorbed by an old episode of the *A-Team*. It was past their bedtime, eight o'clock, but she didn't feel like going through the struggle of getting them off to sleep right then. They would become tired later on and fall asleep in the TV room if left alone.

Smiling gently at Chrissy, Eleanor entered the tiny kitchen and began making herself a cup of hot chocolate. Chrissy looked up furtively, half expecting to be ordered off to her room. She knew it was past bedtime and mommy had already changed into her own nightgown over an hour ago.

Just as Eleanor put some milk on to heat, the doorbell rang, jarring her nerves. Who could that be at this late hour? It was past eight.

"I'll get it," Eleanor yelled at the children, but it was too late, they were already scrambling for the door.

Despite their mom's command, Chrissy and Billy did not stop, causing Eleanor to chase after them all the way to the front hallway. All she had on was a nightgown and she just knew they would invite any visitors right on in. That would be embarrassing to say the least, the hem of her pink gown was so short it was hardly decent. It was a pretty nightgown, with a base layer consisting of a satin material and the outer layer a transparent lighter fabric. She had put it on because of the heat. In the hot Oklahoma summers, light night clothes were a necessity and this was the coolest she had, excluding a few intimate negligees that would not be decent around the children.

Sure enough, Billy opened the door without even checking to see who was outside. Eleanor dodged to the side, thinking to jump out of sight, but stepped on a small Hot Wheels car in the process. Relaxing the force on her foot, to keep from breaking the toy, she lost her balance and began hopping sideways across the hall and into the living room, totally out of control.

When she looked up, Eleanor was shocked to see a pair of uniformed policemen standing in the open doorway. Chrissy and Billy stepped back hastily. Uniforms tended to frighten the children.

"Is your mother home?" a policeman started to ask, but then he saw Eleanor skittering sideways across the room.

Catching her balance, Eleanor approached the doorway timidly. Now that she had been caught in her nightgown, the least embarrassing course of action that she could think of at the instant, was to pretend it was nothing unusual. She felt sick, afraid of what they might want.

"Mrs. Eleanor Hughes, of 7338 74th East Avenue?" the policeman asked gruffly, staring her straight in the eyes.

"Yes," Eleanor responded, feeling abashed and minute, apprehension sweeping over her like a wave.

"I have a warrant for your arrest, Mrs. Hughes. I am afraid you are going to have to come with us."

"What for?" Eleanor cried, feeling faint, tears coming to her eyes.

"You will learn all about it down at the station."

"But, but, my children."

"A social services worker will be here shortly. You need not worry about your children, we won't leave before she arrives. Have you any clothes you would like to change into?"

Eleanor blushed, but she was too scared to feel embarrassed for long. Surely they weren't really going to arrest her, not her? She couldn't go down to the police station. She couldn't allow a social worker to take Chrissy and Billy. Starting to feel panicky, Eleanor struggled to remain calm. An instinctive reaction was to turn and run.

"Mrs. Hughes, are you okay?" the policeman asked, seeing her fright.

"Yes, yes," Eleanor gulped and staggering back a few steps. She could see Chrissy starting to cry. "Chrissy, go and get the policemen a glass of water," Eleanor said. She turned and walked very rapidly toward her bedroom, not looking back to see what was transpiring behind her, although she could hear the policemen entering her home. They were coming inside her home.

As Eleanor entered her bedroom, she quietly shut the door and turned the lock in the handle. She had no intention of going with those men. Fear had replaced reason, she had to escape, she had to get away.

Slowly opening a window, careful not to make any noise, Eleanor pushed the screen out. Placing first one leg, and then the other, out the window, she hoisted herself up and through. The dirt from her flower bed felt cold on Eleanor's bare feet. There was a night breeze out, even though the temperature was still in the high eighties. Racing silently across the backyard, Eleanor felt a chill from the night air, but she did not care, she had to get away, she had to.

As Eleanor reached the back fence, a typical chain link suburban fence about waist high, a pang of guilt assailed her conscience. She was abandoning her children. What else could she do now though? If she stayed behind, the police would take them from her anyway.

Placing her hands between the links on the top bar, Eleanor attempted to hoist herself up. She couldn't make it though, she was too weak. Her arms were shaking almost uncontrollably now. A neighbor's dog was starting to bark, distracted by the sudden racket. Eleanor placed her feet between the links and stepped up. The pressure hurt her toes and feet, but she was able to get up and over the fence. The neighbor's dog was barking something terrible now. Glancing fearfully back toward the house, she saw a policeman pull the drapes aside on their sliding glass door. He saw her, she had been discovered.

With renewed apprehension, Eleanor raced across the backyard of her neighbor and exited though a small side gate to flee between two houses. Crossing a residential street, Eleanor ran for all she was worth.

She had a new friend that lived two blocks away, Susan Rey. They were out of state on vacation, but perhaps, if she could only get to Susan's house, she could hide there. As a result of all the commotion, lights were flicking on in several of the houses up and down the block. Behind her she soon heard footsteps; the police were chasing her.

Eleanor screamed when the fleeter policeman caught her, a rough hand closing about her arm just above the elbow. Lashing out in panic, Eleanor swung with her free hand and slapped him smartly across the face.

Reacting with anger now, the policeman flung Eleanor to the ground. Pinning her roughly to the asphalt, with his knee on her back, he jerked Eleanor's arms behind her and handcuffed her wrists. Now that she was secure, he pulled the struggling woman roughly to her feet. "That is two more charges," he retorted, "resisting arrest and assaulting an officer." Eleanor was sobbing uncontrollably now.

The long march around the block and back to the front of Eleanor's home was both humiliating and embarrassing. Escorted by two uniformed officers, now totally unsympathetic, one on each arm, wrists handcuffed behind her back like a criminal, clad in a short nightgown, dirty, disheveled, distraught, she made quite a spectacle for the neighbors. It seemed as if the entire block, Mrs. Riggs included, had awakened to view her discomfort. Many actually came out of their homes to stand on their front steps, watching with open-mouthed astonishment as they passed.

Finding the social worker had arrived to take custody of the children, Eleanor was read her Miranda rights and forced into the back seat of a police car, under arrest for treason.

19

"So, how's the wife?" Rachel Maris asked, as John Hughes moved away from the phone booth and walked toward her, a brooding expression furrowing his brow. He stopped a few paces short of Rachel, so she stepped toward him.

"I got through to Eleanor again, but no luck reaching Uncle Ellis," John responded.

Rachel brushed the hair back out of her eyes. She had already known, based on the disappointed look on John's face, that he had been talking with his wife. It was the third call to Eleanor that day and each time he had been visibly discouraged. Obviously John's wife was not helping him much. It was okay by Rachel if the wife provided no support or comfort to John, she was only making him more vulnerable to outside advances. John was already opening up to Rachel. He had become a lot more pliable since their encounter with Randy Ostermann.

It puzzled Rachel that John could not get through to his uncle, the situation was kind of ironic. Rachel could reach him if needed, a fellow member of the agency, not really retired, but his own nephew who desperately needed help could not get through. It was sad in a way.

Rachel had known her new assignment involved the relative of a high ranking official within the agency, but what a surprise to learn that the high ranking CIA official was someone she knew, someone she knew very well in fact. Rachel remembered all too well her first meeting with the distinguished Ellis Hughes. She had been a young secretary with the American Embassy Staff in Amsterdam, a young impressionable girl with little experience in the ways of the world, having led an impoverished childhood.

Ellis Hughes had seemed so sophisticated and mature, a true gentleman, aristocratic, courteous, and important. He was a tall handsome man, distinguished looking, catching Rachel's attention from the moment she had first laid eyes upon him. Over the following year they had gotten to know each other quite well.

It was Ellis Hughes, also know as the Baron, who had originally recruited Rachel into the agency. The Baron had seen real potential in the displaced, innocent, little gypsy girl that no one else thought of much worth. She owed him a great debt of gratitude for that. He had taken a personal interest in her welfare, overseeing her overall training, even pulling a few strings for a choice first assignment. Later she had worked for him directly. The Baron had become more than just a friend, he was her mentor.

"You must try again, surely you can reach your uncle eventually," Rachel encouraged John as they once more climbed into that hot old Chrysler and took to the road. They were nearing the Colorado border now.

"Huh...sure, might as well. I have to stop and give Eleanor a call every few hours or so anyway. I hope you don't mind the delays."

John glanced toward Rachel nervously. He enjoyed her company, but her feminine presence was disconcerting. She continually intruded upon his space. Having discarded her blouse, because of the oppressive heat, all Rachel wore was a pair of scant shorts and a halter top. It was hard to deny his attraction toward her, she was so beautiful. In addition, he could relate to her problems, and she seemed genuinely concerned about his. They were both in trouble, both alone, both needing help.

"No, no, I don't mind at all," Rachel spoke, smiling to herself. "You call Eleanor whenever you like. Her target seemed overly occupied with his wife, bringing her up quite often. Rachel knew the woman was bothering him; it was kind of amusing to observe.

"I cannot get anywhere with my uncle's answering service,"

John muttered. "It seems they are purposely giving me a hard time. I certainly would not have such unfriendly people working for me."

Rachel knew that the secretaries John had been reaching were not the average type. If they worked for the Baron, then they would be trained CIA personnel. She wondered if the Baron wasn't purposely avoiding contact with John. Perhaps he saw wisdom in not becoming an accomplice to his nephew's criminal activities. Rachel was sure he would help out though, somehow. She knew Ellis Hughes personally, and he always took care of his own. Surely such loyalty would extend to blood relatives as well as those that worked for him.

"My wife said he did call our home," John continued. "At least he knows I am trying to get hold of him. I just wish he would hurry up and straighten out those bureaucratic receptionists of his. He is the owner of the firm."

"What type of business is it?" Rachel asked, faking a bored lack of real interest. Actually Rachel was dying of curiosity to know what kind of front the Baron conveyed to his family, but she did not want John to think she was prying. So, the Baron knew his nephew was calling. He would know all about the case soon, the Baron had contacts, some legitimate and some not.

"A consulting firm," John answered, as he accelerated onto the freeway.

Rachel wondered if the Baron would try to contact her when he learned she was assigned to this operation. Would the Baron ask his former disciple to help a misguided nephew? It was a real possibility, and here she was assigned to trap the Baron's nephew. Would Ellis think bad of her for operating against a blood relative?

"Are you and your uncle very close?" Rachel asked.

"Yes, extremely so. He was always my favorite, and we did a lot together. Uncle Ellis never had a son of his own."

Rachel frowned, perhaps this assignment was not going to be as much fun as she had thought. She would do her job though, Rachel took pride in her trade, and she never failed. The Baron would understand that; in fact, he would expect it.

"I would keep calling," Rachel offered again. "If you think he might be of help."

"I know one sure way to get to him," John smiled. "I have a cousin that lives near Colorado Springs. She would know how to get through to her own father."

Rachel racked her brain trying to remember. John had a cousin? Did the Baron have a daughter? Rachel could not remember any children directly, the Baron had always lived alone. Then Rachel recalled the pictures of a small gangly daughter in her early years, the only child of a failed marriage. Ellis had never talked much about that marriage, that was why Rachel had been surprised to hear a daughter mentioned now. It seemed odd, thinking of the Baron tied to family members and relationships, he had always been strictly business. The agency was his family.

"Then you might try asking your cousin for a better number?" Rachel queried.

"Yes, or have Gwen call her father for me."

'Gwen,' Rachel mused the name over in her mind. It was the type of name the Baron would give a child, simple, strong, forceful, a good Celtic name. "Where does this Gwen…whatever her last name is, live?"

"It's still Hughes. Gwen is single, not very old, maybe still a teenager."

"And she lives alone, near Colorado Springs you said?"

"She is in college at the Air Force Academy," John spoke with a bit of pride.

"I see," Rachel nodded. That fit what she would have expected from a daughter of the Baron.

"It may not be easy to find her though, in the summer they hold basic training at the Academy. I am not sure Gwen would even be near a phone, let alone available to talk. It might be better to check into a motel, and then call from the motel and leave a message and phone number where we could be reached."

"It is starting to get late," Rachel jumped at the chance of stopping early. If they drove straight through toward Fort Collins, he might try to part company in Denver, where their paths diverged. A night alone with John might have interesting possibilities, an opportunity to draw closer.

"How far past Colorado Springs are you heading?" Rachel asked again. He still had not divulged his final destination, except to say he would take Rachel as far as Denver.

"About fifty miles beyond Denver," he answered vaguely.

"Toward Fort Collins?"

"No, I am afraid not. Denver is about the closest I can get you to home."

"It is probably best to stop early for the night. Then you can reach your destination in the day rather than the middle of night. Where are you going, anyway?"

John stared at the road, unanswering. Rachel decided she was pushing too hard, time to change topics. Leaning her head back, she raised her arms and stretched. "Do you think Randy Ostermann is still following us?"

Instinctively John glanced in the rear view mirror. "I don't know. What do you think, you know the man better than I?"

"Unfortunately, that is true. I suppose the jerk is following. He might be heading for home, searching for me along the way. There is not much chance of him finding us though, especially if we detour south toward Colorado Springs."

As the hours passed, Rachel tried to keep the conversation light but interesting. She was probing her target, learning his interests, his strengths, his weaknesses. Whenever she steered the conversation toward his current predicament or final destination however, he invariably became reserved, defensive, even silent. So Rachel danced around such topics, dipping in the water to test the temperature every so often, quickly pulling out because of the heat. He was cooling to her though, with each passing mile.

On the outskirts of Colorado Springs she hit upon a topic that seemed to really fire John's passions, racial prejudice. Soon the man was talking about genocide of all things.

"The thought of human beings wanting to destroy whole races of their brothers—we are all brothers and sisters you see—anyway, the thought of hating others just because of differences, it is so revolting," John commented with passion, "pure inexcusable evil."

"There is more to it than that," Rachel fed the discussion, enjoying his emotional response. "Usually there is fear involved, the offenders feel threatened."

"No excuse," John countered. "I think that is a rationalization for false pride. Bigots think they are better than others and cannot stand the thought we are all equals."

"You know," Rachel's voice purred. "My ancestors experienced racial persecution. I told you I was Romanian, actually my parents were Roma, or gypsy. Roma is a culture which has often been persecuted because we are different. My parents left Germany for the west because of Nazi persecutions. They hated us more than the Jews."

John thought Goldsmith might have argued that last point. It felt good talking to Rachel, she seemed to share all the same feelings. "Rachel," he said.

"Yes, John."

"What would you do if...ah..."

"Yes, John, go on," Rachel leaned closer, hopefully.

"What would you do, if you ran across something terrible, a threat or plot by a group of powerful people, against another group of innocent people?"

Although the question did not make sense to her, she could tell it was important to John. Rachel knew when to play along, "I would fight against them. It is the moral duty of all people to fight racial prejudice. If we don't, then we are guilty too."

John smiled at her answer, "You would not find fault with what I am doing, Rachel. You might even understand."

Rachel puzzled over his cryptic response. What would racial prejudice have to do with espionage and the space program?

Looking for a motel, John turned from Highway 24 and drove north on Academy Boulevard. "How about this one?" he pointed toward an economy motel, a Budget Twenty.

"No, please," Rachel shook her head. "Let's stop at that convenience store first, I'm thirsty."

"Fine, but don't take too long or we shall never get a room. It is getting late." John gave Rachel a twenty-dollar bill and remained behind in the car, fidgeting nervously while she disappeared inside the convenience store. Rachel seemed to take a lot longer than John expected, but when she emerged, carrying a sack in her arms, with that congenial smile of hers, John's annoyance dissipated.

"I checked in the phone book for a place to stay," Rachel suggested enthusiastically. "There is an Embassy Suites on Commerce Center Drive, at the north edge of town toward the Academy, and a Sheraton on Circle Drive."

"Aren't Sheraton's expensive?" John questioned, recognizing the name of a luxury hotel. He had never heard of Embassy Suites.

"No, not really, but let's go to the Embassy Suites then, I have directions." Rachel would have preferred the Broadmoor over them both, but knew John would never go that far.

Reluctantly John complied, wondering what was wrong with the Budget Twenty they had just passed.

As they drove north on Academy Boulevard, Rachel opened her

grocery sack and produced a sixteen-ounce can of chilled Colt 45 malt liquor. If she had to drink beer, to maintain her country girl legend, she might as well drink the stronger stuff. John was surprised. He had thought she merely wanted a drink of pop or something.

"Would you like one too?" Rachel asked, noticing his interest. She popped the tab and took a deep cool drink. Up until then she had not realized how thirsty or tired she really was.

"No thanks," John responded, eyes returning to the road.

Curious, Rachel asked, "You do drink, don't you?"

"Well...actually...no."

"Why not?" Rachel could not repress a smile.

"I used too," John explained, "but I quit. I don't believe in doing things that dull or inhibit my senses."

Rachel's eyes sparkled, "How long ago did you stop drinking?"

"Let me see, I guess it was about seven or eight years ago."

"Hummm, and you have a six-year-old daughter. I bet that was about the time you got married. Did your wife make you quit?" Rachel teased.

"No, of course not," John answered defensively. "It was a joint decision actually. We saw no real reason for it."

"Okay," Rachel chuckled. She could see right through John, his wife had a noose around his neck with a line so tight he could hardly breathe. He was so gullible and meek it was almost painful. Her initial imaginations were proving to be more correct than she had first thought.

"Is that where you want to stay?" John questioned with amazement, as they turned left on Woodman Road and then north again on Commerce Center Drive, bringing the Embassy Suites into view. It was a big multi-story luxury hotel of white stone brick, with a large clock tower dominated by a blue dome.

"Just pull up at the front entry," Rachel directed. It wasn't the Broadmoor, but it would do. Slipping her blouse back on, Rachel stepped out of the car to check in while John parked.

Inside the Embassy Suites was an open, elaborately furnished lobby with a marble front desk and ornate brass chandeliers overhead. Rachel approached one of the clerks and asked for a room; fortunately they had vacancies. John appeared at her side shortly, as she was filling out the registration form.

"How much?" John asked, still astonished at the type of place she had led him to.

With her pen, Rachel tapped the spot on the registration form where the price was printed. How gauche to ask the price.

"Eighty-five!" John exclaimed in a whisper. "For one night?"

Rachel shot him a stern look that silenced further objections. How embarrassing, eighty-five dollars was not much for a decent hotel. She registered as Mr. and Mrs. John Hughes, and put down a fictitious address in Dallas. "What is the license number, darling?" Rachel asked John.

Half stunned, John was forced to walk back outside to get the number off the license plate of the Chrysler. He returned just in time to pay.

"I put down cash, John darling, is that okay?"

John paid the bill in advance and they left the lobby with a door key for room 434. "You only got us one room?" he questioned Rachel.

"It's okay," Rachel responded. "I've stayed at Embassy Suites before, all the suites have a separate living room and bedroom. I will take the bedroom and you can sleep on the couch. Don't worry, I don't bite."

John started to protest further, but was distracted by the magnificence of the hotel. The rooms faced an open inner courtyard like an indoor arboretum. On each floor the halls ran in wide loops around the building, with an open rail along the inside and the room doors along the outside. On the ground level was a bar, restaurant, and a profusion of indoor vegetation, flowers, palms, bushes, and full grown trees surrounding a bubbling stream stocked with big fish—rainbow, golden, brown, and brook trout.

Room 434 turned out to be quite nice, not eighty-five-dollars nice in John's mind, but nice enough. Inside was a small living room with a TV, sofa, chairs, and a table. A small hallway connected to either the bathroom or bedroom, which offered a queen size bed, dressers, a table, and its own TV.

"I think this will do," Rachel seemed satisfied, "at least for one night."

"Yes, although we could easily have gotten two rooms for far less money at the Budget Twenty."

Rachel wrinkled her nose. "Why, John? If you don't treat yourself nice, no one else is going to either."

"They must have a pool here," John commented. While exploring the suite he had discovered a swimsuit. "I found this on a hook behind the bathroom door. The maids must have missed it also."

"How terrible," Rachel commented. "I'm going to call the front desk right now and complain. They should send someone up to remove it right away."

"No wait," John interrupted her. "I could sure go for a swim, after the long hot day we have been through. I wonder if they have an indoor pool?"

"I suppose so," Rachel said, "and probably a jacuzzi and sauna too. Why don't you go on down, I'll pick out a swimsuit for myself in the gift shop and join you."

"Sounds good," John was relieved to be getting out of the room. The atmosphere was getting a little thick with Rachel so close. Disappearing into the bathroom, John found the swimsuit was way too large around the waist, but he didn't care. As long as it stayed up, he would make do. Emerging from the bathroom he was startled to find Rachel still there.

"I will need some money," Rachel stated, as she unabashedly let her eyes travel up and down his body. She smiled upon seeing how embarrassed it made John. He fumbled around to find his wallet and gave her fifty dollars. Rachel left for the gift shop wondering if that would be enough.

Downstairs, just off the lobby, Rachel found the hotel gift store on the verge of closing for the night. She brushed in anyway, heading for the women's swimsuits. They ran a brisk business in that line of clothing, people that wanted to take advantage of the Embassy Suites indoor facilities but had neglected to bring a swimsuit from home. The clerk was an elderly lady, anxious to close up and head for home, but too polite to rush a customer.

Rachel was beginning to feel tired. As she stared at the clothing her eyes blurred, and for a moment, she felt a pang of consciousness about the way she was planning to manipulate John Hughes. He seemed like such a nice man, a weak person it was true, but harmless. Rachel was so accustomed to working with strong dangerous men, many of them killers. Also, it bothered Rachel that her target was a relative of the Baron, a man she admired greatly. The Baron was her friend, the one who had made her what she was today.

Steeling her thoughts, Rachel pushed such sentiments aside. She would not become weak herself, she would stay strong. Picking one of the tinier bikinis, she resolved not to let emotions interfere with her mission. She was a professional, she would do her job.

As Rachel strolled through the main floor of the hotel toward the pool area, she spotted a familiar figure at the complimentary cocktail bar. It was Randy Ostermann, he was seated at a table with his back toward Rachel, having selected a chair where he could maintain a view of the entryway to the pool area. It was obvious he was keeping a watch on their target. Now dressed as a businessman, his mustache gone, Ostermann was hunkered over a *Wall Street Journal* with a glass of wine at his side, trying to blend in and not attract attention.

Rachel smiled when she realized he was unaware of her presence. Fluidly pulling the F-S dagger out of her purse, and then drawing it from the sheath, Rachel steathily moved in on her adversary, keeping the knife hidden in the hand that also held her purse. She paused for a moment when the knife caught coming out of the sheath. Suddenly a throbbing on her sore ribs reminded Rachel of the malicious blows Ostermann had inflicted upon her in Kansas that morning. Eagerly she swooped in.

"Don't move," Rachel whispered threateningly in Ostermann's ear, as she expertly thrust the point of her stiletto into his lower back. Applying just enough pressure to make her point, but not enough to pierce his skin, Rachel pressed the knife's edge against a soft spot along Ostermann's spine. Cutting a vital artery or nerve center was more effective for a kill; however, the base of the spine was a more interesting spot for the occasion, the pressure really made Ostermann sit up straight.

Rachel had always considered fighting knives her specialty, her preferred weapon of choice, silent, efficient, effective. Although others disdained killing at such close quarters, preferring the impersonal distance afforded by guns, Rachel liked the control it gave her. Vividly she remembered the first man she had slain. Jabbing a spike pattern thrust dagger into his chest, she had held on and watched him die. Blood soaking her hand and arm in a sloppy but effective strike, she had felt the actual moment of his death, her eyes inches from his, the man's gasping last breath hot on her face. She had literally felt him die. Killing by knife was brutally personal.

It was the Baron that had aroused her interest in knives, back when she was a fresh recruit in training at the "farm," Camp Peary near Williamsburg, Virginia.

"Pick a topic to specialize in," the Baron had advised her. "Explosives, guns, disguises, it does not matter what, just choose something to be the best at. Whenever any instruction or training is given on your chosen subject, pay particular attention, become the expert. Your learning process in all areas will improve as well, as your self-confidence grows." Rachel had chosen knives and soon found herself excelling.

Ostermann stiffened abruptly and froze, fear snaking up his spine from the point in his back. He knew Rachel Maris was capable of killing him, right then and there if she wanted. The woman had no emotions, she was a stone.

"Rachel, my dear," Ostermann spoke in a calm even voice, not betraying the sudden rush of adrenaline or increased pulse. "Have a seat and I will buy you a drink."

For what seemed an eternity to Ostermann, there was no answer. He was beginning to wonder if she was really going to stick him. Ostermann considered spinning around in an attempt to knock her hand aside, but decided against it. Rachel was too good for that. He had to do something though, he couldn't die.

Abruptly Rachel laughed, a husky sickly laugh, and withdrew her dagger. "You always were a charmer with the ladies, Randy. I will take you up on that drink, especially since I have no cash of my own." Gracefully Rachel slid into the chair opposite Ostermann's. To any casual onlooker, she presented an image of elegance; one would never suspect the killer in her blood.

Ostermann felt a flush rising to his face and fought to control his anger. He would get back at this slut someday. Ostermann knew his life had hung on a thread, he could just as likely be dead right now, if her fancy had so chosen. Motioning to the cocktail waitress, he tried to maintain his composure. "Things are going well, Rachel. I am pleased with the way you are handling John Hughes."

Rachel smiled and shrugged her shoulders. What a pompous stuffed-up liar, she thought. In actuality Ostermann was undoubtedly plotting her failure, then he could step in and personally save the mission, taking all the credit for himself. Rachel stared at Ostermann intently, coldly, making him look aside.

"Black Russian," Rachel ordered, when the mini-skirted cocktail waitress appeared. She chose Vodka just to irritate Ostermann. As a true red-blooded American, he seemed to think anything with connotations of the enemy was contemptible.

"Any clues as to the whereabouts of the documents?" Ostermann asked, playing the game.

"Not yet, but I think for sure he will confide before long."

"After tonight anyway," Ostermann remarked snidely, smirking lecherously.

Rachel's eyes flashed. Did that idiot Ostermann think this was some kind of brainless honey trap and she was the swallow? Well, maybe in a way it was. "Just see that you do your job," she retorted.

"Right."

Rachel fumed, how she despised Ostermann. He was such a jerk. The waitress brought Rachel's Black Russian and she sipped heavily, anxious to finish the drink and be on her way. When she stood to leave, Ostermann stood also, out of false politeness.

After six malt liquors, and now a vodka, Rachel was already feeling a buzz. Attributing it to the long drive and her resultant tiredness, or maybe the altitude, Rachel left Ostermann, conscious of his malicious stare upon her back. Passing the bar, she ordered another Black Russian, telling them to put it on Ostermann's tab.

Rachel found John inside the pool room, soaking contentedly in a large bubbling jacuzzi. Placing her drink along the edge of the jacuzzi, Rachel retired to the women's room to don her swimsuit.

When she reappeared, John tried not to stare at Rachel's bikini. He should have known the type of swimsuit she would buy. She looked good, although she did appear somewhat unsteady on her feet.

Rachel could tell John appreciated her choice of swimsuits. Stepping into the water, she grimaced, it was hot, very hot. Rachel stood for a few minutes with the water line at waist level, adjusting to the heat, feeling goose-bumps along her arms, and then sat in the water facing John.

"It feels good," John remarked, glad to see her.

"Yes," Rachel closed her eyes dreamily, slumping until the water was just below her chin. "I could stay here for hours."

"If it was not so hot anyway," John agreed. He wondered if the alcohol and this heat was good for her. There was a sign over the jacuzzi warning about such things. Rachel had obviously not seen it, or else did not care.

"We came a long way," Rachel remarked, as she sat up straight and took her drink in hand. "It has been a difficult day."

"For sure. How is your side?" John could not help but notice the large bruise along Rachel's ribs.

"Terrible," she commented with a chuckle, "and I see the side of your face is still swollen."

John liked Rachel, she was so easy to talk to. "I'll bet you will be glad to be home tomorrow." John stepped out of the water, the heat becoming too much for him. He sat along the edge with his feet still dangling in the jacuzzi.

"Not really," Rachel frowned. "Actually I don't have much of a home to return to."

"Tell me," John's voice became more serious. "Why did you register us into the same room?"

Rachel blushed, "I simply wanted to save some money. Each suite has two rooms so there was really no reason to take separate suites. I don't intend to take advantage of you, honestly," she laughed.

Rachel's vision blurred again for a moment, then refocused on John's chest. She liked the way John looked, he had a slim figure with rolling sculptured muscles. She knew John was actually quite weak, he hadn't stood a chance against Ostermann when they had fought, but he looked nice.

"It's okay," John said, worried he had offended Rachel.

"Yes," Rachel mocked good naturedly. "What ever would dear sweet Eleanor think?"

John frowned at the remark, telling Rachel she had said the wrong thing.

"Well," Rachel mimicked John, "I am sure Eleanor would understand. She needn't worry anyway." Rachel rose out of the jacuzzi, she had not lasted five minutes in the water at one-hundred-three degrees Fahrenheit. The motion of standing made her dizzy again though. John watched the water run from her glistening skin. She sat on the edge next to him.

As they relaxed in the heat of the jacuzzi, conversing pleasantly, John began to tell Rachel things he had never planned on talking about. He started out describing his work, the type of job he was currently assigned to, and finally even the program to build and launch a new generation of spy satellites. On and on he went, speaking of satellites and payloads with deadly viruses on board. Rachel knew she had won him over, John Hughes was hers.

She listened attentively as he graphically described the threat of a genocide weapon, an orbiting laboratory of death circling unsuspected above the sky, carrying a virus so deadly it could exterminate the future generations of entire nations.

As he described the threat, Rachel began to feel sick to her stomach—the heat, the drinks, John's apocalyptic words. She realized this poor deluded man was guiltless of any real wrongdoings. He was no traitor, just a decent man caught in the manipulations of a degenerate society. Tomorrow she would help him get in contact with his uncle, the Baron. Ellis Hughes would know how to help. Tomorrow they would contact his daughter, that cadet at the Academy. But first she needed to rest, she needed to get back to her room, she felt herself starting to swoon.

20

Gwen Hughes, Air Force Academy cadet, bolted upright in her bed with a start, blasted out of a deep sleep by a sudden burst of static noise. "Arrghh," she moaned, as her hand sought the off switch on her radio alarm clock. "Must have accidentally hit the tuner knob when I reset the alarm," she berated herself. Instead of being awakened by soft classical music, she had received a blast of chaotic static.

Shutting off the rude little digital box, Gwen Hughes stared at the time, trying to comprehend. It was two o'clock in the morning; good, time for the 'Bear Hunt.' Rising in her bed, the top bunk in a standard cadet unit with a desk underneath, Gwen stretched to clear the cobwebs and then checked on her roommate.

"Fran, Fran," Gwen leaped to the floor and shook the slumbering girl. "I cannot believe you, the alarm has gone off."

A groggy, freckle-faced, sleepy-eyed girl groaned and looked up. She shook her head, her shortly cropped brunette hair falling over her face. "Not tonight Gwen, I am too tired. Let's do it another night."

"No way, Fran," Gwen pulled the covers off her lethargic roommate. "Boomerang and George will be waiting. Come on, get ready."

Gwen Hughes left her friend to struggle out of bed. Stepping in front of a mirror, Gwen hastily brushed her own hair into some semblance of order. Her hair was light blonde in color, also cut short, and she had deep blue eyes that sparkled, showing the laughter of her normally enthusiastic soul.

They lived in Vandenberg Hall, the AFA cadet dorms for a military academy located along the foothills of the Great Rocky Mountains. Their room consisted of two bunk bed units with desks and built-in personal computers, closets, and a sink with counter. They had a window overlooking the terrazzo outside, with lush pine-covered mountains in the background. The room was meticulously clean, no item out of place, ready for a white-glove inspection without notice. It was a sterile military environment, no room for deviation or self expression, except for the one medium sized bulletin board allowed each cadet.

Consequently, the energetic college kids often expressed their exuberance in outlandish activities. Quietly the girls dressed, donning outfits for a midnight expedition; combat boots, dark-colored navy blue sweats, and black parka caps. Except for the white letters "USAFA" printed along the right chest of each sweatshirt, they would be hard to see at night. This evening they were going on a hunt for Dancing Bears. It was time for a little fun.

Hurrying from their room, the mischievous female cadets stepped lightly down the hallways of Vandenberg Hall. Turning a corner, they nearly ran into two other cadets, also similarly attired.

"Watch out, Gwen," Boomerang scolded, as she bumped into him.

"Shhhhh," Gwen whispered. "Be quiet you oaf."

"Hey, you be quiet."

"Shhhhh," Fran insisted, wondering why she had let Gwen talk her into this foolishness. "You want to march tours for a month?"

"You got the stuff?" Gwen asked the boys, her voice mimicking a gangster.

"Sure," Boomerang replied, holding up several small cherry bombs. "Courtesy of Jack's Valley, let's go, Airborne!" Earlier that summer Boomerang had been to jump school training at Fort Benning, Georgia.

"Shut up you idiot," Gwen mocked him. She also noticed the can of comet abrasive cleanser in George's hands. It looked like they were all set.

Quietly the four conspirators descended a stairwell two flights to the terrazzo level, where they exited Vandenberg Hall. The dorms at the Academy were situated on two opposite corners of the Cadet Area, separated by a large grassy square with a terrazzo around the perimeter. Vandenberg and Sijon Halls were six stories high, with rooms on the second, third, fifth, and sixth floors. The first and fourth floors were open except for stairwells and support columns. Each dorm was shaped like a long chain of square links, a most unusual structure.

During the summer, Gwen had been assigned to Squadron H, as part of the cadre for basic training, located on the top floor of Vandenberg hall. Her regular squadron was Thirty-Ninth Squadron, otherwise known by their nickname as Jedi Knights.

Under the light of a brilliant Colorado starlit sky, clear and crisp, free of pollutants, up next to the tremendous mountains of the Rockies, four darkly-clad cadets made their way onto the terrazzo. Feeling exhilarated with the excitement of their adventure, they cut across the thick grassy central square and angled toward the Air Gardens. On each corner of the square were static displays of historic air force airplanes.

Emerging onto the terrazzo again, in front of Mitchell Hall now, the AFA cadet dining facility, they jumped a small wall and descended a slopping grassy hill to a parking area. There Boomerang had arranged for a car, borrowed from a "Firstie."

Piling into the sparkling new Camaro, they drove around to the northeast corner of the Cadet Area and parked by Vandenberg Hall, near the "Bring Me Men" ramp. Now that they had their getaway vehicle ready, they once more entered Vandenberg Hall, this time via a different stairwell. All seemed quiet, with sleeping Basics and their Upperclassmen trainers long since retired from a long grueling day of basic training. Boomerang had scouted out the route. Under his guidance they located the appropriate third-floor Cadet Recreation Room, slipped inside, and shut the door.

"Whew," Fran breathed a sigh of relief. "I don't believe we made it this far without being seen."

"Of course we did," Gwen placed an arm around her buddy in a sisterly manner. "Now we shall see about Speegle. Boomerang, you are sure this Rec Room is directly over his window?"

"Sure is," Boomerang reaffirmed. "The location could not have worked out better, just under that window to the right."

"Let's do it to this Dancing Bear and get out of here," Gwen smiled. She loved a Bear Hunt, the most dangerous, but also most satisfying of cadet midnight pranks.

At the Air Force Academy the Cadet Wing was run by the cadet's themselves. That group of cadets chosen to lead at the Group and Wing levels, were affectionately known by their fellow cadets as Dancing Bears. A prank directed at one of them was labeled a Bear Hunt, dangerous because of the subsequent penalties that would surely follow if caught.

Cadet Speegle was a particularly unpopular Dancing Bear, having distinguished himself over the past year with zealous conformity to officer directions, often at the expense of his fellow classmates, a real brownnoser. He was slated to be a group commander for Fourth Group next year, the group in which Gwen and Fran's squadron was included. Gwen just wanted to start him out with a friendly welcome from the Jedi Knights.

Climbing brashly into the open window frame, Gwen paused while Boomerang and George took a firm grip, one on each leg. Fran stood by the door as a lookout. Taking a deep breath to steady her nerves, Gwen extended herself out the window and reached down with her arms. Boomerang and George braced themselves as she wriggled further out the window, until they were supporting her entire weight and Gwen hung completely upside down.

Feeling the blood rush to her head, Gwen groped out for Cadet Speegle's window, but just her luck, it was shut. Now why would he sleep with his window shut on such a hot day? She stretching to reach the edge of his window frame, hoping it was not locked, if so their plans would be thwarted.

"What in the world are you doing?" Boomerang called down mockingly, as Gwen leaned far to the side. This time she was in luck, the window was cracked open.

Struggling to force her finger tips inside the crack, Gwen lost her parka cap. It slipped off her head and fluttered three stories to the ground below. No big loss, it was probably her only piece of uniformed clothing that did not have her name, squadron, and cadet number stamped or written on it somewhere.

Starting to feel dizzy, Gwen concentrated, renewing her efforts to get the window open. She was not about to give up now. Grudgingly it slid open a bit. That was enough to give Gwen the chance to force her fingers all the way in. Slowly she slid the window halfway open.

Looking back at her friends, Gwen extended an open palm toward them. Boomerang and George were both leaning halfway out the window, each holding onto one leg at the ankle.

"Fran," Boomerang whispered back into the Rec Room, "Hand me a bomb, I can't let go to get one."

Nervously Fran picked up the can of cleanser and selected a cherry bomb from off the edge of a foosball table where Boomerang had set them. The top had been removed from the can of cleanser, in its place was the plastic lid from a can of tennis balls. Rather than hand the items to Boomerang, Fran stepped between the two boys and peered down at her dangling roommate. "You ready for these?" she called to Gwen.

Gwen shook her head emphatically, then whispered, "No, you light it and then hand it to me."

Fran peeled the plastic lid off the cleanser and placed it carefully on the floor. Holding the cherry bomb over the can, she suddenly realized, with an ironic degree of relief, "I have no matches."

"In my back pocket," Boomerang said.

Her hand shaking a bit, Fran struck a match and held it to the fuse of the cherry bomb. When it caught, the sudden flare startled her. With great haste, Fran dropped the small explosive into the powdery cleanser, replaced the plastic cover, and leaned far out the window to place it in Gwen's upstretched waiting hand.

Gwen immediately tossed the canister into Cadet Speegle's open window and then strained to reshut the pane. No sooner had she done so, than a muffled bang exploded inside Cadet Speegle's room, followed by an instant cloud of dense white powder.

"Up, up, get me up!" Gwen yelled, the time for stealth having passed.

As soon as George and Boomerang had safely pulled Gwen back through the Rec Room window, the four of them raced for the door. Running with great zeal, they tore down the hallway and sprinted down the stairs. Tearing out onto the terrazzo, they flew down the "Bring Me Men Ramp," and ran for their Camaro.

Almost instantly they were away from the scene. Circling south, they reapproached Vandenberg hall from the west, parked, and entered the dorms far from the location of their dastardly deed. Quietly making their way back to their dorm rooms, they stuffed their Bear Hunt uniforms into dirty clothes bags and hastily jumped back into bed. They were safe once more; they had pulled it off undetected.

Gwen was thrilled with the experience, she didn't even feel tired. What fun that was! She could just imagine Speegle waking to a cloud of pure white, then stumbling around to find the door and escape his room. It served him right, Speegle was a self-serving twit, and his roommate was no better, typical Dancing Bears. They would have fun cleaning up their room tomorrow morning, everything covered with a fine layer of Comet. He would also probably have a hard time finding a clean set of clothes to wear, and tomorrow was the changeover for the second half of "Beast." Gwen could not help chuckling to herself as she pondered Speegle's dilemma.

Morning came early that next day to find Gwen extremely tired, suffering the penalty of her midnight escapade. It was no real hardship for Gwen Hughes though. She was young and in good health. Rousing Fran first, Gwen made her way to the wash sink and splashed cool water on her face.

Poking her head outside the room's door, Gwen listened for the uniform of the day. A hassled Doolie stood at each end of the hallway; already dressed, they stood frozen at attention, yelling out vital information for the Upperclassmen.

"Sir, the time is zero-six-forty-one hours. The uniform for the breakfast formation is combat boots, fatigues, ascot, and alpha cap. The breakfast menu is french toast, bacon, hash browns, and orange juice, sir."

The Doolie ran through his announcements without flaw; he had to, standing on each side was a stern faced Upperclassman, just waiting to pounce on the slightest error.

Gwen spotted Boomerang halfway down the hall. He winked at her and waved. Gwen smiled back in an exaggerated expression, showing her teeth, and withdrew back into her room.

Dressing quickly, Gwen put on a pair of freshly starched fatigues, the trousers so flat she had to force her feet through the legs. Next she donned an ascot with her class colors and finally combat boots. After brushing her teeth and combing her hair, she was ready for formation, with ten minutes to spare, it was only six-fifty.

Noticing the Doolie at the end of the hallway was one of hers, Gwen approached and eyed him critically. She stood with feet spread apart and arms on her hips, trying to make him nervous. He shouted his message loudly and confidently though, without error.

"Mister Applegate," Gwen spoke sternly.

"Yes, Sir…ah, Ma'am."

"What is my name, Mister?" By calling her sir, he had addressed an Upperclassman incorrectly, a mistake that made him vulnerable for further, unwanted Upperclass attention.

"Ma'am, Cadet Gwen Hughes, ma'am."

"And my home town?"

"Ma'am, Tulsa, Oklahoma, ma'am." All Doolies were required to memorize certain important facts about the Upperclassmen in their squadron.

"That is right, Applegate. Do you want to match shoes, Applegate?"

"Yes, ma'am," he replied loudly, although he would have given up breakfast not to, knowing he did not have much of a chance. But to say no would have brought all the more trouble upon his head.

Gwen placed one combat booted foot next to his. The Doolie looked down and grimaced, the Upperclassman's boot tip shone like polished marble.

"Not too good, Applegate, what is the problem?"

"Ma'am, no excuse, ma'am."

"Think you can do better next time I see you?"

"Yes, ma'am."

"You had better, your new Squad Leader won't be so kind as me."

"Yes, ma'am."

Gwen turned and strode away, leaving the Doolie to hastily make another announcement. Applegate was one of her favorite Doolies. Their conversation had put him off schedule though, and he would soon be in trouble for that from someone else.

Seeing the CCQ (Cadet in Charge of Quarters) waving in her direction, Gwen moved toward the CCQ desk.

"Gwen, you have a phone call," the CCQ called out as Gwen drew closer.

Gwen glanced at the clock, 0654, she only had six minutes to make formation. Who would be calling her on the squadron phone, instead of the pay phone down the hall?

"Cadet Gwen Hughes," she spoke crisply into the receiver.

"Gwen, I finally reached you," a distantly familiar voice responded with relief.

"Cousin John?"

"Yes, I'm surprised you recognize my voice. How are you, Gwen?"

"Fine, but you caught me at a bad moment. Can I return your call a short while later?"

"Sure, I'm in Colorado Springs, I need to talk with you."

"You're in Colorado?" Gwen was surprised. It was a long way from Tulsa for a surprise visit.

"That's right, it's kind of an emergency, can we meet?"

"Well...ah...sure. I will be free for a while at nine hundred hours...ah...that's nine o'clock."

"Thanks, Gwen, where?"

"I will meet you at the steps of the Cadet Chapel. That's an area where tourists are allowed."

"Great, thanks, Gwen. I really appreciate this."

"No problem, I gotta go," Gwen hung up the phone. How odd, to have her cousin John appear out of the blue like that. She hadn't seen him since she was twelve.

Grabbing her alpha cap, Gwen sprinted down the hall and out onto the terrazzo to her position in the breakfast formation, just in time for the inspection of Doolies. With great satisfaction, she noticed Cadet Speegle was absent from his assigned spot at the front of the cadre. Gwen loved it, tormenting Dancing Bears was great fun.

21

Monday, February 19 at Cape Canaveral AFS, Captain Alexander Hamilton II paused in front of a mirror. Smiling confidently, he straightened his tie, ran his fingers over the top of his ears to push any stray hairs aside, tightened the tuck on his blue air force uniform shirt, and checked the shine on his black oxford shoes.

The humidity and heat of central Florida was overpowering, but Captain Hamilton was not one to let a little personal discomfort prevent him from looking his best. He always wore the sharper uniform combination, which included a navy blue tie and matching shoulder epaulets with silver embroidered captain bars. Although a cooler open necked shirt was allowable, one with no tie, Captain Hamilton wanted to look his best. At noon each day he changed into freshly-pressed shirt and slacks. It was important to present a crisp image with nice sharp creases.

Looking professional was a habit with Captain Hamilton, one he had picked up during his days as a cadet back at the Air Force Academy. But even there the custom of changing clothes at midday was only practiced by a handful of dedicated cadets, those that wanted to excel. Alexander Hamilton had been a group commander there, one of the highest of cadet ranks. He was accustomed to excelling, he expected it of himself.

Passing the last minute self-inspection, Captain Hamilton exited the restroom and approached the office of Colonel Roe, the commander of the 6454th STLG at ETR, the Eastern Test Range. "It's essential to make a favorable impression on the colonel," Alexander Hamilton verbally reminded himself, "especially if I'm to make major below the zone."

Stepping into the office area of the commander's staff, Captain Hamilton approached the airman receptionist seated at the desk outside Colonel Roe's office. "I received a message stipulating I report to Colonel Roe at thirteen-hundred hours."

"Yes sir," the airman responded. Purveying Colonel Roe's appointment schedule, he marked a check by Captain Hamilton's name.

The young airman glanced at the captain before him and grinned. Typically he would make social conversation with the colonel's visitors, to keep them entertained while waiting, but the junior officer in front of him had such a strict and solemn look on his face. In mock military formality, the airman rose and snapped to attention, did an about face, and rapped sharply on the colonel's door. "Colonel Roe, sir, a Captain Hamilton to see you!"

"Send him right in, thank you," responded a congenial voice.

"Yes, sir," responded the airman, and did another about face.

"Sir," the airman addressed Captain Hamilton, "Colonel Roe shall..."

Captain Hamilton brushed rudely by the airman without waiting for him to finish his little joke. Stepping into the colonel's office and up to the front of Colonel Roe's desk, Captain Hamilton snapped to attention, saluted, and reported with exact military decorum. "Captain Alexander Hamilton the Second, 6454th Space Launch and Test Group, reporting as commanded, sir."

"At ease, Captain," Colonel Roe responded, motioning toward a chair.

Seated off the opposite corner of the colonel's desk was Chief Master Sergeant Quijano, the first sergeant in charge of all enlisted personnel on Titan IV launch pad LP-55. Captain Hamilton nodded to the chief, acknowledging his presence. Colonel Roe was in command at the launch base, but everyone knew Chief Quijano was the man who implemented and ran operational support.

"We have a new project for you, captain. I am afraid COMSTAR will have to do without your services, now that you have things on track, right, captain?" Colonel Roe had been favorably impressed with his newly assigned officer's performance on the COMSTAR program. After only one year on the launch base, he had exposed a major program foul-up, much to the embarrassment of those red faced, civilian aerospace contractors.

"I am being reassigned to another program, sir?" Captain Hamilton questioned, he thought things had been going well at his current assignment.

"We have a crises on our hands," the colonel continued. "Air Force Program 775 just received a new manifest date, the boys at the Pentagon want that bird up in the air as of yesterday. They have turned the LVIC (Launch Vehicle Integration Contractor) on for a ninety-day prep and launch cycle."

"Ninety days?" Captain Hamilton echoed incredulously.

"That's right, MMC may not be capable of making it, but they are contractually on the hook and the air force has paid for the capability. Pandemonium is breaking loose around here. Lieutenant Colonel Lester and I have been reviewing manning and duty assignments for his project engineers. Major Farr is currently PE (Project Engineer) on 775, but he has PCA (Permanent Change of Assignment) orders for Vandenberg in thirty days. I had a new man slotted to take over, a PCA from SSD (Space Systems Division); but now, in light of this new crises, I think we need someone different, someone who works well under pressure."

Captain Hamilton smiled, it sounded like the type of assignment that could ignite the afterburners on a man's career, a chance to really make a name for himself at the highest levels.

"Captain, I think you are our man, you have demonstrated great potential on that battery recharging fiasco. Why don't you fill the first sergeant in on the details?"

Captain Hamilton, his ego swelling by the moment, began his narrative with false modesty. "Nothing that big," he stated, believing just the opposite. "On COMSTAR they discovered a system design flaw, with regards to their SV NiCad batteries. It seems those babies start heating up once you turn them on, and the hotter they get, the less capacitance they retain. In the flow before launch they typically remove the PLF air conditioning at L minus one hour. It was calculated that the batteries would still have eighty-five percent capacitance by the end of their launch window, which was acceptable if they launched, within spec requirements.

"The problem was, they forgot about aborted launches. In case of an abort, it takes twenty-two hours before safety will allow personnel on the pad to reconnect the coolant ducts. By then the batteries are shot to the point where they have to be reconditioned, a lengthy process they would delay another opportunity for launch by seventy-two hours.

"Of course, it was unacceptable to tie up a launch pad that long for an abort, so a major design change evolved. On the satellite a redundant electrical power system was designed and installed, just for use on the launch pad. It included use of additional batteries on the Centaur just so the original SV batteries could be kept in the dormant mode. Needless to say, in addition to SV mods, there were costly launch tower modifications on LP-54 to support the power system.

"That is where I came in. The launch pad has standard capabilities already available, which everyone seemed to be overlooking. They didn't think to use pad power for this application. Although FPL (Florida Power and Light) is unreliable, diesel power would work just fine."

"What was the big crises?" Chief Quijano asked. There was a problem, but a solution had been found, a common occurrence at the launch towers.

"Don't you see, the generic diesel power at the launch complex could have been used to provide an alternate source of power while on the ground. There was actually no need for additional internal power systems with additional batteries. Meanwhile the program was too deep into pad modifications and SV design changes to back out.

Colonel Roe began to chuckle, "You can imagine their embarrassment. The SPO was furious. Even now the contracts people are negotiating over how much the contractor will have to refund the air force."

"Of course," continued Captain Hamilton, "by then it was too late to discontinue the mods. COMSTAR is going to launch with that lame duck system anyway."

"I'll never let them live it down," Colonel Roe could scarcely contain his glee, thinking of those fat-cat contractors' discomfort.

"I can imagine," Chief Quijano remarked, picturing the scene with great vividness. It was indeed a pleasant thought.

"Now," Colonel Roe became serious, fixing his steely gray eyes on Captain Hamilton. "We need you to ramrod this 775 launch. The national priority is critical. This one has got to go on schedule, and it has got to succeed. Will you accept the assignment, captain?" He asked merely as a courtesy. By military law, his people would serve wherever he commanded.

"Yes, sir, I shall do my best."

"A failure at launch will kill us, heads would roll."

"You can count on me, sir. I will make it work."

"Good man, consider the change effective immediately. Use Major Farr for whatever he's worth."

"Yes sir."

"That will be all then."

Once Captain Hamilton departed, flushed with excitement and the chance for glory, feeling prideful that they had chosen him, Colonel Roe turned to his first sergeant with a questioning glance, "What do you think?"

"Typical Zoomie."

"Yes, but I think that is what we need to get us through this one."

"I agree, we will work with him closely."

"Good, thanks, chief. Have you got a good sergeant for the assignment, one experienced and knowledgeable with this system?"

"I know just the man to help the captain keep his feet on the ground, Sergeant Ramon Garcia."

"Good, put him on it, and have him chaperone the captain day and night. Heaven help us if we lose this bird."

22

Dan Newby arrived at the office uncharacteristically late, so much so that Annette had already called his home to see if he was even coming in at all. Newby felt no guilt about coming in late though. It was Saturday and he had spent an excessive portion of the evening before at work, after which Victoria had insisted they attend a church social which ran late into the night.

Operation Carrier Pigeon was proceeding according to plan, the cumulation of years of tedious research. Newby was aware that this particular case had become somewhat of an obsession, but not without good cause. Soon they would be vindicated for all their efforts.

If successful, they would have the proof they needed to nab Ellis Hughes, the Baron, a traitor to the agency. Not only was he a traitor, the worst kind possible, he was also a despoiler.

Over the years the Baron had been responsible for recruiting and organizing an entire network of traitors, a sinister organization owing loyalty to no one but themselves. They had discarded their allegiance to the agency for a society fed on the self-serving advancement and protection of its own members. No longer dedicated to the protection of the Constitution and our great American form of government, instead they had become a cancerous growth, a parasite that fed off the ideals and labors of others for the benefit of their own corruptly selfish members.

The Baron had to be stopped. His evil organization, if allowed to grow unchecked, would subvert the whole purpose of America's intelligence organizations. Operating under the Baron's leadership, and other as yet unidentified leaders, members of this covert society worked insidiously to promote the careers of fellow members, often jeopardizing important missions, sometimes even compromising entire operations.

Newby had the statistics on his computers to prove it. Everything played together like a gigantic spiderweb, each agent forming a node that comprised a massive network of deceit and self promotion. The Baron sat at the center of that web, directing the actions of his people, growing fat at the expense of non-members.

The man was ruthless; were there no bounds to his ambitions? Didn't he care who got hurt along the way, or whose career was destroyed? Were they responsible for fellow intelligence officers dying in blown operations, sacrificed to promote the advancement of one of the Baron's traitorous disciples? They had to be stopped. If allowed to fester and grow too powerful, this was the type of sinister organization that destroyed whole governments, eating them up from the inside. Despising America's long proven principles of democratic rule, they would grab what power they could for the sake of personal glory.

Dan Newby sat for a full two hours contemplating the events of yesterday, anticipating the plans for the coming day, and dreaming about the eventual downfall of the Baron. It was indeed a glorious time, they were engaged in a good cause, an important mission in which they dared not fail.

Just outside Newby's office, Annette was busily at work typing up reports. Through his open doorway, Newby could see most of her arms and legs, and only occasional glimpses of her face or body. Her hands played expertly across the keyboard of a personal computer; she was an extremely fast typist. Annette's legs were extended under her desk in a relaxed outstretched fashion. She had on nylons and a short skirt, having kicked her shoes under the desk. The hem of Annette's skirt had risen high up her thighs. She was apparently unaware that anyone could see her legs under the desk.

Newby watched Annette type as he fantasized about saving the agency. He considered calling in Andrew Maconey to review their plans for the day, but procrastinated doing so. He was enjoying his thoughts and did not want to disturb his view of Annette.

A phone rang at Annette's desk and Newby watched her knees swing around in a swivel chair. After a brief conversation, Annette stood and approached his office doorway.

"Mr. Newby," she said.

Newby looked up at Annette's face, "Yes, Annette," he cleared his throat.

"That was Joan Moore, Henry Maxwell's secretary. He is going to call you on the secure phone." Annette spoke in her usual bored voice, with an added touch of surliness this Saturday morning. Without waiting for an answer from Newby, having delivered her message, Annette returned to her desk.

Newby wondered if it truly bothered Annette to be interrupted from her typing, or if it was just her natural demeanor. With a sigh, Newby rose from his desk, paid one last glance at the legs, and then left his office for the secure phone room.

Inside that secure area was a small conference table and a few chairs. There were no windows, only a poster with Uncle Sam asleep under a tree like Rip Van Winkle. An ugly Soviet bear was stealing his clothes, leaving poor Uncle Sam, still dozing, dressed in an undershirt and polka-dot undershorts that were red, white, and blue. The caption on the poster read, "Be security conscious. If we're caught sleeping, we could lose everything." Along the table were several phones. One was an old crypto phone, the others were secure dedicated lines.

Dan Newby seated himself at the table, meticulously laid out a pen and pad of paper, and waited for the phone to ring. At the first ring he snatched it up, "Dan Newby here."

"Dan, this is Maxwell."

"Yes sir, what can I do for you?" Newby thought his superior sounded ill; he talked with a rasp and a cough.

"How is the weather in Dallas?"

"It's hot, sir, we just stay indoors all day this time of year."

"Cannot be worse than here. It's so humid at Langley that a person can hardly think. Only the tourists are outside, wandering around the Capitol in a senseless stupor, too stupid to go inside."

Newby chuckled politely, "Well, it may be hotter in Dallas, but at least it's dry."

"Listen, Dan," Maxwell started, but then interrupted himself with a coughing fit. Newby waited patiently until he recovered. "We have a problem."

"Yes sir," Newby waited for the explanation.

"You might know, I am being considered for the position of Deputy Director for Operations."

"That is great sir," Newby was pleased for his superior. With the breakdown of the Warsaw Pact, the agency was undergoing some reorganization, decentralizing to various regional directorships that would operate more autonomously and report directly to the DDO.

"How are the prospects?" Newby felt familiar enough with Maxwell to ask such a personal question, especially since Maxwell had opened the subject.

"Very good," Maxwell responded. "I have been told they have narrowed the choice down to two candidates, and I am one of them."

"Congratulations, I am sure they will pick the right man."

"Well, that is what I am calling about. The other candidate is Ellis Hughes."

"What, the Baron?" Newby felt the hair on the back of his neck tingle. "You cannot be serious. Were that traitor to be placed in a position of such independent responsibility, the damage would be irreparable."

"I am afraid he has probably got the inside track on me. You know he has been managing the European Division for the past five years. That is why I called."

"How can we help, sir?"

"The operation against the Baron must be accelerated. Give it top priority, Dan. If he gains the Deputy Directorship, he'll be in a position to halt all further investigations. We have got to hurry, a decision on this new appointment is imminent."

"We are right on top of things," Newby responded, "all is proceeding as planned."

"Has that female intelligence officer, Maris I believe, taken the bait? When will she reach the Baron with the provocation list?"

Newby hesitated in uncertainty. He knew this phone was not cleared for Albatross level discussion, yet Maxwell was the boss. "She has not reached the list yet, but they are in Colorado approaching the site, and she has attached herself to the target."

"Well, stay on it, Dan, time is critical."

"Right away, sir."

"Good, I know I can count on you. Give me a nightly status report. I am afraid that the Baron will be too powerful to dislodge later. This may be our one shot to get him."

"I have a team of my top intelligence officers on it, and I am giving the Operation my personal attention."

"All right, Dan, don't fail me. I will be expecting your report at twenty-hundred hours each day."

"Yes sir," Newby hung up the phone, feeling anger that the Baron was moving up within the agency. How many honest intelligence officers had he stomped on, gaining unfair advantage, to reach such pinnacles of power?

Returning to his office, Newby called for Maconey, suddenly anxious to receive a run down on the latest status of the operation.

"Waiting for things to happen is going to kill us, Andrew," Newby lamented, after confiding the details of his conversation with Maxwell.

"If they leave Colorado Springs immediately, they might reach the National Park today."

"Yes, but how long will he delay with that Academy cadet, trying to reach his uncle?"

"Ostermann believes the target will be able to reach the Baron through his daughter. I thought that was what we wanted," Maconey commented. "This is an important aspect of the operation, eventually they have to make a run for the Baron."

"Yes, but this is going to take days. I am no longer sure we can afford days."

"May I make a suggestion?" Maconey broke in. "The wife was taken into custody last night. Now, while we are in a waiting mode, why not visit her for questioning? It would give us something constructive to do."

Dan Newby liked the idea. "She's being held in Tulsa?"

"Yes, we could catch a twelve noon American Airlines to Tulsa International and be there by one."

"Annette," Newby called to his secretary. "Call transportation." Glancing at Maconey, he smiled, "We'll do it."

Arriving at the Tulsa city police station a few hours later, Dan Newby and Andrew Maconey approached the front desk. A uniformed officer, seated behind a computer monitor, looked up passively at their approach and wiped his brow. It was air conditioned inside, but only minimally so, with the temperature set by federally recommended standards. He had a private desk fan which helped, but also negated any savings in that room from the higher thermostat settings.

"We are here to visit a prisoner, Eleanor Hughes," Maconey spoke briskly. He felt nervous just being near a jail.

The officer scanned a list on his desk, "Ah yes, Mr. Maconey and Newby?" Annette had called ahead to arrange for badging and the interview with Mrs. Hughes. Maconey nodded and the officer continued. "I will need to see a picture ID and then have you fill out this visitor's log."

Newby signed in with his standard pseudonym and then flinched, the officer had called him by his real name. How could Annette have made such a mistake, using their real names? Hoping the officer would not be paying attention to details, Newby left the false name on the log and gave the officer his real driver's license. Newby then passed the visitors log on to Maconey who followed suit and also wrote down an alias.

"Eleanor Hughes will be waiting in room 203," the policeman stated, and motioned to another officer to escort them upstairs.

Maconey suppressed a shiver as they rode the elevator to the second floor and exited into a barred entryway, then through secure steel doors. This was for real, Maconey thought, a real jail. Down the hall they were taken to a small viewing room. Beyond a two-way mirror, they could see Eleanor Hughes, alone.

She had been taken to a small, nondescript questioning room with a table and four chairs, a phone on the wall by the door, and one barred window opposite the door.

The paint on the walls was pastel green, dirty with age, and the carpet was worn almost smooth. Eleanor Hughes was standing on a chair, which she had dragged under the window. She was still dressed in her nightgown from the previous evening.

Newby was shocked. In an indignant voice, he asked, "Why is she dressed like that?"

"The arresting officers brought her in. Why don't you ask them?"

"You don't know why she is improperly dressed?"

"She resisted arrest. A feisty one, that lady, climbed out the back window of her house and tried to escape, gave the officers a merry chase halfway down the block."

"But, don't you have clothes here?"

"Sure, but she refused them, won't give permission for anyone to return to her home and bring out her own clothes either. Look at her now, trying to get out that window."

"Come on," Newby spoke to his deputy. "Let's have a chat with Mrs. Hughes."

23

Eleanor Hughes was angry and scared, thoughts of despair continually raced through her mind, over and over again. How could this be!? This could not really be happening! To be brutally apprehended by harsh, uniformed officers of the law, mercilessly handcuffed in front of her neighbors, forcefully torn from her frightened children, thrust into a squad car, and taken captive like a vile criminal to be imprisoned at the police station in downtown Tulsa. Who could she turn to for help? Her husband was gone, a fugitive from the law himself, her family was in Minnesota, and she had no real friends in Tulsa. Eleanor hardly knew the names of any of her neighbors. She was truly alone.

After spending the night caged like a dangerous beast, what now? Despairingly Eleanor struggled with the unyielding latch to the only window. They had roused Eleanor from her cell that afternoon and escorted her to this tiny starkly-furnished interrogation room. They had not said why she was there, and Eleanor had been too frightened to ask.

The window was small and high. It would take an acrobat to climb out, but she had to do something. If she could only get it to open. The tension ate at Eleanor like caffeine, driving her to keep moving, allowing her no rest. Anxiously she struggled against the latch.

Suddenly the door behind Eleanor swung open and two businessmen with dark-colored suits ushered themselves in, carefully pulling the door shut behind them. Embarrassed at her attire, Eleanor awkwardly stepped off her chair and stood facing them, head bowed slightly.

The two men looked like accountants. The younger one was skinny and tall, he had blond thinning hair, and large facial features on narrow cheekbones. His suit was tailored and expensive. The older man had a more mature and reserved demeanor. He was overweight, less than average height, balding, and had a reddish plump face. Whereas the younger man seemed impassive, standing stiffly erect, cold, all business—the older man wore a friendly sympathetic smile. He kept glancing at Eleanor's bare legs though, making her all the more self-conscious. Even so, he had a trusting look upon his face and Eleanor felt drawn to him. Perhaps he was someone who could help her.

"Would you like a seat, my dear?" the older man courteously offered.

Grateful for the opportunity to sit, hoping to find partial cover behind the table, Eleanor gently stepped away from the wall. She noticed her own reflection in a large mirror and felt all the more embarrassed. What if it was a two-way mirror? She felt like she was standing under a spotlight. The two gentlemen waited until she was seated before sitting themselves.

"My name is Dan Newby and this is my associate, Andrew Maconey," the older one introduced them.

His kindly voice helped put Eleanor at ease somewhat. "Where are my children?" she asked in a hushed voice.

"Your children are fine. They have been placed in a temporary foster home," Newby began. Then, seeing the shock register on Eleanor's face, he hastened to explain. "Just temporary, for a day or two only, until you are released."

Eleanor clung hopefully to his words, "until you are released." However, the thought of staying for another day terrified her. Eleanor started to speak, but her voice cracked. Swallowing, she tried again, "I don't know why I am here. I have done nothing wrong." Eleanor hoped it didn't sound like she was whimpering.

"Yes, we know my dear. We asked for you to be brought in, for your own protection, merely a precaution."

Eleanor was mortified, they had arrested her even though they knew she had done nothing wrong. They took her children away, they made her spend the night in jail, and now they said it was for her own good. Suddenly the whole situation was all too much for Eleanor. Overwhelmed in self-pity, tears welled up in her eyes and she began to sob.

Newby was devastated by the poor woman's plight and the emotional suffering they had inflicted upon her. Feeling terribly guilty, he passed the sobbing lady a handkerchief to dry her tears. "Are you going to be okay?"

"Yes," Eleanor wept. "When may I go home?"

"We just want to ask you a few questions," Maconey spoke in a monotone.

Newby worried about Mrs. Hughes' health. She looked ill; her hair was stringy and uncombed, her eyes red and puffy from a lack of sleep, and now, her cheeks were stained with tears. It occurred to him that she must be under considerable stress as a consequence of her husband's actions, and they were not helping her situation much. Newby hoped they were not precipitating a nervous breakdown. In spite of her ills though, Mrs. Hughes was a fine-looking woman.

"Perhaps we can move you to a better place, there is no reason to keep you in jail," Newby spoke consolingly.

"When was the last time you spoke with your husband?" Andrew Maconey addressed Eleanor, leaning toward her. His voice was even and businesslike, emotionless.

"Well…ah…" Eleanor stumbled for words, she was afraid to lie. John had not really told her much though, "About five, last night, before I was arrested."

"I see," Maconey had begun the questioning, sensing his boss wanted to play the role of Mrs. Hughes' friend. "Did your husband say where he was going?"

"No," Eleanor drew her breath in.

"Any mention as to his current location, anything at all?"

"No, nothing."

"How about a destination?"

"No, I told you, he never spoke of his location or where he was going in any of our phone calls," Eleanor's eyes momentarily fogged over.

"Why did he do it?" Maconey's voice grew suddenly stern. Newby was silent, fiddling with his fingers.

"Do what?" Eleanor exclaimed.

"You know, steal those documents."

"I have no idea. What did John do? What documents?" She appeared to be on the verge of tears again.

Maconey rose to his feet for emphasis. "Don't pretend innocence with me. You know good and well that John Hughes stole restricted government documents from Krang Enterprises. He is trying to sell vital government secrets to the Russians. Don't try and protect him Mrs. Hughes, or you too will be a traitor to your country."

"That's enough," Dan Newby spoke angrily, standing now also. He had no idea what his deputy was driving at. Maconey had obviously allowed himself to get carried away. Did he want this poor woman to confess to a complicity she was innocent of? Perhaps Maconey was striking out at her because of his hatred toward her traitorous uncle-in-law, the Baron. This helpless woman was obviously innocent, she had suffered enough.

Eleanor Hughes had buried her head in her arms, her frail body racked with sobs of torment and fear because of the mistreatment.

"We shall arrange your relocation to a safe house," Newby spoke to Mrs. Hughes, and then turned to Maconey. "Let's go, we're not accomplishing anything here. Hopefully Maris is having better success with this lady's husband."

24

Danger, Rachel Maris could feel the danger, a chill down her spine, a knot in her stomach, a tightening along the nape of her neck, and yes, the fear.

Checking out of the Embassy Suites early that morning, far too early for sane people, even before partaking of the free breakfast, Rachel had sullenly waited behind at the lobby while John went for the car. The wind was blowing hard off the mountains and Rachel had said she didn't want to expose her hair; the truth was, she rarely felt energetic early in the morning.

From the hotel doorway Rachel spotted the threat, a sinister figure loitering on the sidewalk alongside the parking area. The stranger scared Rachel, he seemed prepossessed with watching John's movements. She recognized a professional, albeit a foolish one to expose himself to such obvious detection. Still, there was no mistaking the telltale signs. The man was an agent of some kind, possibly an assassin.

Rachel exited the doorway when the stranger turned his back. Moving off to the right, she kept both the threatening man and John in view. Rachel took cover next to a loading van, out of sight should the man glance in her direction. Still trying to gauge his intent, Rachel nevertheless stooped to draw a Viper from her right shoe. Either the stranger was merely wanting to keep John under surveillance, in which case the situation was not critical, or else he was planning a kill.

Rachel had the advantage though, she knew of the stranger's presence, whereas he seemed unaware of hers. If he made a move to attack John, then Rachel could swoop in from behind and throw a Viper into the back of his head. She scanned the area for her backup, Randy Ostermann and his crew. Perhaps this stranger had backup also, if so Rachel could not spot them. She glanced nervously behind her own back, hoping no one was watching her from behind.

Ostermann was not far away, he and a subordinate were parked in an Oldsmobile at the other end of the parking lot. Unfortunately they seemed oblivious to the threat. Perhaps this was one of Ostermann's men, a recruit whom Rachel had never met. It would not be unlike Ostermann to set Rachel up for a major blunder, such as attacking one of their own people. Despite the possibility, if this man moved against John, she would have to strike him dead. Her mission was to accompany John and recover the stolen documents, and those orders were not to be interfered with.

Things had been going too easy. Last night John had finally confided in her, confessing his role in trying to obtain the stolen government documents. Last night John had explained his motivations too, and it was not for money. Last night, light-headed from the effects of a few too many drinks and the heat of the hotel jacuzzi, his story had seemed quite plausible. Everyone had their rationalizations though, even murderers.

Now, despite a headache, Rachel could think more clearly, and she wasn't buying it. How ridiculous. An experimental virus to be loaded on satellites? Biological warfare from space? How absurd. Did John Hughes think she was that gullible and naive? No, he actually believed it himself.

Rachel remembered leaving the jacuzzi with John that evening. He had been so relieved to have found someone to finally confide in. Well, that was what she had wanted. Now that she had his trust, Rachel had no doubt he would take her along if she insisted. She had drunk too much alcohol that evening though.

The walk back to their room had been fun. She had played on her intoxicated state to lean heavily upon John, pretending she could hardly stay on her feet. Then she must have passed out, for that was the last she could remember. She doubted John laid a hand on her though, he was too much the perfect gentleman. No, he would not do anything to her, and when she had awoken the next morning, she was alone in the bed, still dressed in her bikini. In a way Rachel had been a little disappointed. John was definitely not her type though, too weak and goody-goody. She liked her men strong and forceful.

Now John was in trouble. When the stranger started forward, Rachel also moved out, pacing him, taking a course that would soon place her directly behind the man. When he reached under his jacket, probably releasing the safety on his handgun, Rachel became apprehensive and quickened her pace.

Rachel hefted the Viper in her palm, her fingers finding the proper location and balance for a throw. This could be tricky, Rachel thought. If she killed the assassin outright, it would surely blow her cover and ruin the mission. If she didn't do something though, the man would murder her target. Rachel glanced anxiously in Ostermann's direction. Where was that idiot, asleep?

Suddenly bracing himself, the stranger went for his gun. John was a sitting duck, an open shot. Instinctively Rachel decided against the knife. Continuing in her role as John's damsel in distress, she screamed loudly, shrieking with all her might, a piercing wail that punctuated the air.

In startled surprise, the stranger swung around, drawn gun in hand. It looked like a Yugoslavian CZ-99. Rachel hoped the man would turn and run, now that he had been exposed, but instead the assassin swung back toward John, apparently still hoping to complete his mission. The interruption had given John the chance he needed though. Alerted to his danger, John dove out of sight between two cars and then rolled underneath one of the vehicles.

The assassin fired twice in John's direction, even though John was already under cover. The 9mm bullets thudded loudly into the metal door of a Toyota. Rachel wondered why the man had fired senselessly. Was it out of frustration and anger? Was he that undisciplined? Rachel saw Ostermann and his partner stumbling out of their car now, running in her direction. The stranger saw them too. Suddenly he turned on Rachel, swinging the automatic CZ-99 around to take aim. Rachel dove for cover as he fired. Rolling to a crouch, she peered over the hood of a car. She saw the stranger fleeing now, with Ostermann's partner giving pursuit.

Meanwhile Ostermann raced up to Rachel's side, an automatic .50 caliber Desert Eagle automatic in hand. "What happened?" he questioned, breathing hard from his sprint across the parking lot.

Rachel shrugged her shoulders and stood up, brushing the dirt off herself. "He tried to kill us," she answered indignantly blaming Ostermann; then, catching Ostermann totally off guard, kneed him in the groin. Rachel had been waiting for an opportunity to do that, ever since Ostermann had slapped her around that day in Derby.

Snorting with sudden agony, Ostermann fell to the ground.

"Put your gun away and get out of sight before the target sees you," Rachel scolded, noticing John Hughes emerging from underneath a car.

Rachel put a distressed look on her face and rushed to John's assistance. "What happened, what happened?" she cried.

"Calm down," John tried to reassure Rachel, as she was frantic with alarm. It was odd how her hysteria had a calming effect on his own feelings. John rose to his feet, glancing about nervously for their assailant. He had apparently run off when Rachel screamed.

"He tried to kill us," Rachel lamented and flung herself at John, throwing her arms around him for some male comfort.

"Come on," John hugged her once and then started to pry her away. When he saw the alarm still on her face, he kept one arm over her shoulder for consolation. Together they hobbled to their Chrysler and sped from the scene, all too happy to be away from there.

The drive to the Air Force Academy was shorter than expected. Almost as soon as they entered Interstate 25, they were at the South Gate Exit. Driving past an abandoned visitor center, they headed along South Gate Boulevard and then Stadium Boulevard toward Falcon Stadium and eventually the Cadet Area. The grounds on base were green and beautiful; acres and acres of lush pine trees and abrupt sloping hills extended along their left, the foothills of the great Rocky Mountains. It was still early in the day and deer were out alongside the road, taking advantage of the rich manicured grass.

"John?" Rachel questioned at last. "Who was that?"

"I don't know," he answered, wondering why anyone would be trying to kill him. It would not be the police or the FBI, so that left the Russians. They wanted that list, but he didn't have it yet.

"You don't know?" Rachel challenged suddenly and loudly, hoping to drive home the concept that his danger was now her danger too. "A man is shooting at us and you don't know why?"

"I did not say that. I do know why, I just don't know who."

"Well then! Why, for heavens sake?"

John looked suddenly ashamed. Pulling over at a picnic area just past Falcon Stadium, he turned to face the questioning woman at his side. "Look, Rachel, there is more to this than I have told you. I'm sorry you had to be exposed to all this."

"What is it, John?" she asked softly.

"There are others after me, and now, possibly you too."

Rachel brushed the hair back from her face and tried to look sympathetic. "I assumed the police would be looking for you, after stealing those documents, and maybe the FBI also."

"I did not steal them, a friend of mine did, a former friend."

"Go on."

"Well...it sounds ridiculous, but I think that man was a Russian.

"What! Are you insane?"

"They murdered Goldsmith, now they are after me, and maybe you too."

"Who is?"

"Russians that's who!"

Rachel covered her face with her hands, giving her a pause to think. She knew from the files that it was actually Ostermann who had shot Goldsmith. "You didn't tell me Goldsmith was killed," Rachel pretended shock.

John shook his head solemnly. It was incredible to Rachel how totally he had swallowed the agency's deception, but who was this assassin? How did he fit in?

"Why was your friend killed?" Rachel questioned. "To recover the stolen documents?"

"Well, not exactly. Goldsmith was already going to give the Russians his documents. They want a list of some type. Don't ask me why, all I know is that they want a list, and it's hidden with Goldsmith's documents."

Rachel sat back thoughtfully. This was turning out to be more complicated than she had expected. There was no list mentioned in the case file. What was it? "You had better tell me everything from the beginning," she said.

"I don't know where to start," John began. "What I told you last night was all true. They are putting those DWARS viruses on the satellites we build. It's all so sick."

Rachel rolled her eyes and looked away. Not again, she thought.

"But how did you get involved?" she asked, prompting John to tell her the whole story, starting with that fateful phone call he had received from Bernie Goldsmith, to the meeting in Goldsmith's apartment, including the appearance of Russians, the attack by the police, Goldsmith's murder, and his own narrow escape.

Then John piqued Rachel's curiosity, as he described being assaulted in the alley by the Russians, over the mysterious list.

Rachel wondered if Newby was aware of this wrinkle. It wasn't in the case file. Was a real defector involved? Had Goldsmith somehow been in touch with former Eastern Block agents without Newby knowing it?

"You have got to understand, this menace is real," John continued earnestly. "They cannot be allowed to deploy the satellite. This goes beyond patriotism, this abomination is so heinous it encompasses all moral standards, transcending all nationalistic loyalties. They have to be stopped at all costs."

"Okay, okay," Rachel didn't want John going philosophic on her. "But how?"

"That is why I am going to Rocky Mountains National Park. First I have to retrieve the documents and prove to myself that Goldsmith was right. Then I'll find some way to stop it."

Rachel's eyebrows raised. This was her first clue as to their destination, Rocky Mountains National Park. "Let me help?" she offered.

"What...?"

"Please, John," Rachel urged. "I can help."

"It's too dangerous."

"You cannot go this alone, John." Rachel moved closer toward him and looked deep into his eyes. She placed a hand on his forearm. Rachel knew how to persuade men, to melt their resistance. "Let me help," she spoke softly.

"I can't, Rachel, you might get hurt," John said firmly, but his tone of voice spoke hesitation.

"But, you said that now they might be trying to kill me too. You cannot leave me somewhere to face those Russians alone. Don't you see, I am already involved. Besides, I can help. This is too important for a person to ignore, morally, you said so yourself."

"Well...ah."

"At least let me go with you to find the documents. You must allow me that." Her face was inches from his, pleading in her eyes, her breath on his cheek. "You cannot keep me from helping, this is too important, morally. I could not sleep without knowing the truth."

"Okay, you can come that far."

"You won't regret it, John, thank you," Rachel slid halfway back to her seat, as John started up the car again. "Now, why are we trying to contact your uncle?"

"I think he might be able to help," John answered. "He may be the only one that can. He used to be in the CIA, but no longer, he's retired."

"I see," Rachel knew better. John's uncle was still very much active in the CIA. The consulting firm was just a front. The Baron had gone under; he was a powerful man in the CIA now. Talk of him brought back memories. She recalled long walks about the streets of Amsterdam, his care, his interest, his kindness.

They turned west on Academy Drive, amazed at how large the grounds were. Passing an officer's club, the base road looped around to the north and came upon a group of modern space-age marble buildings, among which they spotted the well-known pointed spires of the Cadet Chapel.

The parking lot was a good distance away though, next to a planetarium. Walking past the front of a building with letters proclaiming "Arnold Hall," they passed under the administrative building and onto a terrazzo tourist area. Reaching the steps of the chapel, twenty minutes ahead of their appointed time, they approached a nearby wall overlooking the cadet grounds.

Down below the cadets were lined up in formation, squadrons of about one hundred each, patches of blue against the white concrete and marble of the terrazzo which surrounded an immense grassy square. From their vantage point, it appeared as if they were gazing down on the scene of some futuristic science fiction movie.

"This has got to be the most beautiful campus on Earth," John spoke in amazement.

"It is awesome," Rachel echoed his sentiments, as they watched the cadets perform their martial rituals below. There appeared to be some type of inspection going on. Then the color guard presented arms for the Star-Spangled Banner. A small cadre marched forward and was saluted by another group, which then assumed the former's position at the head of the assembled squadrons.

Shortly thereafter the formations were dismissed and the squadrons were marched back to their dorms. As the formations broke up, most of the scattering cadets walked stiffly along marble strips that bisected the terrazzo, although a few, those who appeared to be in charge, walked where they pleased.

"Perhaps now Gwen will be available," John postulated.

They watched the scattering cadets, trying to pick out John's cousin. Rachel noticed a female cadet approaching their position at a brisk pace. "Is that her?" she pointed out the cadet to John.

"I don't know, I cannot tell at this distance," he answered, but then smiled as he recognized her familiar, although now more mature, features. Gwen looked sharp in her uniform: polished black shoes, navy blue slacks, light blue blouse with black and silver shoulder bars, a blue wheel cap with a silver eagle on the front, and white gloves.

She paused in front of them, not sure herself, "Cousin John?"

"Hi, Gwen, how have you been?"

She stepped forward for a friendly handshake. John marveled at how she had grown.

"Who is this?" Gwen asked, gesturing toward Rachel.

"A friend," John answered, not liking the way his answer sounded.

"Where is Eleanor?" Gwen asked, frowning, coming straight to the point.

"Well...ah...she is at home," John stuttered.

"My name is Rachel Maris," Rachel stepped forward, extending a hand. "I am helping your cousin." Rachel sensed the suspicion in the cadet's demeanor, it was so obvious when she ignored Rachel's outstretched hand. Gwen was a lot like her father the Baron, Rachel thought.

"How so?" Gwen asked John, not letting the issue drop.

"She is home with the children. This is strictly business," John was having difficulty gathering his thoughts. "Eleanor is fine, Rachel is simply a good friend."

Gwen stood with arms folded, surveying the pair. She did not like this Rachel Maris, not one bit. She had not expected to find her married cousin in the company of another woman, especially one dressed like this, skimpy shorts and a halter top, make-up to the max, sunglasses and a big floppy hat. Who did she think she was, a movie star? And who was she trying to fool? This vixen was certainly not out on a business excursion, she was dressed to kill.

Rachel, on the other hand, was quite impressed with Gwen Hughes. She was so trim and athletic looking, short light blond hair, piercing blue eyes, and a temper to match. This was definitely a take-charge type person, just what Rachel had expected of the Baron's daughter. She had her father's fire.

"It is okay, Gwen, really," John wanted to ease the tension. He tried to change the subject, "That is some chapel, do you attend services there?"

Gwen frowned at Rachel, and then turned to her cousin and smiled. "I sure do, did you look inside?"

"No, maybe later."

"The top floor is for Protestants, the ground floor is for Catholics, and the basement is for Jews," Gwen explained, thinking the setup quite extraordinary.

"Interesting," John said, relieved his interrogation was over.

"There is a small room in the basement, sort of a shrine for Buddhists or Hindus or whatever," Gwen laughed.

"It is a strange chapel," John concurred.

"The spires are beautiful," Rachel Maris said, trying to join the conversation.

"There are seventeen spires, they symbolize the Twelve Apostles and five chiefs of staff," Gwen explained in all seriousness, then winked at John as Rachel turned to stare at the glistening spires.

"Gwen?" John asked. "We need to talk with your father. Do you have a phone number I can reach him at?"

"Well, yes, but you cannot call him directly."

"I found that out."

"I have a number to call, but then I have to give him a time and place to call me back."

"Does he?" Rachel asked.

"Of course he does," Gwen took offense at the question. "He has never failed to return any of my calls, even from overseas."

"Can you set up a call for us?" John asked.

"Sure. What is this all about?"

"It is personal, Gwen. I must talk with your father and have not been able to get hold of him."

"Okay," Gwen agreed, she was used to not prying into her father's business. He had always been secretive that way. "This is a good time of year for a visit to Colorado. We just finished the first half of training for the new Basics. Did you see any of the changeover? Now I have three weeks of vacation."

"Are you planning to go somewhere?"

"Some friends and I are going camping, tomorrow we were heading for Dinosaur National Monument. I have the evening free today, and I can catch up with them later, if you are planning to stay for a while. I'll show you the sights."

"We really don't have time to visit," John apologized.

"All right then," Gwen responded. "I need about two hours to finish boxing up my things. Should I arrange the phone call for thirteen hundred, ah, one o'clock, at your hotel? You are staying at the Embassy Suites?"

"Yes, but we have already checked out," Rachel broke in, thinking about the assassin.

"Okay then," Gwen thought for a minute. "How about Arnold Hall? Be back here at one."

"Can we go inside Arnold Hall?" John asked.

"Sure, it's a social type building, sort of like a student union on a normal campus."

"Sounds good, we will see you then," John concurred with her plan, pleased that he would finally be getting through to his uncle.

"It is good to see you again cousin," Gwen smiled.

"You too, Gwen," John responded sincerely.

"It was nice to meet you," Rachel said. This time Rachel did not try to shake hands.

As they walked back toward their car, Rachel commented to John, "Nice girl!"

John couldn't tell if Rachel meant the compliment sarcastically. "Yeah, she is something else," he said, having been thoroughly impressed himself.

"You know," Rachel said, "We need to find some place to hide, till one o'clock."

"What?" John turned.

"That killer might be searching for us!" Rachel warned.

25

Thursday, March 22 at Cape Canaveral AFS, it was during a windy, storm threatening week that the rocket engines for the buildup of a new Titan IV launch vehicle began to arrive. Dark angry thunderstorms were graying the sky, periodically releasing harsh furious rain to pound the flatlands of central Florida.

For Captain Alexander Hamilton II, newly appointed project engineer for AFP-775, and his enlisted assistant, Technical Sergeant Ramon Garcia, it had been a busy month. To have actual hardware start arriving at the launch base lent reality to their plans and gave a sense of urgency to their work. The march toward launch had commenced in earnest.

To no one's surprise, Major Farr proved of little help to their endeavors. With less than a month till reassignment, his time was short and his interest factor even shorter. It was evident that he was not the caliber of man that cared enough to do any more than the minimum necessary to get by. In other words, he was worthless.

"Well, there she goes," Sergeant Garcia commented. It was a week and three days later, on a Sunday, April 1. He and Captain Hamilton watched the air force C-141 cargo plane lift off from the landing strip. It rose slowly into the air, its nose pointed upward at an angle of attack that seemed disproportionately high for its slow lazy speed.

"No problems thus far," Captain Hamilton remarked, as if they had just struggled through a major accomplishment.

Ramon Garcia shook his head. They had not really done anything yet, all that had happened that day was the unloading of the Titan IV core. "Wait till we get into testing and checkout, then you will have some problems to solve," Garcia remarked, as he watched the airplane's lazy departure out into the distant sky. "In a way, I envy them."

"Who?" Captain Hamilton questioned.

"The air force crew."

"What for?" Hamilton, who was non-rated, spoke with scorn. He didn't care much for the man First Sergeant Quijano had chosen as his assistant either. What could he expect though, from a typical enlisted weenie?

"Well, their job is done. No problems, no hassles, no worries, just in and out, deliver the load and be done with it."

"So, no honor either. This is where the action is, they're just glorified truck drivers." Captain Hamilton hoped his assistant's attitude problem would not interfere with his work. There was much to be done in the days ahead.

"It was hardly worth the effort of coming to work today, just to watch them unload a plane." The drive in from Merritt Island, where Sergeant Garcia owned a condominium, was no small matter. It was especially irritating on a Sunday. They didn't call this April Fool's Day for nothing.

Captain Hamilton was unsympathetic. "Did you have a hot date tonight?" he remarked sarcastically. It was another sore point he had developed against this sergeant. Captain Hamilton was piqued by the way all the female airmen and contractor secretaries seemed to fawn over his new assistant. There was a young safety airman, a brunette, out at the launch pad yesterday, that was so taken by Garcia she could hardly talk. How revolting, why the man wasn't even an officer.

"I wish," Garcia replied honestly.

"So then, why *not* come in?"

Garcia started to comment on the stupidity of non-value added work, but decided against it. Why bother? With this brainless officer it was pointless.

"I must see to it that Colonel Roe hears about this," Hamilton remarked. "I'm sure he will be pleased."

"What, pleased that they unloaded the core?" Garcia would not let go.

"Sergeant, it is a successful on-dock delivery, right on schedule. I call that a major milestone and I think the colonel needs to know."

"Of course," Sergeant Garcia understood his captain all too well. Self promotion was the driver behind all his actions, kissing up to the colonel, making a name for himself. Garcia had known some ambitiously selfish officers before, but this one had to be the worst.

Together they stared at the shiny metal of the Titan IV's rocket core. It lay serenely prone on a specially designed flatbed transporter, waiting to be pulled away for delivery to the VIB building.

The Titan IV's engines and electronics were shipped separately, loose from the main core which was hardly more than a hollow piece of precision-manufactured, cylindrical metalwork.

The main body of the Titan IV Launch Vehicle System, commonly referred to as the core, was a two-stage liquid rocket built by MMC, the Martin Marietta Corporation, in Denver, Colorado. The two LREs, Liquid Rocket Engines, were built by Aerojet Techsystems and the guidance package by Delco Electronics, as subcontractors to MMC. The processing was controlled by MMC itself, the prime contractor for Titan Launch Systems.

Design of the stage I and II of the core was based on the same basic configuration as the old, provenly reliable, Titan 34D, although the structures had been resized for higher loads and the tanks stretched for increased performance. There were two main tanks in each stage, an oxidizer tank filled with N_2O_4, Nitrogen Tetroxide, and a fuel tank filled with Aerozine 50, which was half N_2H_4 Nitrogen Tetrahydride and half UDMH Unsymetrical Dimethyl-Hydrazine.

Stage I of the Titan IV core weighed 18,500 pounds dry, 369,300 pounds fueled, and was speced for 547,600 pounds of thrust with two nozzles. All would be exhausted in a scant 190 seconds of burn time. The stage II tanks were smaller, yet still weighed an impressive 11,600 pounds dry, 90,600 pounds fueled, and were speced for 103,500 pounds of thrust, and that with only one nozzle. The stage II burn time was a mere 240 seconds.

Delco built the GN&C (Guidance Navigation and Control)

system to provide the necessary autopilot steering that would guide the monstrous rocket in the critical first two stages of flight. The system made heavy use of an earlier program's systems, Transtage, and was totally autonomous from the Centaur upper-stage and the satellite.

The main component was the IMU, the Inertial Measurement Unit, a four-gimbaled carouseling platform system. Initial guidance was based on pre-launch-measured, wind-dependent steering, with on-board load alleviation algorithms. Afterwards a simpler, linear, sine steering was employed.

Surprisingly, during lift-off, the sensed acceleration would not be that great, with peaks at 2.8 g's, 3.2 g's, and 1.5 g's respectively. Where the satellite was stored, acoustic thermal blankets, with an emissivity of 0.86, would hold inner blanket temperatures to less than 125 degrees Fahrenheit, noise levels would be limited to 139.3 dB overall, and the vibration level to 165.6 GRMS (Gravity Root Mean Square).

Delivered by special transporter to the VIB building, the core would have LREs installed, undergo final assembly, and then be subjected to extensive testing and checkout. To maintain schedule, MMC was obligated to successfully accomplish these preps all within an eighteen-day period. After that the core would go to the SMAB building for mating with the SRM stacks.

Once inside the VIB, the core would be erected upon a different transporter, the vertical transporter, which moved by rail from the VIB to the SMAB, and finally to the launch pad, LP-55. All stacking and buildup activities for the Titan IV, prior to launch pad, would be done while upon the vertical transporter.

The entire process was in the hands of highly skilled MMC Cape personnel, under tight air force control and surveillance. Captain Hamilton, as PE for AFP-775, was specifically responsible for the payload, but this core was for his bird and little would go by without his attention. After all, nothing could be allowed to go wrong.

26

Stupefied, Dan Newby hung up the phone, removed his glasses to rub his tired eyes, and then banged a fist noisily upon the desk, a rare display of anger for a normally placid man, but one he found himself doing more and more lately. Curious about the unexpected noise, Annette swiveled in her chair to peek inside Newby's office, but he waved her back.

Andrew Maconey was puzzled by the reaction of Newby also, "What did you learn, Chief?" he asked, not expecting the startling answer he was about to receive.

"An assassination attempt on our target," Newby peered down at the round of his belly, then sat up straighter.

"Could it be a false report?" Maconey offered hopefully.

"No, I do not think so. Judging from Ostermann's description of the events, there is little room for doubt. Someone is trying to have our target killed, but who?"

"There is one likely candidate," Andrew Maconey postulated.

"No," Newby shuddered. "I don't think that even the Baron would stoop to such an act."

"But, who else then?"

"I do not know, but to murder his own nephew?" Newby stood and faced the pastoral picture on his wall. Maconey was familiar with that telltale habit, it meant his boss was pondering an unsavory fact that was mentally hard to digest.

"There is no one else," Maconey shrugged his shoulders, his gray eyes unblinking and emotionless. "The hit must have been ordered by the Baron."

"Why?" Newby asked lamely, already having come to the same conclusion himself.

"Well, he must be trying to stop John Hughes from reaching our list. That's it, the Baron fears the exposure of his network."

Newby turned to face his deputy, "And how could that be? We know Rachel Maris has not seen the list yet. How does the Baron know about the list already? Who compromised the fact that a list concerning the Baron's covert society even existed?"

Maconey's lips twitched in a slight show of emotion, "Another mole?" he muttered.

"Yes," Newby frowned, "and it could be anyone."

"So what do we do?"

"First," Newby returned to his seat, enthusiasm returning to his voice, "no one is to know any more details of the operation, other than absolutely critical information necessary to perform a specific task—No one! Second, recall the urgency this operation has assumed, we must step up our timetable. Finally, we must not let the Baron sabotage the operation. I think we should assign additional men to Ostermann's team. Tell Ostermann to take steps to safeguard the target and Rachel Maris in their journey, to protect them and intercept all would-be assassins."

"Protect John Hughes from his own uncle?"

"That's right. It is critical we expose this traitor before he is promoted to a position of high authority within the agency. We must get that provocation list into Rachel Maris' hands at the earliest opportunity."

"Why is the Baron after that list already? Doesn't he know it's a fabrication designed to falsely implicate him?"

"That's the puzzling part. The Baron must not know the entire truth, apparently he thinks the list is real."

A new thought struck Newby, the answer was so obvious—the computer checks—of course. "Considering all the data we have been compiling, it is possible someone in the Baron's network has become alert to our activities. Once aware of our research, it would not be difficult for the Baron's people to track down the source. In one respect, the Baron's sudden interest in stopping the results of this research, sort of validates our effort. It proves we are on to him."

"Dan, do you think," Maconey asked, "he would actually kill his own nephew?"

"Right now he appears to be trying any means possible to stop the list from being found. He knows that should it fall into Rachel Maris' hands, she would expose her link to his organization. That makes her a target also. I would imagine that if the Baron cannot stop Rachel Maris and John Hughes before they find the list, then he'll do it afterwards, destroy the list and all evidence that it ever existed."

"She'll be taking our provocation list to the Baron like a lamb to the slaughter. Should we stop the operation before she reaches him? He will kill her if she does."

"No, we cannot," Newby felt sick inside. He still felt a paternalistic need to protect Rachel, he still cared about her. "Tell Ostermann to protect them from assassins at all costs, until they reach the Baron that is. Then Ostermann is to let the Baron have them."

27

Arnold Hall, the cadet recreation building at the United States Air Force Academy, is an immense lavishly furnished facility designed in the grand military tradition of officer clubs. Inside is a full-sized balcony theater, game rooms for pool and ping-pong, lounges, (the only place on the base where cadets were allowed 3.2 beer), a snack bar, and the showplace of Arnold Hall, a grand ballroom. Built in an era when money was plentiful, the cadet recreation facility is a magnificent military palace.

John Hughes and Rachel Maris found Cadet Gwen Hughes just outside the marble floored entryway, anxiously awaiting their arrival. She looked markedly different dressed in civilian clothes, wearing jeans and a pink sleeveless sweater. No longer decked out in full military uniform, the dynamic aura of authority and precision was now replaced by one of girlish enthusiasm. Except for the closely cropped hair, Gwen appeared more like an average college girl than a military officers candidate.

"Hurry up," Gwen greeted them with eagerness. "We want to be in place early."

Through the main doors of Arnold Hall, John and Rachel found themselves entering an expansive entryway facing broad dual stairways that led to the cadet theater. Gwen escorted them to the left down the main corridor, past a cadet lounge, and then alongside the balcony-level overlook of an enormous ballroom. The pictures and decor were military in nature, depicting great battle scenes of air force history. It awed John to find such grandeur and luxury in an institution dedicated to learning and higher education.

Reaching an administrative office area, they were greeted by a young gentlemen dressed in the cadet alpha uniform with shoulder braids, white gloves, and wheel cap. "Hi, Gwen," he called, pointing her toward a large office with a mahogany desk. Pictures of fierce grim-faced generals hung on the walls.

"This is a friend of mine, Benjamin Bartholomew," Gwen introduced them. "Meet Rachel Maris and my cousin, John Hughes."

"Everyone calls me Boomerang," the cadet shook John's hand earnestly, a genuinely friendly smile dominating his features. Then Boomerang grasped Rachel's extended hand in his fingers and gave a curt bow. "At your service, let me know if there is anything you need, Ms. Maris, anything."

Gwen shot Boomerang a sideways stare, he seemed to be fawning over Rachel already, in spite of the fact he was more than ten years her junior. "Boomerang is the CIC (Cadet in Charge) for Arnold Hall this evening," Gwen explained. "We can take the call from my father on a phone in this office."

"There is one thing," Rachel spoke, causing Boomerang to face her once more. "We have about ten minutes, could you direct me to the powder room?"

"Yes, ma'am, it would be my pleasure, the restrooms are right down the hall here. In fact, allow me the honor of escorting you?"

"Think you, sir, you are a real gentleman," Rachel smiled. Moving to the handsome cadet's side, she took his arm in her hands and allowed the young man to escort her away. Boomerang seemed delighted by her attention, not noticing the exasperated expression on Gwen's face, as she watched him going mushy over the older woman.

Once alone in the ladies room, Rachel quickly unloosed the belt from around her waist. Inside the cloth belt was the hidden listening wire she had been given to keep in touch with her backup team.

Rachel was bothered by the recent assassination attempt on John Hughes' life. He attributed it to a Russian threat, but she knew better. Rachel was all too aware that the men John originally thought to be Russians, the ones who had killed Goldsmith, were in fact CIA intelligence officers from her own office. It struck Rachel as oddly convenient, the way Ostermann and his men had not been paying attention at the hotel. It was either sloppy or intentional, and she had a good idea which.

The more Rachel thought about Ostermann, the more he worried her. From the beginning he had been trying to sabotage her role in the operation, the man was dangerous.

At first she had attributed his assault to professional jealousy, but maybe his motives ran deeper. It was Ostermann who had killed Goldsmith. Was that really an accident? Was he now trying to kill John too?

Feeling relieved to be temporarily rid of the belt, Rachel had never liked the idea of Ostermann disapprobationly listening in on her, she impulsively thrust it to the bottom of a trash bin by the paper towel dispenser. She threw the small homing device in after it. The trash was a safe hiding place which would not normally be subject to discovery, unless the janitors made their rounds, which one would not typically expect until the end of the day.

An unexpected feeling of loneliness caused Rachel to shiver though. Besides cutting off Ostermann, she had severed contact with all of her backup team. Rachel would be temporarily alone now, at least until after their conversations with the Baron, after which she planned to recover the belt. Feeling the need for some reassurance, Rachel checked the throwing blades in her shoes and the daggers in her purse. Touching them was a comfort. She would also have appreciated a gun, especially with a trained killer on their trail. So she had now cut off any help, that was fine. Rachel would work alone; she was often at her best when alone.

Stroking the handle of her F-S commando stiletto, Rachel withdrew the deadly fighting knife from its sheath. She liked holding it. Something was not quite right though, again the blade had caught coming out of the sheath. Now she remembered it catching the last time she had unsheathed her stiletto, in the Embassy Suites. Another might not have noticed, but Rachel Maris did. Examining the dagger and its sheath more carefully now, Rachel discovered the problem. Her beloved collectors F-S stiletto had been tampered with. Woven into the sheath was a small homing wire.

A chill ran up and down Rachel's spine. Who did this device

belong too? Was it Ostermann? Was it the assassin? One thing for sure, whoever it was, they knew her location. They knew that she and John Hughes were in Arnold Hall at the Air Force Academy.

Rachel fought a chilling fear, the dread of an unknown menace. Just when she had cut off her support too. Some unknown person or persons were trying to kill them. Worst yet, she could not even trust her own people. Rachel Maris was a professional though, one of the best. She had her knives and she knew how to kill. She had done so before, and not always in self defense either.

All this talk by John about satellites and killer viruses and genocide had been getting on her nerves. Now she had to put such worries out of her mind. She was good at her job and she would prevail over her adversaries. After a thorough check to ensure she had no other hidden homing or listening devices upon her person, Rachel disposed of her defiled knife, discarding the stiletto and its sheath into the trash with her belt. Rachel then bade the F-S a good-bye kiss, hating to part with it. That F-S was an authentic WW-II, Wilkinson Sword Company, handmade commando knife, first pattern, and she would not be back for it.

Striding confidently from the restroom, Rachel found the young male cadet still standing just outside the door, waiting patiently for her return, smiling expectantly. He was young and handsome and tall. Rachel felt perfectly at ease in his presence.

As Rachel and Boomerang reentered the office where John and Gwen waited, John looked at Rachel with concern. She appeared paler than normal, and was standing strangely erect, as with false bravado. "Are you ill?" he asked.

Rachel frowned, it was a revelation to learn she did not look as self-confident as she had thought. "No, I am okay. Listen, John, when your uncle calls, don't mention my name or the fact that I am here. It would just be a nuisance explaining me, and might be embarrassing." It was irritating to Rachel that Ostermann had divulged her real name back in Derby.

Listening to Rachel Maris, Gwen shook her head with disgust. That woman knew, good and well, that no rational person would be deceived by her flimsy excuses. What did she want with John?

When the phone finally rang, as she knew it would, Gwen moved forward and lifted the receiver. It was apparent to John, from the smile on his cousin's face, that she treasured these phone conversations with her father. "Hello, Daddy," her voice sang.

"Hi, darling, I received your message. I was expecting you to call once you were finished with basic training. How are things? Have you got those new recruits whipped into shape?"

"Yes, Daddy," Gwen held the receiver close to her mouth, her eyes twinkling. "I am on leave as of one hour ago, but this isn't a social call. I have a surprise for you. Hold on while I put you on the speaker box." Pressing a button, the phone transmitter was switched to a small speaker wired to the phones.

"Guess who is here?" Gwen chirped toward the speaker, talking louder than necessary.

"I don't know," Ellis Hughes chuckled. "Don't tell me you are engaged. If this is a fiancé I don't want to hear about it."

"Dad!" Gwen laughed and glanced toward the others in the room, blushing. "Don't be silly." John thought his cousin was seeming more and more like an average teenager now, sweet and innocent, still Daddy's little girl at heart. The military woman that had greeted them out on the terrazzo seemed far removed.

"Good afternoon, Uncle Ellis," John spoke out.

"John, is that you, John?" The tone of Ellis Hughes's voice changed, as the affection that had been so prevalent melted away.

"Yes, it is," John answered.

"Daddy," Gwen spoke up. "John needs your help with something. An emergency of some kind."

"I see," there was a long pause. "John, do me a favor, please ask Gwen to step out of the room for a moment, would you? I think we had best talk alone." Ellis Hughes spoke in a voice that commanded respect.

"But, Dad," Gwen was upset by the request, not expecting to be excluded from the conversation with her visiting cousin.

"Please, darling," Ellis Hughes' voice was stern, brooking no options for further objections.

"I'll go," Gwen agreed, "but don't hang up afterwards. I want to talk before you leave."

"Agreed," her father concurred.

Rachel Maris shut the door behind Gwen and Boomerang as they exited the room, but stayed inside herself. She was thrilled to hear the voice of her dear friend. He hadn't changed much, there was strength in that voice. The familiarity touched her.

"They are gone now," John informed his uncle.

"What is the idea of involving my daughter in this mess?" Ellis

Hughes spoke harshly, his anger overwhelming, even across a phone line.

It surprised Rachel that the Baron knew John's situation, but when she thought about who John's uncle was, it would have been more amazing if he did not know all about it. John had been trying to contact his uncle for some time, and John's wife claimed the Baron had called their home in response. It would not be hard for the Baron to check into the situation, he had extensive contacts.

"What do you mean?" John questioned, totally taken back.

"You had no right to involve Gwen. No right at all."

"I am sorry," John stuttered, knowing his uncle was right. But if Uncle Ellis already knew about the problem, why hadn't he answered John's phone calls. "What do you know about this, Uncle Ellis?"

"I know you are wanted by the police," Ellis Hughes said, "and also by the FBI, you might as well know."

Rachel longed to speak out, to tell the Baron she was there, to inform him of her presence. Something inside held her back though, as she listened hypnotically to the Baron's voice.

John was impressed, he knew his uncle would be the one to contact. His uncle had friends in the CIA. He was a retired CIA man himself.

Hastily Rachel Maris scribbled a short message on a pad of note paper and thrust it in front of John's face. John read Rachel's question and then repeated it into the receiver. "Is this phone secure?"

There was a long pause, "Yes, as a matter of fact it is. Out of habit I activated a scrambler," the Baron excused his actions poorly.

"I need help…" John started.

"Okay, John, you did the right thing calling me, but promise me one thing. After we hang up, you must distance yourself from Gwen. I don't want her involved!"

"Of course, I never planned to involve Gwen. I just needed help getting through to you."

"Go ahead then, explain your situation. Why are the police after you?"

"It's kind of involved, and I am not sure you are going to believe it."

"Just go ahead, let me judge."

"You know I work at Krang Enterprises, a major defense contractor for military space projects?"

"Yes."

"Well, I am currently assigned to a project, have been for years, that involves a new generation of orbital spy satellites, intelligence gathering."

"Isn't that information classified, the fact that Krang builds those satellites? Should you be saying this to me?"

Again John was impressed with his uncle's keen perception. "I have made so many security violations recently, that it really doesn't matter anymore."

"Go on then."

"Okay, a fellow engineer, at my office, discovered that the air force was planning to store biological weapons on board our satellites; because of that discovery, he was killed!"

"Killed, by whom? The United States has maintained biological weapons for years, everyone knows that. This is no secret worth killing over."

"Not like these," John's voice rose. "This weapon kills future generations. It could wipe out entire nations or races, without the afflicted people even knowing it. It is a genocidal abomination to end all horrors."

"Settle down, settle down. This sounds too fantastic. What proof do you have, John? Tell me what you know."

Rachel was amazed by the Baron's reaction. Why didn't he tell his nephew the whole idea was ludicrous? The Baron, the man Rachel respected more than any other person in the world, seemed to be buying in on the possibility that this insanity might be true. Rachel could tell the Baron was not simply playing John along either, just to be kind, he was actually considering the possibility.

"I don't have any proof, that is why I am here, in Colorado."

"I don't understand, what has Colorado got to do with this?"

"Let me explain. Bernie Goldsmith, the engineer that was murdered, he stole some government documents that supposedly detail our interfaces with these SPL-551 piggybacks. I must see those documents for myself, to know for sure if it's true. This much I do know, Russian agents were interested enough to kill Goldsmith, and the authorities have been chasing after me ever since. They are taking this very serious, and someone even took a shot at me this morning."

"Where are the documents, John?" the Baron asked, causing Rachel's heart to beat a little faster. Perhaps she was now to learn the location? Would this complete her assignment and allow her to recover the stolen documents?

"They are buried at a campsite in Rocky Mountains National Park."

"You know how to find them?"

"Yes!"

"John, you are going to have to check this out before I can help. You must make absolutely sure, without doubt, that this is true. If so, I think I can be of help. I do have some friends in influential positions of government here in D.C. Don't get me wrong, if you discover this is all a false alarm, I will still help. We are going to need evidence, you must bring out everything you find. If it's true, we are going to have our work cut out for us."

"Thanks, I had no one else to call, no one that could help. We are going to have to hurry. The launch of our first satellite is scheduled for August 31. Time is short."

"Can you reach these documents today and get back to me?"

"No, I am going to have to backpack in. I can probably get there tomorrow, then I could call you the next day."

Rachel was totally astonished, the Baron was actually going along with John's wild fantasy. Perhaps there was a possibility this lunacy could actually be true? She felt a numbness in the tips of her fingers and rubbed them to restore the circulation, listening in mute silence to their plans.

As the conversation concluded, John rose and turned to Rachel, he had a look of purpose in his eyes. "I must go immediately. You can stay behind if you want. It is not too late."

"No way," Rachel exclaimed. "I am with you."

Stepping outside the office, they almost ran into Gwen. "I'm sorry," John apologized. "We hung up the phone, I forgot you wanted to talk some more." Gwen did not appear concerned.

John continued, "We have to leave now Gwen, urgent business, you understand. Sorry to rush off. Thanks for arranging the phone call, you don't know what a help it has been."

"Wait a minute," Gwen interrupted impatiently. "I am coming too," she stepped in front of them to block their path.

"What!" John halted in surprise.

"I was listening on another line," Gwen explained defiantly, her feet planted firmly on the floor, her hands folded in front of her, blue eyes flashing. "You aren't going without me, I'm coming, too!"

28

"Are you out of your mind!" John Hughes exclaimed, his frustration getting the better of him. "I cannot believe you, eavesdropping on us."

"Sorry about that, cousin," said Gwen Hughes, a glimmer in her eyes. "But you have to admit, you were being extremely secretive. I'm afraid my curiosity got the better of me. Why didn't you tell me about this DWARS virus from the beginning?"

John was flabbergasted, she knew everything. "Gwen Hughes, you were better off not knowing!"

"What was I to think? You appear out of the blue, no notice, a big mystery, no explanations, a private call to my own father. Come on now!"

"Still!" John was angry nevertheless. "You are not coming with us."

"Oh, and why not, might I ask?"

"Think of the danger. What would your father say?"

"I am an adult now and I make my own decisions. Besides, why is she going with you?" Gwen jabbed an accusing finger at Rachel Maris.

Rachel was beginning to lose patience. Ever since discovering the bug in her sheath, she had worried about enemy agents catching up with them. Rachel glanced furtively down the halls, no one in sight, not yet anyway. She wondered where Gwen's friend Boomerang, that handsome young cadet, had gotten off to.

John could see he wasn't getting anywhere with his cousin. "Look, Gwen, I really don't want to involve you in this mess. You can understand that. Rachel and I will be leaving now, alone!"

Gwen remained defiant though, "John, I already am involved."

"No, I promised your father."

"So, what would Daddy do if he were in my place? I'm sure he would insist on helping."

Rachel had to agree with the cadet. The Baron would never have let a chance for adventure pass him by, especially when he was younger. "It's already too late to keep Gwen totally out of the picture," Rachel spoke up, causing John to look at her with grave concern.

"What are you trying to say?" John demanded.

Rachel hastened to explain, "Right before the phone call to your uncle, I found a listening device hidden in my purse. We have been bugged." Rachel saw excitement sparkling in Gwen's eyes.

"I don't believe it!" John exclaimed with astonishment.

"I do not know who planted the device, or how long it's been there, but whoever they are, they know where we are," Rachel continued. "If it was the man who tried to kill you, John, that would explain how he found us at the Embassy Suites.

"Now he knows we are at the Academy," John stated emphatically.

"Let me see that listening device," Gwen asked, prompting Rachel to lead them to the restrooms. She retrieved her belt and pulled a wire from the cloth to present for Gwen and John's perusal. They flushed it down the toilet.

"It would not take a genius to realize you have a cousin here," Rachel spoke to John, "especially one with the same last name."

"Well, if they listened to our initial conversations," Gwen remarked, "then they know me by name. It's a good thing you discovered that device before Dad called."

"Surely," Rachel agreed.

"What shall we do now?" Gwen asked.

"First," Rachel spoke as if she were experienced in this type of thing, "we have got to assume the worst. We cannot return to the car, there is no way to ensure it is safe. Don't assume a second assassination attempt would fail. We were lucky the first time."

"Abandon the car?" John exclaimed.

"Yes, suppose they planted a bomb in it while we were in Arnold Hall, they have had plenty of time. As a minimum, I would bet they have bugged our car. We need to do some thorough dry cleaning…ah…get rid of these clothes. It's the only way to make totally sure that we too are clean of listening devices."

"This is great," Gwen exclaimed, her eyes wide with excitement. "If we can get over to the dorms, I can get some new clothes for you."

"We?" John questioned.

"Let her come, John," Rachel argued. "I think it's a good possibility she would be targeted for information otherwise. Look at what she overheard, she knows you are heading for Rocky Mountains National Park."

"Do you know a back way out of this place?" Rachel spoke to Gwen, ignoring John's look of exasperation. They needed this cadet, whether John liked it or not. Without her, they might not get ten steps outside of Arnold Hall. Whoever was after them had more than ample time to set up a kill, and Rachel no longer felt she could trust Ostermann for backup.

"Sure, I think we can get out unseen," Gwen affirmed confidently, "and I know someone who will loan me clothes for you, John. I don't know if I can find anything that would fit your friend though," Gwen motioned toward Rachel's hips.

"We are about the same height," Rachel spoke defensively, "can't you loan me some of yours?"

"We are the same height, but you would never fit into my clothes," Gwen could not resist the verbal jab.

Rachel ignored the child's attempt to insult her, this was a serious moment. Rachel did have a more mature figure, she was indeed wider in the hips and fuller in the chest than Gwen, who was leaner, trimmer, and more youthful.

Gwen led them to the east side of Arnold Hall. They descended a long stairwell to the floor level of the great ballroom, hurried past a grand piano, and slipped through some side doors onto a large terraced patio. Jumping a small, marble-topped, concrete wall, they sprinted across a grassy lawn and disappeared into the brush and trees. Following Gwen, they descended a heavily wooded hillside until emerging into the midst of the cadet obstacle course. Working their way south, going around rather than over the various obstacles, they approached Vandenberg Hall from the direction of the gymnasium and field house. It was doubtful anyone could have monitored their exit.

Underneath the dorms, John and Rachel waited while Gwen raced upstairs to procure a change of clothes. Rachel's presence under the cadet dorms caused quite a stir, catching the sudden attention of those male cadets who happened within eyesight. After three weeks of intensive basic training, the sight of a beautiful woman in shorts and a halter-top, was a real distraction. Rachel ignored their stares, she was trying to stick close to John, aware that he was still angry with her for eliciting Gwen's help. Rachel placed a hand on John's folded forearm. At least he didn't pull away.

Gwen emerged about twenty minutes later, having already changed herself. Rachel was relieved, several groups of cadets had actually began to loiter about, smitten by her breathtaking beauty. Gwen was dressed in a fresh set of jeans, a rugged pair of hiking boots, and a stylish long-sleeve cotton shirt.

"Try these shoes on," Gwen said to John, handing him a pair of used, but highly polished, black combat boots. "Sorry it took so long, I had a terrible time finding a size eight extra wide."

"I have high arches," John explained, as he pulled the boots on. They were a good fit, as was a brand new pair of blue jeans and an orange colored sweatshirt with the words "Oklahoma State University" across the front. Cadets were fond of wearing regional reminders from their home states.

"Who's is this?" John asked, thinking of home and, as a natural consequence, of Eleanor.

"It's mine," Gwen smiled. The style those days was to wear large oversized clothes. The sweatshirt was big enough to make a good fit for John.

Rachel could see the cadet had not expended half the effort on selecting clothes that would fit her. Rachel was given an ill sized pair of flimsy white tennis shoes, which were too large, some baggy olive green fatigue pants, one of Gwen's USAFA T-shirts, which was too small around the chest, and a baggy short-sleeve purple sweatshirt. Rachel could just see herself, with the right hairstyle she would blend right in with the punk rocker crowd, or else look like a scarecrow.

Leading them down several long outdoor ramps and stairs, Gwen took her friends to the Cadet Field House, where she made some phone calls while John and Rachel changed in the restrooms. Rachel was thoroughly embarrassed by her appearance. She would not complain though, not if Gwen could get them out of there alive. Still, she felt awkward, especially next to the younger stylishly dressed female cadet.

Meanwhile Gwen had succeeded in borrowing a Firstie's car for their use, a sporty Pontiac Firebird. She disappeared for a few minutes to pick up the keys, and then returned with the impressive automobile.

"I thought all cadets drove Corvettes," Rachel groused, eyeing the tiny backseat, causing Gwen to laugh.

"Maybe in the old days, when you could buy them for five thousand. Besides, if we had a Corvette, there would not be room for you. True sports cars don't have back seats you know."

Their next stop was the cadet recreation supply offices, where Gwen rented backpacks, sleeping bags, bedrolls, a lantern, canteens, cooking utensils, a hatchet, flashlights, and three pup tents. Now they were all set to hit the road. With Gwen driving, a condition of borrowing the car, John in the passenger seat, and Rachel delegated grumpily into the tiny backseat, they departed from the Academy grounds via the North Gate and sped north toward Denver on Interstate 25.

John felt like he was just emerging from a dream and back to cold hard reality. What had he gotten these two women into? With remorse he wondered how his poor wife Eleanor was making do. John hoped she wasn't taking his absence too hard, he hadn't even called her yet that day.

29

Still shaken from her stay in the city jail, Eleanor Hughes resignedly changed into the cotton dress offered by her jailers. She felt worn out. She had been trying to fight the feelings of helplessness and despair. It did not help matters to realize they had obtained the dress, from her house, without her permission. Apparently someone had gone into Eleanor's home, rifled through her personal dresser and closet, and then taken what items struck their fancy. Eleanor felt a sense of personal violation. Those were her possessions and strangers had entered her house to examine them.

It had probably been a man too, judging from the items selected. She could see them clearly. First the closet, flipping through the hangers he had selected four dresses, then a pair of brown casual loafers and a pair of tennis shoes. Next her old oak dresser (she had stripped and finished that old dresser herself before her marriage to John). From the dresser he selected socks, nylons, and underclothes.

None of the apparel he had chosen would go together. Eleanor had been provided dresses only, no pants or blouses, hence the tennis shoes were worthless. Who would wear tennis shoes with a dress? Also there were no slips and, worse yet, no bras. A woman would surely have been more intelligent in picking out clothes.

Selecting a knee-length, yellow print, cotton dress with sleeves and a high neckline, Eleanor had dressed quickly. She felt much relieved to be out of her night clothes and properly attired once more. She had spent the previous evening and the majority of that day wearing a chilly nightgown.

As a result of her interview with a kindly detective, true to his word, Eleanor was soon removed to a safe house, supposedly for her benefit and comfort. It was the least they could do after he verbally admitted she was innocent of any illegal wrongdoing.

The safe house was located in an older section of Tulsa called Maple Ridge, 1616 East 26th Street, near the Arkansas River, north of Cincinnati Avenue. The house was an older home, two-story, brick, and completely refurbished. By Eleanor's standards it was almost a mansion in size.

So this was to be the place of her confinement. A safe house they called it, but for Eleanor it was to be a prison. She had no idea how long they intended to detain her, but it didn't matter, she was not prepared to accept even one additional night of captivity. At the first opportunity, Eleanor planned to escape.

She had two wardens, both female thank goodness, and both about Eleanor's age. One was large and overweight, an ugly powerful woman with gruff hardened features. The other could easily fit the slender athletic stereotype of a female TV cop. She was a redhead with weak but comely eyes, tall and healthy looking, her movements fluidly conditioned. Both women were dressed in slacks and shirts, much to Eleanor's frustration since she had been forced to wear a stupid dress. Each of the police officers also possessed a large, police issue, Beretta 92F, 9mm automatic handgun. Their weapons were holstered in open view like uniformed cops.

Upon arrival at the safe house, Eleanor had been curtly informed of a few simple house rules. She would not be allowed to leave, no phone calls, no visitors, she would not be left alone at any time, and she would obey her wardens. It seemed simple, but at the same time, quite unreasonable. Was this legal? Could they keep her imprisoned without charges or a trial?

After a brief explanation of the rules, Eleanor was escorted downstairs to the TV room. The large officer, who had introduced herself as Officer Blinkerson, excused herself to make a trip to the kitchen, wanting to check out the refrigerator stock. The skinny warden, Officer Pastorelli, switched on the television and casually took a seat on the couch. Apparently they were settling down for a lengthy stay. Flipping through the channels with the remote control, Officer Pastorelli found an old episode of Baretta, which suited her taste.

Eleanor slumped into a large, worn-out, vinyl recliner. Although accommodations in the house were a vast improvement over the city jail, she was still too nervous to relax. Before long Officer Blinkerson joined them, with an overstuffed bologna sandwich in hand.

"Did you make that for me?" Pastorelli asked her partner, half-jokingly.

"Nah, help yourself," Blinkerson answered rudely, too engrossed with her eating to catch her associate's humor.

Eleanor tried watching the TV, but could feel the nervous tension building within her. On the screen a poorly dressed policeman was driving an old ramshackle car with a white cockatoo perched on the steering wheel. Blinkerson was making an excessive amount of noise gulping down her sandwich.

Eleanor's head was starting to spin, she couldn't sit calmly watching TV like this, she had to do something, she had to move. Eleanor realized her face felt clammy. Hesitantly she stood.

"Where do you think you are going?" Blinkerson challenged, Eleanor's movement having interrupted her feeding.

"Are you feeling okay?" Pastorelli asked, a little more perceptive as to Eleanor's distress.

"Oh, I am just dandy," Eleanor responded sarcastically. "I need to walk about a bit, I will be right back." Eleanor started to exit the room. She felt ill and needed to clear her mind.

Pastorelli looked at Blinkerson skeptically, and then rose to follow.

"Tell her to sit back down," Blinkerson grumbled.

"It's okay," Pastorelli replied. "I will keep an eye on her."

As Eleanor passed through the dining room, her nervousness began to ease somewhat and she found herself feeling angry. How dare they treat her like a common criminal? She had rights, she was a free citizen. Eleanor's eyes focused on the gold colored door knob of the front door.

"Hold on there," a firm voice made Eleanor pause. "You know better, it is against house rules to go outside."

"Why?" Eleanor spun on her warden, surprising Officer Pastorelli with the sudden flash of anger.

"Just calm down and take it easy," Pastorelli tried a smile. "We are going to spend some time together and it might as well be pleasant. You probably noticed, Officer Blinkerson is not much of a conversationalist. I would enjoy someone intelligent to talk with."

Eleanor felt her anger dissipating a bit, "But why am I being held?"

"You don't know?" Pastorelli asked.

"No, not really, I have not been charged. It has something to do with my husband."

"You have been charged, with treason and conspiracy," Pastorelli explained. "That's what is on the books anyway, but we both know the real reason you are here, to isolate you from contact with your husband."

"But that is not fair!"

"Not fair," Pastorelli chuckled. "Maybe not, however, it is probably for your own good. You husband has committed an extremely serious crime, espionage against the United States of America."

"I don't believe it, not for an instant," Eleanor defended her husband, although she was beginning to have some doubts. Did she really know her husband? How could he have left her like this?

"Come on," Pastorelli beckoned. "Let's go sit down, watch some TV."

"No, I am not—" Eleanor edged toward the door.

"Don't be difficult."

"What are you going to do, hit me?"

"If I have to," Pastorelli moved closer.

Wondering how far she could push her wardens, Eleanor reached for the door handle. Once outside she could scream for help or something, maybe the neighbors would hear. What was this woman going to do anyway, wrestle her back inside the house?

Pastorelli moved to intercept as Eleanor reached for the door, but a large body pushed briskly past her. It was Blinkerson, moving fast for someone so big. Grabbing Eleanor's wrist as her hand just closed on the door handle, Blinkerson wrenched Eleanor's hand away, and then roughly twisted Eleanor's arm up and around.

"Think you are going somewhere, sweetie? Well I don't take too kindly to disobedience."

Eleanor cried out in pain as Blinkerson jerked her away from the door, twisting Eleanor's arm behind her back. Drawing a pair of handcuffs from off her belt, Blinkerson dragged Eleanor toward the banister alongside the stairs which led to the second floor. She forcefully cuffed one wrist behind Eleanor's back, threaded the other cuff around a banister post, and then snapped it onto Eleanor's other wrist.

"One hour," Blinkerson announced, rubbing her hands together, her breath heavy from the exertion. "I am setting my timer." She pushed a button on her wristwatch with a fat stubby finger, starting a stopwatch function, and then lumbered back toward the TV room.

Eleanor, feeling humiliated, looked to Pastorelli with pleading in her eyes.

Pastorelli had a pained expression on her face. "I have to apologize for this unkind treatment. Please, take my advice, don't do anything to antagonize Blinkerson any further."

30

Friday, March 9 at Cape Canaveral AFS, the last SRM, a Solid Rocket Motor Segment, had finally arrived. Twin seven-segment rockets would soon stand firmly attached to the Titan core, boosting thrust capabilities of the launch system by twenty-five times.

The SRM segments had arrived separately by railroad. There were fourteen segments in total, plus two forward sections, each taken to the RIS building for receiving and inspection. Other inert components went to the MIS building. After carefully ensuring all was in order, the flight-ready segments were then stored at the SRS building ready for use.

Stacking was scheduled to commence on Tuesday, June 4, the operations to occupy an entire week. At the SMAB building, two stacks of five segments each would undergo buildup. Then, upon arrival of the booster core from the VIB on June 12, they would be mated to that Titan core directly on the vertical transporter.

The final two segments, and each forward section, would not be mated to the tops of their stacks until the launch vehicle was at the launch pad. This was necessary due to the tremendous heights of the stacks; the ceiling of the SMAB was simply not tall enough. A new

SMAB was under construction at CCAFS and would someday be able to accommodate complete SRM stacking.

"Where have you been?" Captain Hamilton groused, as Sergeant Ramon Garcia entered the office, nonchalantly placing his cap on the hook by the door.

Now that the major Titan IV components, including the mighty SRMs, were in processing at CCAFS, Captain Hamilton's job had become all the more important. This was no time for schedule delays or slip-ups, the nation needed that rocket.

"Out at the launch pad. Some of us have work to do," Garcia replied, unaffected by the captain's continual surliness.

"What's going on out there? You know stacking operations for the SRMs are scheduled to commence in one hour at the SMAB."

"I'll be there, don't worry. We have plenty of time."

"I'm going on out to the SMAB now, want to come?" Captain Hamilton rose to his feet, straightened his shirt, tightened his tuck, and brushed the lint away from his uniform. Garcia had noticed it was a regular routine for the captain, anytime he left the office.

"I'll be along later."

"What was going on out at the pad this morning?"

"Just checking on a waiver from the safety walkdown," Garcia replied. "Some of the lanyard attach points were not called out correctly in the ICD. It is nothing important."

Captain Hamilton scowled, he knew the real reason Garcia was out at the launch pad, "And I bet her name is Rita, right?" He wished his assistant would grow up and start taking this work seriously.

Sergeant Garcia ignored the captain. He did his job and he did it well. The captain just didn't know how to relax and enjoy life. Working out at the launch base could be a fun assignment, if a person allowed himself the chance to enjoy life's little pleasures, one of the more interesting of which was a cute little airman named Rita Jorgensen who worked in Safety.

The SRMs were built by CSD, Chemical Systems Division of Technologies Corporation. The basic solid rocket configuration was developed on MOL, the Manned Orbiting Laboratory Program. Current SRMs had only minor improvements: the extension by forty inches of the forward closure, and the addition of a welded aft skirt. Also of major significance, the number of segments had been increased to seven, raising the expansion ratio to an impressive 10 to 1.

Each weighed 687,000 pounds and was capable of contributing 1,400,000 pounds of thrust. With the SRMs, the Titan IV would be capable of busting loose from the Earth's gravity, carrying increasingly heavy payloads into space, such as the huge SIGS satellite. After the awesome amount of thrust generated, all within a mere 126.5 seconds after ignition, the SRMs would be separated and discarded to burn upon reentry through the Earth's atmosphere. Once their mission was finished, SRMs were expendable, all for the purpose of placing the precious satellite in space.

31

Randy Ostermann was furious! Rachel Maris, that infernal Romanian, even though now recognized as a traitor, was still managing to make a fool of him. That morning she had the audacity to knee him in the groin, humiliating him right in front of one of his own men. That malicious act still pained Ostermann, his groin area hurting whenever he moved quickly or stretched the wrong way.

Now Rachel Maris had purposely removed his listening wires and spitefully escaped out some back exit of Arnold Hall, intentionally causing Ostermann's field team to lose them. She had done it to put Ostermann in an embarrassing position. What other explanation was there for ditching a backup team? Their mission was to provide support for her. Ostermann glanced at his watch. What was he going to tell his section chief, that they could not find her? He hated that woman with a passion.

Ostermann considered lying to his boss. He had no qualms about doing so, if it suited his purposes. In this case it would be too risky though, he could not control what might happen next and the odds of being caught in a lie were too great. Cursing at that Romanian, his infernal nemesis, Ostermann dialed a secure line and was connected to his home office.

"Hello." It was Andrew Maconey, Newby's smiling errand boy.

"Ostermann here," he spoke gruffly.

"Good, you are right on time, Mr. Newby is with me in the office."

"Good day, Ostermann," Newby vocalized his presence.

"Mr. Newby," Ostermann acknowledged his chief. "Before I tell you the bad news, let me report on our progress. Rachel Maris and the target met with the Baron's daughter this afternoon at thirteen hundred hours. She arranged a phone call with the Baron himself."

"Good," Newby spoke into the line. "Did you record anything incriminating?"

"Well…ah…no."

"I should have known, the Baron is too crafty for that. They did make contact, though. At least we have that on tape?"

"No."

"What, the recorder broke down? A bit of bad luck?"

"Not exactly."

"What then?"

"My men didn't get anything. Rachel Maris removed our wires before the conversation began."

"That makes sense, another indicator of her guilt," Maconey remarked. "She apparently did not want to incriminate her leader. What else?"

"That's all, my men lost them after that."

"What?" Newby exclaimed.

"They gave us the slip, but don't worry, I've got men watching both exits from the Academy grounds, we'll pick them up again."

"What happened?" Newby asked.

"Maris has apparently decided to sever contact."

"Are you sure? This does not make sense, Rachel has not seen the list yet. Maybe they are in trouble."

"I don't think so," Ostermann said with disgust.

"Perhaps they were attacked and had to depart in haste. Perhaps she couldn't recover the wire."

"No, she did it on purpose," Ostermann's voice rose. Why was Newby giving that traitor the benefit of the doubt?

"Okay," Newby continued. "If you are right, it is imperative to find her again, quickly. We must have an established contact when she makes a run for the Baron. You must record and prove the link, Ostermann, that is the main reason for this whole operation. This is a serious setback. How did they get away?"

"We'll find them. If not now, or when they exit the Academy, then later when they go for the documents. I have already sent a man ahead to stake out the entrance to Rocky Mountain National Park, and another all the way in to the site at Desolation."

"That's good, it is fortunate we know exactly where they are headed."

"Yes, and we shall be there waiting."

"One other complication, Ostermann," Maconey broke in.

"Yes."

"This assassination attempt, we think it was one of the Baron's men. We believe the Baron is on to us, at least to the degree of knowing he is in trouble."

"So her own boss is trying to kill her," Ostermann could not help smiling maliciously.

"Don't let it happen, Ostermann, we must have the link established," Newby directed.

"What? She deserves to die."

"What did you say?" Newby was startled by Ostermann's coldness.

"She is a traitor."

"Yes, however, your assignment now, Ostermann, is to protect their lives. Nothing else matters for the moment."

"But, sir?"

"No arguments!" Newby became angry. It had been a mistake to assign Ostermann as case officer over Rachel Maris. She needed help, not another enemy. For some deep borne emotional reason, Newby still clung to the hope he might recover Rachel, even though he was allowing her to march into a sure death.

"Look, Ostermann," Newby allowed his anger to explode. "No more foul-ups! If Maris or the target gets hurt, you are off the case. This entire operation has been one blunder after another on your part. First you killed Goldsmith, now you have lost contact. Mess it up again and you are through. You got that, Ostermann?"

"Yes, sir," Ostermann replied. After Newby hung up, Ostermann slammed the phone down in a rage. He would get that Maris woman, she would pay for this.

32

Driving north on Interstate 25, John Hughes, Gwen Hughes, and Rachel Maris reached Denver in less than an hour with no signs of pursuit. Without stopping they headed northwest on State Highway 36, the road winding amid spectacular canyons, one of the prettiest drives in all of Colorado. Signs warning, "Beware Rolling Rocks" lined the scenic roadway. Reaching the town of Estes Park, just outside the entrance to Rocky Mountains National Park, they paused to stock up on packfood, for they planned to hike into the depths of the mountains.

Rachel had been modestly silent during the drive, not wishing to intrude on John and Gwen's family centered recollections. Rachel did not care who Aunt Jones was dating, how many children the Smiths had now, or how much of Uncle Harry's liver survived the operation. All this talk was depressing to Rachel's spirits. She personally had not known any relatives other than her mother and father, and her father had deserted them when she was twelve, that after taking them halfway around the world to escape Nazi oppression.

Rachel was starting to feel very much alone again. It was not an uncommon emotion for her. Ironically though, it was one which tended to cause her to withdraw even further from the world. She berated herself for never allowing a relationship to mature enough for marriage. It was her own fault, she had known plenty of men who would have been willing. Rachel would sometimes go days or weeks without speaking to another human being. Most of the time she just preferred being alone. There were people Rachel liked, the Baron, or Dan Newby for instance, and there were those who liked her—but none that felt love for her. She was a loner in the true sense of the word, and the reality of her state was depressing at times.

Concentrating on her job, Rachel puzzled over who was trying to kill her target. Perhaps it wasn't Randy Ostermann. He was too stupid to be involved with foreign governments. Besides, the Eastern Block had crumbled, who would defect to their cause at a time like this? Maybe there really were Russians involved? John indicated they were after a list of some type, although he did not know why. Maybe she had acted rashly in severing all contact with her backup team, but how could she be sure? She would never trust Ostermann.

In the town of Estes Park, when John and the cadet visited a local grocery store to buy trail supplies, Rachel excused herself, pretending to be ill. She called a sterile office phone number, an act not normally per procedure, but Rachel felt the circumstances warranted extreme measures, and began leaving a message on the recording machine.

"This is Mary Randall," Rachel stated. The name did not matter, it was the voice that would guarantee her message went to the correct source. Just in case, Mary Randall was a play on Rachel Maris' real name. She had used it before and Newby would recognize it. "This message is for Daddy's ears only." Daddy would be interpreted as her section chief, Daniel Newby. Rachel wanted to limit the dissemination of her message to her boss, although it was unavoidable that clerks would hear it too, one might even be listening real time.

"I lost my purse," Rachel continued, speaking cryptically. "It was stolen this morning, possibly by a close friend. I am continuing on though. Please send money, no checks, I need cash." It was a request for help, a renewal of the backup team.

She was about to give her location when suddenly the line was interrupted, "Rachel, I am pleased you called in. We were worried about you." It was Newby's familiar voice.

Rachel felt a rush of relief. "Dan, I am so glad you were there."

"Are you safe, what is the matter?" Newby felt a surge of pity, she sounded so relieved to have reached him.

"There was an attempt on our lives."

"Yes, I know."

"I have severed contact with my field team."

"Yes, we heard. Ostermann is not happy. Rachel, who tried to kill your target?"

"I don't know for sure. Luckily I was able to abort the attempt. My target thinks it was the Russians, but I don't know."

Newby was not surprised that Rachel questioned the complicity of Russians, she knew how they had deceived the target earlier, back in Tulsa. Was she starting to suspect her mentor, the Baron? He hoped not. If she knew the Baron was responsible, would she still take the list to him? "Who then?" Newby asked, curious as to her answer, his voice straining.

"I think Ostermann is in on it. Can you confirm?"

"No, it's definitely not Ostermann. I would know something. There are too many of our people out in the field with him." Newby felt pained. He longed to tell Rachel of the danger she was walking into, that the man she trusted, the Baron, was actually her worst enemy, one who was seeking her death to prevent his own exposure.

"Are you sure?" Rachel questioned. "There is no possibility he might be in league with the assassin?"

"Absolutely not, Ostermann is still mine."

Rachel was suspicious nevertheless. Newby had answered too quickly, he sounded funny, and she could tell something was bothering him. He had been too anxious to assert Ostermann's innocence, and his voice sounded choked up. Was it possible that Dan Newby had ordered the hit? Not Newby, not her friend.

"Where are you, Rachel?" Newby asked. "Did you learn the location of the documents?"

"Yes," Rachel swallowed, wondering if she was making a mistake to divulge information to Newby. "I am at the town Estes Park. The documents are buried in the National Park here, somewhere along a trail about a day's hike in." She couldn't bring herself to tell him the exact location. Just disclosing as much as she did caused a shiver to run up her spine.

"Okay," Newby's voice trailed off. "I'll send Ostermann and

his team into the Park for support. Be careful Rachel, I don't want you hurt."

Rachel hung up the phone, feeling cold. Was there no one she could trust? Her target, John Hughes, seemed the only guileless person she knew, and she was betraying him. John was so sure of his own motives, the importance of his grand mission to save mankind; the poor, deluded, tormented fool. It was sad. He had genuinely tried to help her; and she, on the other hand, was playing him for a sucker.

"Hi, Rachel, we are back," John called, as he and the cadet rounded a corner and caught sight of her by the phone booth. "You look better," he lied politely, thinking she still looked a little ashen. "I know why you stayed outside," he joked, "too embarrassed to be seen in those baggy clothes."

Rachel smiled, hiding a pang of self-consciousness. She wondered why it bothered her that John thought she looked silly. Rachel could see Gwen grinning, and realized that brat had chosen these horrendous clothes intentionally. If it wasn't for John, and Gwen's father, she would have put the insolent child in her place a long time ago.

Hurrying to obtain camping permits before nightfall, they entered the National Park and stopped at the main Visitor Center by Park Headquarters. While buying topographical maps of the hiking trails, John learned of a smaller ranger station, just outside the Visitor Center, where backpacking permits could be obtained. He started to proceed in that direction, when Rachel caught his arm, wanting to persuade him of the folly in such a course of action. Why buy a permit and take the risk of leaving a trail for pursuers? If they were stopped by a ranger, they could always claim ignorance.

Electing to purchase a one night camping permit for one of the RV campgrounds instead, they selected Moraine Park. It was decided to rest up that evening and then hike in on the morrow.

Reaching their site just as the sun set, they began the task of erecting puptents. Gwen took pains to ensure her own tent was strategically located between her cousin's and Rachel's. She knew better than to trust Rachel Maris with her cousin. The lady's intentions were all too obvious. At least John's motives appeared pure. Still, Gwen remembered the way Rachel had been fawning over her cousin.

Having put puptents together many times before, Gwen was the first one finished, moving with experienced efficiency. John managed to erect his own tent shortly thereafter. Rachel however, could not get past the first step, stymied by the simple task. Gwen would have been content watching her struggle, but John felt compelled to render assistance.

To Gwen's disgust, Rachel gratefully turned the whole task over to John and joined Gwen to watch. It figured, Gwen was the type that felt a need to do things for herself, whereas Rachel felt more comfortable having things done for her.

"Never been camping before?" Gwen asked, not hiding the scorn in her voice.

"I prefer the comforts of civilization," Rachel answered. "Why deprive oneself unnecessarily?"

After John finished erecting the tent, he joined the two women. "I guess we are all set. How about some dinner?"

"Sounds great," Rachel responded. "I am famished, what did you buy for us to dine on this evening?"

Gwen answered, "Beef jerky, dried fruit, and campground water, the same we'll be having for every meal." She expected a reaction from Rachel and was not disappointed, as a look of exasperation furrowed the woman's brow.

They turned in early that evening, exhausted by the events of a long stressful day. Only Gwen seemed to have any reserves of energy, so when Rachel suggested they take turns keeping watch through the night, Gwen volunteered for the first shift. John agreed to be second, leaving Rachel the third shift.

That suited Rachel just fine, she was in sore need of sleep right then. Crawling inside the tiny puptent, Rachel unrolled her sleeping bag, removed her outer clothes, and climbed in. Rachel left the zipper of her sleeping bag all the way undone. She was still hot and she disliked being confined. When the temperature dropped, as the night wore on, she could easily zip up her bag.

Fitfully Rachel drifted off to sleep. She felt terrible, her muscles ached, and noises of the night disturbed her. A pillow sure would have been nice. Sleeping on the ground reminded Rachel of the "farm" and survival camp, a stressful high pressure period during Rachel's early CIA training.

Awakened abruptly in the middle of the night, Rachel was jarred back into consciousness by a rough hand clasping hard over her mouth. It was Randy Ostermann, his foul face not inches from her ear, whispering for her to be still. Rachel started to sit up, but the sleeping bag constrained her. Suddenly Ostermann placed a heavy arm across her chest, inside her sleeping bag, pinning her to the ground.

"Don't move, it's me," Ostermann growled again.

As her initial fright subsided, Rachel calmed herself, although remaining on guard. For all she knew, the man holding her to the ground was a mortal enemy seeking her death. Ostermann was close, too close, inside her tent, practically inside her sleeping bag with her. It distressed Rachel that he had been able to sneak so close without her sensing his presence. Was she getting lax, or perhaps he was just that good?

"What do you want?" she whispered, wishing he would withdraw his arm. Ostermann felt no inclination to do so though, pressing Rachel hard against the ground, and Rachel did not want to verbally acknowledge it bothered her.

"Just wanted to let you know that we are back," Ostermann chuckled. "I am re-establishing contact."

"You need not have come to my tent," Rachel spoke huffily, trying to mask her fear, her breath labored.

"Had too," Ostermann smiled, still pressing Rachel flat on her back. "I was waiting for you to take a shift on watch, but it's almost morning. The target fell asleep on his watch and will likely sleep till daybreak."

"I had better wake him," Rachel moaned. "You can go now, Ostermann."

"Let him sleep, we'll maintain watch for you. By the way, Jeff Murrey spotted a man prowling about just beyond your camp, but he got away before we could catch him."

Rachel's mind spun with thought. Was Ostermann setting up the background for a hit on the target? Or was he telling the truth? He must have been informed about her call to Newby. Ostermann must know she didn't trust him, perhaps he was simply trying to vex her and add to her fears. "I will need a gun, and some ammunition," Rachel requested, testing Ostermann.

"All right," Ostermann surprised her. "We'll make a drop in the women's bathhouse, it will be there when you break camp." He removed his arm at last and started to leave. Rachel breathed heavily, now that the pressure was removed from her chest.

"Ostermann," Rachel whispered, as he slid from her tent. "Just do your job and don't foul me up," she snapped angrily, fighting the urge to kick at him on the way out.

Randy Ostermann sneered and spit on the ground, pure hatred momentarily radiating from his eyes.

Rachel lay pondering her options. She decided not to wake John. They would be safe for the night. If Ostermann had wanted to kill them, he would already have done so. There were probably too many of his own men around, some that might be not involved with the conspiracy. How could Newby still trust that snake? Ostermann was probably just waiting for a more convenient opportunity to strike. It would be up to Rachel not to give him one.

When morning arrived, Rachel emerged from her tent just in time. Gwen was arising also and John was still asleep, resting serenely alongside a log in a grassy spot. Hastily pulling on her fatigue pants and the USAFA T-shirt, Rachel hurried over to John's side.

"Wake up," she prodded John, hoping to save him the embarrassment of being caught asleep.

"What's going on?" Gwen called out, as she crawled from her tent and stood up, seeing John and Rachel together out by the log.

"I just fell asleep," John answered, worried that Gwen had found them together in what might appear to be a compromising situation.

Rachel interrupted, moving closer to John's side. "He was just being a gentleman and served two shifts, to allow me extra sleep."

John blushed, but accepted her alibi. Gwen was staring at them dubiously though.

Standing outside in her bare feet, Rachel found herself starting to shiver in the cold. Gwen's T-shirt was so tight on Rachel it made her uncomfortable, and didn't provide much warmth either.

Gwen was wearing a USAFA T-shirt also. Both shirts had the letters "USAFA" printed in navy blue across the chest, with the name "HUGHES" in smaller letters above the bold print. It annoyed Gwen to see Rachel wearing one of her T-shirts. She had not thought of that yesterday when she had given one to Rachel.

Excusing herself to visit the ladies room, Rachel went in search of the stash Ostermann had promised. True to his word, it was there, a small plastic covered bundle wrapped in a dirty old towel and stuffed into the basin of one of the toilets. Inside the towel and plastic were two seven-round clips of 9mm parabellum and an ASP (Armanent Systems and Procedures) handgun. The automatic ASP was probably an antique, originally developed just for the CIA by modifying a Smith and Wesson model 39.

Breaking camp, John and his female companions drove to the Alpine Visitor Center high atop the Continental Divide. There was parking available there for backpackers, and it was only a half mile from their trailhead. Each of them was equipped with a backpack, their own tent, sleeping bag, bedroll, and miscellaneous cooking provisions. John placed a portion of Rachel's share in his own pack, to help lighten her load. Even so, she felt the weight quite burdensome and unwieldy.

The weather was a little nippy at that altitude, even for a midsummer day. June was still early in the summer for the Rockies.

Rachel had donned her purple sweat shirt over the USAFA T-shirt and was still feeling chilly. The wind had blown her hair past immediate redemption and she had given up fussing over it. Dressed in the clothes Gwen had provided, she was not going to look decent, regardless of what she did with her hair. Gwen had on a 100 percent knit wool sweater which looked comfortably warm. Besides that, her hair was short and the wind didn't make such a mess out of it.

To reach their trailhead, the trio had to journey down a steeply inclined dirt road, the Old Fall River Road, which was open to public vehicles in the up direction only. Balancing the heavy packs was not an easy chore for the novices, and twice they had to stop and adjust straps to more evenly distribute the load.

Reaching the start of their trail, a route which would take them to a back-country site called Desolation, they entered a densely wooded area via a single-file trail named Chapin Creek Trail, which paralleled Chapin Creek. It was however, very steep initially, threading up the side of the mountain through Chapin Pass between Marmot Point and Mount Chapin, the trail rising considerably in elevation.

The climb proved extremely tiring, prompting Rachel to call for a rest stop almost immediately. John agreed readily, feeling quite fatigued himself. Sitting down, he leaned back enough to rest his backpack frame on the ground. Gwen, showing no signs of tiredness, paced ahead, enjoying the scenery.

"She hates me," Rachel muttered between breaths, as she sat down next to John.

"No, I don't think so," John argued politely.

"It's okay, I don't care," Rachel said. "She is just feeling defensive I suppose."

John thought of Eleanor. He trusted the children were not giving her too rough a time. John hoped he hadn't caused his innocent wife too great an inconvenience. Probably not, she was quite capable as a mother.

"John?" Rachel asked seriously, scooting closer, "Do you think you can find the documents?"

"Most assuredly, I know right where to look."

"What then? What happens after you find them?"

"Well, I am hoping to be able to tell if this DWARS virus is a reality."

"And, if it is?"

"I don't know. I suppose we will have to get the evidence back to my uncle. He has contacts, people would believe him. Maybe he can stop the launch."

"But what if he can't?"

"Then I have three months to stop it myself."

Rachel sank back, lying on her pack, staring at the bottoms of the tree branches swaying gently with the wind.

After an interlude, Rachel slipped her pack off and sat upright. She gazed deep into the eyes of the man next to her. "John?"

"Yes, Rachel."

"Have you ever stopped to think, what would happen if we are caught?"

"Sure, we would be sent to jail, probably for the rest of our lives."

Rachel felt a deep sense of sorrow for the well-intentioned, but misguided man sitting next to her. He seemed such a martyr.

John saw the look of anguish creeping upon Rachel's face. Thinking the talk of jail had frightened her, he too felt sudden empathy. He should never have allowed this innocent woman to be caught up in his mess. She was so beautiful. John placed a hand on Rachel's shoulder and squeezed, trying to offer some measure of comfort and support.

Rachel moved closer in response, it was the first time John had touched her. She had brushed against him many times, but he had never before returned physical contact. "It is scary to think about," she whispered, "jail and all."

"I know."

Rachel looked into his eyes again. "What about the others?"

"What others?"

"The Russians, suppose they catch us?"

John grimaced, "I would imagine, if we don't give them their list, perhaps even if we do, they'll kill us."

Rachel used the opportunity to bury her head onto John's chest and snuggle in close against him. He placed an arm around her shoulder. It felt good lying there, next to a man who knew how to care. Rachel wondered how she could ever betray this kind person. She would do it, she had no doubts about that, but the thought made her squirm. She felt so secure with him holding her, and for a few moments, her anxieties seemed to fade.

Suddenly Gwen reappeared from up the trail. They had totally forgotten about her presence. A look of shock crossed Gwen's face, then anger and disgust. John stood up quickly, totally embarrassed. Realizing it was time to go, yet hating for the magic of that moment to fade, Rachel slowly stood up also.

Continuing onward, they fought their way up the side of the mountain, having to stop twice more before reaching the crest at 11,100 feet where the trail leveled off. There were patches of hard crusty leftover snow scattered about in the shade. They were only a half mile up the trail so far.

"John," Gwen accosted her cousin, during a moment when Rachel was lagging behind. "What are you doing with that woman?"

John looked so ashamed it was almost comical. "Nothing really," he stumbled for words. "She was just frightened, that's all."

"You had best be careful," Gwen warned.

"Careful?"

"You know what I mean. If you value your wife, then watch out for that woman. She means you harm!"

33

Eleanor Hughes was left alone to her misery, handcuffed to a banister railing in that miserable old mansion they deceptively called a safe house. Silently she suffered, struggling with her fear, as time passed with agonizing slowness. The stairs rose behind her in such a manner that the bottom of the rail post was waist high where Eleanor was handcuffed. Consequently, even though she slid her handcuffs to the bottom of the post, she was nonetheless restrained in such a manner that she was forced to stand.

Becoming extremely uncomfortable, unable to sit or relax, panic attempted to prey upon her anxious mind. One hour passed, maybe two, why hadn't they let her go yet? Eleanor stifled the urge to cry out, wanting to shout and ask if her time was up. The situation was ironically similar to how her own children must feel, when sent to their bedrooms or a corner for a certain period of time. The principle was the same, disobedience brought a punishment at the whim of the one in charge, only in this case, it was unlawful authority and unjust imprisonment.

Too proud to call out for relief, Eleanor suffered in silence, struggling against cramping muscles, circulation problems in her wrists, and an increasingly distraught frame of mind. Had they forgotten her? The large woman frightened Eleanor, she was cruel, uncaring, and downright mean. At least the other was cordial.

Eleanor was angry with John! How could he have brought this trouble upon her? They said he was stealing secret documents and that he was a traitor. She did not believe it though, not John. Could it possibly be true? For some persistent reason, the thought lingered. Eleanor felt guilty for entertaining such a possibility, for thoughts of disloyalty against her husband, but what if it was true?

"Yee-awh," Eleanor spun around, startled by the sudden appearance of Officer Pastorelli, walking briskly toward the front door.

"I'm going out for some groceries," Pastorelli said, noticing a questioning look upon her charge's face. The policewoman glanced at her wristwatch. "You have ten more minutes and I would not expect Blinkerson to let you off a second early." Pastorelli paused, as if deep in thought, pondering whether or not to speak of something that was troubling her.

With a sigh, Pastorelli said, "Look, I will be back in about thirty minutes. When Blinkerson lets you go, don't do anything foolish. I tell you this for your own sake. Blinkerson will be required to accompany you through the house, not allowing you out of her sight unless restrained. Ah…ah…I would not do anything to irritate her, she doesn't mind inflicting pain, if you get my drift. Just a friendly warning."

Eleanor watched in horror as Pastorelli departed, leaving her alone with that monstrous Blinkerson woman. What on earth was Pastorelli hinting at? The implication was that Officer Blinkerson was not stable, that she liked hurting people. Eleanor's discomfort turned to fear and anxiety. Now she dreaded the passing of those last ten minutes.

All too soon, Blinkerson appeared in the hallway to unloose her prisoner. Eleanor shrank from before the policewoman, bothered to the marrow when Blinkerson brushed against her to unlock the handcuffs. Stumbling to a chair in the nearby dining room, Eleanor sat rubbing her wrists, ugly red marks lined her soft white skin in twin circles. She was relieved to be free, in spite of now having to tolerate Blinkerson's looming presence.

"Let's go in the TV room," Blinkerson spoke, her tone commanding.

"I would rather have a look around the house," Eleanor complained, not wishing to keep company alone with the horrible woman. "If it is permissable?"

"I guess," Blinkerson shrugged.

As Eleanor toured the huge old home, the grossly fat police officer lumbered along behind, following like a trained bear. Her presence made Eleanor extremely nervous, but seemed unavoidable under the current circumstances.

The ground level, upon which the house's foundation sat, was on a hill, four feet higher than street level. Located on the corner of two tree-lined neighborhood streets, the yard was filled with older long growth trees. There were at least two lots there, and a separate garage building apart from the house, with a small room for the maid's quarters.

Just inside the front door was a large entryway facing a set of carpeted stairs. To the left was an isolated living room and to the right the dining room. Through the dining room was the TV room, an addition to the house, and off to the side the kitchen. Past that was a half bathroom and some stairs leading to the basement.

Upstairs were three bathrooms and five bedrooms. The first bedroom was large and had its own private bath. The next two were smaller, sharing a bathroom with the upstairs hall. To reach the master bedroom and its private bathroom, one had to pass through the fourth bedroom, which was furnished like a small sitting room.

Eleanor wondered where she was to sleep, but was leery about asking.

"You ready for bed?" Blinkerson queried, noticing Eleanor staring at the bedrooms with a questioning look.

"No, I was just curious." Eleanor shuddered involuntarily.

"I guess you can have that first bedroom," Blinkerson decided. "You get a choice, either we handcuff you to the bed, or else one of us sleeps in there with you. If you choose the latter, and it's me, then I get the bed and you can have the floor."

Eleanor wondered why Blinkerson had to be such a distasteful person. Some people seemed to like tormenting others. Maybe it made them feel important in some way, compensating for weak self-respect.

At that moment they were disturbed by the noise of Officer Pastorelli returning with the groceries. They all adjourned to the kitchen for a feast of microwaved burritos and tortilla chips with salsa dip. Once her hunger was satisfied, Eleanor announced her intentions to retire for the night, even though it was still quite early. She took no pleasure in the company of these two police officers. Eleanor chose the handcuffs, of course, regardless of the humiliation, and consequently had to endure one wrist being cuffed to a post on the headboard of her bed.

Eleanor hardly slept that night, bothered by a persistent nightmare in which she was naked and being chased through the mountains by bloodhounds. Despite the dream, Eleanor stayed in bed late that morning, far past her normal waking time, having no real reason to rise. In time she was forced out of bed though, when Pastorelli poked her head inside to announce the arrival of a visitor. Startled, Eleanor grabbed frantically for her covers, and pulled them to her chin.

"Relax, it's only me," Officer Pastorelli laughed. "Get dressed and hurry downstairs," she ordered, unlocking the handcuffs from Eleanor's wrist. Hastily Eleanor donned one of her more casual dresses and the two of them hastened downstairs to the living room.

Waiting patiently was the same gentlemanly detective that had questioned Eleanor at the police station. "I only have a few moments," he spoke with a friendly voice, and ushered Eleanor toward the couch. "Just stopped by to see how you are doing."

"I am better," Eleanor responded, taking a seat on the soft flowery living room couch. The detective sat down in a matching chair directly opposite her, causing Eleanor to cross her legs and tug the hem of her dress down over her knees.

"Tell me the truth," the detective leaned forward seriously. "How are you really doing?"

"Okay I guess, a little scared."

"That's only natural," Dan Newby leaned back in his chair, satisfied with a more honest answer.

"My children?" Eleanor asked.

"They are doing fine, staying with a nice foster couple that is seeing to their every need. Don't let their welfare concern you in the least, I personally have seen to their care."

"Thank you," Eleanor responded, and then wondered why she was thanking the man responsible for her unlawful arrest and detainment. He had taken her children away from her, and she was thanking him for seeing they went to a decent home?

"I'll be checking up on you periodically, and the children,"

Newby reassured Eleanor.

"Thank you," Eleanor said again, and then clenched her fist, annoyed at herself. "Tell me," she asked, as strongly as she could, "Where is my husband?"

Newby eyed the engineer's housewife, turning the question over in his mind. What would it hurt to tell her? She was secure, and she might be of assistance at some later date. "In Colorado," he answered.

"Colorado, but why?"

"Your husband is involved with another engineer from Krang Enterprises. The other man hid several stolen documents in the mountains of Colorado. Your husband is trying to recover them. Together they tried to sell those classified documents to the Russians."

"I don't understand," Eleanor moaned. "John is a family man. We don't have a lot of money, but we aren't hurting either. We even manage to save a modest amount each month, for the children's college you understand." She looked pleadingly at Newby, eliciting a nod of sympathy. "So why would John commit treason?"

Newby spread his hands in a gesture of befuddlement. "Who can say? There may be extenuating circumstances. We have an officer with him, undercover."

"Then why doesn't he arrest John and put an end to this mess? Bring John in and let's find out what is really going on."

"Well...ah...we are waiting till the right moment. Then she will do just that, recover the stolen material and arrest your husband."

"She?"

"Yes, a female intelligence officer, one of my best."

34

The back country trail to Desolation was quite scenic. Although strenuously steep at the beginning, the trail leveled off partway up the side of the mountain at Chapin Pass. Barely below the timberline, an altitude where trees could not grow, three weary travelers, burdened by their loads, took a short respite before continuing onward. After a steep descent of 350 feet, the trail soon emerged into a beautiful valley with a small sparkling stream snaking through the richly green valley floor. The Chapin Trail wound along parallel to Chapin Creek until running into Poudre River Trail along the west side of the Cache la Poudre River, skirting in and out of the forest, occasionally crossing lush meadows and soggy marshes.

"How much further?" Rachel Maris complained, as they reentered the shade of the woods after crossing a large sunny meadow. She felt like they had been hiking for days instead of hours. "I am so hot, and this backpack is killing me. What are we, beasts of burden?" The occasional stretches of trail across open areas exposed to the direct heat of the sun were difficult on Rachel, making her sweat profusely and appreciate the cooler shady parts of the trail.

"Don't be a pansy," Gwen mocked her. The cadet didn't mind

a little sweat. In fact, the exercise felt exhilarating to her active system.

"I can manage just fine," Rachel defended herself, "but I take no pleasure in manual, pack labor. How some people could call this fun, it's beyond me."

"I like the scenery," John remarked softly. "It's great to be outside in the mountains. You didn't see such trees back in Kansas I'll bet."

Rachel started to make a snide remark, but then thought better of it. John was just trying to be helpful. Letting her pack slip to the ground, Rachel stretched and tried to rub the small of her back where a persistent ache had developed. When she removed her sweatshirt, she noticed her shoulders hurt too. The cool breeze felt nice against the fine sheen of sweat along her arms and back, rejuvenating her. Rachel stuffed her sweatshirt into a side pocket of her backpack and started to remount her load, when Gwen halted also, to remove her cotton shirt. Underneath she too had on a USAFA T-shirt.

"Want to take a rest break?" John asked. He thought about calling them the Bobbsey Twins, but decided against it. Neither one of them would likely appreciate the pun. They did not seem to get along with each other.

"No," Rachel responded, waving her arm through the air. "The bugs are thick here, let's keep moving."

As they continued hiking along the meandering valley trail, Gwen took pains to ensure, whenever possible, that her cousin and this provocative stranger were isolated from each other. The task had not been difficult, as the society lady tended to lag behind most of the time anyway. On this particular occasion however, spurred by a horde of insects, Rachel hurried to don her pack and took up the lead, with John following close behind.

Whenever the trail widened, skirting out across grassy meadows, Rachel would slow, maneuvering to allow John to catch up and walk beside her. At such times Gwen followed close behind, listening to their conversation. Gwen could not forget the picture of this tart, trying to snuggle up next to her cousin, and to think she had found them together first thing that morning too.

The more Gwen pondered the matter, the more irritated she became. Finding herself close upon Rachel's heels, Gwen stepped out suddenly, catching the back of Rachel's foot and causing her heel to step out of her shoe.

"Oh, I am sorry," Gwen exclaimed, pretending it was an accident.

Rachel spun around, almost losing her shoe altogether, trying to stay calm. "That's okay," Rachel responded politely, with controlled breath, as she bent over to place her heel back in the tennis shoe. Suddenly the awkward weight of her pack caused Rachel to lose balance and almost pitch forward onto her face. With rising frustration, Rachel was forced to remove her backpack in order to get her shoe back on. After struggling to get her backpack replaced upon aching shoulders once more, Rachel had no sooner taken two steps when Gwen stepped on her heel again.

"My goodness," Gwen exclaimed, with mock abashment. "How could I be so clumsy?"

Rachel struggled to control her anger. "It happens," she spoke evenly, in a tempered voice. It was bad enough she was the only one without hiking boots, but now this harassment too. Rachel wiped the sweat off her face, wishing the trail would stay more in the shade.

"How about I walk in front of you, so this doesn't keep happening?" Gwen offered sweetly.

"How about you just watch where you are stepping?" Rachel fumed.

"I am sure it was an accident, Rachel," John interrupted, not wanting an argument. Gwen just smiled and shrugged her shoulders.

Cursing to herself, Rachel removed her backpack and grudgingly slipped her heel into the shoe once more. As she was kneeling down to tighten her laces, Rachel caught sight of something suspicious, something that drove all thoughts of the irritating cadet from her mind. It was a glint of sunlight in the woods, a few miles ahead, a reflection on something shiny, perhaps a rifle scope or field glasses. Rachel worried about who it might be. Was it one of Ostermann's men? Was it the assassin? Were they one and the same?"

"I'll take up the rear," Rachel conceded, no longer feeling a desire to squabble. Once her companions were moving down the trail, Rachel lagged behind even further, until she could feel safe slipping the ASP 9mm and a clip of bullets from her backpack. Quickly she dropped them into the front pocket of her fatigues. One good thing about those ugly fatigue pants, they did have large pockets, it was pretty much their only redeeming feature.

Alert to danger now, Rachel put her self-centered worries aside; the heat, the dust, the mosquitoes, the aching shoulders, her appearance, the cadet, would all wait. It would take all her skills to see them through this venture alive and she certainly could not count on Ostermann for help, not if she planned to stay alive.

Suggesting they break for lunch, Rachel took the opportunity to slip away, excusing herself for a visit to a private part of the woods, to use the bear's restroom, as Gwen called it. She instead began working her way in a circle toward the north, hoping to approach the area where she had last seen that flash of sunlight reflecting through the trees.

What she had thought would be a ten minute hike, stretched out into a lengthy hour. The woods were thick with fallen logs, making progress slow, with frequent obstacles sometimes necessitating climbs over tangles of fallen tree trunks. If not for chancing upon a deer trail part way up the ridge, Rachel might have taken two hours to reach her objective.

Rachel Maris knew her business though, and the fact that she had spotted her opponent, and hopefully he did not know it, was an advantage, thanks to a little help from the sun. Managing to approach the source of her investigation from behind, Rachel came upon a scene that distressed her greatly.

It was indeed a sniper of some type, or at least an armed spotter. He was situated on a protected vantage point with a clear view of the crossroads where Poudre River and Mummy Pass trails intersected. Leaning against a nearby fallen log was a high-powered hunting rifle with a scope, a Weatherby Mark V. Should Rachel, John, and Gwen continue along their planned route of travel toward Desolation, they would soon be in a position for the spotter to pick them off with relative ease.

The sniper was a stranger to Rachel Maris. Again the question haunted her, was he an enemy assassin, or simply a new member of Ostermann's backup team. There was no way for Rachel to tell for sure. Should she kill him, she might be taking out a CIA fellow intelligence officer. She could not ignore him though. One hour had already passed since Rachel had slipped away into the woods, there wasn't time to work her way back to John and redirect them onto another trail. John and Gwen might already be looking for her. Any minute now they might show up searching along the Poudre River Trail, right into the sniper's sights.

Deciding to take him out, but not slay him, Rachel circled until directly behind the man. She would have to get close, for if he saw her too early and swung that Weatherby around, then she would be forced to kill him.

Slowly and carefully Rachel approached the man, Viper ready in the right hand, ASP in the other. Calming herself, Rachel focused her energy, moving in for the kill, the faster her heart beat, the slower she moved.

Creeping within ten yards, to move any closer would invite discovery, Rachel slowly rose to a full standing position, sheathed her knife, and pointed her handgun. In a firm commanding voice, a threatening voice, she called out, "Don't move!"

Her quarry froze, sensing a loaded pistol. "Throw the rifle aside," Rachel commanded. He complied without hesitation, so she moved closer, within a few feet of the man. "Now lay spread eagle."

Fearing his life was lost, the man stood unmoving, "Don't shoot," he begged.

Rachel drew even closer, "Put your face in the dirt. If you have another weapon, tell me now or it will cost you a bullet in the leg."

"In my shoulder holster," he mumbled, eyes shut. "Please, I have family, a baby girl."

"I'm sure your wife would have little trouble finding a new husband to be your baby girl's daddy, if you don't do exactly as I say."

In the distance Rachel could hear John calling her name. They were coming up the trail. That fool, he knew there was danger about, why was he calling her name? She would have to hurry. Standing directly before her helpless captive, ASP pointed at his face, Rachel commanded for the last time, "Draw your weapon and toss it to the side. Then you get on the ground!"

Fearing all was lost, the man pretended to comply, but then lunged desperately at Rachel, swinging hard to ward her gun hand aside.

Rachel was prepared, she had expected him to try something, and merely stepped into the man, smacking him hard across the temple with the barrel of her pistol. He fell heavily to the ground unconscious, a nasty gash across his forehead, blood flowing into the dirt.

Rachel could hear John coming closer, she had no more time to waste. Hastily she retrieved the injured man's rifle. He was lucky, if it were not for the approaching footsteps of her friends, she might have slit his throat.

Drawing the man's pistol, she discovered a CZ-99. That made her feel better, this was no ordinary hunter. Ditching the pistol, Rachel grabbed up the hunting rifle, it was a Weatherby Mark V Safari Grade, a very nice high-velocity magnum rifle.

Laying the Weatherby down where it could easily be seen, Rachel hid herself in the trees, watching the trail below till John and Gwen had passed. Once they were safely up the trail a ways, she worked her way down to the trail behind them. Putting on a frightened look, she cried out hysterically and begin running in their direction.

John heard Rachel's distress and raced back to meet her, with Gwen following quickly behind. "What happened?" he cried out in alarm, his eyes widening at the sight of Rachel's fear.

Rachel stumbled up before John, wheezing for breath, trying to look frightened. "When I was in the woods, I became lost. After wandering about for hours, I finally chanced upon our camp, but you had left without me. I started to follow down the trail, when I heard some arguing up a hill. Some men were fighting and they had guns. One of them has been hurt terribly. I was so scared, I didn't know what to do, John." Rachel took hold of her target's arm for support.

"Why didn't we hear anything?" Gwen asked with amazement.

"Come and see," Rachel cried, leading them back down the trail and up a tree covered slope toward the injured assassin, telling them how she had seen three, maybe four others, attack and beat this lone man.

As they reached the site of Rachel's fallen sniper, John and Gwen froze in open-mouthed amazement. "Looks like a hunter," John surmised, staring at the unconscious bleeding man, a churning sour feeling building in John's stomach. "I wonder why he was attacked?" John questioned, as he picked up the man's fallen Weatherby rifle.

"We have to get help," Gwen remarked, stooping to take his pulse.

"No, we cannot," Rachel argued. "We have to get out of here. The men who did this may be looking for us."

"But we cannot just leave him," John groaned.

"Once we are out of the woods, we'll notify a ranger, send help back," Rachel proposed anxiously.

"This man is no hunter, look at this," Gwen pointed to a walkie-talkie, and the injured man's empty handgun holster. "He must have friends somewhere in the woods, on the other end of this walkie-talkie."

"We must hurry away," Rachel cried. "His friends will be looking for him soon. This looks like the man who tried to kill us back at the Embassy Suites."

"Rachel's right," John agreed. "Let's get out of here before we are discovered." John liked the feel of the man's rifle. "Should we take the rifle with us?" he proposed.

"I'll keep it," Rachel offered. "You have a heavier pack." Gwen was startled by the sudden transformation in Rachel's demeanor, her fright seeming to have disappeared all of a sudden. John didn't seem to notice though.

"Rachel, I think it would be best if I took the rifle," John said. "A loaded gun is a dangerous thing." Taking the Weatherby in his hands, John turned the weapon around, admiring the flamboyant styling like an appreciative child with a new Christmas toy.

"Why, do you know how to use it?" Rachel argued, knowing they would be in a better position to fight off assailants if she kept the weapon.

"Well, as a boy I went hunting a couple of times with Uncle Ellis, and I have had hunter safety training. Have you had hunter safety training, Rachel?"

"No," she admitted grudgingly. Rachel couldn't tell him she was a rated expert marksman.

"Well then, I'll keep it," John smiled.

Rachel was exasperated at the irony of her cover story. Of course an innocent city girl would turn the weapon over, men were the supposedly stronger sex.

John slid the chamber open, checking for bullets. "It's not loaded."

"Here you are," Rachel began emptying the pockets of the wounded man. When she looked up, she saw John and Gwen staring at her with shock. Rachel ignored them and put two boxes of .460 caliber bullets into John's hand. She noticed Gwen eyeing her suspiciously. The cadet knew something was not right, she was not buying Rachel's story.

"Are we going to stand here talking all day?" Rachel declared, prompting them to race back to the trail and continue onward at a jog until reaching the cover of some trees, at which point they settled into a fast walk.

Upon Rachel's suggestion, they traveled more carefully now, taking pains to stay always under the cover of trees. The one exception was a footbridge that had to be crossed when the trail forked to the right over Cache la Poudre River, as they switched to Mummy Pass Trail which followed Hague Creek.

By late afternoon they reached the remote back-mountain campsite named Desolation. It was prettier than Rachel had expected. Probably because of the name, she had anticipated a bleak, barren, windswept area. Instead Desolation was an idyllic one-party campsite, located in the pine trees about fifty yards from the waters of a rushing snow-swollen stream, Hague Creek. It was distinguished by a massive smooth-surfaced boulder, larger than the height of a man. Next to the boulder was a small clearing in the trees. From Desolation, although surrounded on all sides by trees, one could still hear the relaxing rush of waters flowing against rocks in the stream.

"This is it," John exclaimed. "That boulder will make a good point for us to keep watch from."

Rachel did not bother correcting John. Although a sentry on top of that boulder would have a good view, it would be a poor choice of location, he would be too exposed. A good sentry should be well hidden first of all, and then have a good view. A guard was of no value if intruders could easily avoid or dispose of him.

"Okay," John removed his backpack and dropped it to the ground. He laid the rifle against a stump and begin rummaging inside his pack for a small folding shovel. Both women watched him expectantly.

"Is it close?" Rachel asked impatiently.

"Yes, buried at a radial of thirty-nine degrees from this boulder. You two can relax for a moment while I dig it out."

Rachel decided to scout around a bit, as Gwen curiously followed John to watch the excavation. Rachel had not gone far when she spotted one of Ostermann's men, then another, this time both people she recognized, Jeff Murrey and Eddie Sanders. Rachel wondered if they knew about the man she had bloodied back along the trail. When Sanders waved to Rachel, she returned the acknowledgment. They had the area surrounded, a complete perimeter surveillance. That bothered Rachel, Ostermann's men seemed to have already been set up before they had arrived.

It would all be over in a while, Rachel thought. As soon as John finished digging the documents up, she would give the signal and Ostermann's men would close in for the arrest. Rachel wondered why she was feeling so sick. She should be feeling elated, another successful mission, another outstanding performance for her files.

Rachel meandered back to camp, thinking about John. He was such a nice guy, she would hate to see him go to jail, but then, he had brought this on himself. It wasn't Rachel's fault he was stealing government documents. Why was she feeling so sick? Visions of deadly micro-bugs, released by satellites, raining down from the sky, suddenly filled Rachel's mind. Genocide, genocide, the death of a race, the annihilation of a people, Rachel placed her hands over her ears to shut out the sounds of her imagination.

John suddenly reappeared from behind the boulder, he and Gwen were smiling broadly. "We found it," he called excitedly to Rachel. Then, seeing her face, asked, "What's the matter? You look ill."

Rachel sat down suddenly in the grass. She felt clammy all over. Inwardly Rachel moaned to herself and silently exclaimed, "I cannot cope!! What am I to do!!"

35

John Hughes approached Rachel Maris with optimistic enthusiasm in his step. She was reeling with nausea, but he hardly noticed. John's attention was engrossed by the knapsack he had recently unearthed, which he dropped on the ground with a plop next to Rachel. Opening the damp, dirt caked bag, excited with anticipation, like a small child unwrapping a birthday gift, John uncovered a cache of documents bound securely inside a plastic trash bag.

Out of the bag he pulled a thick document with red cover sheets on the top and bottom. There were no titles on the cover sheets, only the number "113," in large bold letters. John turned the cover sheet to read the document's title page, "Mission Targeting Specification." How did Goldsmith get this out of the building? John shook his head in amazement. He laid the spec aside and peered into the knapsack, selecting another document.

Rachel felt bile rise up into her mouth. "John," she called softly, after forcing it back down. "I don't feel safe here, perhaps we should move on."

"I agree," Gwen Hughes concurred. The sun was just beginning to set and it made her shiver. "We shouldn't camp so close to the trail." She kept thinking about that man Rachel had discovered, beaten half senseless, whose gun they had stolen.

"John, put those papers away and let's move to a safer spot for the night!" Rachel spoke shrilly, startling John with the intensity of her words. Rachel hoped Ostermann would let them leave alive. She closed her eyes for a moment. What was she doing? Why couldn't she call in Ostermann to make the arrest? Why did the thought of betraying John sicken her?

Gwen pulled out the topographical park map to look for a safer location. "Here we are at Desolation," her finger pointed to a spot along Hague Creek. Earlier they had studied out and planned their route in great detail, originally thinking to hike out of the mountains along the same route they had followed in.

"There are trails all along this side of Hague Creek, and also deeper into the park," Gwen remarked. "However, if we cross the steam into 2H and 3H, those areas are marked as unimproved. I would suggest we camp for the night in one of those isolated areas, across Hague Creek. Then tomorrow we can make our way back to the car along the unfrequented sides of Hague, Cache la Poudre, and Chapin, and then possibly no one will see us."

"It's a good plan," John agreed, "but there are no bridges across Hague Creek."

Listening to their discussion, Rachel felt strangely relieved. Now, if only Ostermann would let them leave in peace. He might, for all Ostermann knew, not all of the documents had been retrieved. Perhaps he did not know they had recovered any of the stash. According to their plan, he was not to move in and make the arrests until Rachel gave the signal.

As John placed the Mission Targeting Specification back into Goldsmith's knapsack, he noticed a dull aluminum cylinder, about three inches tall and a half-inch thick. After holding it curiously in his palm for a moment, he started to place the cylinder into a pocket.

"What's that?" Rachel asked, also curious.

"I don't know." John unscrewed the top of the cylinder. Turning it upside down, he shook a rolled piece of folded paper into his palm. Careful not to tear the yellowing piece of paper, he unrolled and then unfolded it.

"Names," John remarked. "This is significant, this must be the list that the Russians are after."

"Let me see," Rachel reached for the list, but John pulled away.

He refolded the paper and then rolled it, so that it fit back into its cylindrical container. "First we move camp, then we'll have time to examine this in detail."

"I'll keep it," Rachel volunteered. "I have a free pocket." She recognized that type of metal container from her days in Europe, it was of East German manufacturing origins.

"No," John thrust the cylinder into his left front pocket. "The Russians are deadly serious about this list. I should be the one to assume the risk if we're caught. No one but Bernie Goldsmith and myself knew this list was buried with the documents, and that might explain why a Russian has been trying to kill me. They must have figured the list would be lost forever if I was dead, which would suit their purposes almost as well as if they recovered it themselves."

Rachel shrugged, she knew there were no Russians involved. She would bide her time, John had said she could examine the list later.

John finished repacking Goldsmith's knapsack, which was much heavier than any of the backpacks they had brought in, and slung it over his shoulders. He also insisted on retaining the rifle. Rachel was forced to take John's backpack. She hated that. The hike had been so much easier since she had lost her own backpack.

They decided the only way across Hague Creek was by wading, but, upon closer inspection, the task appeared more difficult than anticipated. The waters were rushing deep and swift at that point. However, with dusk starting to settle into night there was no time to search for a more suitable crossing area.

"I vote we cross," Gwen asserted, as they argued the options. "What else can we do? If our clothes get wet, then so be it."

"We can't," John countered. "It's already getting cold and the temperature is dropping fast."

"I for one don't want to freeze tonight," Rachel offered. "But they'll find us if we don't cross."

"Now that we have the list and the documents, we are of no value to the Russians alive," Gwen continued. "If they catch us we'll be killed. We must cross."

"We cannot get wet," John exclaimed. "It might drop below freezing tonight."

"I have an idea," Rachel offered. "We'll take off our shoes and pants so our clothes don't get wet when we wade across, going separately of course. Once on the other side, we can dry off and redress in nice dry clothes. We needn't get our shoes or pants wet at all."

John looked at Gwen skeptically, but she shook her head in approval. Practically speaking, there was no other way, John could see that. Going first to test the waters, John took both backpacks, after placing his combat boots, socks, pants, and shorts inside one of the packs. Gwen and Rachel crouched behind nervously, watching the forest with their backs to John and the water.

The first step was a shock. Hague Creek was bitterly cold, a product of melted snow. Although his feet hurt from the cold, John continued onward. Soon they were so numb it didn't bother him. Stepping slowly and firmly, planting each foot solidly before moving the next, John inched across. He couldn't afford to fall, if he did so they would lose both remaining packs and all their gear.

At the deepest point, midway across the stream, the waters lapped at John's waist, but the task proved doable, as long as he was careful and did not rush. The current was fast, but the greatest danger lay in the shifting, slippery rocks all along the bottom. A firm footing negated any risk though. Reaching the other bank, John scrambled up an incline to a tall grassy area. Relieved to be across, he brushed off what water he could and then dressed, making extra sure to get his feet dry before putting on his socks.

Looking back for the women, he saw them still crouched with their backs to the river. "Okay," John yelled in a hushed voice. "Watch for shifting rocks, and make each step secure, then you'll be okay."

It was difficult for John to sit with his back to the river while the women crossed, not being able to see how they were doing, wondering if they needed his help. Gwen was supposed to come across first with the heavy knapsack of documents. If she lost it, their entire journey would be in vain.

After what seemed an eternity, John heard a rustling in the grass as Gwen approached from behind. "That was exhilarating," Gwen exclaimed, throwing the knapsack down. "Don't turn around yet," she added needlessly, for John had no intention of turning till they were all fully dressed again.

"I'm glad you made it," John exclaimed with relief.

"Of course I made it," Gwen responded good naturedly. "Compared to the Bayonet Assault Course in Jack's Valley, this was a piece of cake."

"How is Rachel doing?"

"She just started across," Gwen responded, while pulling on her hiking boots. "All she's got to carry is the rifle. Her pants and shoes are already here, stuffed into this knapsack with mine."

Moving with what seemed like reckless speed, Rachel was almost safely across when disaster struck. The sudden crack of a high powered rifle echoed across the valley, causing Rachel to pitch forward onto her face, shot from behind. Gwen stood up, screaming in horror, and then bolted toward the stream, rushing to Rachel's side.

"Wait, wait," John called after Gwen, and then he too began to run down the hill to help Rachel.

Rachel felt the impact of the bullet smashing into her left shoulder, the force knocking her face-first into knee-deep water. Instinctively she flung the Weatherby ahead onto dry land. As of yet feeling no pain, Rachel struggled to her feet. Soaked thoroughly with water and bleeding profusely, she lunged forward to escape the icy stream. Reaching the bank, Rachel frantically grabbed for Gwen's extended arms and was pulled up out of the water. They dove for immediate cover at just the right moment, as another crack split the air and a high velocity bullet thudded harmlessly into the soft mud beyond their heads.

John, startled by the second shot, dove for the Weatherby Mark V and rolled behind a small bush. He lay flat on his stomach, afraid to move, afraid even to load the rifle.

"I'm hit, I'm hit," Rachel cried out in a panic, as pain now laced along her shoulder and ran through her arm. She clung to Gwen wildly. Rachel had never been shot before, not in all the field assignments and undercover jobs of a long career. The pain seemed unendurable.

"John," Gwen yelled across the bushes. "We've got to make a run for it, get back to the tall grass."

"No!" Rachel screamed. She was hurt, but not incapacitated to the point she had lost her reason. "He won't miss again. We cannot make it that far."

Suddenly there was an exchange of sporadic gunfire across the river. Rachel, even in her pain-wracked state, grasped the significance. Someone was shooting at the sniper, hopefully her backup team. He would be distracted. "Now!" Rachel screamed frantically, struggling to regain her feet. "Run now!"

With Gwen supporting Rachel by her good arm, the two frightened women raced up the short hill toward the tall grass. John, seeing them go, grabbed the rifle and sprinted after them, running harder than he had ever run in his entire life. Upon Rachel's frantic insistence, they continued running past the grass, heading the short distance further for cover in the woods on the slope of Flatiron Mountain.

John paused long enough to recover the knapsacks and one backpack, then continued chasing after them. Reaching the trees, he dove into the dark, expecting at any moment to be shot from behind.

As John lay in the pine needles breathing so hard he thought he was going to die, he saw Rachel clinging to Gwen like an injured child, crying and moaning with pain like she was being tortured. Looking into Gwen's face, John was surprised to see tears streaming down her cheeks. This was real. Rachel had been shot. Someone was trying to kill them.

Rolling into a sitting position, John found a box of bullets and fumbled to load a few into the Weatherby's chamber. Once armed, he located a safe position, with cover, from which to watch the stream. If anyone tried to cross in pursuit, he was prepared to shoot at them.

Gwen, deathly concerned about the loss of blood from Rachel's shoulder, calmed her own fears enough to turn her attention to first aid. Rachel was shivering uncontrollably, her sweat shirt soaking wet, and she appeared to be going into shock. Gwen knew she had to stop the bleeding first.

Removing Rachel's soaking sweat shirt, Gwen saw where the bullet had entered Rachel's flesh, just beside the shoulder blade, high up on her back. There was no exit wound, so the lead was still lodged inside somewhere. A tourniquet was out of the question with a shoulder wound, and those were only to be used as a last resort anyway. Although preferable to bleeding to death, a tourniquet could result in the loss of a limb.

Opening Rachel's knapsack, Gwen searched for a cloth to press into the wound. She saw a funny, sharp bladed knife with a push handle, and two small throwing blades, but thought nothing of it at the time. Withdrawing Rachel's fatigue pants, Gwen cut off the legs and then cut strips of cloth, pressing the heavy green material over Rachel's bloody wound. Rachel cried out in pain and shrank away, but Gwen held the press firmly in place.

Once the blood flow subsided, Gwen replaced the bloody cloth with fresh strips, and then tied a wrap around Rachel's torso. Now that the immediate danger of bleeding to death had been stanched, it became urgent to find some way to make Rachel warm. They hadn't brought a first-aid kit or any medicine, so there wasn't much she could do for the pain.

Gwen felt so sorry for the afflicted woman. Taking off her own sweater, she dressed the wounded lady in the sweater and cut-off fatigue pants. In the process, Gwen discovered a startling surprise, she found an automatic pistol and two clips of ammunition. Placing these aside, Gwen put Rachel's socks and shoes on her. Having done all she could, Gwen took Rachel in her arms for added warmth.

Gwen was holding, almost rocking Rachel, when interrupted by John. "I don't think they are following us," he whispered. "We need to move on, further into the woods to hide. Can she move?"

"I can walk," Rachel answered, surprising them both. Rachel also realized they could not stay there, although she was loathe to leave the comfort of a sympathetic embrace.

Gwen helped Rachel up onto her wobbly feet, supporting most of her weight. Rachel found herself weaker than she had expected, feeling quite faint from the shock. John took the last backpack and placed it onto his shoulders. Grabbing the rifle in one hand and knapsack of documents in the other, he followed. It seemed strange to John, observing how Gwen was taking such pains to care for and comfort Rachel, knowing how much Gwen had disliked the woman.

The going was extremely rough, up the side of a mountain, through uncleared woods, in the dark. Forest rangers protected the park against forest fires and the ground had accumulated a massive tangle of fallen trunks and branches. There was no straight route up the hill either, and they often had to backtrack and circle around huge pile-ups of dead fallen trees. To make matters worse, the ground was soggy in places, as streamlets of melted snow flowed off the mountain toward Hague Creek below. John was so burdened down he thought he was going to faint from fatigue, but they couldn't stop now; fear drove them on into the night, deeper into the woods.

Finding a deer trail, they followed the level path running parallel to the side of Flatiron Mountain. Due to sheer exhaustion, they could not have climbed higher against the tangled logs anyway. Walking for what seemed an hour, having traveled as far as their strength could endure, they finally halted for the remainder of the night.

It was cold outside, the temperature near freezing, and they were all shivering from exposure. None of them had coats. Gwen had only a T-shirt and jeans. Rachel had a sweater but her hair was wet and her fatigue pants had been cut into shorts. They only had one pup tent, one bedroll, and one sleeping bag between the three of them. It would have to do.

John set up the tent as quickly as his numb fatigued hands could manage, and all three crawled in, lying on the bedroll, using the sleeping bag like a blanket. None of them bothered to undress, and they placed Rachel in the middle to benefit from the most body warmth. Huddled together against the cold, they were soon warm enough for sleep, which came quickly to their over-fatigued, over-stressed bodies.

36

Very early the next morning, John arose first, having been awake off and on through the night, uncomfortable from the cold and from aching muscles. Their tent had kept the morning frost off and helped contain body heat, but it was still cold. John's left side felt warm and soft, where he had lain next to Rachel, but his right side was cold and distant. The contrast was startling and disconcerting. Rising quietly so as not to disturb the women, John slid out from under the sleeping bag, crawled out of the tent, and stood on his feet. The calves of his legs felt like they wanted to contract into knots, but he endured.

The forest looked entirely different now, in the sunlight of early morning. Last night the darkness and gloom had seemed impenetrable, like they had taken refuge in the bowels of a great cavern; now the woods were open, a panorama of varying shades of green. They had inadvertently chosen a spot for their tent on the top of a slight crest. At night he had thought them well hidden, but now they seemed vulnerable. One could see through the vegetation for hundreds of yards.

Feeling nervous, John softly called to his friends, hoping they were awake.

"It is so cold," Gwen complained, as she rose to a sitting position.

"You gave me your sweater," Rachel muttered, sitting up also, causing John and Gwen to both stare at her with concern. Rachel smiled feebly and pulled the sleeping bag up about her chin for warmth.

Gwen smiled, "You were in bad shape last night, and your clothes were soaking wet. How is your shoulder?"

"It hurts," Rachel attempted to move her arm, but then winced in pain.

"You look a whole lot better," John commented, remembering the sweat soaked, clammy whiteness of her face last night, the vacantness in her eyes.

"It hurts a lot," Rachel repeated again. "I need a sling to hold my arm." She was suffering, but not to the point of incapacitation. Rachel knew she needed medical help though, her body's energy reserves were rapidly dwindling.

Gwen rose and began rummaging about their backpack for some material to make a sling. She found a few strips of cloth, left over from Rachel fatigue pants, but also ran across Rachel's handgun and knives again. Now was not the time to challenge Rachel about them, although their presence made Gwen all the more suspicious of her cousin's friend.

"I'll fold the tent down," John commented, "if you feel up to the hike in? Otherwise one of us could go for help."

Rachel looked at John with amazement, "You cannot leave me here." She tried rising to her feet, but the movement made her dizzy and she had to sit back down. Rachel was puzzled to notice the pant legs of her trousers had been unevenly cut away. She was having trouble remembering anything that had happened since falling into the water. Realizing the 9mm ASP and her own familiar knives were no longer in her pockets, Rachel felt a moment of panic, but then quieted herself. She was hurt, she was unarmed, but she was still alive.

While Gwen fashioned a sling for Rachel, John scouted about, checking for signs of pursuit. "I don't think we have been followed," he reported back to them. "Let's break camp and try to get back to the car."

"I think we should wait till nightfall," Rachel recommended, realizing her own limitations and a need for further rest.

"Wait till night?" John questioned.

"If we don't, they'll see us. Spotters are probably searching for us all over these woods. Remember how hard it was to see your own hand at night, even right in front of your face."

"But, you need medical help." Gwen protested.

"Not really. I'm not bleeding anymore, and there shouldn't be any danger from infection yet. What would a few hours hurt?"

"We'd better hide the tent a little better," John suggested, agreeing with the wisdom in Rachel's words. "I saw a depressed hollow over that ridge."

Once the camp was moved, Rachel, badly in need of more sleep after the exertions of being up even for a short while, was given the tent to rest in. Meanwhile, John began the task of sorting through the documents Goldsmith had stolen, the material Goldsmith had lost his life over, while Gwen watched with curiosity.

As John searched for the proof of Goldsmith's assertions, a grim look deepened across his features, darkening steadily as the picture unfolded before him. It did not take John long to establish the facts and remove any lingering doubts. With disgust he slammed the last document shut and lay back onto the ground.

"Well, well?" Gwen queried, wanting to hear him say it.

"It's all true."

"How do you know?"

"First off, there is the ICD for a piggyback payload, just like Bernie Goldsmith claimed. No one even knew there was a secret payload attached to the bottom of the bus, fitting there so innocently, hanging down in that empty cavity inside the adapter, just above the Centaur."

"What does that prove?"

"Well, when you look at the characteristics, it tells a lot. The cryogenic system for cooling, the hydrazine RCS jets for propulsion, the shape designed for reentry, the composite heat-reflective material."

"So, it is a carrier for biological weapons?"

"Yes, I'm afraid so! It even has its own autonomous cooling system to maintain frozen temperatures and preserve the DWARS virus. It has its own propulsion system to separate from the main satellite and deploy, and it is designed for reentry through the atmosphere, to attack some location on Earth I suppose." John was beginning to get excited, his voice starting to get a little loud.

Rachel lay on her back trying to shut him out, trying not to listen. She had known he would find it to be true. She had hoped the opposite would be the case, that John would find no solid grounds for his suspicions, but it did not surprise her. The fact that their beloved democratic government would develop and deploy such weapons, a literal doomsday device, was no shock to Rachel.

"Worst of all," John continued, "look at these specs, these requirements for maintaining a sterile contamination-free environment, and for creating precise sub-freezing temperatures inside the piggyback. The device has no other possible function that I can ascertain, no sensors for surveillance, no optics, no transmitters, nothing. There is no other possible purpose. It is purely a storage box with limited memory capability, enough to process deployment and reentry instructions. There is nothing else it could be!!"

"Shut up!!" Rachel screamed suddenly, quieting the man. "Do you want to wake the bears?" she scolded, and then covered herself with the sleeping bag. "So what," Rachel muttered to herself. She did not care. What was it to her?

"What now?" Gwen asked her cousin. Now that their fears had been substantiated.

"If they were capable of killing Goldsmith, they are capable of killing us too," John muttered.

"What?"

"To protect their secret. Don't you see?" John's face was flush and his eyes looked wild, scaring Gwen somewhat. Rachel had seen the look before. He was losing control.

"We have got to stop them," John rose to his feet. "To think, I helped build this monstrosity."

"Sit down," Rachel shouted and threw her covers aside, hurting her shoulder.

Gwen leapt to her feet also. "Calm down, John! Dad will help us."

John began stuffing the documents back into the knapsack, then suddenly halted, sweat glistening on his forehead. He moaned audibly and sank to his knees. "How could this be happening?" he groaned.

Gwen glanced toward Rachel, who shrugged in response. The cadet placed a hand on John's shoulder, "You knew it was true all along," she spoke sympathetically. "Don't try to carry this burden alone, we're here to help. Now, let's relax, at nightfall we'll find a way out of here."

"You're right," John regained a bit of composure. "I'm sorry, it's just that I feel so tired."

"We all do," Gwen responded, wondering if there was any way possible to escape this adventure turned nightmare.

37

Wednesday, April 25 at Cape Canaveral AFS, the Centaur upper-stage vehicle arrived at the landing strip by C-5 military airlift. Built by GDSS in San Diego, the Centaur was a key component in the Titan IV launch vehicle system. Its purpose was to take the SIGS satellite from low Earth orbit, where the Titan core dropped off, to a deep elliptical orbit far out in space.

Ramon Garcia walked beside his PE, Captain Hamilton, noticing the man seemed preoccupied with the memory of their recent viewing of the Centaur, now housed in the VIB. "What a bomb," Garcia remarked, wanting to irritate the captain.

"What are you saying?" Captain Hamilton stopped.

"A bomb," Sergeant Garcia repeated. "The Centaur is nothing more than a large flying bomb."

"The upper-stage," Captain Hamilton retorted, "is an intricate, highly technical, space vehicle, designed and manufactured to the most stringent of standards. The idea of man placing satellites deep into orbit about the Earth, thanks to upper-stages like the Centaur and rockets like the Titan IV, is an achievement our ancestors never even dreamed possible. The Centaur is a technological wonder.

"Okay, it's a wonder bomb."

Captain Hamilton scowled with disgust, the sergeant was hopeless. How could anyone work in the space program and not be inspired with a sense of man's grand destiny.

"Say," Sergeant Garcia casually remarked, "I'll meet you back at the office, I'm going to the NASA cafeteria for lunch."

"Is there time?" Captain Hamilton asked, glancing at his wristwatch. "They are going to commence installation of the payload fairing around the Centaur at thirteen-hundred hours."

"I'll be back," Sergeant Garcia started toward his car. "The operation will take hours anyway, I don't need to be there when it starts." Garcia didn't think he needed to be there at all, actually.

"I don't know," Captain Hamilton murmured.

"See you soon, I'm meeting an airman there for lunch, so I need to get going."

Captain Hamilton shrugged. "An airman," the sergeant had said, that meant Airman Rita Jorgensen, his latest fling. There was no keeping the sergeant away from his women. If he paid as much attention to rockets as to girls, he'd be a better assistant. Let him go, he wasn't really needed anyway.

Centaurs as a group were not new, General Dynamics had been producing the powerful liquid stage vehicles since the early sixties. They had flown on Atlases and Titans before, and the Centaur had an excellent record of demonstrated reliability. Out of seventy flights in the A through D series, (including D-1A and D-1T models), only eight failures had been attributed to the Centaur for an 88.57% success rate, which was acceptable for such complex space transporters.

One of the last major disasters attributed to a Centaur, (prior to Centaur G's) occurred on March 26, 1987. During the Atlas boost phase of flight, a lightning strike resulted in an erroneous DCU (Digital Command Unit) command that yawed the engines hard over, causing vehicle break-up. The RSO (Range Safety Officer) was forced to activate the command destruct, ending that mission in a fiery but safe explosion.

Although proven in the past, this modified Centaur G Prime version was a relatively unproven system. Much as the GDSS contractors liked to claim it was the same type bird, the space community perceived it as a new system. Larger, more powerful than any previous Centaur models, the Centaur G Prime was essentially an unproven upper-stage.

Mounted on the forward interface of the booster vehicle, the Centaur would support the weight of the satellite during launch and ascent. The mission of the Centaur was to provide the final velocity thrust necessary to achieve a park orbit, and then the necessary propulsion, guidance, and control required to place the satellite into the desired extended Earth orbit.

Arriving at the CCAFS landing strip by C-5 military airlift, a double-bagged Centaur G and its 2492 adapter had been unloaded on April 25, six days late. Lifted onto a specifically designed transporter by a sling assembly, the Centaur was set upon special aft and forward shipping adapters, and was driven to the VIB.

Inside the VIB, the protective outer bags had been removed from off the Centaur. It was then rotated to the vertical position, lifted off the trailer, and placed on the VIB floor. Unbolting the Centaur from the shipping adapter, it was next installed on the 2492 and 2490 adapters, resting on a support stand in Cell 3, a Class 100,000 clean room inside the VIB.

Once the forward shipping adapter was removed, the stretch adapter and sling were installed and stretch applied. At last the final protective bag could be removed in preparation for system buildup and testing. The Centaur had to pass receiving, inspection, and a series of power-on testing called CCET (Centaur Combined Electrical Test).

Then testing commenced on all systems, including pneumatics, propulsion (Liquid Hydrogen LH_2 and Liquid Oxygen LO_2 feed systems and the main engine), hydraulics, structures, the N_2H_4 RCS system, avionics, electrical (including ordnance), and instrumentation (including radio frequency RF). Many of these would be repeated during additional last-chance testing at the launch pad.

With only minor solvable anomalies, the Centaur had passed and the umbilicals had been disconnected, the stretch sling removed, and the Centaur rebagged. At that time a 22 hard-point truss had been installed, which would eventually support the all important SIGS satellite.

The next major task, scheduled to commence that afternoon, was the installation of the base payload fairing, to be erected around the Centaur. First the stretch sling would have to be reapplied and access platforms installed, for later systems buildup and testing. After the payload fairing bolt-on system installations were completed, and end-to-end hydraulic testing run, a flight events demonstration would be conducted, a combined electrical readiness test run for certification, and electromagnetic compatibility testing conducted.

If satisfied with the results, the Centaur would be bagged again and loaded onto a modified Viking transporter for delivery out to the launch pad.

38

Despondently Eleanor Hughes stared through the kitchen window into the shady backyard of her picturesque suburban prison. Tremendous oak trees rustled as lush green leaves on nut-burdened branches caught the breeze. Two squirrels raced across the grassy yard, pausing periodically to watch for neighborhood dogs, their only predator, but even the dogs, which chased more for fun than for food, were no real threat to the squirrels.

Eleanor sighed, longing to fling the kitchen door open and flee outside. If only she had the nerve. She had tried bluffing her way out once, upon her first arrival at the safe house, and as a punishment that Blinkerson woman had handcuffed Eleanor to the hall banister for an hour.

She would just have to be patient and bide her time. When the opportunity arose, she would be gone. Eleanor felt no moral or legal obligation to stay in captivity, and only the threat of force kept her in place. They had illegally arrested and detained her and they had no real authority to hold her a prisoner, none that would stand up in court anyway.

"Get away from that door," a stern voice warned, startling

Eleanor and causing her to jump. Blinkerson stood by the refrigerator, next to the stairs leading to a dark old basement. The policewoman seemed to know what Eleanor had been thinking.

Huffily, Eleanor stomped from the kitchen, the angry movements causing her cotton dress to swirl. Eleanor hated Blinkerson, she was a monster, a blimpish ogre.

Lumbering after her charge like a heavy bear, Blinkerson followed Eleanor through the house and into the living room. There Eleanor had run into a dead end and could go no further. Spinning around, she turned on Blinkerson with anger. "I want to speak with Dan Newby. Call him on the phone right now!"

"What for, sweetie?" Blinkerson asked, amused by the futile display of anger.

"I want to arrange a phone call with my husband."

"Why?"

"I think he will come back, if I ask him to."

Blinkerson laughed, "Mr. Newby doesn't want your husband to come back."

"What do you mean?"

"Put two and two together, sweetie. He has an intelligence officer with your husband. If Mr. Newby wanted to, he could arrest your man right now."

"I don't understand?"

"He's using your husband, stupid. Mr. Newby is after bigger fish, he wants your husband to play some role in one of his little schemes."

"You don't know what you are talking about." Eleanor stammered, feeling confused and angry.

"Sure," Blinkerson enjoyed Eleanor's discomfort. "Maybe your husband is the bait to lure dangerous felons into a trap. Although, more likely, Mr. Newby is just practicing, field exercises for his intelligence officers, you know, real life training."

Eleanor was appalled. What bothered her the most was the truth in Blinkerson's words. Detective Newby had told Eleanor he had an undercover officer with John, a female one. Why hadn't they arrested John? And why had they isolated her from contact with her husband? This whole affair was sick. "I must talk to John," she muttered to herself.

"You cannot," Blinkerson taunted. "Besides, I doubt he'd come back voluntarily anyway. He has one of Mr. Newby's female intelligence officers to escort him about. You know, practice her trade craft on him. I rather imagine your husband likes the attention, if you get my drift."

Angrily, Eleanor lunged at her tormentor, swinging the palm of her hand to slap that ugly mouth and shut the taunting voice. Blinkerson easily blocked Eleanor's attack though, her fat hand closing about Eleanor's slender wrist.

"You should not have done that," Blinkerson mocked. Twisting Eleanor's wrist, the police officer forced Eleanor to her knees in pain. Eleanor's strength was no match for the behemoth.

"That's enough," another voice called from the doorway. It was Officer Pastorelli, who had been watching the entire episode, silent until now.

Blinkerson released Eleanor's wrist and shoved the helpless woman with her knee, knocking Eleanor to the floor. "Did you see her try to hit me?" Blinkerson smiled.

Pastorelli nodded, there was a look of disapproval on her face.

"I'll let it go," Blinkerson said, turning her back to Eleanor. "But next time I'm going to break her arm, or at least a finger," Blinkerson snorted, chuckling at her own joke.

Eleanor stifled a cry. She had to escape somehow.

39

At midday Rachel Maris awoke from a deep sleep. The sun had heated her tent to the point where it had become intolerable. Insects were flying about, annoyingly lighting upon her bandages. Rachel was surprised that she had slept so deeply for such a long period of time. Perhaps her body was trying to recover from the trauma of taking a high-velocity bullet in the shoulder.

Was it luck they had not been discovered? No, luck could not explain that much good fortune. Chances were, Ostermann's men had found their camp and placed them under surveillance. Why hadn't they moved in though? Was Ostermann unaware that John had already recovered all the stolen documents? Was he still waiting for her signal to move in?

Rachel's shoulder and arm were hurting again, now a deep dull pain that caused her great distress. She tried not to dwell on the hurt. If she wasn't careful, the agony would build to overwhelming proportions. As long as she relaxed though, and kept her arm still, it was bearable. If only the insects would leave her alone.

The firefight last night was a puzzlement. Someone had engaged the sniper and given Rachel and her friends the relief they needed to escape into the woods? It had to be Ostermann's men, but why? Was Ostermann faithfully trying to do his job and protect them from a hostile agent? It was uncanny though, three times now an assassin had found them, no thanks to their backup team. How could one explain the way Ostermann and his people were never quite alert enough to prevent the attempt, always showing up a minute too late? But if the assailants were working with Ostermann, which seemed almost a surety, why did Ostermann's men abort the sniper? Maybe some members of the backup team weren't a part of the treachery.

Rachel couldn't take the pain any longer. The daylight was only half gone, she couldn't just lie there and suffer till nightfall. Her backup team would have a first-aid kit. Rachel had to find a pain killer, she needed medical help, she needed something to calm her mind.

Poking her head out of the tent, Rachel saw John and Gwen sitting in the shade along a large fallen tree trunk. If she strained, she could just hear their words. They appeared to be arguing.

"It's nothing," John was saying.

"Nothing," Gwen retorted. "You call an automatic pistol nothing.

Rachel was shocked, John and the cadet had discovered her 9mm ASP.

"Look at the circumstances," John rationalized. "People are trying to kill us. I'll admit it's unusual, but I can understand carrying a gun. Look at the conditions in which I found her."

"John, a pistol is not normal, and she also had knives."

"Well, maybe she found them on that hunter, when we took the rifle. Remember, he had an empty holster."

"Then why didn't she say something? That whole story seems awfully strange to me."

"You cannot tell for sure. Why don't we just ask Rachel when she wakes up?"

Rachel was touched by John's defense of her, he really wanted to believe in her.

"I've hidden the gun and knives in the pack," Gwen said. "Don't tell her I have them."

"Okay," John agreed, although he knew his cousin was overreacting.

"When we get ready to leave," Gwen changed the subject, "we

can only take necessary items, to facilitate a speedier travel through this dense tangle of dead trees. If we don't, it will be impossible to get out in one night."

"Fine," John agreed. "But we need the rifle, and the knapsack with Goldsmith's documents. The tent, sleeping bag, and all our camping gear, are not critical."

Rachel stood up then, allowing them to see she was awake. She felt unsteady on her feet though.

John noticed her first. He smiled congenially, "You are looking better."

Rachel frowned, "What time is it? I feel as if I fell off a circus trapeze."

"It's almost noon," Gwen responded.

"Oh, I couldn't have slept that long."

"You've been dead to the world," Gwen said, not looking Rachel in the eyes.

"Are you hungry?" John asked. "Eat all you want, we are going to leave all our supplies behind at nightfall."

"Sure," Rachel said, but then turned her nose aside at the beef jerky. "On second thought, I need to walk around a bit."

"Are you sure?" John asked incredulously. "I don't think it wise. Are you up to it Rachel?"

"I just want to scout around, stretch my muscles a bit," Rachel stuttered, trying to make it sound plausible.

"You had better not, remember your shoulder," Gwen recommended.

"I am okay, really." How could she forget her shoulder, Rachel wanted to scream. She had to get something for the pain.

"Look, I'm hurt in the shoulder, not in the head!" Rachel snapped, cutting off further objections. She could tell they thought her crazy, but she needed to get away, regardless of how bad it looked.

Trying to act confident, Rachel swung around abruptly to leave, but the sudden motion made her dizzy. Steadying herself, she walked away from her bewildered friends. As Rachel disappeared up a small crest, she could feel their concerned stares upon her back. Once out of sight, she circled around behind them. It was important to make sure they weren't going to try and follow.

Rachel listened for a few moments, until satisfied they were paying her no attention. They had settled into another argumentative conversation, this one about her erratic behavior. She began working her way up the hillside, searching for a member of her backup team.

"Hey," Rachel call out softly. "Anyone about?"

"Over here," came a hushed response.

Relieved, Rachel worked her way toward the voice. It was a familiar one, a young field operative out of Newby's office, a fairly new recruit of about two years. As Rachel neared a large fallen fir, the boyish face of Eddie Sanders materialized from cover. "Eddie, is that you?" Rachel called.

"Yes, over here."

Rachel drew up next to him, eyeing the young man cautiously. She did not know if he could be trusted. "Have you been watching the camp long?"

"Just an hour, I begin my shift…oh, you don't mean me personally. We picked up your trail at daybreak and found your camp a few minutes later. You look terrible."

Eddie Sanders felt nervous talking to the infamous Rachel Maris, in person. Although he had never worked an assignment with Rachel Maris personally, her reputation had preceded her. Sanders held her somewhat in awe, not just because of her success on the job as one of Newby's experienced top intelligence officers, but also because of her devastating beauty. Even though a bloody mess at the moment, he thought she was one of the most gorgeous women he had ever seen.

"I'll survive," Rachel said. "But I need something for the pain." Rachel stared into his eyes, searching for a clue as to his real intentions. She realized right away that her peer had a crush on her.

"Come on then, I'll get you back to our base." Eddie Sanders thought about taking Rachel by the arm, to help steady her along the trail, but her attractiveness frightened him.

Rachel followed the new recruit back to Ostermann's temporary base of operations, a scant five minutes down the trail. There she saw three more intelligence officers, besides the kid, and one of them was Ostermann. Rachel decided to play dumb and assume they were allies. For now she could not allow Ostermann to know she was on to his treachery.

As they saw Rachel entering their camp, all the men sprang to their feet. Ostermann approached first, eyeing Rachel suspiciously. He was limping slightly. Rachel wondered if his limp was a result of her kneeing him in the groin yesterday. She hoped so, he deserved it.

"Why did you break contact with the target?" Ostermann asked, challenging her with an accusatory tone of voice.

Rachel ignored him, addressing Eddie Sanders instead. "Have you got any first-aid?" she asked, drawing everyone's attention to her injury. Soon they were crowding around her, concerned about her condition. Only Ostermann hung back. Rachel was frightened by the sudden attention, but it soon became apparent that the others were genuinely worried about her.

"Don't touch," Rachel exclaimed, as Murrey begin to undo her wrappings. Jeff Murrey had the most medical training of the group and had naturally fallen into the role of team medic. "You must not disturb my bandages or you will blow my cover," Rachel cautioned.

"This does not look good," Murrey argued. "The first aid is sloppy, and it looks like an infection has already set in."

"Just give me something for the pain, and I'll survive," Rachel said.

"I could apply penicillin, under the bandages, to combat the infection."

"Fine, what about the pain?"

"We have aspirin, or maybe extra strength Tylenol."

"Come on, I need something stronger."

"Well…ah…morphine, but that's for extreme injuries."

"And you don't call a gunshot wound extreme. Give me the morphine."

"Rachel, you don't want morphine," exclaimed Eddie Sanders with concern. "This medication will cause you more difficulties than you can handle. How can you continue the operation under morphine?"

"Give it to me," Rachel demanded, the anger in her voice forestalling further argument. Murrey carefully unwrapped Rachel's emergency bandages and applied a salve to her wound. Then he gave Rachel a shot of morphine. Rachel felt much relieved, even before she could feel the effects; she could cope once more.

The bullet is still in your shoulder," Murrey announced. "You need a doctor, it cannot be left inside to fester. You know you are bleeding again."

"Just put the wrapping back on," Rachel frowned. "We are going to break camp at sunset, and I must get back. If we can get out of the woods this evening, I promise, I'll get medical help. Believe me, I'll not let this shoulder go unattended."

Rachel stopped herself, realizing she was saying too much. It didn't matter though, it was foolish to think they could sneak away from or lose Ostermann and this team of professionals. What could she do? Ostermann would have them killed before they escaped these woods.

Rachel had been assuming Ostermann was still unaware that John had recovered all the documents, otherwise why didn't he move in and make the arrest? But now she began to wonder. They did not seem very interested in recovering the documents, no one had even asked her about them. Something was not right.

Rachel saw Ostermann watching her with an obscene smirk of pleasure on his face. He was leaning against a massive tree like they were hanging out on some street corner. He was so cocky, so prideful. Rachel could feel her anger and frustration mounting. Approaching Ostermann for a confrontation, Rachel was already starting to feel a buzz from the morphine; she drew up until her face was inches away from his, still he didn't budge.

"Did you get the sniper?" Rachel demanded.

Ostermann shrugged his shoulders, still leaning casually against the tree. "Nah, he escaped into the woods before we could reach him."

"You fool, you let him get away again. You incompetent jerk."

Ostermann straightened up, feigning indignation, although he could scarcely contain a smile. "Hey, we saved your tail. You were a dead broad."

Rachel almost exploded, "Saved me!" How audacious, he was the one responsible for her troubles. Restraining her emotions, Rachel struggled to calm her voice, "I need another weapon."

"Take mine," Ostermann answered, pulling his jacket open to expose a large automatic handgun, daring her to reach for it. He was so vain.

Hanging from a shoulder strap around Ostermann's chest was an automatic Desert Eagle .50AE. Manufactured by Israeli Magnum Research, the .50 caliber Desert Eagle was possibly the most powerful handgun on the market, typical of his ego. Suspended in buckskin sheaths off Ostermann's belt were two large hunting knives, one was a Bowie and the other an Arkansas Toothpick. Instinctively, Rachel reached for the knives first, but hesitated before drawing the closest off his belt. He stood there facing her, with that ugly smirk on his face, just goading her to try and get it. Rachel could feel the stares of their compatriots, watching them.

She could not resist the challenge, slowly she drew the large Arkansas Toothpick, a long, wicked looking, two-edged blade. Once the knife handle was firmly in her grasp, Rachel lunged at Ostermann, her arm a blur of precise motion. He did not have a chance, slouched off balance, posturing to intimidate her, too sure of himself, so confident in his masculine superiority, knowing he could bluff the female down.

Thrusting the hilt of the Arkansas Toothpick hard against Ostermann's diaphragm, just below the center of his rib cage, Rachel forced him back into the tree, pinning him there. Then, before Ostermann could react further, Rachel rotated her hand until the point was against his chest.

Before he knew what had hit him, Ostermann found himself pinned against the tree with a razor sharp blade beneath his ribs. He could hardly let his breath out or his chest would drop and he would be cut. "You're a crazy woman," he hissed indignantly, to hide his sudden fear.

"Shut up!" Rachel screamed. "Now listen up everyone," Rachel flung her head back to get the hair out of her face. "Starting right now, I am relieving Randy Ostermann from duty as case officer."

"Now wait a minute," Ostermann interrupted. "You have no authority to do..."

Rachel jabbed the Arkansas Toothpick inward cutting him off. The move was effective, but a little overzealous, for she soon felt a trickle of warmth, his blood oozing onto her hand. Still she held the knife in place. "Who is the second in charge? I have firm reasons to believe Ostermann is working with the enemy."

"You are insane," Ostermann sputtered, in spite of the sharp pain at his stomach.

Rachel was desperate though, "I know he is working with the sniper," she screamed. "I want him relieved until the situation can be reported back to Dan Newby."

Ostermann paled at the thought. What was this wild woman trying to do to him?

"Watch him or he'll never let me out alive," Rachel caught Eddie Sanders' eyes, causing him to take a step forward. "Sanders, you are in charge now. Promise me you'll see this is reported to

Newby," she plead, but Sanders hesitated, unsure of himself. "Promise me, or I'll gut him right now and end this threat to my life."

"Okay, you have my word," Sanders conceded. He considered jumping Rachel but decided against it, she was just distraught enough to actually kill Ostermann.

Now Rachel turned to face Ostermann again. That cocky smirk was gone from his face. He knew his life was in her hands, a wounded she-tiger had him at her mercy.

Glaring at Ostermann, but still speaking to the others, Rachel continued, "Tell Newby about the assassination attempts, how he always seems to find us, how he always seems to slip in unhampered. Three times now, once in Colorado Springs, once along the trail, and now again at the stream crossing. Tell Newby how he always gets away."

While talking, Rachel relieved Ostermann of his Desert Eagle. It felt obscenely large in her hand. She had to use her injured arm to take it, the pain was not too bad though, the morphine was starting to do its job.

Rachel had to trust someone, or she had no chance of escape. At least she hadn't been shot in the back so far. For some reason, she had picked the kid to trust, Eddie Sanders, the new recruit. Maybe it was his boyishly innocent face. Suddenly Rachel released Ostermann and stepped back, at the same time raising his Desert Eagle, finger resting on the trigger.

She stumbled backwards, unsteady, and almost fell into Sanders, but his hands steadied her. "Hey, we are on the same team," he said.

"No one follows," Rachel cried, as she backed out of his grasp.

"You fool," Ostermann shouted at Rachel, causing her to swing the automatic pistol in his direction.

"Shut up, or I'll kill you!" Rachel threatened.

"You idiot," Ostermann continued anyway. "It's not enemy agents trying to kill you." Sanders, Murrey, and Jones were stunned by the hatred in Ostermann's voice and the utter loathing upon his face. He had lost all control. "It was one of the Baron's men," Ostermann taunted. "Your own mentor is trying to kill you!"

Rachel was shocked. In a bewildered quandary, she continued backing away. No, that could not be true. Ostermann was laughing hysterically, no longer concerned about his safety, or the blood oozing from his stomach.

"I want all contact broken off, till you get further orders from Newby," Rachel cried. "If I see anyone following, I'll consider it a hostile act and shoot to kill."

Rachel realized she must sound like a maniac. Turning fearfully, she ran with all her might, soon disappearing over a ridge.

Sprinting along the trail until her breathing became labored, Rachel slowed to a walk. Her vision started to spin and she felt light-headed, fuzzy. It had to be the morphine, everything felt surreal. At that moment, if Ostermann had come after her, he could have had her. She would not have resisted, she wasn't capable, she felt tired, so tired.

She had to get back to John. The thought spurred her onward. John would help, he was her friend, maybe her only friend. Could it be true about the Baron? No, it was a lie, he would never hurt her. She had to get back to John. It was so hard to think. Rachel stumbled and dropped to her knees, then picked herself up.

It was already getting dark. She hoped they hadn't left without her. If they did, John would go to the Baron, and he might kill John. No, the Baron was their friend, Gwen's father. Ostermann was lying.

Rachel felt delirious. The realization that she had left John unprotected from the sniper frightened her. Ostermann said the assassin had escaped, that meant he was still after them. Now Rachel had demanded that the backup team withdraw. John had no protection at all, she had to get back.

Awkwardly Rachel stumbled again, falling softly into the spongy leaf covered dirt. She lay still, unmoving for a few minutes. She was so tired, but she had to go on, she had to. If only she could get up.

40

John Hughes frowned, deep in thought. Looking up at his cousin, he shook his head despairingly. "I feel so sorry for Rachel Maris, but you know, it doesn't surprise me that one of us got hurt. Poor Rachel."

"At least we're all still alive. I had my doubts last night crossing Hague Creek," Gwen Hughes' eyes sparkled with amazement. She was thriving on the excitement.

"I'll never forget the way Bernie Goldsmith was murdered," John spoke in a depressed voice. "He was about ready for retirement too. He had a wife and grandchildren. They had recently bought a fancy Airstream trailer to tour the country in. I'll never forget Goldsmith."

"Was he a close friend of yours?"

"No, not really. He was just someone I worked with. We never did anything together socially, but he was a good decent man."

"Did you hear something?" John questioned suddenly, glancing furtively toward the bushes behind their camp.

"No, why?" Gwen responded, her cousin's jittering making her feel nervous now also.

"Must be the squirrels," John tried to relax.

Gwen glanced at her watch, anxious to be moving on. The flies seemed to be congregating in larger numbers with time. "If we stop this death satellite," Gwen offered consolation, "then perhaps Goldsmith's death will be vindicated."

"A big if."

Gwen continued, "The cost of failure would be a catastrophe for the entire human race. Think of it, sterile children, how reprehensible to build such a weapon. The thought is horrendously revolting."

"Yes," John agreed, "and you cannot argue that the virus would never be used. The same people who could rationalize developing and deploying such a device, would also be capable of justifying a reason to use it."

"I cannot imagine what type of person would build such a weapon," Gwen shivered.

"Mostly innocent engineers and technicians like myself," John replied dejectedly. "Sheep just following orders, just trying to earn a living, never bothering to ask why, never questioning."

"Yes, but what excuse do the bosses have, those that gave the orders, those that knew?"

"They have no moral excuse, none at all! Although really, neither can any of us justify our actions. We all have a moral duty to know what we are doing. It is too easy to let them keep you in the dark, to pretend you are not responsible because you did not know."

"It makes me sick thinking about what those in power do to the people under their authority."

John realized this was a fairly deep philosophical issue to be debating with someone so young in life, a college student, a girl just barely out of the home, hardly out from underneath her mother's skirt so to speak. Yet college students were usually at the forefront of political reform.

"Are you holding up okay?" John questioned, wondering about the pressure Gwen was being subjected too, both physical and mental.

"Sure, I'm not even tired," Gwen responded. In fact, she looked almost fresh. "I'll get some more sleep later, before we break camp. Is there anything worth reading in the knapsack?"

"Just technical papers. What are you majoring in at the Academy? Do they offer any engineering degrees?"

"Sure, four or five different ones. In fact, Boomerang is majoring in astronautical engineering, that's your field, isn't it? The academy is perhaps the only college in America offering separate bachelor of science degrees in astronautical and aeronautical engineering. Myself, I am majoring in poly sci, that's political science. I find international affairs extremely interesting."

"These technical papers would be boring to you," John nodded toward the knapsack. "To tell the truth, I find them boring myself, and there is still the matter of security classifications to consider. If you expose yourself to these documents, there would be extensive debriefings to endure once this is all over, including polygraph testing."

"Oh, I've never had a lie detector test. It sounds like fun."

"Believe me, it's not."

"What about the cylinder containing that list the Russians are after?"

"I had forgotten about that," John drew the small cylindrical metal container from his pocket. He opened the lid and removed a yellowing rolled-up piece of paper. Unrolling and then unfolding the list, John began to peruse the typed words. "I wonder why the Russians were so interested in this list?"

Curiosity drew Gwen to John's side. There were two columns of words upon the paper, both in English. The first column contained a large number of names arranged in alphabetical order. Alongside those names was a second column of cryptonymns or code words. "This is from an East German spy?" Gwen mused.

"Supposedly, he offered this list to Goldsmith as proof of his intentions to defect."

"Then maybe it truly is a list of East German spies, and this second column could be their code names."

"Yes, that's possible, or it could be a list of Americans who are spies for the East Germans."

Suddenly Gwen's eyes widened in astonishment. "Look John, there is Rachel's name!"

John could not believe it, but sure enough, there it was in black and white "Rachel Maris" and next to her name was the cryptonymn "Gyrfalcon."

"This is insane," John exclaimed. "Why would Rachel's name be on this list?"

John continued to stare at the list in disbelief. He was heartbroken that she had deceived him. "It was a setup all along. I thought she needed help, but it was all a lie."

"Do you think Rachel knows she is on this list?" Gwen pondered.

"No," John concluded. "This came straight from the East German to Bernie Goldsmith, who buried it, and now we have it."

"Do you see the implications?" Gwen prodded her cousin. "Being on that list means Rachel is..."

"Working for the Russians," John finished.

"Yes, or for the CIA. A double agent."

"This is unbelievable. Did the government send her to help me, or did the Russians?"

"To help you!? Neither, John, she is definitely not helping us. Either she is working for the government to trap you, or—worse yet—for the Russians."

"This is too much. I cannot accept this."

"Quick," Gwen became suddenly nervous. "Put that list away before she comes back. Better yet, let's pack up camp and get away from here."

"You want to leave Rachel behind?"

"Do we have a choice? She is the enemy, John. She might even be a traitor, or a spy."

Disbelieving, John glanced at Rachel's name one last time, and then hastily put the list back into its container. "Gyrfalcon, gyrfalcon," John repeated Rachel's code name. "What is a gyrfalcon?"

Gwen answered as she threw the knapsack over her shoulder and stood to leave. "It's a type of falcon of course. The Academy's mascots are falcons you know. Most falcons are brown or tan colored, but a gyrfalcon is a large, beautiful, white-feathered bird. Their natural habitats are arctic areas, although occasionally in the winter they range as far south as the northern states, or to England. In medieval days they were used for sport. The peregrine and kestrel falcons were used by earls and priests, but the gyrfalcons were reserved for royalty."

Gwen helped John to his feet. She was anxious to be off before it was too late. "One thing about the gyrfalcons, they are fierce hunters. Most falcons prey on field rodents and small ground animals, but gyrfalcons prey on other birds, weaker members of their own kind."

41

Eleanor Hughes was not the type of woman accustomed to abuse. Never in her life had she truly been mistreated before, never physically beaten. Now, under threat of that abominable woman, Officer Blinkerson, Eleanor found herself not only mad, but consumed with a desire to exact revenge. All of Eleanor's frustrations and anger had become focused on Blinkerson. Although that ugly policewoman was not the root cause of Eleanor's difficulties, she was a violent immediate contributor.

Eleanor had eliminated options of physical revenge, even though the thought was appealing. To shove Blinkerson down the stairs, hit her with a pan, anything that hurt, the idea was tempting but not practical. To cause Blinkerson the most injury, Eleanor wanted to beat the policewoman at her own game, and that involved escaping. To do so would be a personal victory over Blinkerson, and that would be the best revenge. Escape was no longer an end unto itself, it had become personal, between her and Blinkerson. To keep it personal, she would need to make her escape when Pastorelli was out of the house, as was often the case when someone went out for food. Then it would be just Eleanor and Blinkerson.

Early that evening, Eleanor watched with intrepid anticipation as her wardens decided on Chinese take-out food for dinner. They had not bothered to ask Eleanor's opinion, she did not matter. She felt so innocent, sitting quietly in her little cotton-print dress, listening, waiting for her chance. Eleanor wanted to escape from Blinkerson, not Pastorelli. Unfortunately, it was decided that Blinkerson should do the shopping, Pastorelli had gone the past two times.

"No wait," Eleanor interrupted, as Blinkerson stood to leave. "Let Officer Pastorelli go?" Eleanor spoke firmly. There was a challenge in her voice.

The two policewomen exchanged puzzled looks. "What for?" Blinkerson asked, suspecting ulterior motives. Ever since the prisoner had arrived, her partner was the one who had been so worried about their prisoner's feelings, acting so nice. Blinkerson had never pretended even the least friendliness, so why would their prisoner ask for her company?

Eleanor turned red in the face. What could she say? How could she explain her request?

"What have you got in mind?" Blinkerson demanded, her voice almost a growl, obviously irritated. She was such a repulsive person, not her body but her personality, Eleanor shuddered.

"I want you to stay," Eleanor made a face.

"What did you do that for?" Blinkerson moved forward threateningly.

"I just wanted it to be me and you," Eleanor said, in a voice that spoke of challenge.

Blinkerson chuckled in a snorting manner and sat back down.

"I suppose that means I'm elected to go again?" Pastorelli questioned irritably.

"Sure are," Blinkerson answered rudely. "Our little prisoner doesn't want YOU keeping a watch on her. She has something in mind and I do not want to miss it," Blinkerson glared at Eleanor. "In fact, I think this may turn into a very interesting evening."

Shrugging her shoulders, Pastorelli gave in. "All right, all right, if that is what the both of you want."

Once Pastorelli was gone, Eleanor sat for a few moments, thinking, gathering her courage before putting her escape plan into effect. Noticing her hands were trembling, she took several deep breaths, trying to calm her nerves. This had to work, if it didn't, she was sure to suffer the wrath of Blinkerson.

Closing her eyes, Eleanor said a silent prayer. When she opened them, she found Blinkerson staring her in the face from across the room. The cruel policewoman was primed, she knew something was up, she realized Eleanor was planning some type of confrontation. Blinkerson was actually looking forward to the challenge. It almost made Eleanor lose her nerve, but no, it was now or never, she had to try.

Springing suddenly to her feet, Eleanor darted from the TV room, running as fast as she could go. She was hoping to take advantage of Blinkerson's obesity, which would make the policewoman slow on her feet. Officer Blinkerson called out in anger for Eleanor to halt, but Eleanor paid her no heed. She raced across the dining room and into the kitchen before Blinkerson could even get herself off the couch.

Bounding through the kitchen, Eleanor slammed into the back wall of a narrow hallway, just to the side of the refrigerator. To her right was a small bathroom, to the left a door to the basement. Springing into the bathroom, Eleanor turned on the light switch and flung open the small window. Quickly she stepped back into the hallway, pulling the locked door shut behind her. With her diversion set, Eleanor hurried through the basement door and onto the top cellar step. There she halted, closing the door behind her.

With heart pounding, Eleanor tried to control her breathing, listening to see if she had been fast enough. Within seconds Blinkerson came thundering into the kitchen and then halted, she didn't know which way her charge had fled.

Seeing a light shining under the bathroom door, Blinkerson yelled angrily, and took hold of the locked door handle, mistakenly assuming Eleanor had locked herself in. Blinkerson tried to force it open, but the little door held amazingly firm.

"You come out of there!" Blinkerson demanded, panting hoarsely from her physical exertions.

Slowly Eleanor tiptoed down the stairs into the dark basement, carefully feeling each step, anxious not to make the ancient wood creak underneath her weight. Eleanor's plan was simple, to sneak downstairs and climb out a basement window while Blinkerson was preoccupied with the bathroom.

"Is there a window open in there?" Eleanor heard Blinkerson yelling into the bathroom, as she slammed her large body against the door, creating an awful racket. "You stay out of the window," Blinkerson ordered. Actually that window in the bathroom was too small for a person to climb out, but Blinkerson apparently did not know that, for she suddenly hurried out of the hall, hastening around to the outside.

"Don't rush, don't rush," Eleanor cautioned herself, as she felt another step and applied weight, careful to place her foot toward the back of the step. She had to hurry though, as soon as Blinkerson got outside and around to the bathroom window, she would realize no one could fit out that small an opening. Then Blinkerson would know Eleanor had tricked her.

Suddenly Eleanor felt something brush against her face. She let out an involuntary cry and sat back upon the steps. Eleanor froze in horror, but it was only the string to a ceiling light bulb. Fortunately Blinkerson had not heard the noise, Eleanor could still hear the policewoman fumbling with keys to the kitchen door leading outside.

Fighting waves of anxiety, Eleanor continued on and soon felt smooth cement underfoot. Good, that meant she was down the stairs. The basement was quite large, the main feature a monstrous antique gas furnace, squatting in a tangle of venting and pipes. Stacked along the walls of the basement was an odd assortment of old furniture, lumber, and boxes. There was a workbench on the far wall and an old shower, of all things, in one corner. In another corner of the basement, two interior walls had been framed to make a small extra bedroom.

That bedroom was the object of Eleanor's movement. On an earlier tour she had noticed a small window in the room, high near the ceiling. Moving in the dark was hard but necessary. Had she turned on the light bulb, Blinkerson would surely have noticed the light coming from under the door at the top of the stairs.

Groping out into the dark void away from the stairs, Eleanor felt for the doorway to the bedroom. Where was it? The basement air felt cold and musty. Eleanor did not like it there, she was scared. Reaching the walls, she moved to the right until her hand slid into the doorway molding.

Stepping into the doorway now, she was relieved to see the window, opaque with dirt, framed in light up near the ceiling. Strewn about among the shadows in the bedroom were old rusty weights, apparently a previous owner had used this small cool room as a tiny home gym. There was a bench for pressing weights, barbells, dumbbells, and stacks of loose irons scattered on the floor.

Eleanor dragged the weight bench under the window. She had to stand upon it in order to reach the window's latch. Hearing Blinkerson reentering the house, Eleanor strained frantically, pressing her fingers against a rotating slide latch. The old rusty metal cut into her skin, but she persisted with quiet desperation.

All of a sudden the latch unfroze and gave way to her pressure. Immediately Eleanor shoved the window open, the rush of fresh air and the brilliance of sunshine was refreshing, giving her hope.

"Are you in the basement?" Blinkerson's voice called loudly from the top of the stairs, as she pulled the string to the ceiling bulb, flooding the downstairs with light.

Eleanor cried out in alarm and crouched down. She wanted to hide, but there was no place to go, she would surely be found. Eleanor could hear Blinkerson descending the wooden stairs, stepping heavily with great weight, coming down hard on each foot.

Frantically Eleanor leaped at the window, trying to get her upper body onto the bottom frame so she could hoist herself out. Her head banged into the top of the window frame though, causing her to fall back and stumble completely off the small bench. Eleanor had scraped her arms, they were bleeding from several cuts, but she could not pause. Desperately she leaped again, this time successfully getting her arms, head, shoulders, and chest out the window.

Wiggling through the opening, Eleanor worked her hips out and almost had one knee through, when a heavy hand suddenly grabbed her by the ankle. Pulling forcefully, Blinkerson unceremoniously dragged Eleanor back through the window and into the room, allowing her to fall onto the floor with a painful thud.

"Stand up," Blinkerson shouted, frightening Eleanor further. Hurting from her fall, Eleanor rose with her back to the wall, fearful of what her large jailer might do, but never expecting what came next. Blinkerson angrily struck at Eleanor with a closed fist.

Crying out in pain, Eleanor shrank toward the corner, but then Blinkerson hit her again, and then again, punching at her furiously. The third swing caught Eleanor on the chin, shoving her head back against the cement wall. Terrified, Eleanor dropped to her knees in a frightened effort to escape the fists.

Blinkerson was out of control. Having her victim helpless did nothing to abate her fury. Angrily she slapped at the top of Eleanor's head. The force of the blow drove Eleanor to her hands and knees, but there, right under Eleanor's face, she found a weapon. It was a five pound iron dumbbell.

Grabbing the weight with both hands, Eleanor lifted it above her assailant's toes, slamming the metal downward with all the force she could muster. Howling in pain, Blinkerson stumbled backwards and fell clumsily upon her back.

Instantly Eleanor was fleeing for her life. Stumbling to her feet, she lunged for the bedroom doorway. As she exited the room, Eleanor saw Blinkerson drawing her Beretta 9mm pistol from its holster. Screaming in horror, Eleanor dodged sideways, frantic to escape from Blinkerson's line of fire.

That was a mistake though, for now she had no place to flee. If she ran for the stairs, Blinkerson could shoot her in the back, and Eleanor had no doubt that the fiendish woman would do so. Circling around the monstrous furnace, Eleanor ran into a cluttered, dirt covered, workbench. Crying with fear, Eleanor turned to see Blinkerson limping across the concrete toward her.

Eleanor nearly fainted with fright at the sight of her approaching assailant. Blinkerson's face was red and puffy, contorted with rage, and her pudgy hand was holding a large Beretta. She was limping on one foot, for the other was bloody with broken toes.

"Throw it down," Blinkerson roared, as she moved ever closer, waving the revolver in front of her.

Eleanor hadn't realized she still had the dumbbell clutched in her hands. Shrieking with fright, she threw the weight to the side and fell to her knees, sobbing uncontrollably.

Blinkerson approached, beside herself with pain-maddened anger. Grabbing Eleanor by the hair and jerking her head, she lifted the terrified woman to her feet with no more effort than a child lifting a doll. Then, shaking Eleanor cruelly, Blinkerson began dragging her shrieking victim across the cellar floor toward the old rusty shower.

"You want a shower?" Blinkerson shouted, thrusting Eleanor under the showerhead. "Well, maybe this will cool you down." She cranked an old handle, causing the pipes to bark and spurt as air and then cold water flowed through the rusty tubing. As a spray of icy water emerged, Blinkerson rotated Eleanor's face toward it, causing her to gasp and sputter for breath. Blinkerson released Eleanor's hair and grabbed at the back of Eleanor's dress where it buttoned.

Jerking roughly, she ripped the dress apart, causing buttons to fly.

Panicking beyond reason, Eleanor lunged away from Blinkerson, slamming into the concrete, pipe-lined, walls of the cellar. Now Blinkerson's massive weight worked against her. Caught off balance by the unexpected move, Blinkerson slipped on the wet cement and lost her footing. They fell together, Blinkerson dragging Eleanor down on top of her.

Desperately Eleanor pulled free and rolled to the side. Regaining her feet first, she now had the advantage again, Blinkerson was still flat on her back. Racing away from the scene, Eleanor sprinted up the basement stairs. Leaping to the outside kitchen door, Eleanor was disappointed to find Blinkerson had relocked the door with a padlock upon coming back into the house. The front door was the same story, locked tight.

Scared for her very life, Eleanor fled up the stairs to the second floor. Inside her bedroom, she slammed the door shut. There was no lock on it though, and she knew she could never hope to hold it shut against Blinkerson's strength.

Desperately Eleanor dragged a heavy dresser in front of the door and then leaned against it, waiting. After what seemed like an eternity, she heard Blinkerson ascend the second floor stairs and pause opposite her bedroom door.

Eleanor moaned, what had she done? Why had she thought to fight against that monster? She crouched low behind the dresser in case Blinkerson tried to shoot a bullet through the door. As Blinkerson attempted to open the door handle, Eleanor pushed against the dresser with all her might. Could anyone save her from that abominable woman? Where was John?

42

John Hughes and his cousin Gwen worked their way south through the woods of Rocky Mountains National Park, attempting to stay two-thirds of the way up the side of a ridge, paralleling Cache La Poudre River. They were an odd sight, Gwen thought, tramping along a deer trail through the giant Douglas firs of the great mountains. Their intent was to avoid the well-traveled paths of the National Park, yet keep their directions by paralleling the same beautiful alpine valley through which they had traveled the previous day.

John Hughes was troubled though, and with each step further away from camp, his anxiety grew stronger. Gwen was aware of his consternation, having noticed the perturbed expression on his face, the deep furrows creasing his forehead.

"Are you okay?" Gwen drew closer, peering at him intently when he paused.

"I'm worried about Rachel," John spoke apologetically.

"What ever for?" Gwen questioned, disturbed by her cousin's unsaid thoughts. "Forget her, John. She is not your friend."

"I know, but still, it's hard to believe."

"Let's keep moving," Gwen prodded, prompting John to take up the trail once more. She knew her cousin was too trusting. Gwen had never liked nor trusted that maneuvering dark-haired woman from the beginning. It did not surprise her in the least to learn Rachel was a spy. She had been using John, whether for the CIA or the KGB, she was a threat to their safety.

John accepted the fact that Rachel had manipulated him into leading her to the Goldsmith documents, but could not understand why. If she had wanted the government papers, why hadn't she taken him the moment they had uncovered them? She had her gun then. Was she merely wanting him to carry them out of the park for her? Someone had shot Rachel. She had enemies, people who wanted her dead also. Was it the same Russians who had tried to kill him, or was Rachel working for those Russians? It didn't make sense.

John could picture Rachel's apprehension when she returned to camp and found them gone. It pained him to visualize her dismay. They had deserted Rachel, left her to die with a bullet still lodged in the flesh of her shoulder. There were no doctors available in the woods, and she didn't have any medicine. If Rachel had been shot in town, an ambulance would have been sent for and she would have been rushed to the hospital for immediate emergency medical attention. In the woods she was on her own, miles away from help. Could she make it out alone?

Poor Rachel, they had left her there to die. If her enemies didn't kill her outright, she would surely perish from exposure and the loss of blood. John could clearly see and feel the anguished look of helplessness and fear upon her face. He could see her wandering the woods, desperate for help, wounded, dying, alone.

The remembrance of a different face haunted John—back in Wichita when he had been the one who was hurt, after the fight with her former fiancé. It was a look of real concern, of compassion. No, he couldn't accept the conclusion that Rachel didn't care for him, he had seen it in her face, in those dark chestnut eyes.

"I have to go back," John exclaimed, halting suddenly.

Gwen groaned, she had just known he was going to say that. "She might kill us, given the opportunity," Gwen offered one last futile argument.

"I cannot believe that," John contradicted her with conviction. "Rachel would never do anything to hurt me."

Gwen couldn't argue, although she thought her cousin was a dupeable fool. Why did men allow themselves to be manipulated to such extremes by a pretty woman? Gwen had seen it herself, in the boys she had dated in high school and in college. For some stupid reason she had expected mature men would eventually outgrow that characteristic, but apparently some never did. If a woman was nice to look upon and knew how to smile the right way, then she had to be guileless. How ridiculous.

Rachel was a good case in point. That woman was self-centered, uncaring, mean, and emotionally handicapped. It was so obvious to everyone but John. He seemed blinded by her beauty and a pretty smile. Couldn't he see Rachel for what she really was? Why, the woman was withdrawn to the point of being a manic depressive. She was incapable of truly caring about anyone else, only to the extent they intruded into her own limited world. Why couldn't he see beyond her facade?

Following behind John as they retraced their steps through the woods, Gwen fumbled in her backpack to find Rachel's pistol. It wasn't loaded so Gwen slid a clip of bullets into the handle. John spun around suddenly at the sound of the weapon being readied, a puzzled look on his face.

I'm just being prepared," Gwen explained herself. Then, to drive home her point, Gwen remarked, "Remember, Rachel is a spy. She probably works for the KGB, don't get too close to her."

John shook his head in amazement. Why was Gwen being so melodramatic? Rachel did not want to hurt them. As he searched for some sight of Rachel, John's thoughts were plagued by the revelation in his pocket. Rachel was an enemy spy, the Gyrfalcon. What an odd code-name, a falcon that preyed on inferior birds. Was it apt? Was Rachel a predator that found prey in lesser beings of her own kind?

He could picture Rachel digging her fingernails into the throat of a helpless victim, killing like a giant bird of prey, heartless, without mercy, unfeeling. John fought the illusion, but his mind persisted, haunting him, sending shivers up his spine.

When they found Rachel, the unpleasant sight was quite different than expected, shocking in a strange way. Rachel looked like a wild woman; her hair was a tangled mass of black, half obscuring her face, her clothes soiled and ripped, with bloody rags tied about her shoulder and chest in an amateurish attempt at first aid. In one hand she clutched a giant Desert Eagle .50AE automatic pistol, in the other a large unsheathed hunting knife. The worst were her eyes, which had a vacant, half-attentive look, like a deranged person oblivious to her surroundings.

Rachel was stumbling through the woods, barely staying on her feet. At first John thought she was half asleep or only semi-conscious, then he realized she must be crazed from shock and fever. Was this the same beautiful self-confident woman he had rescued from an abusive fiancé in Derby, Kansas? She looked so different now, stripped of the vestiges and cosmetics of civilization.

When Rachel first noticed the presence of others, two people halted in her path a short distance down the deer trail, staring at her with muted wonder, she reacted instinctively. Dodging three steps to the left, Rachel dove for cover behind a fallen fir tree. It was intended to be a dive anyway, but in Rachel's impaired condition, the dive turned into more of a stumbling fall.

She struck the ground hard, the impact momentarily jarring the breath out of her, sending ribbons of pain lacing through her shoulder and down her left arm. The impact caused Rachel to drop the Arkansas Toothpick.

Recovering her breath, Rachel rolled for cover, only to find that infernal cadet standing not two feet away, legs spread apart, an ASP 9mm pointed at Rachel's chest. What was wrong with her, Rachel wondered about herself? It wasn't till halfway through her leap that she had realized it was only her friends, and how could she have allowed such amateurs to approach so close before noticing them. Now Gwen had the drop on her. Was she losing her skills? Had she sunk so far that a child could outmaneuver her? Rachel resolved to shape up and stop being so lazy. If she didn't, she might not live through this affair.

Realizing there was dirt and decaying foliage in her mouth, Rachel spit and coughed to clear it out, as she struggled to her feet. She tried to ignore the distant twinges of pain in her shoulder, they seemed unreal. The morphine made everything seem distant. Why was Gwen still holding that handgun pointed at her chest? She would have to be careful or the cadet would blow her away by accident. Rachel's eyes focused on the trigger. She could see the gun was cocked.

"Drop it," Gwen barked nervously, her hand, the one holding the automatic ASP, shook visibly.

Rachel's eyes dropped to the Desert Eagle in her own hand, she had forgotten she had hold of the large gun. Stupidly Rachel stared at the barrel of Ostermann's Desert Eagle, of course the cadet had been frightened. Relaxing her grip on the pistol, Rachel allowed it to slip through her fingers and fall into the foliage at her feet. She heard Gwen shifting, and became startled. "Be careful," Rachel cautioned. "That gun could go off by accident."

"I have handled firearms before," Gwen retorted, still waving the ASP at Rachel.

"You look hurt," John cried out, crossing into Gwen's line of fire as he approached Rachel with concern.

"Get back!" Gwen screamed and moved sideways to align Rachel in her sights once more. "We have to search her for weapons."

"What?" John protested.

"Look what we've found on her in the past," Gwen said as she handed her cousin the cocked ASP 9mm. "If she moves, then shoot her in the leg." Cautiously Gwen moved toward Rachel. After kicking aside Rachel's gun and knife, Gwen frisked her to ensure she had no hidden weapons.

Rachel did not protest, submitting silently to the searching. Her head was swimming with dizziness and she did not feel like arguing the matter. When Gwen touched her injured shoulder though, Rachel involuntarily cried out, which caused Gwen to jump back with a pained look in her eyes. Rachel knew then, that Gwen would never have been be able to shoot her, even if she did have a loaded gun.

Rachel despised the amateurishness of Gwen's frisking. She bypassed the obvious hiding places, the crotch, the bosom, inside the shoes. Why, even concealment knives taped to the small of her back or the inside of her thighs would not have been discovered by such a clumsy effort.

Unfortunately though, Rachel had no hidden weapons, she was effectively disarmed again. It was embarrassing to have been taken by a layman, a mere child. She deserved her own misfortune, stumbling around like she was oblivious to the world.

Seeing that Gwen was satisfied, John relaxed and allowed his pistol to drop to his side. He had kept the weapon trained on Rachel, as Gwen had wanted, but had not been willing to put his finger on the trigger.

"Where do you keep getting these guns?" Gwen questioned, as she retrieved Rachel's fallen handgun and the Arkansas Toothpick.

"I...ah...I don't feel good," Rachel spoke in a pleading voice. She had no answer to Gwen's question, and she really did feel ill, so much so it was taking an effort to stay on her feet.

"Are you in pain?" John drew close now, placing one supporting hand under Rachel's arm, and the other against her forehead. "You are running a fever. We need to get help."

Rachel felt like crying at the show of sympathy. She really did need help. Silently she moved into John, burying her head on his chest. He responded by taking her into his arms, careful not to touch her injury, and holding her tightly.

Gwen was not so tolerant, "We know who you are, Gyrfalcon!"

Rachel's head shot up in surprise. Gyrfalcon, that was the old cryptonymn she had been assigned back in East Berlin. "I don't understand," Rachel moaned. "What are you saying?" She took great comfort in John's embrace.

"It is all on this list," Gwen mocked her unrelentingly, "your name, and your code name. Who do you work for Rachel, the CIA? Is *Rachel* even your real name? We know you set us up. Who do you *really* work for, the KGB?" Gwen had a look of disgust in her eyes.

"I need to sit down," Rachel moaned, her mind was spinning again. John allowed her to slip from his arms to the ground.

"Are you going to make it?" John asked, as he sat down beside her, propping her back for support.

Rachel snapped her head up like a thought had just struck her. "We have to be moving," Rachel announced suddenly. "I was being chased. They are trying to kill me."

"Kill you?" Gwen challenged skeptically. "The venom in her voice causing John to rise and move protestingly in front of Gwen.

"Not just me, all of us. We have to keep moving," Rachel implored them pleadingly.

"Let's go then," Gwen mocked. "On your feet, you are the one sitting around."

Demurely Rachel raised her arms to John. "Help me, please."

Without hesitation John moved to Rachel's assistance.

43

Thursday, February 22 at Cape Canaveral AFS, portions of the payload fairing, known as the PLF, were the first major pieces of flight hardware to arrive at CCAFS for AFP-775. Although first to be delivered to the launch site, according to the nominal launch flow plan, the upper sections of the PLF would be the last major components to be installed as part of the total Titan IV launch system stack.

One final time Captain Hamilton reviewed the PLF schedule for processing at CCAFS. He knew the major milestones by memory. Glancing at his watch, he saw it was 0745. In fifteen minutes he was scheduled for his now daily status briefing to the colonel. It had been Captain Hamilton's idea to report daily at 0800 hours to Colonel Roe. Each day Captain Hamilton tried to highlight a different major component, this morning he was emphasizing the PLF.

"Sergeant Garcia," Captain Hamilton bellowed from his desk, knowing his assistant could hear him from the office next door.

"Yes sir," Garcia appeared at the doorway smiling.

Captain Hamilton frowned. Why did that mustache make

Garcia appear to be smirking whenever he smiled? "Did you call the colonel's office to ensure he will be in this time?" Hamilton questioned.

"Yes, sir, I was just hanging up the phone with his receptionist when you yelled."

"And...is he in?"

"He's in all right, but he canceled our morning meeting."

"What!" Captain Hamilton exclaimed. "That's three days in a row."

"Yes, sir," Garcia commented. For Alexander Hamilton these meetings were the most important event of the day.

Was the sergeant smirking again, Captain Hamilton wondered, his anger rising? "That will be all, sergeant," he dismissed his assistant and turned his eyes upon the PLF schedule charts, which he had prepared for nothing.

On February 22, six PLF tri-sectors had arrived at CCAFS by railroad. They had immediately been taken by truck to the MIS building for receiving, inspection, storage, processing, and necessary flight preps. On April 28 the aft tri-sectors were taken to the VIB for Centaur processing. The remaining three forward tri-sectors would go to the launch pad for storage to await arrival of the rest of the Titan stack. Not till after the satellite itself had been mated and tested, would these tri-sectors be installed, completing final close out.

Manufactured by MDAC, the McDonnell-Douglas Astronautics Corporation in Huntington Beach, California, the PLF was vital to the success of the launch. Designed as a protective shell that would be placed over the Centaur upper-stage and the fragile satellite, the PLF was built to shield these delicate space vehicles from the harsh environments experienced upon launch and subsequent flight through the Earth's atmosphere. Once in space, the PLF would be discarded as useless space debris, its one-time function completed.

Fairings were manufactured to match a range of sizes for various boosters and different payloads. For Titan IV booster rockets, the PLFs were a full 200 inches in diameter, with four advertised lengths. The NUS (No Upper Stage), 403 and 405 configurations came with a variety of PLFs. The IUS upper-stage 402 configuration required a 56-foot-tall PLF. For heavy payloads, the powerful Centaur G upper-stage 401 configuration, PLFs of 66 feet, 76 feet, or even 86 feet were available. The largest of PLFs weighed a total of 14,000 pounds, a massive protective structure.

The MDAC PLFs for Titan IVs were the same isogrid design that had previously been used on Titan 34D and Delta launches with much success. Full-scale development tests were performed at the factory in California to conduct nodal surveys, check out the structural capability, and test the separation function of each and every PLF before shipment.

For ease of installation, a tri-sector design was employed so that sections of the PLF could be individually placed around the satellite and then attached firmly together. Once safely in space, when the time came to separate, the PLF would peel off like a giant banana. Each PLF was specifically tailored to satisfy individual satellite requirements and provide critical thermal acoustic protection during launch and ascent. On the ground, unique access doors were cut to facilitate satellite ground testing and box replacement directly on the launch pad.

At the VIB building, the base payload fairing was integrated into the Centaur processing early in the flow. After Centaur erection, still in its original shipment bagging from the Centaur factory in San Diego, the aft PLF tri-sectors were installed around the vehicle. Seven weeks later, upon completion of Centaur checkout in the VIB, the combined Centaur and aft PLF would be transported to LP-55, scheduled on June 19, via a modified Viking transporter. The next day the Centaur would be hoisted by special slings and cranes to be mated atop the waiting Titan IV core vehicle.

The Titan IV core was scheduled to complete its assembly and checkout at the VIB on June 11 and then be taken to the SMAB where it would be mated to five SRM segments. This was a four-day process after which the Titan would also be delivered to LP-55 for installation of the final two SRM segments.

Final closeout of the space vehicle with the last three PLF segments, the forward tri-sectors, was not scheduled to take place until August 16 through 18, a mere two weeks before launch, just before the commencement of the final readiness countdown.

44

"All right Mrs. Hughes," Officer Pastorelli sternly called through the barricaded bedroom doorway. "Would you please come out now?"

Eleanor considered ignoring the police officer, but decided it futile to think she could hold them at bay indefinitely. After having held out against Officer Blinkerson for a whole of five minutes, it had been such a relief to hear Officer Pastorelli arriving back at the house.

Could she count on Officer Pastorelli to protect her though? Especially after listening through the door with dismay as Officer Blinkerson described to her partner the recent fight, cursing at Eleanor like a foul-mouthed she-devil. It was obvious Eleanor had incurred the endless hatred of that demented sadistic woman. What had she done though? Tried to run away? Defend herself when Blinkerson was beating on her face? Eleanor felt no sympathy for Blinkerson's broken toes.

"What are you going to do?" Eleanor called through the tightly shut door, her buffer from that Blinkerson monster.

"I want you to come out, now!" Pastorelli responded. There was no anger in her voice, only firmness.

"Is Officer Blinkerson still there?" Eleanor asked. She wanted to come out, but had doubts that the more rational police officer could constrain her irascible bellicose partner.

"I am still here," Blinkerson growled ominously.

"You will not be harmed if you cooperate," Pastorelli added, now irritated at her associate. Didn't Blinkerson want their prisoner to come out willingly?

Eleanor moved hesitantly to the side of the protective dresser and shoved it across the carpet away from the door. She was apprehensive of course, and her jaw still hurt from their recent fight. The door was no longer blocked, but no one opened it. They were waiting for Eleanor to come out on her own. Timidly she grasped the door handle. Her palm felt sweaty as she slowly swung it open.

Officer Pastorelli gasped in surprise as she saw Eleanor's battered face, bruised and bleeding from the large pudgy fists of Officer Blinkerson.

"Turn around," Blinkerson ordered angrily, startling Eleanor with her fierceness. Roughly Officer Blinkerson shoved Eleanor up against the wall and slapped a pair of handcuffs onto Eleanor's shaking hands. "You can expect attempted escape and assaulting an officer to be added to your charges," Blinkerson threatened.

Grasping Eleanor's bound arm just above the elbow, Blinkerson squeezed cruelly and escorted her captive forcefully down the stairs. Too frightened to cry out from the pain or from fear, Eleanor did not resist as she was taken to the main floor, through the dining room, through the kitchen, and into the back hall—but there, at the head of the basement stairs, she balked.

"Where are we going?" Eleanor cried, pulling against Blinkerson, causing the officer to tighten her grip even further, fingers digging into Eleanor's skin. "You are hurting me," Eleanor cried out, but to no avail.

"Shut up," Blinkerson commanded, jerking her relentlessly down the stairs. Once in the basement, Eleanor was unmercifully led to the same spot where Blinkerson had tried to force her into the shower. The cold cement floor was still wet from water. "Over there!" Blinkerson shouted, pointing to a spot next to the wall.

Meekly Eleanor stood where requested, as Blinkerson removed her handcuffs. The policewoman then attached one cuff to Eleanor's right foot and the other to a dirty copper pipe extending up from the concrete of the basement floor. It was cold and damp downstairs, and Eleanor found herself starting to shiver again. She saw Officer Pastorelli watching from the foot of the stairway.

"You'll just have to stay down here from now on, sweetie. A troublemaker like you does not deserve to be in a house. Down here it's more like a cell, a place for criminals."

Eleanor was dumbfounded, shocked at her mistreatment. She was afraid to complain though, lest they hurt her physically.

"Oh," Blinkerson stepped back to survey her handiwork. "I see that I ripped your cutesy little dress, sorry about that."

The dress was an old favorite, one that Eleanor had owned and worn for many years. Silently she pulled at the torn fabric to more fully cover herself.

The two officers departed up the creaking basement stairs, Blinkerson was chuckling to herself like a madwoman. Pastorelli had a grim, set expression on her face, but did nothing to alleviate her prisoner's predicament, intentionally avoiding eye contact with Eleanor.

As they reached the head of the stairs and exited the basement, one of the policewomen turned off the lights and shut the door, leaving Eleanor in total darkness. She started to sob. They surely couldn't leave her like this. Eleanor tried to sit, but the floor felt cold and wet.

Soon the darkness began to press ominously upon Eleanor's distraught nerves. She was all alone, her solitude uninterrupted except for the sound of someone boarding up the basement windows from the outside, a distraction that only added to her sense of despair.

As night drew on, doubly dark in the confines of the basement, devoid of outside star or moonlight, Eleanor's fatigue grew heavy on her. Small creaking noises in the woodwork of the older home constantly disturbed and distracted her, making Eleanor think animals or spooks were about. She needed to lie down, but couldn't bring herself to do more than sit on the cold unyielding cement floor. Where was her husband? What was he doing? How could she endure the night, alone and frightened, captive in this basement dungeon?

45

John Hughes held tightly to Rachel Maris as they fled through the woods, stumbling along a narrow winding deer trail. It was night, yet they had no problems with visibility, the moon and stars providing sufficient light with which to see. The world seemed strange to Rachel Maris as she drifted in and out of consciousness. Her motions seemed unreal, imaginary. At times she felt like she was floating, being pulled along like a large human-shaped balloon. Then she became aware of her feet, realizing they hurt, that she had blisters. The awareness of that pain made Rachel smile. As she considered her feet further, they begin to grow heavy like rocks, then her legs became heavy too. It soon took a tremendous effort to keep them moving.

"Let's rest," John gasped and eased Rachel's arm off his shoulder, allowing her to slip to the ground.

Rachel realized then how much support John had been providing, why, he was practically carrying her. "You're so strong," she complimented him, smiling churlishly.

"She's losing it," Rachel heard Gwen mutter, her voice sounding distant through the fog of Rachel's mind.

"She's burning up with fever," John lamented.

"Do you think she will last till we can get help?" Gwen questioned.

John looked startled. "Last? What do you mean last? She's not dying." He sat down next to Rachel, leaning his back against a tree, his breathing heavy. Rachel moved against him like a small child seeking comfort.

"John?" Gwen queried.

"Yes."

"You were right to come back for her. If we hadn't, she would have died."

John smiled, appreciative of the apology. It was true, if Rachel had any other friends in the woods, they were making no effort to save her.

Rachel raised her head suddenly, a lucid look momentarily crossing her eyes. "Why have we stopped?" Rachel protested. "They are following us. They will kill us if they can."

"Who, Rachel?" John questioned, feeling a tingle run down his spine. He shuddered involuntarily. Rachel had such a wild look in her eyes. She was terrified.

John took the frightened woman into his arms again, hugging her in an attempt to soothe her fears.

As Rachel's hands moved around his back, John almost recoiled, as a strange but stark vision came hauntingly into his mind. He could see Rachel's fingernails pressing into his shirt, biting into his skin, but now it wasn't a hand on his back, but a giant talon sinking razor claws into his flesh. His confused mind tortured him with the image of a huge malevolent gyrfalcon, reaching out to claim him as her prey.

Shaking his head in wonder, the vision disappeared from John's head. Nevertheless he pushed Rachel's arms away.

"Can we go, John?" Gwen questioned nervously, glancing down the trail behind them. At that moment they heard a twig snap, just beyond their sight, back in the woods somewhere. "Hurry," Gwen exclaimed, crouching low.

As John scrambled to his feet, assisting Rachel up off the ground also, Gwen took up the pack with Goldsmith's documents, along with the Weatherby hunting rifle they had stolen from the sniper. Gwen had Rachel's two automatic pistols and her knives tucked into her belt, leaving John free to devote all his strength to assisting Rachel. Still very unsteady, Rachel was leaning upon John almost to the point of having to be carried.

"Give me a gun," Rachel moaned, but they ignored her. How ironic, Rachel thought, dwelling on their stupidity. She was the one that needed a weapon, not that silly cadet. Rachel knew how to fight, but how could she protect them without a weapon? As John started forward though, she felt the security of his strong arm around her waist but her head was swimming, dizzy from standing, and she almost passed out.

Hours lapsed and it seemed to Rachel as if they were walking into eternity. She felt herself becoming one with John. He was her life support, her strength, her savior. She loved John.

When they stepped into icy water, Rachel was totally unprepared. Screaming with fear, she drew back suddenly, almost toppling John.

"Shhh," Gwen cautioned, glancing about fearfully. "Geez, not when we are out in the open. You must keep her quiet, John."

"It's okay, Rachel," came John's soothing voice. "We are simply crossing Chapin Creek. I'm afraid the water woke you. The trail leading out is on the other side of this valley, through the creek. Then its up a short hill, over the top of a ridge, and down to Old Fall River Road. We're going to make it." He spoke smoothly and continuously, his voice allaying her fears.

Rachel grimaced as they waded into freezing waters up to her waist. It was cold, so cold, like ice, and the current was so strong. She clung desperately to John. They hadn't bothered to remove their clothing for the crossing, not this time, desperately hoping to escape the park soon.

Successfully crossing Chapin Creek, they struggled up a slope into the woods and collapsed for a moment of exhausted rest, their bodies demanding the respite.

"I don't get it," Gwen spoke, after catching her breath.

"What?"

"We've been moving awfully slow through the woods. As fast as we could, but still slow, and quite noisily too, right?"

"Yes, I suppose. What are you getting at?"

"Well then, why didn't our pursuers catch us?"

"Perhaps we lost them," John spoke hopefully, "or," his face turning to a frown, "perhaps they..."

"Didn't want to catch us," Gwen finished.

"They are probably right behind us," John glanced across the mountain valley, to the spot where they had exited the woods.

"Why are they doing it? Why are they simply following us and not shooting?" Gwen despaired.

"I don't know," John looked grim.

"You go ahead with Rachel," Gwen suggested. "I'll hide here and see if anyone does follow, then I'll catch up with you at the road."

"No way," John was insistent. "We are not going to split up." For all he knew their enemy was before them, rather than behind, having anticipated their direction of travel.

The climb to the crest of the trail, up through Chapin Pass, nearly finished them, in spite of several lengthy stops. By the time they reached the crest, their overwrought muscles were so exhausted they had to stop again, not even having the strength to start down.

It was noon when they finally reached Old Fall River Road and emerged from the woods. It had taken them the entire night and morning to escape. Now on a one-way, well-maintained, but uphill road, composed of dirt and gravel, they had a half-mile to go, up an extremely steep grade to the Alpine Visitor Center and the main highway, Interstate 34.

Trudging up that incline, John thought his legs were going to split, the top of each thigh straining mightily with each step. They spotted a bicyclist far down the hill, working his way up the same road, his gears set so that his feet seemed to spin without resistance. He seemed to be cycling in slow motion, hardly moving forward for all the speed of his pedaling, but nonetheless caught up with their position in short order. John thought about calling out for assistance, asking the biker to send help, but didn't.

They must have appeared like an odd trio to the biker. The man was so engrossed with his own task of endurance, he hardly noticed them though, not even enough to discern their distress or see the blood upon their clothing. Discouraged by the apparent rhythmic ease with which the bicyclist traversed up the grade, John realized they were not going to make it themselves. The top was too far, the hill too steep. John felt like crying, he was so tired, and they were so close.

"Oh look," Gwen called out with relief, directing John's attention to an approaching car. It was a station wagon of all things, a family automobile pulling a Coleman tent trailer. What had possessed them to deviate from the normal paved roads, John could not begin to guess, crazy tourists.

"We must flag them down," Gwen spoke urgently, expressing the necessary fact that was on both their minds.

John looked at his younger cousin critically. Would the tourists stop for them? Gwen appeared haggard and beat, and her face was covered with sweat. Despite the physical conditioning of Academy regimentation, she too was suffering from their deprivations, the long grueling march through the night, the lack of recent nourishment, the strain of being hunted, the fear of death.

"You flag them down," John directed grimly. "We'll commandeer their car, force them out, and make a run for the hospital. Give me one of the pistols."

"No," Rachel interrupted, surprising them. She shifted her weight off John's shoulder to stand, swaying unsteadily on her own two feet. "We cannot leave witnesses behind."

They stared at her in dismay, shocked by the idea of such a heartless suggestion.

"I mean, do not leave them behind to call the police, take them with us as hostages, make them drive." It hurt Rachel to realize that John had thought she was suggesting murder.

Nodding with understanding, John watched as the car neared. He felt himself starting to shake out of nervousness. This was not going to be easy. His head was suddenly clouded with a sharp aching pain.

The family wagon pulled to a slow stop alongside them, the windows were down. A concerned young couple was inside, they couldn't have been married more than a couple of years.

"My goodness," the woman cried out with astonishment, eyeing Rachel with unexpected horror. The blood on Rachel's shirt and arm presented a frightful sight.

"She's been shot," Gwen pleaded frantically. "Can you take us to a hospital?"

"What happened?" the young husband exclaimed, as he leaped out of the car to assist John in loading Rachel into the back seat.

"Poachers," Gwen answered, taking a seat in the front as the woman scooted toward her husband to make room. The wife looked at her charitable mate despairingly. The young lady sliding in next to her was soaking wet from the waist down, and covered with dirt from head to foot.

"There is a hospital in Estes Park," the husband exclaimed, as he gunned the car, gravel flying.

"Careful," his wife cautioned, suddenly alarmed at his driving.

John considered drawing his weapon then, but felt hesitant. If they were going toward medical help anyway, why risk trouble?

"I think we should stop at the visitor center and alert the rangers," the driver's alarmed wife asserted practically. "They can call ahead for an ambulance and maybe have it meet us on the way."

He had to do it, John grimaced, knowing his duty. In spite of his promise to never threaten innocent people again, he had no choice. Drawing the 9mm ASP, John pointed the wavering barrel at the back of the driver's head.

"Just keep right on going," John directed, and cocked the hammer for effect.

"He's got a gun!" the wife glanced back and then screamed, causing her husband to swerve violently and almost plunge over the edge.

"No one is going to get hurt," Gwen reassured the panicky couple. "Just get us to a hospital."

As they sped through the national park, down scenic winding Interstate 34, Rachel Maris struggled to stay conscious. The situation was critical. Pulling close to John, she attempted to speak. He had to be warned, she had to tell him not to assume they were no longer being followed by those in the woods. The men chasing them had radios, they would have anticipated their moves, tails would have them in sight before they could get anywhere.

Rachel's head was spinning though, the message could wait. She snuggled against John, allowing herself to relax. The warmth of his body felt good and she wanted to drift off into sleep. Rachel was overwhelmed with an outpouring of emotions toward John. He was such a good person, and he had come back for her. More than risking his life for her sake, he was risking his cause for her.

Rachel's hand moved against John's side. Her fingers touched something metallic. She realized her hand was coincidently inside John's pocket. Instinctively she lifted the small metal cylinder from John's pocket and slipped it into her own. A moment later she was fast asleep.

Reaching Estes Park after dark, they found it to be more of a clinic than a large medical facility, and worse yet, it was closed. John ordered the young couple to continue on toward Denver. They could not afford to wait for small-town medical personnel to respond to an after-hours emergency phone call, nor could they turn to the police for help, John was a wanted man.

In Denver, Rachel would have a much better chance, at a major hospital with a trauma center. There Rachel would receive the type of attention she needed.

Approximately one hour later, Gwen directed them to the emergency entrance of Denver General off Bannock Street near downtown. Rachel was worried about pursuers and made them promise to drop her off and then escape into the streets of Denver.

At DGH they exited their commandeered vehicle and rushed Rachel Maris into the emergency entrance, taking the frightened wife along with them as a hostage. The poor girl was scared to the point of hysteria, and they felt it unlikely she would do anything other than cooperate. The husband was directed to circle the hospital and park across Delaware Avenue near the main entrance loop.

Once inside, John and Gwen regretfully but promptly abandoned Rachel, leaving her in the hands of capable and experienced medical attendants. Hastily working their way through the large crowded hospital with their terrified hostage in tow, they exited the main entrance and crossed the parking areas to find the husband waiting anxiously as instructed. Giving the frightened couple the opportunity to escape their nightmare at last and flee back to a life of normalcy, minus a car but otherwise unhurt, John and Gwen left them standing in the parking lot of DGH and disappeared into rush-hour traffic of the large cosmopolitan city called Denver.

46

"Here you go, Annette. I'm done with these files. Please bring me the next set." Dan Newby slid a stack of three documents toward his disinterested personal secretary, who was standing just off the corner of his large oak desk. To an unknowing observer, the identity of those documents was masked, each had a blue coversheet stapled to the front and back. Emblazoned on those coversheets was simply a number, "88," symbolizing the local program identifier for that compartment.

As Annette scooped the heavy documents into her arms and sauntered from her boss' office, Andrew Maconey entered, unintentionally blocking his superior's view of Annette's retreating figure. "It's almost time, sir," Maconey reminded his boss of their scheduled conference call.

"Sit down, Maconey," Newby invited his deputy inside. "I'll have Annette transfer the call into my office instead."

Maconey took his customary seat off the front right corner of Newby's desk. Outside the office doorway they could see Annette stooping to dig through the bottom of a heavy five-drawer safe. She had worn a tight miniskirt that day. As she stooped and twisted about, almost sitting on her heels to shuffle through a drawer overstuffed with files, the dress rode well up her shapely thighs.

Maconey saw a chance to tease the Chief, who was also his friend, "You've been keeping Annette busy with the files all day, I see."

Newby felt himself inadvertently turning red. He had a suspicion, a nagging worry, that Maconey always seemed aware of his private thoughts. "Yes," Newby coughed. "I have been very busy today. Doing a little research on my own, you know."

Maconey saw he had Newby in an embarrassing position. Leaning forward conspiratorially, he asked in a hushed voice. "Sir, have you ever considered asking Annette out? She is quite an attractive lady, although a bit young."

"What?" Newby appeared genuinely shocked. "Good heavens no, the thought never crossed my mind. What would Victoria ever think? You know I am a happily married man. What ever has gotten into you, Andrew?"

"Never mind," Maconey sat back in his chair, smiling good naturedly. He and Newby had a special relationship, more like friends than the typical subordinate to manager. Truth was, Dan Newby was one of the few people Maconey felt at ease around.

Together they watched Annette working with the files, until startled by the sudden ring of a phone. Annette swiveled around and stood up, turning to approach her desk and answer the office phone. Both men turned aside, Maconey to stare at some papers on the desk and Newby to gaze at the picture of a ship on the wall.

"Hello," Annette answered, an inadvertent wrong number would have no idea who or what office had been reached. Unfortunately Annette spoke the word "hello" with such formality and lack of emotion that no one would mistakenly think they had reached a home. She sounded like an office worker.

Maconey and Newby listened expectantly, anticipating it was their conference call. Operation Carrier Pigeon had taken on such important dimensions that all other activities and normal office duties now seemed insignificant. Tracking the progress of Rachel Maris and Randy Ostermann, closing in on the notorious Baron, it seemed to consume the energies and thoughts of the entire department. Although Carrier Pigeon was a limited dissemination program, protected under the Albatross Control System, everyone seemed to be aware of the effort to one degree or another.

When Annette announced a confirmation of their expectations, a Carrier Pigeon call from the field team, Maconey snatched up the phone in Newby's office. "Hello, Ostermann?"

"No, this is Sanders," a younger voice replied. Eddie Sanders was a new man, Maconey had recruited him a little over a year ago, from the crypto division, a brilliant innovative young man who had been wasting his talents.

"Eddie Sanders?" Maconey questioned. It was odd not to have Ostermann, the case officer, reporting, and doubly odd to have a junior member of the team reporting in his place. "Where is Ostermann?"

"He is unavailable, sir."

Maconey noticed a questioning look on his boss' face. "Hold on a moment while I switch on the squawk box. Dan Newby is in the room with me."

"Eddie Sanders?" Newby questioned, as soon as Maconey hung up the receiver.

"Yes, sir?"

"What is the difficulty? Is Ostermann not in a position to report in?"

"No, sir. We have a situation difficult to explain."

"Has he been injured? Have any of the team been hurt?" Newby felt suddenly anxious for Rachel Maris' safety.

"No…ah…we are all okay physically. Wait, I take that back. Rachel Maris was shot in the shoulder."

Newby bit his lip, he knew it. "Is she seriously hurt? What is the extent of her injury?"

"She's in bad shape sir, lost a lot of blood. You know Rachel Maris though, continuing on with the mission. She made contact with our back-up team early yesterday. Murrey cleaned the wound and gave her a pain killer."

"How could this happen? I left strict orders." Newby felt his anger rising. What was going on out there?

"It was the assassin, sir. Took a shot at her when they were crossing a mountain creek. We reacted in time to prevent him from finishing her, but there was no way to anticipate or prevent the attack."

Newby couldn't accept an answer like that, there were always ways to prevent an attack, if one did his job correctly. Things were starting to go sour on this operation. He had a bad feeling in his stomach, too many foul-ups, too much carelessness. The ruthlessness of their adversary, the Baron, was unbelievable. To think another member of the company, a highly decorated, much admired leader, was heartless enough to try and eliminate one of his own operatives.

Calming himself, Newby continued, "Okay, Sanders, where is Maris now?"

"In a hospital sir, in Denver. They have left Rocky Mountain National Park."

Newby was stunned. Was it all over? Had Operation Carrier Pigeon failed?

"What about the documents?" Maconey asked, also concerned about the continuation of the operation.

"Hughes recovered the Goldsmith documents."

Newby wanted to ask about the provocation list, his bait for the Baron, but couldn't. Sanders would not know anything about their planted trap, he had not been briefed on all the details, he wasn't Albatross cleared.

"Get Ostermann to a phone right away," Newby ordered.

"Sir…ah…that will be a problem," Eddie Sanders stammered. "I am afraid Ostermann has deserted."

Newby and Maconey were shocked. Had their best field intelligence officer gone over? What more could go wrong? Newby sat in a stupor as Maconey continued the conversation with Sanders. "What happened? When and why did he leave?"

"We tried to restrain him, sir. He seemed to have lost control. The man was totally enraged. I have never seen anyone so insanely mad. He went berserk and took off pursuing after Maris."

Newby felt a twinge of guilt, the ache in his stomach had developed into a sharp pain. Had he pushed the man too far? He had told Ostermann that he would be relieved if there was another slip-up, or any harm befell Rachel Maris or Hughes, and obviously Rachel had been shot.

"What caused this madness?" Maconey asked incredulously.

"I guess it started when she kicked him in the groin," Sanders paused. They could hear someone speaking to him in the background. "Ah…" Sanders continued, "that was the day before. Today, she held Ostermann at knife point, disarmed him, and relieved him of his command. It must have been too humiliating for him, sir."

Newby was amazed. Not that he did not believe Sanders' report, on the contrary, it very much sounded like something Rachel might do. It must have been something to see.

Sanders continued, "After Maris left us, Ostermann went crazy. He tried to take Murrey's gun. I fully believe he intended to shoot her in the back. We held Ostermann at bay, having to forcefully restrain him until Rachel was out of sight."

"Go on."

"Well, then we followed Rachel, at a discrete distance. She caught up with John Hughes and the Academy cadet, then they made their way out of the Park at night. They even stole a car to do so, kidnapping a young couple in the process."

Newby's mind was spinning. Ostermann was the only member of the field team that knew their plot against the Baron. None of the others had been briefed on the full details of the plan. They did not know it was all a big sting to lure Rachel Maris into making a run for the Baron, to implicate him with the covert society and force him into revealing himself.

"Who is in charge of the field team?" Newby leaned above the squawk box, feeling a total loss of control over the operation.

"Well, ah, I guess I am, sir."

"What, the men elected you in charge?"

"Well, no, not exactly. Rachel Maris put me in charge when she relieved Ostermann. She claimed Ostermann was teamed with the assassin, sir, that he had gone over to the enemy. She insisted I report that suspicion personally to your ears."

"I see," Newby exclaimed. Rachel was too much for them, too strong, too resourceful. His men needed help.

"Where is Hughes now?"

"They...ah...escaped. We lost them sir. After driving Rachel to Denver General Hospital, Hughes and the cadet gave us the slip."

Newby was further stunned. What more could go wrong? What more could happen? "Tell me, you said Rachel is at Denver General Hospital?"

"Yes, sir."

"Okay, Sanders, listen now, this is very important. You said they have the stolen documents. Did Rachel also recover a small metal cylinder with a rolled piece of paper inside?"

"I don't know, sir. I did not see one. Why?"

"Never mind. Where are the documents?"

"Hughes has them, they are gone."

Newby groaned audibly. He had no way of even knowing if Rachel had obtained the provocation list.

"You have the hospital under surveillance?" Maconey questioned.

"Yes, sir. I also have people out searching for Hughes. It's a long shot though. Should we call in the Denver police?"

"Yes, have them picked up. Also, we need you to get hold of Maris' belongings. See if she has that cylinder."

"What about Ostermann?"

"If he shows up, send him back to Dallas. When was he last seen?"

"In the park, sir. When Maris and Hughes hijacked the car, he flew into another rage, thought we had lost her and became verbally abusive. He broke away from us, running by foot back toward our vehicles. We could hardly shoot him in the back, not one of our own men."

"What was he after?"

"Said he was going after Rachel Maris on his own. Said he was going to catch her himself and teach her a lesson. He's gone mad, sir. I'm afraid he intends to murder Rachel Maris."

47

"What happens now?" Gwen Hughes questioned, as her cousin drove down Broadway toward downtown, leaving Denver General Hospital and Rachel Maris behind.

"I don't know," John responded, as he made a left turn on Colfax Avenue, plotting a zig-zagging course through downtown. "Do you think we are being followed?"

"No one appears to be following."

"Poor Rachel," John worried. "I hope she will be okay." John hated leaving Rachel Maris alone in the hospital, especially with a killer on their trail. Hopefully no one would attack her there.

"Don't worry about her," Gwen said thoughtfully. "I'm sure she'll receive the best of care at DGH, they are known for their trauma center and treatment of gang related gunshot victims. She needed medical attention." Gwen noticed her cousin seemed unconvinced, "You did the right thing!"

John's concern was mystifying, especially considering the way Rachel Maris had deceived him. "We could not very well stay!" Gwen asserted. "If you had not gone back for Rachel in the woods, she would be dead right now. You did enough."

"I guess you are right. We were extremely fortunate to get out of the mountains alive. It's a miracle those killers didn't murder us all in there."

"I'll say," Gwen relaxed. "What a relief, but what now?"

"Well, we need to get hold of your father."

"Right, and to do that, we need a place to call from."

"How about the Academy?" John proposed.

"I don't think so," Gwen demurred. "Our enemies would probably be watching for us there."

"How about a motel then? We could hide there till you reach your father."

Driving past the downtown district, John and Gwen searched down Park Avenue for an inconspicuous roadside motel. They selected an older establishment, the Country Town Motel, with three rows of units in the shape of a U, some of which had parking out of sight from the street. Although cheap in appearance, the grounds and buildings looked clean and well cared for, and best of all, it had a vacancy sign.

John could not help comparing their frugal accommodations to the Embassy Suites, that luxury hotel Rachel had insisted on staying in at Colorado Springs. Rachel was not the type of woman that would have been satisfied with anything less. Strangely enough, John missed her.

Pulling into a parking slot backwards, so the license plate would not show, John left Gwen seated in the station wagon with the engine running. Inside a tiny front office was an elderly gentleman from India. John made up a name for the registration, paid cash for the night, and received a brass room key, number twenty-four. It was a small one-room motel unit with a worn double bed, ancient dresser, a battered table and chairs, and a brand new color TV with cable channels. The furnishings were modest, but it was tidy and well cared for. It would do.

"First priority, I want to try and call Eleanor," John declared, seating himself on the bed next to a small nightstand, which supported a gaudy lamp and the phone. He had been unable to reach Eleanor since they had entered Rocky Mountain Nation Park. It pained John whenever he allowed his thoughts to linger on Eleanor. He almost felt as if he were being unfaithful, although his motives were pure.

"Good idea," Gwen sank into a chair and propped her feet up, on the wobbly table. "Let's hurry and get our phone calls out of the way, I'm dying for a long hot shower."

Suddenly John realized how tired he had become, his fatigue seeming to hit against him like an ocean wave. Dialing zero, and then his home phone number, he asked the operator to place a collect phone call from Edward Foulke. It was the name of Eleanor's grandfather, who had died last year, she would understand who was calling. Unfortunately there was no answer.

"I don't like it," John grumbled, placing the receiver down gingerly.

"No one home?" Gwen questioned.

John shook his head negatively. "I have not been able to raise anyone for some time now, something is not right."

Gwen bounced to her feet. "Let me put a call in for my daddy."

Marveling that she seemed to still have so much energy, John stood to move aside, stiff overwrought muscles protesting painfully.

After leaving a short message for her father to call, including the phone number of the motel switchboard and their room number, Gwen retreated to the bathroom and her long awaited shower. John switched on the TV and watched the news, waiting for his turn to be freed of the dirt and sweat from their flight through the mountains.

It was almost forty minutes later before Gwen emerged from the bathroom. "Feel better?" John asked, knowing from the refreshed look on her face that she did.

"Oh, you don't know how much," Gwen beamed cheerfully.

"I'll find out soon enough," John countered, finding the energy to saunter into the bathroom.

"I just wish we had some clean clothes to change into," Gwen mused.

All John wanted was to take a shower and then crash for some much needed sleep. Once under the water, he washed his hair twice and then began scrubbing himself with a soapy washrag. It was amazing how his muscles responded, most of the aching actually went away. He felt great.

After dressing again, John returned to the main room. Gwen was already fast asleep, having kicked off her shoes and climbed in under the covers with her clothes still on.

John sat in one of the chairs and closed his eyes. It was no good though, he was too tired to get comfortable. Lying on top of the covers, next to his cousin, John closed his eyes and relaxed. It felt like heaven and within a few minutes, he too was sound asleep.

An hour later the phone rang, jarring the two of them back into consciousness. Gwen sat up, instantly alert. "Hello," she called into the receiver.

"Hi, Gwen," it was the familiar voice of her beloved father. "Are you safe? Thank goodness you called."

"I'm okay, Daddy."

"I've been worried sick, darling. You're not hurt?"

"No, Daddy, I am fine."

"Where are you, Gwen?"

"We're in Denver, at a motel."

"Who is there with you?"

"Just John. We are both unharmed, but a friend that was with us, she was shot."

"Shot!?"

"In the shoulder, she is going to be okay, we took her to the hospital. Daddy, we have the documents."

"Listen, Gwen, I want you to get away from John. Go to the motel lobby, call a taxi, get out of there quick."

"But, Daddy, we have to talk," Gwen protested.

"No, Gwen, you just do what I say."

"Daddy," Gwen complained, knowing he was one person you couldn't argue with.

"Just do it."

"I am going to put John on the phone," Gwen spoke angrily, full of pent-up frustration. Why did her father insist on treating her like a minor?

John could see his cousin was upset. In a huff, she threw the phone on the bed and stomped across the room, eyes flashing, arms folded tightly.

John picked up the phone, "Uncle Ellis."

"Don't uncle me. I cannot believe you dared to involve my little girl in these illegal escapades. I trusted you, John. You have hurt me very deeply my boy."

"I...ah..." John was flabbergasted for a moment. "We really had no choice. She insisted on coming and we had people pursuing us. I could not very well leave her behind."

"Give it up, John," Ellis Hughes spoke harshly. "You must turn yourself in to the police immediately."

John was dumbstruck. What had happened? What had caused the complete turnaround in his uncle's demeanor? In their original conversation he had been encouraging, he had even recommended John try to obtain the proof. Now that they had proof, Uncle Ellis did not even want to know what they had found.

"It's all true," John blurted out hastily.

"What!?"

"The DWARS virus, the genocide weapon. It is all true."

"That is absurd."

"No! It's not!" John asserted fervidly. "They are actually going to put that abominable weapon into orbit. I think they must be insane."

"You think THEY are insane! Look John, I order you to turn yourself over to the authorities. I will finance your legal council."

"You are not going to help us," John stated softly, not wanting to believe his own conclusion. He had been so sure Uncle Ellis would have all the answers.

"Sure I am, John. You've been deluded. I will help, but first you have to turn yourself in."

"They have to be stopped."

"What! Look, we'll check into it, John."

"They have to be stopped!"

"You keep my daughter out of it, my boy. Let her go."

Silently, John hung up the receiver. He felt angry, a dark cloud seemed to be covering his mind, making it hard to think. He knew one thing though, the people who had deluded him and his fellow employees at Krang Enterprises, into building a satellite for that genocide weapon, were not going to get away with it.

Gwen nodded knowingly, "My father thinks we are fools."

"We have to be going," John replied grimly.

"Yes, Daddy is probably calling the police right now, but where are we going?"

"Ever been to Cape Canaveral, Florida?"

Gwen's eyes glistened with surprise. Smiling, she reached for her shoes.

48

Friday, June 1 at Cape Canaveral AFS, Captain Alexander Hamilton smiled with anticipation, a rare change to his normally austere, rigidly professional demeanor. "This is great. A night launch is supposed to be one of the most magnificent sights on Earth."

"Yes sir, quite a fireworks show. It should really light up the sky." Sergeant Ramon Garcia stood off to the side of Captain Hamilton, smiling with odd amusement. "Have you ever seen a night launch, sir?"

"No, but I have been involved with several launches back at Vandenberg, of course." Captain Hamilton, as a matter of policy, hated to admit a lack of knowledge or experience in anything relating to his job.

This enlisted man was a constant irritant. Sergeant Garcia seemed quite capable, but never took anything seriously, and to Captain Hamilton that was a sin. For Alexander Hamilton, everything relating to their job was deadly serious, and he had no tolerance for horseplay or joking behavior when it came to matters of such great importance. What seemed to bother Captain Hamilton the most about his sergeant though, was a nagging suspicion his assistant did not even take him seriously.

The two men were standing just off Control Center Road on the NASA Causeway, next to several stands of white-washed bleachers amidst a lush grassy parking area along the north side of the road. This was a choice location where the press and other privileged spectators typically gathered to view Space Shuttle launches. Looking north up the Banana River, one had an excellent unobstructed view of the Space Shuttle launch pads.

There was no Space Shuttle to be launched that evening though, and only a few, in-the-know on-lookers were on hand. If all went according to schedule, there was to be a Titan expendable launch vehicle sent up into space that night. It was a classified military launch, and, although the press had obtained and announced the date, quoting unreleased but reliable sources, there was no official press allowed on base.

Sergeant Ramon Garcia had not been surprised when Captain Hamilton announced his intentions to personally view this Titan DSP launch. Garcia would have preferred to spend his evenings at home, or walking the beaches with a lady, but he had strict orders from Chief Quijano to accompany the good captain everywhere, and Sergeant Garcia obeyed orders. Still, they didn't pay overtime wages in the air force and he would much rather have read about the launch in the morning newspapers.

Garcia had known Captain Hamilton would insist on being there. Why, he had even dressed in his uniform for the event. Sergeant Garcia, on the other hand, wore civilian clothes: jeans and T-shirt, never missing an excuse to dress casually. The good captain felt it was his duty to personally oversee everything that impacted his own mission, including this DSP launch. Garcia knew they were going to be in for some long nights over the next few months.

"It is now 2317 hours," Captain Hamilton announced the time in military fashion. "The launch window has now begun."

"How long is the window?" Sergeant Garcia asked, as they both stared north toward launch pad LP-55. Heavy floodlights lit up the area around the rocket, illuminating the launch complex as if in daylight. Even at this distance on the Causeway, the gleam of the shiny Titan rocket was clearly visible.

"Eighty minutes," Captain Hamilton responded. The launch could take place anytime during the eighty-minute window, although typically they tried for the beginning to allow contingency time for minor delays. Once the window closed, if they had not launched, it would mean shutting down for the night and waiting for another window tomorrow, when the Earth's rotation lined up again for the correct orbit.

"There she goes," Ramon Garcia called out suddenly, as a flash of light erupted from the launch pad.

As directed flame shot off to one side, billowing in a cloud of brilliant smoke and gases, the rocket slowly lifted off the ground. At that moment the thunderous noise of the blast reached the position of the two men, now insignificantly minuscule against the backdrop of the monumental forces unleashed by the controlled man-made monster. The very ground itself shook with the noise and the night fled before the combustion of the Titan booster.

The magnificent Titan IV sped upward, and before long, all that was visible was the flame of the monstrous engines. The flight path was arcing to the north and east. Soon there was a flash as the SRMs separated and the flame broke into three separate fireballs, two hanging momentarily motionless before arcing into a descent, and the third continuing upward with increasing acceleration.

A short time later there was another flash as Stage 1 separated and fell away from the upwardly thrusting launch vehicle. Up into the night air the Titan IV shot, until disappearing altogether from view, lost from sight in the starry darkness as it struggled to pierce through the grip of the Earth's gravity.

Sergeant Garcia took a deep breath as he lost sight of the rocket. These launches never failed to leave him speechless with wonder. He felt overwhelmed with a surge of patriotic pride and the sense they were attempting something grand, something immortal. Garcia felt like cheering, and indeed there was clapping and shouts from some of the other awe-struck spectators.

"Another successful launch," Garcia whispered in awe.

"Yes," Captain Hamilton exulted, his voice also flush with excitement. "She's off the launch pad. Now it's ninety days, and then we'll have our turn!"

49

Rachel Maris languished in bed, wearied with boredom, sleeping restlessly in an uncomfortably sterile hospital environment. Dozing, half-awake, half-asleep, a movement in the room caught her attention, someone dressed in white. It was a nurse. Rachel watched the blur of white scurry out the door in a rush.

Shifting in discomfort, Rachel examined the dressing securely fashioned over her shoulder and under the left arm. It was going to hurt when they took those bandages off. There was an IV alongside Rachel's bed with an anesthetic tube and needle inserted into the top of her hand. Turning restlessly, Rachel pulled on her sheets. The mattress was uncomfortable and the linen was stiff and cheap. At home Rachel had luxurious satin sheets.

There was another bed in the room. Although half-obscured by a partially drawn curtain, Rachel could see it was unoccupied. There also was a reclining chair next to each bed. A medium-sized TV hung on a bracket attached to the wall up near the ceiling.

Rachel noted a remote controller for the TV, on a cord between the twin hospital beds. She switched the TV on to see if it was working, but then immediately back off when a sportscaster appeared on the screen. Rachel raised the inclination of her bed until she was half sitting. She eyed the telephone thoughtfully.

Rachel knew she should call the office, but felt reluctant. Who could she trust? Besides, she felt tired right now, maybe after she slept a bit longer, maybe then she would call in.

Wondering if Ostermann and the others had followed them to the hospital, Rachel lowered the back of her bed into the full reclining position. Of course Ostermann's team had followed them but why had no one been up to see her? Perhaps they were just being discrete. Rachel hoped Eddie Sanders reported her suspicions to Newby concerning Ostermann.

She debated the odds of John and Gwen Hughes having escaped with the documents. John was such a nice man, it was a shame he was in such trouble. She liked John. The antagonism Gwen had openly displayed toward her in the mountains was distressing though. The cadet had even called her "Gyrfalcon." Somehow they knew one of her CIA operative labels, her cover had been blow, but how?

The cylinder! Suddenly Rachel remembered the small cylinder that had been the object of such mystery. Supposedly an East German defector had stashed it with those stolen Goldsmith documents. Fortunately she had lifted it out of John's pocket, but what had she done with it? Rachel tried hard to remember. She was too sleepy though.

Maybe in her own pocket, but her clothes were gone. All Rachel had for attire now was one of those strange hospital gowns that are left uncomfortably open in the back.

At that moment a doctor emerged through the doorway to Rachel's room, number 808, followed by the nurse whom Rachel had seen leaving in such haste. He looked young for a doctor, maybe not even as old as Rachel. A tall, skinny man, with bold pointed facial features.

"Good morning," the doctor greeted his patient cheerfully, while examining papers attached to a clipboard. "I am Doctor Abernathy, the one that was cutting on you last night, up on the seventh floor," he chuckled at his own joke, but his delivery was bad. Rachel, although not amused, managed a polite smile.

"How are you feeling?" Doctor Abernathy continued, thinking his rapport had now been established.

"Fine, just fine," Rachel sat up, but then closed her eyes.

"That is good. I need to ask you a few questions, for the paperwork."

"Okay," Rachel opened her eyes and looked into the doctor's face attentively.

"Let's start with your name. I don't even know your name." He grinned once more, as if that was another joke.

"I don't remember," Rachel turned away.

"You cannot remember your name?"

"No."

"Do you have insurance?"

"I don't know."

"No need to be uncooperative, Miss. You don't have head injuries, so I think we can rule out amnesia."

"I cannot remember."

"Who brought you to the hospital?"

"Friends."

Doctor Abernathy laid his pen and clipboard upon the small shelf near the head of Rachel's bed. He leaned forward confidentially, his hand resting on a lowered rail alongside her bed. "In the state of Colorado there is a law requiring doctors to file a report with the police whenever treating a patient with gunshot wounds. I removed a high caliber rifle bullet from your shoulder, Miss. This wound was old, the bullet had been in the muscle of your shoulder for at least twenty-four hours. We also found traces of morphine in you blood samples. Now, are you going to tell me who you are?"

Rachel started to lie down, stubbornly refusing Doctor Abernathy's questions, but then had a different thought. There was no reason to make this doctor angry, she was under his medical care and might need his cooperation on other matters later. Reaching instead for a control button to her bed, Rachel raised the back to the highest setting position, allowing her covers to slide onto her lap.

"Doctor," Rachel placed her hand over his. "I need your help. I was not shot in a hunting accident, it was deliberate."

"What?" Doctor Abernathy straightened up, as much surprised by her conspiratorial tone of voice as by her message. "Was someone trying to kill you?" he asked in a hushed voice.

Rachel opened her mouth to answer, but then looked the other way, a miserable expression on her face.

"Are you trying to protect someone?" the doctor's demeanor had melted to compassion.

"If I tell you who I am," Rachel stifled a sob. "Then you would know..."

"Please, calm down." Doctor Abernathy placed his other hand over Rachel's and squeezed reassuringly.

"I don't feel very good," Rachel spoke softly. "Could you help me to the bathroom?"

Rachel noticed the doctor's stare, poorly disguised, upon her shapely bare legs as he assisted her out of the bed. He walked her slowly across the room. Rachel knew her hospital gown, although not very comely, was extremely short.

When Rachel returned from the bathroom a short while later, she found the doctor waiting patiently.

"I understand how you might feel," he began, as Rachel sat back into bed. "We really must have your name if we are to help, you understand. We doctors at DGH can be quite understanding."

"It's Rachel."

"That's better," Doctor Abernathy reacted as if he had just extracted a great secret. "Rachel is it," he jotted her name upon his papers. "Now your last name?"

Rachel looked down.

"I see."

"Doctor?" she looked bewildered.

"Yes."

"Where are my things?" Rachel had the small cylinder from East Germany in mind.

"You did not have much with you, no identification, no money, and your clothes were ripped and covered with dried blood."

"My purse?" Rachel asked, intending to ease suspicion, knowing she had no purse. That was the first thing any woman would be expected to ask for though.

"I didn't see a purse."

"Where are my clothes then?"

"We did not save them, except for your shoes and socks. They are in the top of the closet here," he pointed across the small room.

"Anything else?" Rachel persisted.

"Personal possessions? Well...ah, yes, a small cylinder with a piece of paper in it."

"You opened it?"

"Yes. Just looking for identification you understand."

"May I have it?"

"Sure, it's in the closet also, but I feel perhaps you need some more rest now. I am going to give you something that will make you drowsy. It will help with the pain also."

"Thank you, doctor."

"By the way, how does your shoulder feel?"

"I do feel tired, so tired," Rachel took the opportunity to terminate their conversation.

"We'll talk later then," the doctor arose smiling. He placed a hand on Rachel's good shoulder. "You need not be afraid here. We shall take good care of you."

Rachel smiled gratefully, "Thank you, doctor."

By the time the doctor and his nurse left the room, Rachel had indeed drifted off to sleep. Many hours later though, upon awakening, the first thing on her mind was that small metal container and the contents therein.

Ignoring the buzzing in her ears, and some dizziness when she rose to her feet, Rachel slipped out of bed and staggered over to the closet. Inside, on the hat shelf, she found those oversized tennis shoes which the irritating cadet had given her, a pair of socks, and a plastic zip-lock bag containing the object of her curiosity.

Eagerly Rachel clutched the bag and stumbled back to the security of her bed. Her heart was beating rapidly. Good grief, she felt like a schoolgirl shoplifting in a local department store. Waiting till her breathing slowed to normal, Rachel lay with her prize held tightly between her fingers, hidden under the covers.

Not very professional, Rachel thought. She held one hand in the air to check for steadiness. Not bad, no shaking, were she a surgeon she could have performed an operation. She was not a surgeon though, she was an intelligence officer, a spy by profession, and sometimes life or death, her own included, could hang in the balance based on the unwavering execution of her skills and training.

Carefully Rachel removed the zip-lock bag from under her covers and examined the contents. The cylinder was of East German manufacturing design, no question of that. Opening the lid, Rachel removed a small piece of paper. It had been folded and then rolled to fit inside the cylinder. Unfolding the paper, Rachel noticed the words were typewritten, not the product of a computer or word processor, another indication it was not American.

John had insisted that Russians were the ones Goldsmith had first contacted, and that those Russians were after this list. He consequently assumed Russians were responsible for the assassin who had been dogging their trail, eventually shooting Rachel in the shoulder.

Nervously Rachel glanced toward the window. That assassin, whoever he was, could still be about, and she was the one that now had his coveted list. Rachel felt naked, not from the lack of clothes, but rather from the lack of a weapon.

Patiently Rachel allowed her eyes to scan the typed words on the list. Almost immediately they focused on her own name, right there on the paper. Next to it was "Gyrfalcon," the cryptonymn Gwen had called her in the woods.

Rachel closed her eyes momentarily. What did it mean? How did her name come to be on this list? Carefully reading each name and code word, Rachel found others she knew, mostly people from her days on assignment in Berlin. The last entry on the list had no name attached, simply a cryptonymn standing by itself, "Welshman." That was a common code name for Ellis Hughes, the Baron.

Again Rachel closed her eyes. This was a list of intelligence officers associated with the Baron, there was no doubt about it.

This list was dangerous, an attack on the Baron and his friends. John thought Russians were trying to get the list, but that did not make sense. Why would Russian's care about a list like this?

No! Rachel remembered Ostermann and his taunting words in the mountains. He had implied it was the Baron who had been trying to kill them. Maybe he was the one after this list? That could not be true though, it just couldn't.

Suddenly the phone at the side of Rachel's bed rang, interrupting her thoughts. Rachel picked up the receiver after the third ring, "Hello."

"Hi, Rachel!"

"John, it's you!" Rachel's heart leapt. She was so glad to hear from him.

"I wanted to check on you, see how they are treating you." John Hughes' pleasant voice was soothing to her ears.

"I'm feeling much better. Where are you, John?"

There was a long silence. It pained Rachel that John apparently did not trust her enough to say. Rachel broke the silence before he would have to make an excuse. "John, listen to me. Don't call your uncle about the documents."

"It's too late, I already have. Why do you say that?"

"What I'm going to tell you may not make much sense, but

please do it anyway," Rachel spoke urgently. "You have got to change locations immediately, get away from the place where you called your uncle from. You must hurry!"

"Why?"

"You're in terrible danger there," Rachel's voice rose. "Don't delay, you must leave now!"

"We already have," John said, much to Rachel's relief. "What do you know about this matter?" John questioned. "What are you not telling us, Rachel? Who do you work for?"

"Does it matter?"

"Yes, it does to me."

"I work for you, John."

"Oh come off it," John sounded bitter.

Rachel was hurt, "It's true, I've crossed over to your side, John. You converted me to your cause."

John silently cursed. She was such a liar, he thought.

"John," Rachel pleaded desperately, aware that she was losing him. "Have I ever done anything to harm or betray you?"

The silence on the phone was an answer in itself.

"Have I?"

"No," John had to admit. He had never quite figured out why, if Rachel was his enemy, they had still managed to escape, and who had shot Rachel?

"I never will, John, I never will. Let me help you. You need me."

"What can you do?"

"What instructions did your uncle give?"

"None."

"None?"

"Uncle Ellis is not going to help us. He wanted his daughter back and for me to turn myself over to the police."

Rachel pondered the implications. It must be a ploy on the Baron's part, trying to throw them off track. Rachel's heart ached, she could not believe Ellis Hughes had betrayed her, and his own nephew also. The one man she had ever admitted any degree of love for was Ellis Hughes, up until now maybe.

Rachel continued, "John, don't bother contacting your uncle again. It is better this way, and he must never know your location. I believe he may be the one responsible for the assassin who was trying to kill us."

"That's ridiculous."

"There is more to this than you or I know about, John. You have got to believe me on that."

"Rachel," John said, concern in his voice once more, as when he had first called.

"Yes, John."

"Did anyone follow us to the hospital? Those men from the park. Did they...?"

"Have they harassed me here in the hospital you mean?" Rachel was touched by John's concern.

"Yes."

"I've not seen them."

"Be careful, Rachel."

"I will, John. What are you going to do now?"

"Gwen and I are going to Florida. We have got to stop the deployment of that DWARS virus somehow."

"But how? You cannot stop them alone."

Suddenly there was a rap at the door and in walked Dan Newby. Rachel was aghast, Dan Newby, in Colorado, at Denver General.

"I have to," John continued. "That evil payload cannot be allowed to deploy. I must stop the launch of that Titan IV."

Entering the room, Newby gave Rachel a friendly knowing smile, and then stood quietly by, waiting politely for Rachel to finish her conversation.

"Listen, John," Rachel started, but suddenly remembered the list she had left out, and almost dropped the phone. Dan Newby couldn't be allowed to see that list, not with her own name on it. Glancing about frantically, Rachel discovered, with partial relief, but also with apprehension, that the paper was lying next to her far side, opposite Newby. Quickly Rachel raised her knees to obscure it more fully from his vision.

"Rachel, are you still there?" John spoke into the phone.

"Yes," Rachel cupped the phone and turned away from Newby. "John, please," she whispered. "Let me help?"

It was no good, Rachel thought. Her boss could hear everything she said.

"Where can I find you?" she asked anyway.

After a tension filled pause, John answered, "Near the pier at Cocoa Beach, in the crowd at twelve noon. Lay out on a beach towel, sunbathing or something, I'll watch for you and make contact.

Rachel felt an inordinately euphoric wave of relief. He trusted her, a heavy burden was gone. Suddenly remembering her situation though, Rachel whispered into the phone, ready now to end the conversation, "Someone is in my room."

"Good-bye, Rachel, I'll be watching for you."

"Good-bye, John," she hung up the phone, pleased beyond measure.

"Was that John Hughes?" Dan Newby asked, causing Rachel to start.

"Yes, it was," she stuttered nervously. "What are you doing here, Dan?" Under other circumstances, Rachel would have been delighted to see Dan Newby. He was one of the few people she genuinely liked.

"I flew up this morning," Newby answered, moving closer to Rachel's side. "I have to take care of my people, especially when they are injured." He smiled, looking at her congenially.

It made Rachel nervous though. If Dan got too close he would discover her list, still exposed on top of the covers on the opposite side of her legs, and he kept looking in that direction too. "Excuse me while I go to the restroom," Rachel said. She folded the covers off her legs and over the list, hiding it completely from sight.

"Of course," Newby responded and backed into the doorway to give Rachel room to climb out of bed.

Rachel rose and walked nervously toward the bathroom door. She felt a bit embarrassed as she turned her back to Dan, knowing her gown was wide open in the rear. Dan would surely turn the other way though.

Upon returning to her bed, Rachel stealthily slipped the cylinder and its list permanently out of sight as she slid under the covers. She felt confident Dan hadn't seen them.

"How is your shoulder?" Newby asked.

"Better, much better, thank you."

"So where is John Hughes now?"

"Ah, still in Denver, but didn't you know? Did Ostermann lose him?"

"Well, yes. I'll have to fill you in on some changes. Did the engineer give you any clue as to where he was headed?"

This could be a test, Rachel thought, best not to lie. "He did say they were going to Florida."

"Good, and he still thinks you are on his side," Newby concluded.

Rachel felt a pang of guilt. Was she on John's side? She had just managed to convince him that she was. Rachel decided not to tell Dan about the arrangements for their planned rendezvous.

"I am afraid Ostermann is no longer with us, Rachel," Newby held his hands behind his back, unknowingly making his stomach stick out all the more. "Randy Ostermann has gone rogue, set out on his own, vowing to stop you and Hughes at all cost. I hate to tell you bad news, but Ostermann said he was going to kill you."

"Great," Rachel felt her head spinning. First assassins, sent by her old friend Ellis Hughes, and now Ostermann vowing to murder her. How could she ever hope to survive? Perhaps she had been mistaken in not trusting Dan Newby.

"If you feel up to it," Newby questioned, "why don't we go over the details of the past few days, give me a full field report."

Dan Newby was dying to ask Rachel about the list his men had planted for her to find. Had she seen it? Their entire operation hinged on that provocation. If she had not discovered it, then everything had been in vain. He dared not even hint about the list though, for if he did, Rachel would become suspicious. Newby worried, even if she had seen the list, had Ostermann blown the operation by telling her that Ellis Hughes was behind the assassin? Would she still run to the Baron? Operation Carrier Pigeon was a mess!

Rachel started at the beginning, telling of her first contact with John Hughes. She elaborated how Ostermann had actually physically injured her that day, and reviewed the entire story up until awakening that morning in the hospital.

As Rachel spoke, hope begin to swell within her breast. Perhaps Dan might believe John's story. Maybe Dan would understand John's motivation and declare him a hero rather than a traitor. With the agency's help, perhaps this DWARS virus could be stopped. In spite of her hope though, Rachel was nevertheless cautious to omit any references to the list with her name on it.

As Rachel spoke, Newby sat listening, spellbound. He liked the way Rachel's covers molded about her scantily clad body, her figure was matchless. Rachel was beyond pretty, to Newby she was flawlessly beautiful.

As Rachel finished her story, she looked at her boss expectantly. Newby rose and paced across the room, stopping to gaze out the window. He had to consider his answer very carefully. Rachel was obviously on the verge of believing this story of John Hughes', and that might not be a bad thing. The main thrust of this operation was stopping the Baron.

"So," Newby stated, "John Hughes has gone to Florida intending to stop the launch of this satellite."

"Yes, sir."

"Good, at least we know where he is headed."

"You...you don't believe him?"

"It doesn't matter whether the engineer is correct or not. Of paramount importance is recovering the stolen documents."

Newby needed an excuse to put Rachel back in the field, hope she had seen the list, and give her a chance to run for the Baron. "It looks bad for the department you know, losing the engineer like that, not recovering the documents. I don't blame you personally, Rachel, but the whole messy situation needs to be cleaned up. I shall send men to Florida to try and pick up the engineer; but in case we cannot, I also want you to head for Florida as soon as you are released from the hospital. You know the man's habits, find him if you can, and get those documents back."

Rachel was sorely disappointed. "Yes, sir," she responded glumly.

"I'll have a guard posted for your protection, no need to worry about assassins or Ostermann, we will see to that. Tonight we shall also change hospitals as a precaution."

"Thank you, Dan."

"I guess Ostermann has lost all control," Newby continued. "The men told me he was saying a lot of wild things, things that make no sense at all." Newby was hoping to discredit Ostermann and minimize any damage from statements revealing the Baron's complicity with the assassin. "I'm not putting any stock in anything Ostermann said," Newby concluded. He noticed Rachel's eyes starting to droop.

"Are you sleepy?" Newby asked.

"Sorry," Rachel sat up. "They gave me a sedative."

"I'll be going then. You are safe here, Rachel."

50

For Rachel Maris the next couple of days passed in a haze of frustrated hospital confinement and drug assisted sleep. Rachel's body fought to recover from the wound of a rifle powered projectile tearing into the flesh of her soft shoulder, the subsequent operation, and a deep-set angry infection. Sleep was Rachel's only relief from the long marching hours of inactivity. Slowly but steadily her strength returned.

Rachel liked the stupor of thought and gentle dreaminess induced by the painkillers Doctor Abernathy was so kind to provide. She had an affinity for drugs, Rachel knew that. She could easily have become a junkie, had circumstances been slightly different, or temptations more readily available during her teen years. As it was, she occasionally took sickness as an excuse for excessive use of prescription medication.

Now at the Presbyterian Denver Hospital, she could easily justify the need for drugs especially to Doctor Abernathy. He had become very cooperative ever since the CIA sent someone to have a short chat with the good doctor, cutting off any improper questions. Readily agreeable to the need for secrecy, Doctor Abernathy had become Rachel's friend, spending time with her, making life more bearable. Even when Newby had Rachel moved to PDH off 19th Avenue, he had insisted upon continuing as her personal physician. She had a much nicer room at PDH, number 1710 on the second floor of the TCU, with a window and a nice view.

Two dark unknowns still bothered Rachel though, making her otherwise peaceful rest a trial of endurance. The first was concerns about John's safety. She had to find him as soon as possible somehow. He needed her help, he needed her protection. The second concern was that bothersome list with her own name in the print. The hours Rachel spent scrutinizing and pondering those names, should she warn the Baron, he was obviously in jeopardy, or should she fear him? Was the Baron trying to kill her because of this list?

Early one evening, shortly after the sun had set, as Rachel drifted lazily between sleep and wakefulness, she was startled into full alertness by a sudden thud outside the door. Rachel sat upright in shock, as if awakening from a horrible nightmare, although she could not recall dreaming. She wasn't sure if the noise was real or a dream.

Rachel felt a drip of sweat originate under the bandages between her shoulder blades and run down the curvature of her spine, making its way along the small of her back. She shuddered involuntarily, realizing her entire body was covered with a sheen of sweat. Rachel touched a hand to her forehead, alarmed that she was radiating heat. A painful headache testified to the existence of a fever.

Another thump along the outside corridors, beyond her doorway further alarmed Rachel. Listening intently, Rachel could now discern the sounds of a struggle. The grunts and groans, the sounds of scraping against the walls and floor, it sounded like two men wrestling, she was convinced of it.

Rising quickly, Rachel paused, listening again with apprehension. The coolness of the air-conditioned room against her sweat-covered skin made Rachel shiver.

What could she do? Should she open the door and confront the danger? Rachel felt dizzy from the fever; apparently Doctor Abernathy's sedatives were wearing off. She felt a craving for more medication. The memory of that morphine in the woods lingered strongly in Rachel's mind. It would have felt so good right then.

Rachel decided against opening the door. What could she do in her weakened condition anyway? Dan Newby had said he would post guards about the hospital to protect her. Perhaps one of those guards was struggling right now to prevent the entry of some evil.

Alarmed at the thought, Rachel retreated across the room away from the closed doorway. Peering out a closed window into the dark, Rachel surveyed the environment outside. Dusk was starting to settle, but the night lights of Denver kept the area from ever becoming really dark. Looking down from the second floor she could see a parking lot, dotted with cars, stretching out in front of her until interrupted by a parking garage. Directly below her the hard asphalt of the parking lot extending right up to the emergency and ambulance entrances of the hospital.

Rachel opened her window and felt a rush of night breeze swirling in about her. The window had three vertical panes with the two sides slideable toward the middle. She could easily fit out the window, if she wanted, and then drop to the ground below. It could be done.

Hearing a frighteningly repetitive thump, thump, thump, outside her door, Rachel spun around. The image in her mind was graphic, it sounded like someone bouncing a head against the floor in rapid succession. Afterwards, there followed an eerie silence, which bothered Rachel more than anything. Someone had won, the struggle outside her doorway had concluded.

Rachel's arms hung stiffly at her side, her hands clutching the hem of her hospital gown, as she watched the doorknob slowly turn. Was this it? Would the assassin finish her now? Was she now to die? Rachel longed for one of her beloved Vipers. That was all she needed, just one simple throwing knife.

Then the door swung open, and in lunged a haggard, disheveled man, breathing heavily from his recent exertions, blood running from a cut above his left eye. Clutched in his hand was a large Colt 10mm Delta Elite automatic pistol. His homicidal eyes frantically darted about the room, locking on Rachel's shivering figure.

Sucking in her breath at the sight of him, Rachel backed up to the open window. The man's appearance was so frightening that at first she did not recognize him. With sickening dread she soon discerned his identity, it was Randy Ostermann. He looked bad, not just physically, but emotionally. The look in Ostermann's eyes was that of the insane.

Seeing Rachel helpless before him, Ostermann snickered gleefully and stepped further inside, carefully shutting the door behind his back. Advancing ominously to the center of the room, no longer in any hurry, Rachel's enemy held his 10mm Colt leveled at her heaving chest.

Rachel felt like swooning, but fought the sensation. She was totally in Ostermann's control. If she lost consciousness though, she would have no chance at all. The fear had to be controlled, her knees were wobbling to the point they were actually striking together. Looking up, tears starting down her face, Rachel pleaded for her life, afraid to die. "Please," Rachel begged. Ostermann was going to kill her, she knew it. She couldn't die though, what had she done with her life? Would anyone mourn for her passing? Would John care?

"You thought you could treat me like scum, and get away with it," Ostermann croaked dryly, enjoying his moment.

Rachel took hope. He was talking. If she could only keep him talking. People did not shoot when they had something to say.

"Randy," Rachel gasped, hardly getting the words out. "What is the matter? We are partners."

"No, never, you despised me from the beginning," he sneered.

"No," Rachel pleaded. "We are fellow CIA officers. I am on you side."

"Liar," Ostermann accused, taking another step forward. He was smart enough not to get too close though. Ostermann respected Rachel's abilities, he'd had enough experience with her skills first hand.

Desperately Rachel tried flattery, "Randy, you have misjudged me, I have always admired you." She had to soothe his anger. He was on the verge of pulling the trigger, she could tell. Her words sounded so emotionless and unconvincing though.

Ostermann scowled at her, she looked pathetic, standing there shivering, clad in that white hospital gown, a scared pathetic little girl. Could this be the renowned CIA officer everyone though so highly of? She was just a girl. He did not want her admiration. "You humiliated me," Ostermann croaked.

"We were rivals," Rachel sobbed. "You were the only one man enough to be a challenge."

He appeared to hesitate.

Rachel continued. "Sure, Randy, you know the score, the others are all weaklings. I despise them, not you. You are the only real man in our department."

Ostermann had a confused look on his face.

He's not thinking straight, Rachel thought. If she could only get her hands on him. Rachel allowed her arms to drop, then crossed them in front of her, attracting his attention to her bare legs. Then she folded her arms tight against her stomach, drawing the gown in to reveal her figure and cause the hem of the gown to rise up a little higher. When Ostermann looked up at her face, Rachel tried to smile demurely. She was shaking too much though, Rachel just knew she did not appear that enticing.

Randy Ostermann was wavering though. Then they heard footsteps running down the hallway toward their door, heavy shoes slapping loudly on the tile floor.

This is it, Rachel thought. Now he'll finish me.

"What is going on!" they heard a loud voice exclaim, calling to the fallen guard Ostermann had left lying unconscious upon the floor.

Ostermann lunged toward the door and swung it open. There in the hallway was the hawk-nosed kindly Doctor Abernathy, stooping over the prone figure of Newby's disabled man. Ostermann moved to attack the doctor and kicked him violently in the side. A splitting sound, like the breaking of ribs, followed by a painful scream, filled the air.

With the Colt no longer aimed at her chest, Rachel shifted into action. Moving on instinct, she climbed into the open window behind her. Expecting at any moment to feel the shock of a bullet slugging into her exposed back, she leaped with all her might into the night air.

Rachel jumped out as far as she could, hoping to clear any curbs below. As she fell, her body picked up speed and she experienced a momentary instant of panic, almost losing her breath. Suddenly she crashed into the hard unyielding asphalt of the pavement, scraping her legs as she hit and rolled.

Even though Rachel fell, rolling onto her good side, the jarring to her injured shoulder was painful. Arresting her tumble, Rachel leapt to her feet and dodged back against the hospital wall. Sprinting for the sidewalk along High Street, she ran in a crouched position.

As Rachel reached the corner of the parking garage, she glanced back before racing around the edge. There was Ostermann, pistol in hand, looking out the window, casting his eyes about searchingly.

Rachel was safe though, and she felt exuberant. She had escaped, she had beaten him, she felt like a conqueror. The adrenaline was still pumping through her veins. Leaping back into Ostermann's view, Rachel taunted, "Over here, stupid!"

When Ostermann looked her way, Rachel gave him an obscene gesture and then dodged back past the corner.

Out of anger, Ostermann fired a futile shot at her, even though she was already out of sight. Rachel laughed and sprinted away into the dark. She would hot-wire a parked car and soon be gone. In the distance she could hear Ostermann, raving at the night air like a madman, cursing her obscenely and vowing an endless quest to see her dead.

Rachel laughed again, Ostermann was a fool. He was no match for her, she was the Gyrfalcon.

51

It was a crisp sunny day in Dallas, Texas. In the windowless division offices for the CIA however, the sun was not shining so brightly. Dan Newby entered the large conference room and glanced sternly around the table. All of his people were there, everyone involved with Operation Carrier Pigeon. Everyone except Rachel Maris that was, and of course Randy Ostermann, who had disappeared. Newby stood behind his seat at the head of the table. Now that they had all been fully briefed on the details of Program 88, no longer to be kept in the dark on aspects unrelated to their specific tasks, he could speak freely to them all.

Just to his right was Andrew Maconey, Newby's deputy. Good old Maconey, professional to the last, steadfastly loyal to a fault. Up until yesterday's debacle, Maconey and Ostermann had been the only ones besides Newby who were fully briefed. Maconey had been with Newby from the beginning on this one. Together they had tried valiantly to close the net on the Baron's infamous spy ring, but it had all been for naught.

Eddie Sanders was there, Jeff Murrey, Sally Jones, and all the other members of Randy Ostermann's now defunct field team. Who could have anticipated such a skilled group of trained intelligence officers failing so miserably? Why, the new recruit had been forced to assume leadership. Randy Ostermann had gone rogue, the case officer struck out on his own in an insane attempt to murder Rachel Maris, the fellow intelligence officer he was assigned to protect.

Karl Helmick was there, an older intelligence officer of German origins, who had posed as an East German defector to fool Goldsmith and Hughes and plant that ill-fated provocation list. Of course, there were no real East Germans or Russians involved, just Newby's abused intelligence officers.

Even Annette was there, with her long legs crossed under the table, looking as bored as ever. The secretary had to be included, since she probably knew as much or more than any of the others. Annette sure looked nice that morning, in spite of her cross attitude.

"Okay, listen up," Newby rapped on the back of his chair to gather everyone's attention. "You have all been briefed on the details of Operation Carrier Pigeon, level 88, so now I have an announcement to make."

Newby leaned over the table, then announced, "Operation Carrier Pigeon is officially dead, canceled."

Before continuing, Newby paused to gauge the expressions on his employees' faces. Those the most involved showed greatest consternation. Newby went on, "Starting henceforth, we shall no longer be pursuing any further investigations into the Baron, Ellis Hughes, or those associated with him."

"What about his organization?" Maconey protested lamely.

"Forget about them." It pained Newby to say that. "At least for now," he retrenched a bit. "We have a more immediate emergency to deal with for the present, one of our own doing." Newby paused to take his seat, angry that the Baron had beaten them, for the present anyway.

"What could be more important than the exposure of a covert society infiltrating the intelligence networks of this country?" Maconey deplored. It was unlike Maconey to react so negatively to orders, Newby thought. He was taking it hard.

"I'll tell you what," Newby expounded. "A multi-million-dollar Titan IV rocket system with a billion-dollar satellite perched on top. The stakes are high, think of the investment of national resources. I have been told that we, no the nation, cannot afford to lose this one."

Newby continued, with building emotion, "Times are continuing to change gentlemen, the game is different now. These orbiting spy satellites are now our primary source of intelligence. This one in particular is extremely important; it has to be deployed immediately."

Then Newby's voice became almost apologetic, "Before calling this meeting, I had just talked by phone with the boss, Henry Maxwell, who has been involved in a series of high-level cabinet meetings with the DCI (Director of Central Intelligence), the military chiefs of staff, the secretary of defense, and some meetings even with the president. Maxwell is under intense pressure because of us, gentlemen. They have been discussing our failure, our section, us and our operation against the Baron.

"But why the high-level attention?" a voice asked. Newby did not even pay attention as to who was questioning.

"Nothing must threaten that rocket and its precious little satellite," Newby answered. "No matter how remote the danger, any perceived threat is a matter of national emergency. We have manipulated and driven a man into considering the unthinkable, sabotage of the Titan IV."

"What are his odds though?" Eddie Sanders asked skeptically. "I presume you mean the engineer, John Hughes."

"Yes, John Hughes, the target we have been playing our games with. The man we should have picked up at the start in Tulsa. The man that has somehow completely eluded us. If this were the KGB, we would all be executed for such an inept set of blunders."

"But what are his odds?" Sanders persisted.

"It does not really matter. Any probability is too grave a risk to tolerate. Our friends in the FBI give him a fair chance. Think of it, he knows the setup at the launch pad, he knows the local environment, and he is intimately familiar with the technical design of the satellite. The KGB could not hire a more perfect saboteur. He has proven himself quite resourceful in the field, he is motivated, and he has skilled friends."

"You mean…Rachel Maris?"

"Yes, one of our own."

"But what is Hughes after?"

"Well, from the best I can determine, the man learned of some new type of weapon onboard the spy satellite, an experiment or something. He objects morally and feels partially responsible. He's determined to stop the launch."

“What type of weapon?” Sanders questioned.

Newby stared at the junior intelligence officer, “Does it really matter?”

“I guess not.”

“How could Rachel Maris fall in with such a madman?” Sally Jones exclaimed.

“Do you blame her? Rachel surely knows by now that we tried to set her up. She probably feels betrayed, and justifiably so.”

Maconey interrupted, defending their actions, “Let’s not forget about Rachel’s duplicity in this. She is one of the Baron’s moles.”

“Forget the Baron,” Newby whispered. “We’ve got to find Hughes, and we have got to do it quick, before he can jeopardize the Titan launch. Henry Maxwell is taking personal heat from the highest levels for authorizing Operation Carrier Pigeon. We must salvage what face we can by capturing the engineer.”

Newby nodded to Maconey, who proceeded to unroll a large detailed map of the eastern coastal area of central Florida. Stretching out a pointer, Maconey begin. “This is Cape Canaveral Air Force Station, just east of NASA Kennedy Space Center. In seventy days the Titan IV rocket is scheduled to launch on the morning of August 31 from here,” he slapped the map at the location of Launch Pad 55.

“We can assume John Hughes is already in the area or else enroute. He has been missing four days since our last sighting. He is accompanied by an Air Force Academy cadet, his cousin Gwen Hughes. We can also assume Rachel Maris is heading in that direction. Yesterday she disappeared from the Presbyterian Hospital in Denver where she was receiving treatment for wounds sustained from an unknown sniper in Rocky Mountains National Park.”

“All right, gentlemen,” Newby spoke, once Maconey was finished. “We have limited manpower, so, effective immediately, we are all dedicated one hundred percent to this effort. We are expected to cooperate fully with the teams being deployed by the FBI, the DIA, and also other departments with the agency.

“However!” Newby’s voice rose hoarsely. “I want us to be the ones to nab John Hughes! Now, let’s have some ideas.”

52

Monday, July 2 at Cape Canaveral AFS, on a hot steamy Florida day at a runway guarded by armed military police, a large military transport aircraft landed carrying a precious cargo. That cargo, tucked securely within the cavernous body of the large airplane, was intricately delicate and insanely expensive. More valuable than the air force plane which carried it, the production, development, and building of that single piece of cargo had in fact cost the American taxpayers more dollars than a squadron of large cargo planes.

It was a classified SIGS satellite, SIGS-4, built by Krang Enterprises. Some satellite designers and engineers at KE had spent their entire careers developing and overseeing this one all-important project. Now the moment of truth was fast approaching, but first the precious satellite had to be delivered to the care of the launch base personnel at CCAFS.

On hand to witness the arrival of the military air transport was a contingent of military security police and aircraft servicing personnel. Also there were Captain Alexander Hamilton II, Technical Sergeant Ramon Garcia, and an ugly old alligator named George. Any unauthorized visitors, other than the alligators, would be warned off by a flashing red light on Skid Strip Road and by armed military SPs.

The covert arrival of a classified cargo was handled a little differently from typical operations. Once the behemoth airplane had landed and taxied into position, it seemed to sit as if paralyzed. There was no air force loadmaster with his MAC (Military Airlift Command) crew immediately busy removing cargo as one might expect. There was no satellite transporter in sight to greet the delivery of a new satellite at the launch base.

All operations for this cargo would wait till nightfall and the cover of darkness. It wasn't that security was concerned about snooping spies hiding in the bushes. Times had changed, the spies to worry about orbited thousands of miles above the Earth, Russian optical spy satellites.

Captain Hamilton took great satisfaction in watching the large military aircraft arrive. He knew what was inside; SIGS-4 was finally there.

Only George seemed particularly unimpressed. George had seen them come and go over the years. The security guards changed, the air force crews changed, the CCAFS project engineers changed, but George was always there.

George had been lying out on the grassy banks earlier that day, soaking up the rays of the early morning sun. The heat of noonday and the sudden influx of visitors had disturbed his slumbers though, driving him back into the nearly stagnant waters of his swampy drainage-ditch home.

George was a particularly large and fat alligator. He lived there in the drainage canal that flowed under Skid Strip Road by the guard post. His presence was well known by the local contractors and security police. George had frequent guests himself, humans out on noon-hour lunch walks, people stopping by to visit on an almost daily basis. Occasionally a portion of the onlooker's lunch made its way off the bridge, into the waters, and eventually into George's stomach.

Of course, all was not always pleasant. A large scar ran across George's face near one eye, a gift from a visitor who threw a jagged piece of tin at George one day, meanly trying to make the lazy alligator move. On some occasions visitors just happened to be carrying entire raw chickens, George liked those. It was illegal to feed wild alligators in Florida, but George seemed to have little trouble finding ample food there by the landing strip. In addition to the lunch-time visitors, his best friends, the security police, sometimes gave George the accidental road kills from on base, sometimes even full-sized deer.

George closed his eyes, snoozing lazily. Floating contentedly in the water, the reptile's eyes and the tip of his nostrils were all that protruded above the surface of the algae-covered stagnant pool. It was hot out for people, but George was comfortable. The arrival of a military transport and its expensive satellite did not excite him. They would soon be gone. George would still be there though, he would outlast them all.

"Well, Sergeant," Captain Hamilton began. "Now our work will begin in earnest."

"Yes sir, I hope things go as well as they did with the adapter."

The spacecraft adapter was a flexible but sturdy supporting structure, placed on top of the Centaur upper-stage, to which the satellite could be mated. It had arrived at CCAFS fifteen days earlier and had already been taken out to the launch pad. Prior to that, the Centaur had been lifted and mated to the top of the Titan core. With the adapter now securely bolted to the top of the Centaur, they were ready to receive the satellite, a new generation spy satellite, a replacement for the nation's failing ears in the sky.

"It is good to see old Spooky here at last," Garcia remarked jokingly.

"Spooky, what the devil are you talking about?" Captain Hamilton did not appreciate the wisecrack.

"Spooky," Garcia repeated. "That is what they call this satellite." Captain Hamilton was so predictable, so easy to irritate.

"That is what *who* calls the satellite?"

"People up at the Blue Cube, CSTC, the Consolidated Space Test Center, where the satellite controllers are."

"I don't believe it," Hamilton turned slightly red. It was an affront to think of such foolishness.

"Sure," Garcia goaded him further. "The one that just failed was named Siggie. The other two are called Shelley and Sindy. This one is Spooky. I know, I have a cousin there."

Alexander Hamilton ignored his assistant. It was not amusing how freely "almost classified" information floated about.

Garcia continued, "They are calling this one Spooky because they don't trust it, don't think it's going to work. I've heard that this is the first military satellite this new defense contractor has ever built, and their civilian space ventures haven't a good track record for success."

"Let's go," Captain Hamilton interrupted. "Nothing more is going to happen here for a while."

"Going home for some sleep before tonight?" Garcia asked, knowing that they would be up all night monitoring the off-loading and transportation operations.

"Can't, we have too much work to catch up on. Let's head back to the office."

Later, after dusk, the CCAFS satellite transporter appeared at the landing strip and off-loading operations began. Captain Hamilton and Sergeant Garcia were there to watch the proceedings, which proved excruciatingly slow and meticulous, as in all such delicate operations. Although dark outside, the entire area was lit with floodlights to the point of being as bright as day. That was okay with security, ground lighting did not reveal anything to orbiting optical satellites, which were capable of providing useful data only in the daylight.

Off-loading of the satellite onto the transporter expended the majority of the night. As evening expired, the satellite, still in its shipping container, had to be taken to a large hangar where it would be parked out of sight for the upcoming day.

Once the sun set for the following night, operations would resume and the satellite would complete its journey to LP-55, safely under the cover of darkness once more. Before long SIGS-4 would be lifted and mated to the Titan IV stack. Soon Spooky would be ready for the journey to its new home in deep space.

53

Endurance—one sometimes wonders how much true enduring they are capable of. Around children, patience often wears thin extremely quickly, strained and broken in a instant, but what about solitary confinement, the opposite type of strain, with absolutely no human contact? Add to the isolation a lack of outside communication, telephone, radio, or even television, and a removal of familiar environments, sights, smells, and sounds, and you have a real test of endurance.

It was just such a predicament into which Eleanor Hughes found herself innocently thrust. As the hours and days passed, five entire days and nights, Eleanor endured her suffering in the silence of total solitary isolation. She was alone, and in the process of her trial, discovered within herself a strength and power she never dreamed existed. While others might have broken and lost control in such madness, Eleanor grew stronger.

Left in the basement, handcuffed to a copper pipe, nothing within reach except a raw aging concrete wall and the rusty pipes of an ancient shower, nothing to sleep on except the cold cement of the basement floor, no light, no company, nothing, Eleanor endured.

After her initial wave of panic had subsided, after she realized she was unharmed, after she learned the mental self-control to fight back the occasional attacks of despair or self-pity, Eleanor internalized her situation and resolved to accept it, knowing it would not last forever.

Over the days a steel-like resolve grew firm within Eleanor's soul. She would not beg for mercy. She would not ask for relief. When her captors brought meals, Eleanor would cover her eyes to protect them from the sudden flood of light, and then proudly leave them covered until her enemies had left and the lights were again extinguished. She would not speak to them. She would not give them the satisfaction of seeing her acknowledge their presence or beg for deliverance.

Eleanor proved herself over those days, learning who she really was, and she liked what she found. Eleanor came to realize she was no average or ordinary person, she was someone strong.

She could wait for the moment when freedom would come, it was inconceivable that the law would allow such treatment of one of its citizens indefinitely. Then, knowing she had beaten them, she could hold her head high. They could not break Eleanor Hughes, and she would proudly look that Blinkerson animal straight in the eye, for Eleanor Hughes no longer feared the woman.

As inevitable as the rising of the sun, the day of her release finally did arrive. When lights flooded the basement again, Eleanor covered her eyes as usual, somehow knowing it was to be different this time. Eleanor counted two sets of footsteps walking down the stairs, but still she did not look. They halted beside her, but there was no sound of plates or silverware being placed on the concrete, and still Eleanor did not look.

Eleanor felt hands on her feet, as her captors unlocked the manacles binding her a prisoner. At last, her ordeal was over, at last, she had survived, she had won. Slowly lowering her hands from over her eyes, Eleanor blinked, adjusting to the light.

"Get up, sweetie," Blinkerson mocked, as unkind as ever.

Eleanor struggled to her feet. Officer Pastorelli offered her a hand, but she refused it. Once standing, Eleanor stared at the two policewomen with increased confidence. They did not look so bad anymore, the truth was, they even looked physically smaller.

"Upstairs," Blinkerson ordered roughly, giving Eleanor a shove on the shoulder. Eleanor stepped forward eagerly, anxious to be out of the basement; when Blinkerson took Eleanor's arm to forcefully escort her up the stairs, Eleanor halted suddenly and jerked her arm out of Blinkerson's grasp. They glared at each other for a moment, then Eleanor turned to continue on.

Single file like some silent troop, they plodded up those creaking stairs and out of the basement. Eleanor exulted in her freedom. She was flush with pride and a strong deep-set feeling of accomplishment. As they led her toward the living room, Eleanor saw the reason for her release. She had a visitor, one of the detectives who had initially brought her to this safe home.

Eleanor halted, suddenly embarrassed by her appearance. She started to shrink back, but then caught herself. No, she was not going to be cowed. Standing erect, she faced the man proudly.

Dan Newby blinked his eyes, startled by the disheveled sight of Mrs. Hughes. The police officers had tried to warn him, but who would anticipate anything so outrageous? The poor woman had obviously been abused and subjected to grievous mistreatment.

Turning toward the policewomen, Dan Newby fumed with rage. They had planned for him to stage a display of anger at this time, over Mrs. Hughes' imprisonment in the basement, but now there was no need for Newby feign anger, he was truly livid. Struggling to find the control to speak, Newby sputtered, "What has been going on here? How dare the two of you treat this prisoner in such a disgraceful manner?"

Fixing his eyes on Pastorelli, Newby ordered, "Go and get some proper attire for this woman! I hold you, as the senior partner, personally responsible. You knew this woman was under my care. Now go!"

As Officer Pastorelli hurried upstairs to Eleanor Hughes' bedroom, Newby fixed probing eyes on her accomplice, Officer Blinkerson. She was a large heavy-set woman, massive in size and height. Blinkerson had her head slightly bowed, standing at ease, her weight resting mainly on one foot. Obviously she wasn't taking Newby too seriously, or else she still thought this was all part of his act. It was no joke to Newby though.

Pastorelli returned shortly with a clean dress, slip, and appropriate underclothes. Eleanor accepted them gracefully and walked stiffly away toward her bedroom. Neither of the police officers tried to follow, perhaps neither dared.

Once Eleanor was alone in her bedroom, she shut the door behind her. It was the first time she had been given such privacy without being restrained in some manner. Eleanor was in no hurry to change, let them wait. At the rear of her bedroom was a large bathroom with an old fashioned built-in tub.

Drawing the tub full of steamy hot water, Eleanor opted for a long leisurely bath before dressing. She felt a sense of control now, there was no one who dared disturb her peace. She was the one that had been mistreated, and she would have her day in court.

It was over an hour later before Eleanor emerged from her bath. She leisurely dressed, combed her hair, and descended the stairs to join her impatient captors below. No one spoke a word about her discourtesy. Newby had insisted they wait, offering Eleanor some meager time alone to compensate, in a small way, for the injustices of the past few days.

Newby rose at Eleanor's entrance. "Mrs. Hughes," he said politely.

"Yes," Eleanor responded, feeling more equal to the man, now that she was cleaned up and dressed as a human being once more.

"I have decided to move you back to the police station."

Eleanor paused as if pondering a petition. "That is not acceptable. Isn't it time you released me?"

"I am sorry, we cannot do that. Your husband is still at large. I shall arrange a private place of confinement though. Rest assured, you will not be thrown in with common criminals."

"My treatment here has been barbaric," Eleanor tried to pressure the man. "I must demand you bring me before a court of law without further delay. I want to see a lawyer, a fundamental right which has been denied me, and I would like to see a judge."

"Well...ah...technically you are not under arrest."

Eleanor was again amazed at the blatancy of this total disregard for due process. "I was arrested! I was taken to jail! And I have been illegally confined ever since!" she corrected him.

"Purely for security reasons. We could not allow you to jeopardize the federal investigation currently under way."

Eleanor was almost speechless, "Am I not to be charged?"

"No. Sorry about the inconvenience."

"Then, I can go now?"

"Not exactly. We would like to keep you under custody until your husband is apprehended."

"Absolutely not! This is unconstitutional! I demand to see a lawyer!"

"Fine, when we get back to the police station, arrangements will be made."

Eleanor could not believe the audacity of these people. How could they think to get away with unlawfully holding her in jail? This was America, a democracy. It was astonishing to think this could be happening here in Tulsa, Oklahoma. She didn't live in a dictatorship, it just didn't make sense. Eleanor had grown up thinking people's freedoms and rights were guaranteed.

Well, whatever the ordeal, Eleanor would endure it with honor. She would not beg for mercy nor ask again for her rights. However just her case might be, Eleanor would not humiliate herself.

Stiffly Eleanor accompanied Mr. Newby outside to his sedan, an official, navy blue, government furnished automobile. He courteously opened the front seat passenger door for her; but she declined, choosing instead a position in the back seat.

Newby drove through the beautiful tree-lined streets of Mapleridge and turned onto Peoria Avenue. Instead of heading north toward downtown and the police station though, he turned right, intending to drive all the way to 71st Street and the southern area of Tulsa where Mrs. Hughes lived.

"We'll stop by your house on the way," Newby spoke, trying to spark a conversation.

Eleanor did not bite though, sitting solemnly in the backseat, lost in her own sullen thoughts.

"You do want to stop by your house?" Newby raised his voice ever so slightly.

"Why?"

"I thought you might like to pick up a few personal effects: clothing, cosmetics, whatever."

"Sure," Eleanor answered glumly. Apparently the detective thought she was in for a prolonged stay at the police station.

"You know," Newby tried to sound hopeful, "once this ugly mess is all cleared up, after we apprehend your husband, then you can get back to a normal life. This inconvenience is only temporary."

"A normal life without my husband," Eleanor retorted.

"Why do you say that?" Newby tried to steer the conversation. "We'll find Mr. Hughes." Newby wanted to ask Mrs. Hughes if she had any clues as to the where her husband might have fled.

"Yes, but what then, a jail sentence for the rest of his life?"

"Well, not necessarily. There are extenuating circumstances. He may not actually be a traitor. We will find out more once we bring him in."

"I don't believe he is a traitor," Eleanor defended her husband.

"No, perhaps not. He may have been motivated by the best of intentions, although his actions were strictly illegal."

"May I speak with him?" Eleanor asked skeptically. "One phone call and I might persuade him to return."

"Well...ah...we want the stolen documents located first."

"He'll bring them back. I am sure he will. Let me talk to him, please."

"There is a problem."

"What?"

"We don't know where your husband is."

Eleanor was flabbergasted, "You lost him? I thought your undercover agents were keeping him under surveillance."

"They were," Newby shrugged, a bit embarrassed. "I don't know how to explain it, an inexcusable slip-up."

"What about the female agent that was traveling with John?" Eleanor thought it strange of this detective to be telling her all this. She was not about to complain though.

"They were separated and she lost him also. She is on his trail though. We shall find him eventually."

Eleanor was totally amazed, "Are they still in Colorado?"

That was the question Newby had been patiently waiting for. Now to plant his seed. "The last time we saw him was in Denver. He has left the state of Colorado though. We know the area where he is headed, but not the specific location. Your husband is going to Florida planning to stop the launch of that satellite built by Krang Enterprises. He might even be there now, only we cannot find him."

Eleanor was lost in thought. So John was on his way to Florida. She was familiar with the names of places where he frequently stayed on business trips. He always stayed in the Cocoa Beach area, usually at the Cape Winds or Royal Mansions Condominiums, or, if the condos were full, at the Hilton.

As they drove the southern outskirts of Tulsa along 71st Street, Newby exited right on 70th East Avenue and entered the middle-class suburban section of town where the Hughes' lived. He asked Mrs. Hughes for directions and allowed her to steer him to 74th East Avenue, where her home was located.

Eleanor strained for the first glimpse of her house. Funny how she missed home, it seemed like months since she had last been there. Suddenly nervous, Eleanor feared the house would not be there, burned down in a fire, vandalized, or something. As they rounded the bend and she saw the familiar ranch-style house, she relaxed with relief, her unfounded fears dissipating.

Newby fumbled in his pocket for a key to the front door as they proceeded up the driveway and walked onto the porch of Mrs. Hughes' home. He unlocked the front door handle and then stepped aside, allowing her to enter first. As Eleanor walked through the door into familiar surroundings, a feeling of foreignness seemed to pervade. Everything was in its place, yet seemed so lifeless. Without the presence of its family, the house was just a shell.

"I'll just be a moment," Eleanor spoke and headed for the master bedroom.

"Take your time," Newby responded. He seemed strangely relaxed and overly cooperative.

Alone in her own house, in her own bedroom, Eleanor sat on the edge of her familiar bed to think. She had to collect her thoughts. Why had Newby allowed her into the bedroom alone? There was the window she had climbed out, trying to escape that day when they had first arrested her. The screen was still off, but at least someone had shut the window.

Should she try and escape again? What was to prevent her from climbing out that same window? Was this a test? The thought was tempting, there was no one to chase her except for that overweight middle-aged detective. Eleanor noticed her purse on the dresser, right where she had last laid it. Checking the contents, she saw with relief that her money, credit cards, and identification cards, were all in place. Eleanor slung the strap onto her shoulder. She decided to change out of her dress and into jeans and tennis shoes before tackling the window again.

Suddenly a loud crash distracted Eleanor's attention. What had the detective knocked over? Rushing out into the living room, Eleanor found Dan Newby sprawled out flat on his back, a lamp and overturned end-table lying next to him. Newby's face was ashen and he was gagging for breath.

Horrified, Eleanor rushed to his side. She had been trained in CPR several years ago, but could she remember any of it? What was she to do? As she fell to her knees next to the choking man, he convulsed, clutching at his chest with both hands.

"Pocket, pocket," Newby groaned desperately. "Nitroglycerin."

He was having a heart attack. Frantically Eleanor searched through the dying man's pockets. In the front right pocket of his white shirt, she discovered a silver pill box. As Eleanor examined the box, looking for a latch, Newby reached out frantically for the box, clumsily knocking it out of her hands and onto the floor."

"Help me," he cried between spasms, "Pill."

Eleanor snatched up the box again and popped the lid open. Inside were several little tablets. "How many?" Eleanor cried.

"One," Newby rasped.

Nervously Eleanor picked out one of the minuscule pills and placed it between Newby's quivering lips. He seemed to settle down and relax almost immediately, relieved just to get his medication.

"Shall I call an ambulance?" Eleanor asked. She realized her heart was pounding rapidly itself.

Newby nodded his head in the affirmative and closed his eyes. His spasms and coughing had subsided.

Wasting no time, Eleanor hurried into the kitchen and dialed 911. She gave her address to the operator and then returned to Newby's side. He was resting more calmly now, but still breathing heavily. Eleanor considered taking the opportunity to escape, but could not bring herself to desert someone in such desperate trouble. Stepping outside the front door, she watched anxiously for the ambulance, ready to flag it down.

Exactly seven minutes later, the flashing lights of a paramedic vehicle appeared down 74th with siren wailing. Eleanor rushed into the driveway, arms waving, and within seconds the emergency medical crew was at Dan Newby's side. Checking a few vital signs, they called in to the hospital and reported his condition as stable.

Eleanor stood by in a daze as they loaded Newby onto a stretcher. It was all happening so fast. There were neighbors up and down the street watching with great curiosity.

"Do you need a ride to the hospital?" an aide asked Eleanor, startling her.

"What?"

"Would you like to ride in the ambulance with your husband?"

"Ah...no, I'll drive myself, so I have a car there."

"Could you sign this release, please? These other forms need to be filled out also, but you may do that later at the hospital." He passed several papers into Eleanor's hands. She watched as the driver hurried around to his seat and fired up the engine for a hasty departure.

As the ambulance doors closed and the vehicle sped away, making a noisy emergency exit, the heart patient inside stirred. Suddenly flinging his covers to the side, he sat bolt upright. "Is everything in place?" Newby demanded.

"Yes, sir," smiled Eddie Sanders, one of Newby's CIA intelligence officers.

"Good," Newby said. "We had better not lose this one."

Eleanor Hughes moderated her steps, slowly pacing back up the driveway and into her home. She did not want to rush and arouse further suspicion from the neighbors, especially Mrs. Riggs, who was watching all that transpired from her living room window across the street. Once inside her house, Eleanor flung the door shut and threw the deadbolt. She could not believe it, she was actually free.

Eleanor's first thought was for the cars. In the kitchen she found the keys hanging next to the phone on a pegboard, right where they had been left. Her heart pounding, Eleanor hurried over to the door leading to the garage and flung it open. Both cars were there, they were actually still there. Eleanor felt like shouting with joy.

To think, just a few hours ago she was chained up in a pitch black cellar, no, a dungeon, like a wild animal. Now she had the means to really make good her escape.

Racing into the bedroom, Eleanor pulled out some large suitcases and began hastily packing clothes for an extended trip. She was in such a hurry, she couldn't think straight.

"Calm down, calm down," Eleanor told herself. "Don't be in such a rush, no one could be looking for you yet."

She had given the ambulance drivers a fictitious name for the detective, so they would not know who he was or call his office. Of course they would search through his billfold eventually, especially when Eleanor never showed up with the paperwork. Others might be expecting Newby back at the police station, but not yet.

Besides packing clothes, bathroom articles, and cosmetics into the suitcase, Eleanor stacked up a pile of blankets, sheets, a pillow, and some towels. There was no telling how long she might be gone. Pulling a small cooler out of the closet, she noisily emptied ice trays into the cooler and then cans of pop and other foodstuff that would not need extended cooling: bread, sandwich meat, mustard, chips, cookies, anything available.

At last she was ready, but what had she forgotten? Looking at her watch, Eleanor was shocked to see she had wasted thirty minutes. She had to hurry. Once the police missed Mr. Newby, they could call a patrol car and have policemen at her home in minutes. A map, she needed maps, Eleanor thought, starting to get frantic with hurry. In the study Eleanor found an old road atlas.

Choosing the larger Chevrolet Celebrity station wagon over the economy Ford Escort, Eleanor threw her things into the back. The Celebrity was worse on gas mileage, but it was newer and a lot more reliable than the old Escort. She would not have as much worry about the Celebrity breaking down on a long road trip.

Pushing the remote controller for the garage door opener, Eleanor backed out into the driveway. As the sunlight poured into the windows of her car, she felt a sudden rush of euphoria, things were finally going her way. Pulling out onto 74th, she drove past a parked telephone service truck and headed for the freeway.

Eleanor considered striking north for Minnesota, where her parents lived, but no, it was such a sunny day. Why not go on a vacation? She had always heard Florida was a nice place to visit.

54

"Three weeks and not a clue," Dan Newby complained, as he wiped drops of sweat from his brow. It was so hot and muggy Newby felt like it was a strain just to breathe sometimes. How could anyone live in Florida with such stifling heat, anyone other than the skinny teenagers that seemed to thrive basking in the sun?

Newby stared out at the rising surf. A narrow strip of green inhospitable vegetation, sea oats and other scrubby ground plants, separated a small parking lot from the sands that bordered the relentless, rolling ocean waves. The attraction offered in tourist posters was an illusion. Beaches, sun, bikinis, water, fun, it was all there, but the view was always the same, never changing from day to day. It didn't matter which beach you visited, there was the sand, the water, and the sun, always the sun.

Filled with a sense of optimistic urgency, Newby and his people had relocated to Florida. They had fully expected the fugitives to be located within days. Their goal had been to beat the others to the prize, win back some measure of self-respect by being the team to recapture the engineer, and remove any threat to the satellite.

Now three whole weeks had passed, and nothing. Where had

the engineer gone? Had the earth opened up and swallowed him? Had he ever truly come to Florida? What an ironic joke, if he was sitting smugly in another state, laughing at their futile efforts to locate him. Why did it have to be so hot this time of year? Why did they have to be there in July? Where was John Hughes?

Newby swiped at the sweat on his forehead again. What was the use, his shirt was already soaked with growing rings of wetness under each arm. Where was Maconey, they were supposed to meet at twelve? Newby had to get out of the sun, he felt like he was going to croak.

At last a beige Grand Prix, Maconey's Avis rental car, pulled into the parking lot and circled over toward Newby's position. Opening the passenger door, Newby climbed inside and slumped into his seat, grateful for air conditioning. Good old Maconey had the fans on "Max Air," blaring away with instant comfort.

"Any luck?" Maconey asked, as they circled the parking lot back toward the street.

"Nothing, no sign of anything," Newby responded pessimistically. Every minute of the day and night they maintained a constant surveillance on Mrs. Hughes. It had seemed like such a great idea at first. If anyone might lead them to John Hughes, or have some clue as to where he might be hiding, it would be his wife.

Newby had sent half his intelligence officers directly to Florida to set up an immediate search for Hughes, while the others executed a subtle plan. Allowing Mrs. Hughes to escape from police custody, they hoped she would make a run for Florida to try and find her husband.

At first things looked promising, Mrs. Hughes drove straight for the eastern coast of central Florida, to an area called Space Coast. Newby's men had secretly attached homing devices to her car, and on the third day, they tailed her to a small city on the Atlantic Coast called Cocoa Beach. It was a good start, a place where one might expect to find her husband. Cocoa Beach was located just south of NASA's Kennedy Space Center and the air force's Cape Canaveral Air Force Station.

Mrs. Hughes seemed to have a definite destination in mind, more than just a certain city. Stopping at a gas station, she had searched through a phone book, apparently looking for a specific address. Mrs. Hughes then checked into the Cocoa Beach Hilton Hotel, right on the strip. Things did look promising. Newby had postulated that this was the hotel her husband typically stayed at when on business trips. It was a good lead and, although a thorough check-out of all registered guests did not turn up anything, Newby felt confident she had led them into a high probability area, a good central location in which to concentrate their search.

That hope proved to be fleeting though. From that day on, Mrs. Hughes settled into a disappointingly regular pattern of futile searching. She spent the morning and early afternoon hours walking the beach, and the late afternoon and dinner hours visiting the malls and shopping areas. She was obviously searching randomly, with no real idea where to find him. They kept Mrs. Hughes under constant surveillance anyway, but her value had apparently been spent. If only they had some other clues to pursue.

Dan Newby had just come from the beach himself, where a pair of his men were observing Eleanor in her daily walk. Again there was no sign of her husband.

"Care for some lunch?" Maconey asked his boss, as they stopped at the turn onto Atlantic Avenue.

"Fine with me, where would you care to go?" Newby looked particularly discouraged that day, discouraged and hot. He always looked uncomfortable though, the heat did not set will with his portly frame.

"How about Sonney's barbecue?" Maconey suggested, he loved their baby back ribs.

"Sounds good, but let's stop by the FCC (Field Command Center) first and see if Annette's received any secure messages."

As they drove along Atlantic Avenue, Newby noticed a pair of young college girls clad in scanty two-piece swimsuits. Newby realized he had gotten so hot out on the beach, that he had momentarily lost interest in girl watching. Cooling off under the air conditioner, Newby was noticing the pretty ones again. Mrs. Hughes was not bad looking herself, although she wore too modest a swimsuit, a one-piecer. Eleanor Hughes was a nice lady though, and Newby almost felt like she was a friend.

Newby's group had set up a covert Field Command Center at the Sandcastle Condominiums, just south of the Hilton where Mrs. Hughes was staying. There Annette maintained a twenty-four-hour office in room 105, a ground-floor condo. It was necessary to have a local office so Newby's people could call in with information and status reports, or to receive messages. Annette tracked the location of all members of the team at all times.

Lodging in the FCC, Annette took one of the two bedrooms for her own sleeping quarters. She set up the computers and phones in the living room, a reception office, and organized the second bedroom for meetings or as Newby's personal office. The Sandcastle was conveniently located and served their needs well. Newby's men, along with himself, took other condos in the complex for their own personal accommodations.

As they approached the door of the FCC, appearing innocent enough to the casual tourist, Newby noticed a short man in a dark suit come out, blinking at the sun. When he spotted Newby and Maconey, the man lingered by the door, apparently wanting to talk. Newby recognized him as Louis Piche, part of the FBI contingent and in charge of the coordinated search for John Hughes. The FBI had been given jurisdiction over managing the search, which was an affront to the CIA.

"We should have gone to Sonney's first," Newby muttered to Maconey. They greeted the FBI agent cordially with a shake of hands. Newby was smiling diplomatically.

"Just who I wanted to see," Piche spoke in a booming voice, loud for such a short man. The volume of Piche's greeting made Newby nervous, they were having a hard enough time maintaining a low profile there at the Sandcastle.

"Let's step inside out of the heat," Newby suggested. Entering the condo was almost a shock, Annette kept it very cool inside, almost cold, just how Newby liked it.

On the kitchen table Annette had an IBM PC with an HP laser printer and removable forty megabyte disk drive. Annette was seated at the table behind her keyboard, wearing shorts and a pastel-colored blouse. She was barefoot. Newby wondered if Annette thought this was a big vacation or something? She probably did, never having been outside the state of Texas before in her life. Newby had yet to complain about her casual dress though.

Taking the only single chair in the living room, Newby forced Piche and Maconey to take seats together on the couch.

"Any new developments?" Piche asked, in a strictly business-like manner.

"Not a thing," Newby answered in an equally businesslike tone.

"Do you still have the wife under watch?" There was a tone of contempt in his voice.

"Of course," Newby spoke briskly. "She has not led us to any new developments though."

"Just continue to maintain the surveillance."

"We intend to."

"And you will notify us of any leads."

"Of course." Newby did not bother asking if the FBI had developed any leads of their own. Information would flow up, but not necessarily lateral, not against the current of inter-agency rivalries.

After some meaningless chatter about the weather, Louis Piche finally took his leave and departed. Newby and Maconey had made no effort to cause the man to feel welcome.

"I don't like that person," Annette complained, once Piche was out the door. "I had already told him we had no new information. You know he calls daily."

"People like that tend to put a damper on cooperation," Maconey agreed.

"Uh-huh," Newby concurred. "Do not let him get us down though, at least he is not as bad as one of our own." They both knew who Newby was referring to. CIA headquarters had set up their own FCC, of which Newby's office was a branch, and the head of that effort, Alex Boruchowitz, was even more obnoxious.

It puzzled Newby the way his own boss, Henry Maxwell, had put such an abrupt halt to Operation Carrier Pigeon. It was indeed disturbing. Sure the operation had turned into an embarrassment, to lose the engineer, and now to have him endangering a vital space launch—but the need for Operation Carrier Pigeon was still there. The danger from the Baron and his covert organization had not disappeared.

Why had Henry Maxwell halted the operation so suddenly? Why the refusal to even discuss objections to his orders? Was he afraid of something, further embarrassments maybe, what? Why was Maxwell now so adamant about pursuing it no further?

55

John Hughes frowned with disapproval as his cousin Gwen approached the tent. She insisted on wearing daringly racy swimsuits. Although a one-piece suit, it was more revealing than old-fashioned two-piece bikinis. Almost coming to a point in front and back, it had no sides, leaving the hips entirely exposed. John started to reprove her, but held his words.

Gwen noticed the critical look on his face. "Don't worry," she excused herself. "We've been here what, six days now? No one has identified us yet."

"Still," John could not hold back. "Why do anything that would attract attention?"

Gwen shrugged her shoulders and disappeared into her dome tent.

John decided not to let it bother him. They could not allow the strain and tension of their situation to make them start being irritable with each other. He really had no reason to complain. Gwen was sacrificing a lot to be there, and what did it hurt if she worked on her tan at the same time? He knew how the young kids adored tans these days, and Gwen was not that old. Thus far, since reaching sunny

Florida, a day had not gone by that Gwen had not spent at least a few hours baking under the sun. At least she tried to be discrete, shunning contact with the boys on the beach and politely putting down any advances.

They had taken up camp at a Brevard County campground area called Jetty Park. John had thought it safer to avoid all the hotels and condos he typically patronized during business trips. He still wanted something close though, and Jetty Park Campgrounds seemed ideal.

Located just south of CCAFS were two small beach cities, Cocoa Beach and Cape Canaveral. Built all along the strip were luxury skyrise hotels and condominiums. The tourist trade was very good there, thanks to the combination of hot weather and the beach.

Secluded just to the north of those two cities, tucked in next to a large man-dredged canal, was Jetty Park Campgrounds. A short distance further to the north, past the Port Canaveral canal and a Trident submarine turn basin, was the air force launch base of CCAFS. John had stumbled onto the campgrounds almost by accident on a previous business trip. He had been staying at the Royal Mansions, one of the northmost condos, and had gone for a long walk up the beach. When he had run out of beach, John had cut inland and there it was, a county park with a small overnight campground for tourists.

Jetty Park was an ideal place in which to take refuge—secluded, off the normal highways, not appearing on most maps, and isolated. Who would ever think to look for them there? People were always coming and going at Jetty Park, it was a place where strangers would not draw attention. They chose a campsite to the rear of the campgrounds, away from the beach, a dark shady area reserved for tent campers only. No one had to walk by their campsite on the way to the beach or the restrooms. Of course, a pretty young girl like Gwen would naturally attract some attention, just by her mere presence, but she did take precautions.

Gwen soon emerged from her tent wearing a pair of white shorts and a sleeveless T-shirt with a smiling green alligator on the front.

"Look, Gwen," John apologized, "I did not mean to criticize."

"It's okay," Gwen smiled. She did not take offense easily.

"It's time for me to leave for work," John glanced at his wristwatch. "Do you want the car?"

Their drive from Denver to Florida had completely exhausted

John's petty cash. Taking a northeasterly route, they had first headed to Chicago and exchanged cars, buying a fairly new Celebrity station wagon with only 20,000 miles on it. Finding a wooded area outside of town where frequent illegal dumping took place, they ditched their stolen vehicle.

While in Chicago they had taken pains to disguise their identities. Gwen tried dying her hair brunette and also bought a couple of wigs for varying appearances. John decided to grow a beard and also bought some wigs. Stocking their station wagon with provisions, including clothing, tents, and camping gear, took all the remainder of John's stolen funds.

Gwen was willing to donate her savings account to the cause. She was young and felt no commitments or responsibilities. Nevertheless, John insisted she allow him to repay her at a later date, otherwise he could never have felt right about taking his cousin's money. Transferring all of her savings into her checking account, Gwen withdrew the full amount. They knew this might leave a trail for the FBI, but did not plan to stay in Chicago long.

It had surprised John to learn how much money Gwen had saved, almost four thousand dollars. As a cadet at the Air Force Academy she had no expenses for tuition, books, dorms, food, uniforms, anything. Besides that, she received a salary equivalent to one-half the base pay of a second lieutenant. It was not a bad deal for a college student working on a degree.

Leaving Chicago, they drove east to Washington D.C. along a northerly route through New York State. They had thought to blend in with the crowd and planned a route with high volumes of traffic. Throughout the journey they picked motels off the main highways, always checking in at least an hour apart and taking separate rooms. On the road they either ate their meals in the car, or else at separate tables, and sometimes even different restaurants. It became kind of a game for them, and Gwen especially enjoyed the intrigue.

By the time they reached central Florida, four weeks had passed. Knowing the scheduled launch date for the SIGS satellite, John had planned their arrival in plenty of time to do what needed to be done. They still had approximately two weeks until the ideal time in the launch flow for gaining access to the satellite.

John took a job working in the kitchen at a nearby restaurant called Captain Ed's. With Gwen's funds also beginning to dry up, they had both been forced into the necessity of working. Gwen was employed part-time as a waitress, during the lunch hour, at a different restaurant called the Sailors Choice. *Florida Today*, the local newspaper, had been filled with an abundance of ads offering work opportunities, mostly part-time jobs in support of the tourist industry, with many positions at hotels, condos, curio stores, and restaurants. John had even managed to find a position at a seafood establishment within walking distance.

"I think I'll stay home, sit in the shade, and read," Gwen responded to John's question. "You can take the car." She knew her cousin would prefer driving over walking, especially in this stifling mid-summer heat.

"Fine. By the way, did you ask for the day off tomorrow? Rachel was down by the pier again today."

Gwen stiffened, not particularly receptive to what her cousin was planning. "No," Gwen muttered, "but I can call in sick, if need be. Do we really want her help, John?"

"I think so. We really could use her."

"Can we trust her though?" Gwen hated the thought. She had not forgotten how easily Rachel Maris had manipulated her cousin in the past.

"Every day she comes to the beach and sunbathes, all according to my directions. She is always alone, no signs of anyone watching."

"That doesn't really mean much."

"No, you're right, but look, she wants to help. We have been over this before, how else can the plan work? We need three people. Besides, if Rachel had wanted to turn us in, she had plenty of opportunities in the Rockies. I believe her, she wants to help."

Gwen muttered something inaudible under her breath. John could tell she was not going to argue any further though. "You take the car and I'll walk," John suggested. "I think it would be wise if you picked up a new wig and another set of clothes. Tomorrow we will contact Rachel, and don't worry."

• • •

"How I hate this," Rachel Maris complained to herself, as she lay out in the hot blistering sun at twelve noon, sunbathing on a sandy beach next to the Cocoa Beach Pier.

Rachel was an indoor person and, although the warmth felt pleasant at times, and her skin was turning a rich mahogany tan, she much preferred being shielded from the weather. Rachel hated being hot, or cold for that matter. A controlled, comfortable, air-conditioned environment would be so much more civilized and enjoyable than lying out in the sun like a savage, with nothing against her skin other than a beach towel and dirty sand all about.

Rachel glanced at her wristwatch, a dainty gold-plated time piece she had received as a gift from an acquaintance in Greece. The watch was propped up on Rachel's beach bag, she had taken it off so as to not leave a tan line. She hated tan lines, that was why she wore a swimsuit that was hardly more than strings and a few attached pieces of cloth. Another half hour and she could go in, Rachel sighed. She glanced disapprovingly at her arm, turning it around to examine the skin from all sides. The sunlight was drying her skin out unbelievably. Producing a bottle of ointment from her beach bag, Rachel begin smearing additional oil over her sweat-glistening skin. She ignored the glances and stares of the males lying nearby.

John had done one thing right, Rachel Maris thought. He had chosen a nicely crowded area for a rendezvous point. Obedient to his instructions, Rachel came to this beach, just to the south of the Cocoa Beach Pier, and lay in the sun each day. He had said to be there at twelve o'clock, so she laid out, as close to the same spot as possible each time, for thirty minutes before and thirty minutes after.

Although Rachel had disguised her appearance somewhat by dying her hair a light blond color and cutting it short in a Dutch-boy style, lightening her eyebrows, and wearing blue contact lenses, she was confident John would still recognize her, if he came. To make herself easier to spot, she wore the same string bikini she had bought at the Embassy Suites in Colorado Springs. It was daringly skimpy to be wearing outside, but did not seem unusual or out of place on the beaches in Florida.

For weeks Rachel had been sick with worry that John Hughes would fail to contact her. He had said on the phone to meet him there, but would he really come? Yesterday Rachel had been much relieved to spot him up on the pier. Watching out of her peripheral vision, Rachel had discovered John, and she knew he had seen her too, for he was staring. Although John didn't make contact that day, or the next, she no longer worried. John was just being cautious—perhaps today or perhaps tomorrow.

Rachel thought back, to that moment when she had first noticed John's presence on the pier. At the time her reaction to the sight of him had disturbed her greatly, to find her heart suddenly beating rapidly within her chest and her breathing unexplainably labored. What had been the matter with her? She had never reacted that way to a man before. Who was John Hughes anyway? He was nothing. John was not even that handsome, just slightly better than average.

Rolling over onto her stomach (it was Rachel's habit to turn over every fifteen minutes), she reached behind her back and undid the strings to the top piece of her swimsuit, allowing the straps to fall along her side. If she had to cook in the sun, at least she would have a smooth unbroken tan all the way down her back. Rachel was already seeing good tanning results. She refused to wear suntan lotion, just expensive body oils.

Suddenly Rachel was distracted by a young girl, perhaps fourteen or fifteen, maybe even younger, walking in her direction. She had caught Rachel's eye because her line of travel would pass right over Rachel, and the child did not seem to be paying attention. Rachel hated the thought of having sand kicked on her if the girl passed too close. The young teenager's hair was braided in pigtails and she wore a pastel-colored child's one-piece swimsuit with a frilly short skirt. She also sported gaudy florescent pink sunglasses and carried a large beach bag.

As the young girl swerved to pass behind Rachel's feet, she stopped for a moment, stooping to brush the sand off her sandals. When she did so, the teenager discretely opened her hand, exposing to Rachel's view a small piece of paper, tucked securely in her palm. Dropping it on the sand, the girl then stepped on the paper and stood up. Twisting her foot as she rose, the girl buried that piece of paper into the sand and then walked away.

It was obvious that she was trying to pass Rachel a note, yet Rachel made no effort to retrieve it, nor showed any signs of recognition. Rachel did not know the girl, but if she was trying to be that secretive, then it was wise not to give her away.

When the fifteen minutes on her stomach had expired, Rachel refastened her top piece and rolled over onto her back. Still she made no effort to retrieve the note. Not until she was picking up her things to leave, did Rachel discretely brush her hand into the sand, snatch up the paper, and slip it into her beach bag, without even pausing to read the message.

If it was one thing Rachel prided herself on, it was patience. She had come to the conclusion that the young teenager had to be Gwen Hughes, although Rachel would never have known it by recognition. It had to be the cadet though, she was the right height, and who else could it be? Once safely in her rental car, Rachel examined the note. The message was short and terse, "Tomorrow at lunch, Sailors Choice."

Rachel was excited, at last she would get the chance to be with John again. She did not recognize the name Sailors Choice, but she had a day to decipher the meaning, and the fact that the first letters were capitalized meant it was probably a restaurant or bar. She would probably find it in the phone book. It was too bad she had to wait another day though. Hopefully John would not try anything stupid before she could reach him.

The next day Rachel did not go to the beach, she instead gathered up all her things and checked out of her hotel, the Holiday Inn on Merritt Island. Once Rachel found John again, she was not planning to lose him. The Sailors Choice turned out to be a restaurant, located on highway 401 just off the south entrance to CCAFS.

Strolling into the restaurant thirty minutes past twelve, it had been a bit difficult to find, Rachel noticed that most of the patrons were men. The reason was obvious, the waitresses wore tight T-shirts with mermaids on the back, and brief black shorts.

Gwen was sporting a shoulder-length, long-haired, blond wig, she was one of the waitresses at Sailors Choice. The contrast from yesterday's young teenager was most amazing. On the beach Gwen hardly looked old enough to be a teenager, now she appeared to be in her early thirties, a fully grown mature woman. Gwen seemed to have a real talent for altering appearances, not always an easy task.

When Gwen came to her table, Rachel ordered a bacon cheeseburger, fries, and a bottle of Michelob. Rachel was careful to pretend she did not know Gwen, and the cadet showed no sign of recognition either. Not until Rachel had finished her meal, a second beer, and was leaving, did anything happen. Gwen had written another note on the back of Rachel's receipt.

In her car again, Rachel read the message, "Jetty Park, snack bar roof, two hours."

All right, Rachel smiled, surely John would be there. Two hours would not be too much longer to wait. Rachel had been worried about John's welfare, but now she could watch over him again, protect him, see that he was not hurt. It would be so nice to be with John once more.

56

"There she is!" Gwen Hughes pointed toward the approaching blond-haired woman. "I told you about the bikini she was wearing at the beach yesterday, now look at the way she is dressed." Gwen remarked with disapproval, making no effort to hide the scorn in her voice.

"I know," John responded, staring down and out across the parking lot for a glimpse of Rachel Maris. John felt a sense of anticipation at the prospect of being around Rachel once more.

"Well," Gwen quipped. "Why does she dress that way?" Gwen was understandably concerned, worried that the Romanian lady had aspirations toward her cousin.

John did not think Rachel looked so bad, in fact, she appeared very stylish. He had to smile though, for all his cousin's complaining, Gwen had on quite a daring swimsuit herself. Of course, that was different.

Rachel was wearing a short pantskirt and the top half of a yellow bikini. Her hair was blond now, and she looked very much like a Norwegian.

"Up here," John called down to Rachel and waved. He and

Gwen were standing on the deck of the snack bar at Jetty Park. The flat, tar roof was designed for sunbathers. It also provided a good view of the surrounding park and nearby beach.

Rachel smiled radiantly toward John and returned his wave.

Jetty Park was a beautiful spot tucked alongside the Atlantic coast with a nice stretch of sandy beach and a modern set of public facilities. On the beach side of the park was a long boardwalk paralleling the sand. North of Jetty Park was a large channel where fishing trawlers and luxury liners frequented. To the south one could find beach homes, condominiums, and luxury hotels. The park belonged to Brevard County and was administered by the Canaveral Port Authority.

Along the beautiful boardwalk were some delightful buildings consisting of a snack bar, restrooms and showers, a bait and tackle shop, and the exposed rooftop sunning area. Further inland was a small parking lot, a playground picnic area, and the campgrounds. It was an ideal area for tourists, a relaxing peaceful little park hidden away just below the nation's space launch centers.

As Rachel joined her friends on the roof, John had nervously half-expected her to embrace him. That would have been more Rachel's style, but instead she stood off a bit, not allowing their eyes to connect, acting strangely shy.

"I'm glad you came, Rachel," John greeted her.

Rachel smiled nervously, still glancing downward.

"How is your shoulder?" John asked.

"Oh, much better," Rachel felt so awkward it was embarrassing. What was the matter with her?

"I wondered if you were coming," John remarked.

"You knew I would come," Rachel asserted, then noticed Gwen staring at her with disapproval.

Gwen was annoyed by Rachel's presence and the obvious attraction she displayed toward John. It sickened Gwen to see that Rachel woman, already trying to manipulate her cousin.

"Let's head back to our tents where we can talk in private," John suggested, noticing the tension between the two women.

As they walked through the campground toward the tent area at the rear of Jetty Park, John related to Rachel all that had transpired since their separation that dreadful night in Denver, after Rachel had been shot. Rachel's shyness was starting to leave her, and she literally hung on every word John spoke. Gwen interrupted on several instances, bringing up the name of John's wife at least three times during that brief walk.

"It sure is odd that Eleanor cannot be contacted," Gwen commented again, as they reached the two dome tents. "She seems to have totally disappeared and no one, not even Eleanor's own parents, knows where she is, or where Chrissy and Billy are either."

"I'm sure Eleanor is taking good care of Chrissy and Billy," John murmured.

"So, this is home," Rachel remarked, eyeing the two medium-sized dome tents skeptically. Rachel suppressed the urge to complain, but were they actually to sleep in tents, day after day? "They are very lovely," Rachel spoke at last, but not too convincingly.

"They will do for now, or for at least another two weeks," John responded.

"So where do I put my things?" Rachel asked. "I checked out of the Holiday Inn, my luggage is in the car."

John seemed totally perplexed by the question, the dumbest expression appearing on his face. They only had two tents, should they buy a third?

"Oh, you can sleep with me," Gwen said with disgust, turned off by the look on John's face and by the thought of sharing a tent with that woman.

"Great," Rachel responded, "and I must say one thing, you two have done an excellent job of keeping out of sight. This hiding place is perfect, and Gwen has the most wonderful disguises. By the way John, I like a man with a beard, although you do need to get it trimmed. A neat well-manicured beard is an asset to any masculine face, but if you don't trim it, you look shaggy and unkempt."

John wondered if it would be possible to continue in hiding, now that Rachel was living with them—one man and two beautiful women, especially one as gorgeous as Rachel. Every person in the campground was sure to notice her. He could tell Gwen was not at all happy about the prospects. Still, Rachel was such an interesting person to have about.

"Well," Rachel placed a hand on John's shoulder, drawing close. "What now? How are we going to stop this DWARS thing-a-ma-jig?"

"Well, ah..." John fumbled for words. "The hard part is getting up on the launch tower, alone with the satellite."

John noticed Gwen scowling at him. She did not seem to like the thought of him giving their plans away. Apparently Gwen still did not trust Rachel. She had originally been sent to trap him, and that list they found did indicate Rachel might even be a spy for some foreign intelligence network. John did not care, she had proven herself by not betraying them in the Rockies.

"Suppose you do get access to the satellite and sabotage something?" Rachel asked earnestly. "Won't they simply delay the launch until it can be fixed?"

"There is the possibility I can disconnect some vital function that won't be discovered till they try to launch it."

"Sounds risky, trying to get into the launch pad and up on the rocket."

"Not really, I have been up there many times before."

Rachel shuddered and moved closer yet toward John. "Can you really get in there?"

57

Tuesday evening, almost midnight, July 3 at Cape Canaveral AFS, Captain Alexander Hamilton II stood on the asphalt pad deck of Launch Pad 55 at the base of a looming tower, the place of final processing and launch for Titan IV rockets.

Captain Hamilton strained to catch a glimpse of the approaching spacecraft transporter. This was an important day, within hours they would take receipt of the precious SIGS satellite, to be stored snugly atop the Titan rocket, perched safely out of harm's way like the fragile egg of an eagle secreted high in a cliff-top nest.

Noticing a film of sweat on his forehead, Captain Hamilton drew a handkerchief from his pocket and wiped the moisture from his brow. It was hot and muggy that evening with no trace of the typical Florida coastal breeze. Acting out of habit, since he already had his handkerchief out, Captain Hamilton also stooped to wipe the dust from his shoes. He took satisfaction in the black, billiard-ball shine on the tips of his shoes. Even in the night he could see his reflection.

While the majority of eastern Florida slept, life at LP-55 was swarming with activity. Although it was a dark night outside, the launch tower and surrounding grounds were lit up like an outdoor baseball field. It gave one the feeling of being in a dream, an artificial environment, distantly surrounded by the nighttime darkness of reality.

Things were transpiring at the launch pad, events were rolling by with a momentum almost too huge for puny mortals to grasp. At times Captain Hamilton felt insignificant. Although he had a major role in the monitoring and supervision of events, the flow of the timeline had an inertia of past planning that was like a living beast, marching inexorably toward launch.

Now the jewel was about to arrive, the prize possession for their titanic launch beast. Once delivered up by its creators, they would take the delicate satellite and mate her to their explosive rocket, soon to flee the planet and hide the gem thousands of miles away in the dark recesses of orbital space.

As the satellite transporter finally came into view, Captain Hamilton felt a twinge of nervousness in his stomach. He paced a bit to clear his head. Once they turned the satellite over to his launch processing crew, then he would be directly responsible.

"Where is Garcia?" Captain Hamilton muttered with a scowl. He had been standing there a few moments ago. Captain Hamilton had last seen his assistant flirting with that female airman, as on other all-too-frequent occasions. That petite brunette who worked with the safety office seemed to be catching Garcia's eye a lot lately. Captain Hamilton would bet money she had his attention even now.

Meanwhile the transporter rumbled up the road and through the south gate with painstaking careful slowness, its speed never exceeding ten miles per hour. The transporter cab pulled an extra-wide girdered platform, built specifically to haul large delicate satellites. Secured to the top of that platform was the spacecraft shipping container. The container resembled a black miniature barn, as tall as two men and as long as six.

"It's about time," Garcia remarked unexpectedly, causing Captain Hamilton to jump.

Ramon Garcia was now standing just behind Hamilton, the little brunette airman conspicuously at his side. They showed no obvious signs of familiarity, hand-holding and other such non-professional displays were strictly against regulations while in uniform. Indeed, they knew such actions were not the type of thing that would ever be tolerated by an officer like Captain Hamilton.

Even so, it was obvious there was more to the acquaintanceship than mere business or simple friendship, the couple stood so close together it was apparent to all.

"Where have you been?" Captain Hamilton asked briskly.

"I've been here," Ramon Garcia retorted, the question amusing him. The launch crews were working two ten-hour shifts and Garcia had been putting in more than his share of non-paid overtime trying to help monitor and track key activities.

A tremendous amount of work had been spent by air force and contractor personnel in preparing the launch pad for the fast approaching big day. All was set, the fifteen ton MST (Mobile Service Tower) crane hovered overhead in readiness and the UES (Universal Environmental Shelter) tower doors were gaping wide open. Even the winds were being surprisingly cooperative.

"You want some coffee, Ramon?" the female airman offered, surprising Captain Hamilton. Surely she was not going to leave now and miss seeing the commencement of hoisting.

"Sure, thank you," Garcia responded, and off Rita Jorgensen went, around the tower and down the hill toward the Ready Building.

There was plenty of time, the transporter had a tight U-turn maneuver to perform at the junction with the Pad Perimeter Road. From there it would back toward the launch tower along the prescribed path, clearly marked with a yellow strip on the asphalt pad deck, until halting under the lift point.

Garcia's girlfriend was back long before the tractor had completed its job. Together they watched as the huge fifteen ton crane now came into play as busy workers attached it to the shipping container sling. As the cover came off the satellite, a sense of excitement electrified the crowd of onlookers. It was their first view of the actual spacecraft, although still completely wrapped in an enormous protective bag and surrounded by an immense handling frame. Still, the sheer size of the satellite was impressive.

Pad crews scurried around the transporter connecting electrical grounding lines and air coolant ducts. The spacecraft was rotated to the vertical position and a lift sling attached. Tag lines were set up with great care, long nylon ropes extending from the spacecraft like a circus act. It was an unconventional human touch in the otherwise automated mechanical process. Ten lines in all: four ran high up the launch tower to the 250-foot level where the spacecraft would eventually mate, two others ran to level nine for stability, and four were manned at ground level. After a weather ruling on the winds, the standoff fittings and trunnion caps were removed, and the satellite was hoisted into the air.

Captain Hamilton watched the procedure with mixed emotions. At this point he was merely a spectator to the process, his job having been to ensure that all the equipment, procedures, and personnel were ready and in place. Coordinating the launch processing of this mission would be the highlight of his assignment to CCAFS. A successful launch would be just the thing to light the afterburners on his career.

The satellite was slowly raised to a height just over 250 feet and pulled into the launch tower above the top of the Titan IV stack. Perched upon the Centaur upper-stage was the spacecraft adapter, a gridwork of composite material that was developed for strength and lightness. Onto this frame the satellite would be bolted for the journey into space.

Once actual hoisting began, Captain Hamilton and Sergeant Garcia left the pad deck and entered the launch tower, climbing the east set of stairs up to the mating level, wanting to watch the actual mating from up close. Airman Jorgensen remained behind to watch from below; she was not on the access list for entry to the UES during hoisting.

The UES provided a tightly closed and controlled sterile environment for operations upon actual satellite flight hardware. As the hoisted spacecraft came within reach, technicians inside the UES began removal of the lower portions of the contamination bags. Once ready, the spacecraft was lowered the final inches and mated to the adapter. Cooling air flowed through the UES for contamination control as the massive outer doors of the tower closed to seal the environment.

That was it! Now the spacecraft was his. Captain Hamilton felt a surge of power. This was what life was all about, this was what he lived for. He was in charge now and nothing would be allowed to stand between him and the accomplishment of his destiny.

58

Andrew Maconey regarded the chief with quiet unobtrusive concern. Dan Newby seemed lost in thought. He had been suffering from the pressure lately and it showed, his distress readily evident to Maconey and the others. It was more than just their failure to complete Operation Carrier Pigeon, or their inability to locate the engineer; no, there was something deeper, eating at his mental well-being. Maconey had never seen Dan Newby so stressed and nervous before, even in life threatening situations. Operations had failed in the past, so why was Newby so devastated this time, so emotionally vexed?

"You say Maxwell is coming to meet with us, I didn't even know he was in Florida," Maconey tried continuing their last line of conversation, hoping to rouse his boss from his introspective thoughts.

"Neither did I," Newby spread his hands in an exasperated gesture. They were sitting at a Denny's restaurant, brooding over old cups of weak coffee.

Henry Maxwell was head of the CIA Western Hemisphere Division, a powerful position within the agency reporting to the deputy director of operations. He was also Dan Newby's direct line supervisor. Newby was section chief of the Southwest U.S. Special Support Office located in Dallas, Texas. More than being his boss though, Henry Maxwell was also a close associate of Dan Newby, a mentor.

Whatever brought Maxwell to Florida was beyond Newby. Men in such high positions within the agency never visited the troops out in the field. It was unusual even for a section chief of Newby's rank to be there. Was it because of the tremendous embarrassment Newby's office had caused Mr. Maxwell? Could it have something to do with Maxwell's rivalry against the Baron, each aspiring to the office of deputy director of operations?

Annette had summoned Newby and Maconey by beeper earlier that morning at 11:00 A.M. Responding via cellular car phone, they received the disconcerting news, Maxwell wanted to see the two of them, in person. Although it was now fast approaching their appointment time, and they had finished their breakfast, Newby was loathe to leave, leery of what bad news the meeting portended. Were they to be fired and sent packing back to Texas? It was a distinct possibility.

"You know," Maconey commented dryly. "Perhaps we are wasting too much time tailing Mrs. Hughes. I don't think she is going to find her husband, something would have come up by now."

Newby had to agree, but what other options did they have? They had no solid clues.

Maconey continued, "Rachel Maris said John Hughes had agreed to rendezvous with her in Florida."

"True," Newby looked at his companion hopefully, perhaps Maconey was on to an idea.

"Well, then why don't we concentrate instead on finding Rachel Maris. If we locate her, then we'll find our man."

"We have even less of an idea where Rachel Maris might be. Perhaps she did not come to Florida? Perhaps she went north to warn the Baron, like we had originally hoped?"

"Who knows?" Maconey shook his head. It was just an idea.

"I don't want to give up on Mrs. Hughes just yet; besides, where would we look?" Newby asked.

"I don't know," Maconey continued. "Leave the rest of the team working on Mrs. Hughes," he proposed. "You and I could search for Rachel. We know her the best, and we are really not doing the men much good, looking over their shoulders."

Speaking of Rachel Maris put Newby back into thought. The loss of Rachel was a disturbing matter. She must have realized they were on to her, that they knew she was a double agent and were trying to manipulate her, to use her for live bait. She must have figured it all out, Rachel Maris was too smart to be deceived for long. It was not surprising she had run at the first opportunity.

Randy Ostermann was another matter. Ostermann had been Newby's best intelligence officer, overly cocky and prideful, but no traitor. Why had he turned against them? It was true Ostermann had been fouling things up, and Newby was putting him under pressure, but that would not explain going totally rogue. The idea did not sit right with Newby.

Rachel's accusations against Ostermann were haunting. There was a ring of truth to them. She claimed Ostermann was working with the assassin, that he was trying to kill her, and that he had indeed turned traitor. Could Rachel be right? What was she trying to accomplish by casting doubt on Ostermann's loyalties? They had always assumed the assassin worked for the Baron, was that wrong? Did Ostermann work for the Baron too? He was the one that blew the cover off Operation Carrier Pigeon, shouting the truth to Rachel in a moment of unbridled rage. What was going on?

"We had better be going, it is twelve-thirty," Newby spoke reluctantly. He had to admit, hunting for Rachel Maris was something constructive to do. He was sick of waiting around for a lead to turn up.

They reached the Sandcastle Condominiums in a matter of minutes, a short jaunt across Atlantic Avenue. Entering condo 105, they found it deserted. Where was Annette? It was gross negligence on her part to leave the phones unattended. What if Maxwell had arrived early and found no one at their station?

"She must be around somewhere," Maconey voiced concern.

"Probably out by the pool," Newby grumbled, his facc flush with anger. "You stay here, I'll go check."

Stepping back out into the sun and hurrying around a corner, Newby saw her from a distance. Sure enough, Annette was indeed lying in the sun, stretched out in a lounge chair by the aqua-colored swimming pool. She was wearing a fashionable two-piece swimsuit, a pair of dark sunglasses, and a large straw hat. On the ground next to Annette was a plastic glass filled with ice tea. She looked like the picture one might find on a travel poster.

"Annette!" Newby called. What did she think this was, a vacation?

Annette sat up suddenly, blinking in the sun at her boss. "Hi, Dan," she responded in puzzlement, as he approached.

"We had better get back to the office. Maxwell will be here soon," Newby spoke curtly, trying not to say something he would regret.

Annette stood up gracefully, stretching lazy sun-baked muscles. She gathered up her towel and ice tea, not the least bit embarrassed at having her boss find her loafing out by the pool.

"What were you doing out here?" Newby finally had to ask.

Annette frowned at the question, then looked shocked as she realized why Newby was acting angry. "I am on my lunch break," she defended herself.

Then Newby noticed she did have a cordless phone under her towel. He chickened out on his plans to reprove her for leaving the office unattended. Anyway, it was not prudent to make Annette angry.

At exactly one o'clock sharp, Henry Maxwell arrived at the FCC in the Sandcastle Condominiums. He wore a long-sleeve, freshly-pressed, white shirt, dark tie, expensive slacks, and sports jacket—the typical look for a Washington businessman, unusual however for Florida, especially in the summer when even executives wore short-sleeve shirts.

"Come in, Mr. Maxwell," Newby greeted his superior. Newby's apprehension grew as he noticed Maxwell's driver had remained behind with the car. That was not standard practice.

"Good afternoon, Dan," Henry Maxwell greeted him cordially, "enjoying this sunny Florida weather?"

"No, sir, not really, we have been much too busy to take in any tourist sights." Newby felt himself starting to feel sick, he fought the beginning of an urge to vomit, and there was the sensation of clammy sweat upon his face. It was grotesquely odd how cool Mr. Maxwell looked, even in those dark hot clothes.

Maxwell retrieved one of the chairs from the kitchen table and dragged it into the living room. "Have a seat gentlemen," he gestured toward the couch.

Newby and Maconey sat as requested, sinking into the cushions of the couch, feeling uncomfortable, like school children called into the principle's office.

"Annette," Maxwell smiled crookedly, "could we be left alone for a few minutes?"

"Sure," Annette replied and rose from behind her computer CRT monitor. Newby feared for a moment that she still had her swimsuit on, and was much relieved to see she had changed into a modest summer dress.

"Take the phone," Newby spoke to Annette as she exited the front door, and then felt embarrassed when Annette glared back at him. Of course she was taking the phone.

As the door shut behind her, Maxwell's countenance became suddenly serious. "This operation has gone from bad to worse," he scowled. "I see no good way out of it now."

"No sir," Newby replied meekly. "We are still trying to locate the engineer. We do have a good lead with his wife, and feel sure he is in the area."

"I do not care about the engineer, that is not why I am here," Maxwell interrupted, and then fell silent, allowing them to wonder, allowing a little suspense to build.

"We have bigger problems," he started speaking again.

Dan Newby and Andrew Maconey remained dolefully silent, waiting for the hammer to drop.

Maxwell hesitated, "I take that back. I do care about finding that engineer. If he harms that stupid rocket we are all finished. We'll be looking for new jobs if that happens gentlemen."

"Yes sir," Newby shook his head in exaggerated agreement.

"Meanwhile," Maxwell's voice lowered. "I hear you still have feelers out investigating Ellis Hughes. Is that true?"

"Well, yes, sir, back in Dallas our research department is continuing the investigation, and our liaisons with the Office of Central Reference, and the Office of Information Services, and the Office of Personnel are..."

"I want it stopped, now!"

Newby was shocked, "But, sir, we know the covert organization exists. How can we let it alone?"

"Stop all investigations immediately! That is an order, and I want all research data boxed and filed in a secure condition. No one is to have access without my personal approval."

"Yes sir," Dan Newby was flabbergasted. He wanted to ask why, but did not dare.

"Tell me about field operations," Maxwell looked at Newby anxiously.

"Operation Carrier Pigeon has been aborted," Newby explained.

"We have all of our intelligence officers down here at the moment."

"Good," Maxwell sat back. "As far as I am concerned, it never took place. What about Maris, the suspected double agent?"

"Well…ah…yes sir, she is still in the field somewhere, hopefully with the engineer."

"Does she have the false provocation list? Is there still a chance she might run it to the Baron?"

"I could not say for sure. There is that chance," Newby was at a total loss as to what Maxwell was driving at.

"Call her back," Maxwell ordered resolutely. "Tell her the list was a phony and it was all a big mistake. Get her off the case."

"Yes sir," Newby was afraid to tell Maxwell that the operation had been blown to Rachel Maris, and she might even be actively aiding the engineer.

"Good," Maxwell pulled a dark well-used pipe from the pocket of his jacket. Slowly he filled it with tobacco and lit up. When he spoke again, it was in a more friendly tone. "Gentlemen this is important, more than important, it is vital."

"We shall take care of it, sir," Newby responded quickly.

"Good, that is what I want to hear." Maxwell rose as if to leave, prompting Newby and Maconey to struggle onto their feet also. "I know I can count on you, Dan," Maxwell extended a hand.

"Yes sir," Newby replied, as he shook hands with his boss.

Next Maxwell shook hands with Maconey, eyeing him intently for a moment, as if evaluating his worth.

Once the boss was out the door, Andrew Maconey turned to Dan Newby, "Whew, I wonder who he is trying to protect?"

Dan Newby scowled crossly, no longer feeling sick. Now he felt angry.

59

"Do you have any questions?" Rachel Maris asked Gwen Hughes, having finished a small training session on explosives.

"Nah, it seems easy enough," Gwen shook her head in the negative. Much as she disliked Rachel Maris, she had to admit, the lady knew her business. She no longer thought of Rachel as some floozy trying to get her claws into John. To think, Rachel was a CIA intelligence officer and she had them believing she was just your average mistreated cowgirl from Colorado. Now Gwen knew just how dangerous Rachel really was.

"You're positive?" Rachel queried. Explosives were so unforgiving of mistakes.

"Don't patronize me, I'm not stupid," Gwen retorted.

"Fine," Rachel began packing up her hardware. The young cadet was so touchy.

Rachel Maris had managed to lay her hands on the explosives just last week in Miami. She knew how to develop the necessary contacts, having done so before in previous assignments. Driving down the East Coast to the right neighborhoods of Miami, asking the right type of questions, eventually being steered to a Cuban source who would discretely sell her the explosives, it had not been difficult. John and Gwen had been lucky to have her along though, they would surely have gotten into trouble trying to buy explosives on their own.

Unbeknownst to her friends, Rachel had also taken the opportunity to rearm herself with a new automatic handgun, a Firestar Model 43, a small but powerful Spanish pistol from Star/Interarms that used heavy .40 Smith &Wesson ammo. Much to her delight, she had also been able to obtain several Canadian Vipers, the only throwing knife she would use, another F-S British stiletto, only a black Third Pattern design this time, and an interesting boot knife by A.G. Russell, one of her favorite knifemakers, straight from the Ozarks of Arkansas.

They would need the explosives soon enough. With the help of CIA intelligence officer Rachel Maris, and his cousin Air Force Academy cadet Gwen Hughes, John Hughes had developed a daring scheme to gain access to the SIGS satellite. The goal was simple, to get John inside the launch tower, up close to the DWARS piggyback. Once alone with the add-on payload, John knew how to fix things right.

Their first hurdle was to gain the proper access badges, an absolute necessity, without which they could not even get onto CCAFS. With the right badges they could go anywhere and John knew just the place to find some.

There was one man in particular who would have the perfect set of badges, Alfred King, a fellow employee from Krang Enterprises. As pre-launch activities got underway with the satellite, there would be large groups of KE engineers down at the launch base. Alfred King was the engineer responsible for contamination control and maintaining the proper cleanliness environment around the sensitive satellite.

He would have access to go anywhere, including the UES, the controlled environmental shelter where the satellite was located. The UES was that part of the launch tower which surrounded the satellite while perched on top of the Titan IV booster, sealing it from all outside contaminants.

Another good thing about Alfred King was his physique, not too much larger than John's own. Although the two men looked different in the face, they were approximately the same age and height. John figured he could dye his hair black and easily pass for Alfred King.

According to John's memory of the launch flow, based on the last schedule he had seen before departing KE, they had to be somewhere in the sixty-day period following arrival of the satellite and mating with the Titan stack, hopefully still prior to closeout of the payload fairing. If John's calculations were correct, they were likely nearing the end of "standalone testing."

During the standalone testing the satellite received its final checkout by the manufacturer. They had allocated fifteen days for the testing, barring time critical anomalies. Thc next set of tests was the "integrated testing" series between the satellite, the Titan, and the Centaur.

It was during integrated testing that John wanted to make his move, for afterwards came RCS propellant loading, during which access was severely limited due to the danger of hazardous operations. Shortly thereafter, the forward payload fairing would be installed around the satellite and he would be physically closed out.

John knew that Alfred King would be on hand in Florida throughout the critical periods of both standalone and integrated testing, so the only problem was how to locate the man. John began by calling the hotels and condos where KE employees typically stayed. Asking the hotel switchboard operators for Alfred King, he received a positive response on the second try. John hung up before King could answer, now he knew King's location, he was at the Hilton in Cocoa Beach.

Time was critical, so the very next day John and Rachel set out to reconnoiter the area around the Hilton. It was necessary to visually identify Alfred King, to point him out to Rachel Maris and, if possible, determine his room number. They felt fairly secure in their disguises. But one factor John and Rachel did not anticipate was the presence of someone who would recognize John no matter how clever his disguise.

• • •

Eleanor Hughes stood on the beach in the smooth wet sand of the Atlantic Ocean. She scanned toward the north and the south, visually searching for a familiar face among the mass of humanity packed along that narrow strip of sand called a beach.

Eleanor tried to determine a logical direction for her search that morning, but it really did not matter. She sighed wearily at the prospect of another fruitless day. The enormity of her task had fast become a reality, after days of disappointment. She had stupidly thought to come waltzing down to Florida and find John right away. Now Eleanor wondered if she would ever locate her husband. The task seemed hopeless.

Still, she was better off in Florida searching for John, than back in Oklahoma a prisoner of an unlawful arrest. Eleanor desperately wanted to find her husband. It was the only way to straighten out this whole mess. So she spent her days tirelessly searching the beaches and stores and restaurants of Cocoa Beach, Cape Canaveral, Merritt Island, and even Cocoa.

Walking north toward the pier this time, Eleanor felt the burning heat of the noonday sun upon her slender back and petite shoulders. For protection she had liberally applied a good portion of suntan lotion, Panama Jack SPF-15. Eleanor was always careful with her skin and had not received any sunburns. The first few nights her legs ached from walking in the sand, but they had eventually adjusted to the constant long hours of use.

Eleanor stepped along lightly, just beyond the reach of the lapping waves. The sand was more solid there and gave the firmest footing. Even so, it was extra work walking on sand and maintaining any kind of pace faster than a stroll. Eleanor wore a navy blue swimsuit with a pink strip down and across the front like a sash. She felt cute in that swimsuit, cute without being overly exposed.

When Eleanor first caught sight of John, she could scarcely believe her eyes. At a distance she could hardly make out her husband's face, but there was no mistaking that peculiar gate of his. Her first impulse was to rush forward and confirm her sighting, but luckily she restrained herself. John was not alone; he had another woman with him!

As they drew closer, Eleanor was mildly surprised to see her husband sporting a heavy beard, and he had allowed his hair to grow long. Ever since the day they were married, John had always been clean-shaven. He had on sunglasses too, but she knew it was him. There was no doubt as to his identity.

Eleanor wondered if the woman alongside John was the undercover police officer she had heard about. The woman was beautiful, a short-haired blonde with a tiny two-piece swimsuit that caused Eleanor a rush of jealousy. Her husband and that female were walking side-by-side down the beach, conversing with apparent familiarity. They sure seemed to be enjoying each other's company.

Suddenly panic set in and Eleanor felt her head starting to spin.

This was all wrong! She felt jealous and angry, she had to get away. Turning her back to them, Eleanor started retracing her steps back down the beach at a brisk pace. She was sure they hadn't seen her yet, if only she could get out of sight without being noticed.

Eleanor's head was hurting, a sharp throbbing pain that laced across her temples. She wanted to run, but that would draw attention. Glancing nervously over her shoulder, Eleanor hurried down the beach until reaching the boardwalk that led away from the sand and up to the Hilton. Climbing seven sandy wooden steps, she paused atop the boardwalk; from her vantage point she hoped to watch them pass and then thought to fall in behind and follow.

Who was that woman with John, and why was she walking so close? Could she possibly be the police officer that the detectives in Tulsa had mentioned? If so, then the police must know John's every move. Why were they playing him along like that? Worse, why was he letting that woman play him for a dupe? Was John that gullible? Eleanor was going to kill him. She was his wife, and if John needed help, why didn't he turn to her?

To her surprise, Eleanor saw they too were heading toward the Hilton, angling away from the surf directly toward the same boardwalk upon which she stood. Retreating further up the boardwalk, Eleanor entered a small patio area reserved for Hilton guests. There was a swimming pool, with sunning chairs and tables, and an outdoor bar. Across the patio was a side entrance to the Hilton, a single glass door next to a tar removal station.

Hastily Eleanor rushed into the safety of the hotel. She turned down an immediate side hallway and halted just outside the ladies restroom, a good place to hide. She wanted to keep them in sight. But what if they bypassed the side door and continued on out into the parking lot?

Eleanor would die if she lost track of John now, after searching for so many days. John needed her help, but what could she do? If she approached the couple openly, it might precipitate his arrest. Why did he have to be sporting about with that woman? John was such an idiot. It made Eleanor so angry. Carefully she slipped back down the hall, just enough to bring the doorway into view.

Eleanor thought maybe she would allow John to catch sight of her, just a glimpse to gauge his reaction, but suddenly they entered the back door to the Hilton, startling her. Without thinking, she retreated down the hallway and into the ladies room. With the door nearly shut, peering through the barely open crack, Eleanor watched them turn down the same hallway and continue in her direction.

Letting the door slide shut, Eleanor spun around to find herself in a cramped little bathroom. It had a sink with a mirror and two stalls, one of which was closed for plumbing repairs. Fortunately the stall door to the other toilet was open. Moving into the enclosure, Eleanor shut and bolted the stall door. She counted seconds, trying to figure when they would pass by, so she would know it was safe to exit.

At just the moment Eleanor figured they were passing, she heard a hand on the door handle, and in stepped the blonde. Eleanor berated herself for not locking the outer door; but then relaxed, this strange woman would not recognize her anyway.

Placing her eye up to the crack between the stall door and its supporting frame, Eleanor could see the woman's back. She was facing the mirror looking at herself, preening and fussing with her hair. Eleanor could tell the woman was quite vain; she seemed to enjoy turning her head this way and that to gaze at her own face from different angles. To think John would have anything to do with such a shallow person. And that swimsuit was scandalous; she was practically naked.

Eleanor felt a flush of anger toward John. How dare he run off cavorting with this vixen and leave her abandoned in Oklahoma to look after the children and be hassled by the police. If he was in trouble or needed help, what excuse was there not to include her? They could have solved his problems together. After all, she was his wife.

Suddenly it occurred to Eleanor that the blonde woman might be waiting for her to vacate the stall. Making some noise with the toilet paper, Eleanor flushed the toilet, paused a moment, took a deep breath, and then exited the stall. She stepped out behind the strange blonde as if desiring to use the sink. Eleanor dared not exit the restroom, John might be waiting in the hall.

The woman made no move to take Eleanor's place in the stall though, but continued grooming herself with apparent selfish unconcern. She had removed a small bottle from her beach bag and was applying some moisturizing oil to the skin of her face. Eleanor studied her from behind, noting with satisfaction that the woman was not a natural blonde. The dyed hair color did not suit her very well, either. Her skin complexion did not blend with that shade in an aesthetic manner; she would have looked much better with her natural hair color. Eleanor took great satisfaction in that observation.

Rachel Maris stood in the bathroom of the Hilton Hotel at Cocoa Beach, Florida. She was hot from a recent walk in the sun and her throat felt parched. The burning rays of the sun and the drying salt air was terrible on her skin. Besides her immediate physical discomfort, there was a strange woman behind her who was staring, and that added to Rachel's feelings of irritation. Could the odd lady be an agent or an informant of some type?

Professionally Rachel knew it was best to ignore the woman, so she hid her concern and never allowed their eyes to lock. Finishing up at the sink, Rachel removed some spare clothes from her beach bag and slipped a beige T-shirt and a matching pair of shorts over her swimsuit. She also placed a pair of latching sandals onto her feet.

John Hughes was waiting patiently for Rachel just outside the ladies room door. He too had donned a light shirt and pair of sandals. As Rachel joined him, they walked casually into the interior of the hotel. John proceeded in the direction of the front desk to inquire about Alfred King, but was halted by Rachel.

"Wait a minute," Rachel touched John's arm. "Let's not rush this. We need to assess the area a little further before speaking with anyone. Let's rest a moment." Rachel was still feeling apprehensive because of that peculiar lady in the bathroom.

Thus far they had seen no sign of Alfred King, and John was feeling impatient. How he wished for a detailed timeline of the launch flow. For all he knew they were running ahead of schedule. He had to reach the satellite at precisely the right moment, before they closed out the payload fairing.

Rachel noticed the hotel bar was open and doing a brisk noon-hour business, so she steered John to a booth near the back. While John fetched her a scotch on the rocks, Rachel surveyed the area. She saw nothing to further arouse her suspicions. John returned shortly with Rachel's drink and a lemonade for himself. It felt nice to sit in a cool air-conditioned environment with a drink to appease her thirst. Rachel nursed her scotch for longer than was necessary, purposely stalling. She could tell John was feeling impatient, but impatience could lead them into making careless mistakes.

After a rest, they approached the front desk, hoping to learn Alfred King's room number. The chances were slim that a clerk would give the information out to a strange woman alone, and even less to a single man, but a couple would allay suspicion. There were two young desk clerks on duty, both barely past their teens. Rachel approached the one young man and smiled congenially, "Good afternoon," she spoke, looking directly into his eyes.

John smiled when he noted the involuntary blush appear on the young man's face. "How may I help you?" the clerk offered.

"We were supposed to meet a friend in the lobby, but he did not show. Could you tell us what room Mr. King is in?" Rachel leaned over the counter edge.

"Of course," the clerk responded. He typed some keys on a computer terminal, and then smiled when the desired response appeared. "We have two Kings registered."

"Alfred," Rachel responded.

"Yes, Alfred King, he is in room 408."

"Thank you so much," Rachel was pleased.

John could hardly keep the grin off his face as they departed with the desired information. Rachel was good.

At that point Rachel thought it prudent that they gain a feel for the layout of the hotel, at a later date they would be back and it would be wise to know their way around. Taking one of the two elevators up to the fourth floor, they found the appropriate hallway and strolled innocently by room 408, Alfred King's room. After locating all exit stairwells, making particular note of the one that had access to the roof, they departed down the ocean-side stairs to ground level.

"We should not loiter here any longer than necessary," Rachel advised, even though they had failed to see Alfred King.

John was all too glad to comply. He felt extremely nervous sneaking around the hotel like a thief. It was amazing how calm and composed Rachel appeared.

As they exited the Hilton and stepped back out into the sun via the patio, John received the shock of his life. There she was, Eleanor, his wife, standing across the patio in stark reality. John could hardly believe his eyes. Eleanor was not in Oklahoma, she was there, in Florida, standing right before him, staring at him intently, her hands folded tightly in front, a scowl upon her features. How could it be?

Rachel noticed when John suddenly went tense and froze in his tracks. The look of shock on his face told her something terrible was wrong. Following his eyes, Rachel saw that strange woman across the way, that same peculiar lady Rachel had encountered earlier in the ladies restroom.

It had to be someone whom John knew. They had been recognized and that meant trouble. They had to get away quickly. Taking hold of John's arm, Rachel jerked him toward the boardwalk. "Who is she?" Rachel questioned, "someone from work?"

"No, it's Eleanor," John replied with total astonishment.

Rachel was shocked. Realizing the magnitude of the situation, she was appalled by their immediate danger. If John's wife was there in Florida, there could only be one explanation, it was a trap to lure them out into the open. There would be spotters around, perhaps they had already been seen!

"We have to get away from here right now," Rachel spoke urgently to John. "Your wife is surely being watched! We are in grave danger!"

"I cannot just leave her!"

"You must, we can find her again later."

"But...but...Eleanor is here," John was confused beyond rational thought.

"Come on!" Rachel demanded. She dug her nails into the skin of John's forearm as she pulled him toward the boardwalk.

John allowed himself to be tugged across the patio, but his eyes never left the face of his grieving wife. Eleanor was making no move to follow. Could it really be her? John's mind was in a daze. He could not fight the wisdom in Rachel's words or the demands of her arms. They could not risk being caught, not now. Turning with despair from his wife, he and Rachel Maris fled down the boardwalk toward the crowded beach.

As they disappeared among the mass of humanity packed along the sand, hoping they had not been identified by any of Newby's men, an oddly dressed tourist arose from his stool at the corner of the outdoor bar, next to the hotel pool. He watched the crestfallen Eleanor, as her defiant stance dissipated and her anger turned to bitter disappointment. He watched as she ran weeping back into the hotel; and he grinned.

It was Randy Ostermann and he had arrived just in time to see Rachel Maris. Too late to act, with Newby's spotters about it was too dangerous for rash moves, but that was okay, for he had seen something almost as good. This woman she was his key. He had finally found a way to reach Rachel Maris.

60

Dan Newby slumped in a poolside lounge chair, basking in the sun next to a sparkling swimming pool at the Sandcastle Condominiums. It was a brief respite from the pressures of his job, yet he could not bring himself to relax. Even when off duty, Newby could not bring himself to stray far from his FCC, even though he had a beeper and a cellular car phone. Something was bound to break soon, he could feel it.

So Newby spent his off hours hanging around his condo or lounging at the pool area. He glanced at the bulge of his extra-thirty-pound, lily white belly, and frowned. He sucked in his stomach to make his waistline thinner, if only for a moment. He was hot and uncomfortable, and did not even know why he had come out to sit by the pool. He did not even like the sun very much.

Annette liked the sun. In fact, she spent so much time lying out in the sunlight one would think she worshipped the fiery heat-giving orb. Newby glanced toward Annette, sleeping in a lounge chair flat on her stomach. Newby had seen her out by the pool from his condo window, perhaps that was what had enticed him out to get some fresh air.

As of late, Dan Newby had been bothered by feelings of failure and ominous imminent disaster. His worries ran so deep that physiological manifestations were developing, such as a deep aching in the top of his stomach. The pain had been with him ever since the hour his boss, Henry Maxwell, had arrived in Florida, personally curtailing all investigations into that sinister organization run by the Baron.

Operation Carrier Pigeon was dead, and Newby had no justifiable idea as to why. True, things had been totally botched, but was that a good reason for canceling a worthy cause? Operation Carrier Pigeon was terminated, but the need was still there, the danger still threatening, the objective still obtainable. They knew the Baron's organization existed, they had proven it statistically by the computer. The only task remaining was to expose the traitor and gain the needed proof.

The idea of planting a provocation list on Rachel Maris was logically sensible. It was a proven tactic which had been used with great success in the past. Why did Maxwell terminate the operation? He was the source of the original information that first started the investigation. Now that they knew Rachel Maris was a member of that secret combination, their one solid clue, their long awaited breakthrough, provided by Maxwell through a reliable source, how could they stop now? With that piece of knowledge, they could prove a link between her, the Baron, and the organization. Then they would have him.

Annette rose from her reclining position. She stretched lazily and then lowered herself slowly into the cool waters of the sun heated swimming pool. She looked in Newby's direction, but his eyes were shut as if sleeping. Annette swam lengthwise across the pool for a few laps, and then drew herself out of the pool via a ladder on the side, water dripping from her wet tan skin. Contentedly she returned to her place in the sun.

As Newby's mind pondered more depressingly morbid thoughts, he allowed himself to sink further into his misery. They could not find that stupid engineer. As if that was not bad enough, he had also lost his two best intelligence officers. Where was Ostermann? Did they really push him over the edge? People just did not go crazy that often, it just did not happen.

Ostermann had been wrong for the assignment from the start, and killing Goldsmith was unforgivable. Newby berated himself for not pulling Ostermann from the case immediately. Accidents of that magnitude could not be brushed over, they destroy a man on the inside. The killing of a civilian could eat away at a man's sense of purpose, take his objectivity away. Was that the beginning of the end for Ostermann? As failures mounted, tension must have built up until he could not handle the pressures anymore. Newby felt bad. He was Ostermann's boss, he should have foreseen the disaster. Ostermann was one of his children.

The coincidences were disturbing though. Things were not as they seemed, it simply did not add up. What a monumental quirk of nature, to give them a man who just happened to be the living blood nephew of the Baron. They had jumped too quickly, they had wanted the opportunity too badly. Newby was feeling sicker all the time. It was odd how Ostermann had killed Goldsmith, once John Hughes was implicated, forcing the Baron's nephew to become the central character. They had manipulated the engineer into going after the documents. Why, Newby realized, he had even arrested the man's wife so she would not talk him into giving himself up. They had been so absorbed with passing that counterfeit provocation list to Rachel, that it had blinded them to all decency.

Why had the assassin failed so miserably in his many opportunities to kill John Hughes? Judging from the field reports, almost any amateur could have succeeded in those circumstances. The assassin never intended to be successful, it was the only logical explanation. The thought made Newby shiver.

If that was true, then where else had they been deceived? Was the death of Goldsmith no accident? It made Newby feel nauseated to think that the aged Jewish aerospace engineer might have been murdered. Death was so final, it could not be undone. How do you make restitution for killing? How do you compensate for the price of a human life? Was it possible to repent of murder?

Newby rose wobbly to his feet, ready to leave. He was feeling overwhelmed. It was hot, he had to get out of the sun, he had to lie down. Perhaps he would seek out Maconey and they could take comfort in their shared misery. Maconey was a good man.

Maxwell, Maxwell, he could not get Maxwell out of his mind. Why the sudden termination of Operation Carrier Pigeon? Newby knew that Maxwell and the Baron were competing for a key promotion within the agency. With the operation halted, how could the Baron's guilt be exposed? Was the traitorous Baron now to win the influential post as DDO? Would he then grow too powerful to ever stop? Why the personal insistence by Maxwell that all investigations be terminated? What was Maxwell's true involvement with the Baron?

Newby walked alongside the pool, his shoulders stooped from tension, his head slightly bowed from deep cumbersome thoughts. He had the weight of the world on his back. He was a man who had lost everything, who had lost the war and now saw inevitable defeat descending upon all that he held dear.

Annette raised up on her elbows and watched Newby pass by and exit through a wrought-iron gate, shuffling wearily away without so much as even a glance in her direction. How strange, not to have him watching her.

61

Back at Jetty Park Campgrounds, amongst the shady trees of the tents-only area, secluded from the busy RV sites, a heated discussion took place. Although emotions ran high, discretion kept the volume of their voices low.

"We cannot just leave her there!" John proclaimed fiercely.

"Why not?" Rachel demanded, equally as intense.

"She must think I deserted her. I cannot abandon my wife like that." John knew all too well the emotional turmoil his wife would be suffering, after their chance encounter outside the Hilton Hotel earlier that day.

"No, John," Rachel turned aside, her stubborn anger masking the hurt inside. Why did she have to develop feelings toward a man who was already married? The thought of having John's wife around made Rachel feel ill. "If you want," she insisted, "we shall call the whole operation off right now. Otherwise we play it safe."

"Let's be reasonable," Gwen Hughes interjected. "I think you both need to calm down and look at this rationally. I agree with Rachel though, we cannot risk bringing Eleanor into the group."

John was stung that his cousin agreed with Rachel against him.

"It's not such a bad thing," Gwen explained. "Eleanor knows you are in trouble with the law, she knows we are being hunted by the police. I think she would understand."

"Ha," John spoke indignantly. "You don't know Eleanor, she would never understand seeing me with another woman."

"Is that what this is all about?" Rachel spun on him angrily. "You would risk our lives so your poor little wife doesn't feel jealous?"

"Don't make fun of her," John defended his wife. "You know there is more to the issue than that."

"Well I am sorry!" Rachel spoke, her voice heavy with sarcasm.

"Stop it," Gwen countered, fearful the bickering would attract attention. "Eleanor did come all the way from Oklahoma."

"Yes," John seized on the opening, "and I think she deserves better. Gwen and I risked being caught to contact you, Rachel."

"That was different," Rachel retorted. "You needed my help. Besides that, I was alone and we know for a fact your wife is being followed. Your wife is here as the bait for a trap and we all know it."

"I don't know it," John protested.

"Oh come on!" Rachel allowed no slack. "Why else would she be here? Besides, she is of no value to us. Our plans have been made, we do not need her. She would just be in the way."

"Okay," Gwen said, "we all can agree it is probably a trap. I think there is too much risk. If we blow it now, there is no one left to stop this DWARS virus from being launched."

"One phone call?" John asked lamely.

"Don't be a fool," Rachel chided, unwilling to give an inch. "You know they have her phone bugged."

"I'll keep it short so they cannot trace the call, and I'll make no mention of our whereabouts."

"Then why call at all?" Gwen questioned.

"To reassure her, to tell her not to worry."

"Oh please!" Rachel said disgustedly. "She sure must have kept you on a short leash. I'll bet you never left the house without asking her permission first."

"Stop it!" Gwen cut Rachel off.

"You cannot call," Rachel retorted. "To tip the police that we are in the area would be unforgivable. Besides, we have to go back to that same hotel to obtain King's access badges. If you call your wife, there will be so many spotters all over that hotel we will never get in."

"Then I'll go in person," John insisted defiantly. Rachel had aroused his anger and pride beyond the point of ever giving in.

"Fine, but count me out!" Rachel's eyes flared.

"Good!" John exclaimed.

"I am going back to Texas," Rachel snatched up her purse.

"Go on then, leave!" John spoke with anger.

"I'll visit you in jail some day," Rachel turned so John could not see the tears forming in her eyes.

"No wait," Gwen interrupted! "Stop it, I'll go."

They both turned to her in surprise.

Gwen shrugged her shoulders, "We cannot risk your getting caught, John. You are the only one that knows the satellite."

"But..." protested John.

"It's no big deal," Gwen spoke softly, her blue eyes firm with resolve.

"You are both fools," Rachel muttered. "Either you will lead them right back to us, or else they will arrest you on the spot."

Gwen ignored her, "Let me change my clothes and I shall go now."

"Wait, at least till tomorrow," Rachel interjected. "We can go into Titusville first and I will help you with a disguise that no one will penetrate." Then Rachel turned to John, "It can wait till tomorrow can it not?" she quipped.

Shortly after noon the next day, Gwen Hughes made her appearance at the Cocoa Beach Hilton. She had traveled from Jetty Park to the vicinity of the luxury highrise by catching a city bus down Atlantic Avenue, the congested main business artery through Cocoa Beach. A few miles north of the hotel, at the pier, Gwen had exited, walking the remaining distance down the sidewalks of town.

Gwen felt secure in her disguise. Rachel Maris had been true to her word and together they had altered Gwen's appearance to the point that even her own father would not recognize her. From a vibrant appealing young lady, Gwen had been transformed into a broken-down, aged, drunken, homeless, male street bum. Buying a wig and false beard in Titusville, they had dragged them in the sand and dirt until the hair looked stringy and matted. Her clothes they procured from a secondhand store. With a little abuse they too looked soiled and torn. It was an exceptional disguise, no one would ever suspect.

Now at the Hilton, Gwen avoided entering the hotel by the main doors, knowing her degenerate appearance would arouse a quick response. Instead Gwen circled the hotel and entered the patio pool area from the side entrance. Swaggering like she was intoxicated, Gwen steered clear of people and planted herself in a chair off to one corner.

"Just stay put and wait," Rachel had advised. "Sooner or later Eleanor will show up, if not today, then tomorrow. Don't move about or make a commotion and everyone should leave you alone. No one will want to come near you, they will avoid you like an ugly spider. If the staff confronts you, just leave and we'll try something else."

Obediently Gwen sat in that chair for over an hour, pretending to doze in a drunken stupor. When she finally caught sight of her cousin's wife, Gwen could hardly contain her excitement. Eleanor had been by the pool all along, just out of her line of view.

Okay, step one was complete, she had found Eleanor. Now for step two, observation. Not moving from her chair, Gwen carefully monitored Eleanor's every move, waiting for an opportunity to speak with her. Eleanor was making herself quite visible, apparently hoping for her husband to return, frequently pacing out onto the boardwalk to take long searching looks down the beach.

It was another hour and a half before Eleanor finally tired of waiting for her husband to appear. Restlessly she exited through a side gate into the parking lot. Gwen waited a moment and then pretended to awaken from her drunken sleep. Clumsily she staggered after Eleanor, hoping she was not being too obvious.

Passing through the pool gate, a disturbing sight greeted Gwen's eyes, a suspicious looking man speaking to Eleanor, having pulled up his car to block her path.

"I don't know," Gwen heard her cousin's wife responding negatively.

"You must come quickly," the man urged Eleanor. "John Hughes wants to see you."

The stranger in the automobile was tall and ruggedly handsome, although even a first impression portrayed an image of haughtiness and conceited pride. With alarm, Gwen recognized him, the homicidal man whom Rachel Maris had warned them to be on the lookout for, Randy Ostermann.

"Why would John send you?" Eleanor questioned in puzzlement, taking a step back.

"Well, he could not very well come himself, could he. It would be much too dangerous, people would recognize him."

Gwen's heart pounded. What should she do? How could she warn Eleanor without giving away her disguise.

"Where is John?" Eleanor asked.

"I was instructed not to tell you, but I will take you there."

"Is he hurt?" Eleanor asked, moving slowly forward.

"John Hughes is fine. He wants to see you, that is why he sent me for you." From inside the car, Ostermann pushed the passenger door open.

Gwen felt like screaming, but she couldn't, she was immobilized, paralyzed with apprehension.

As Eleanor reached the car and pulled the door fully open, starting to enter, she hesitated, "How do I know John sent you?"

"Get in, he is waiting," Ostermann beckoned to her.

"He told you nothing you might say, to let me know you are a friend?" Eleanor questioned.

"What could he say, something about work? Any fool could fabricate a convincing enough line about work."

"About work?" Eleanor straightened suspiciously.

Ostermann realized he might have made a blunder, "Aren't you an associate from Krang Enterprises?" he asked hopefully.

"I am his wife," Eleanor stifled a scream and stumbled back away from the car.

"No you don't!" Ostermann yelled. Rushing from the car, he sprang around the vehicle to grab his quarry by the wrist.

"What do you want?" Eleanor cried.

"I am looking for someone and I think you might be of help. Now get into the car!" Ostermann twisted her wrist harshly, causing pain and then fear to contort Eleanor Hughes' face.

Witnessing that act of cruelty against someone she knew and cared for spurred Gwen into instant action. Disguise or no disguise, she could not let that vicious stranger kidnap Eleanor. If Ostermann was half as bad as Rachel described him, he was a murderer or worse.

During last fall's intramural seasons back at the Air Force Academy, Gwen had played on the squadron rugby team. At the Academy all those cadets not on intercollegiate teams were required to participate in intramural sports. With three separate seasons each year, and a rule that required cadets to change sports between their first and second years, they became familiar with a multitude of team sports.

Although Ostermann was a good half foot taller than Gwen and over fifty pounds heavier, she knew how to tackle. Racing toward him at top speed, she tucked her head and dove into Ostermann, driving her shoulder into the small of his back.

Ostermann did not know what hit him. Violently slammed up against his car, he momentarily lost hold of his startled victim's wrist. Frightened as she was, to her credit, Eleanor seized the opportunity to escape. Scrambling out from under Ostermann, she broke away and bolted into a dead run.

Her assailant soon recovered his senses and started to follow, but quickly saw the futility of trying to catch the woman and then drag her back to his car kicking and screaming. The interfering street bum had slipped off. Cursing vehemently, Ostermann trotted back to his car, jumped into the vehicle, and sped away, hoping to avoid capture himself, now that Newby's men must surely be aware of his presence.

The events had taken place so quickly and suddenly that no one else had seen the episode. Onlookers were starting to gather though, their curiosity aroused by the noise and commotion. Gwen noticed Eleanor staring at her from across the way. Her disguise as a street bum had not yet been compromised, although she had to assume some of the people starting to gather were policemen assigned to watch Eleanor.

Gwen decided to try one of the scenarios she and Rachel had rehearsed. She was supposed to fall to the ground as if drunk and then, hoping Eleanor would have compassion and pause to offer assistance, speak to her. Having been told of Eleanor's kind nature by John, they felt the odds were good she would stop to aid a person in distress.

Staggering a few steps, Gwen fell to her knees as if dizzy. Immediately Eleanor rushed forward to see what was wrong, thinking the unfortunate street bum that had just saved her life was hurt.

"Eleanor, it's me," Gwen muttered softly, as Eleanor bent over her.

Eleanor straightened in shock, "What the…"

"Shhhh, it's Gwen, your cousin. John sent me."

Through the disguise Eleanor recognized the gangly teenager. A feeling of elation enveloped Eleanor's whole being. "Is John okay?" she whispered.

"Yes, but he is worried about you and insisted on getting a message through."

"Where is he?" Eleanor exclaimed.

Gwen had not planned on giving their location away, but could not resist, "We are at Jetty Park Campgrounds."

"Jetty Park Campgrounds, where is that?"

"You must be careful," Gwen cautioned. "You are being watched." Then Gwen had an idea, after two days they would be finished with their plans to abort the launch of that abominable DWARS satellite. "Wait at least three days, and then come at night," she told Eleanor.

"Gwen, I am so glad to see you," Eleanor exclaimed.

Past Eleanor, Gwen could see a man approaching. Quickly she said, "John loves you, Eleanor. Now go, leave me and run back to the hotel."

"Thanks, Gwen," Eleanor stood to leave, but then stooped down again with a word of warning. "That woman John was with," Eleanor exclaimed, "she is not who she seems. She is working for the police." With those words, Eleanor turned and left in haste.

Groaning, Gwen slowly struggled to her feet. She had delivered her message, and what did it matter if poor Eleanor knew where they were hiding, in two days they would commence their operation against the Titan. Now, if only Gwen could escape this area without being apprehended by the authorities.

The long walk across the parking lot of the Hilton and out to Atlantic Avenue was torturous. At any moment Gwen expected someone to call, ordering her to halt. She wanted to run, yet forced herself to walk slow, agonizingly slow. She had to stagger, she could not hurry, and for sure she dared not look back.

As Gwen almost reached the sidewalk, a car pulled by, exiting the Hilton, the man inside looking her over intently. Gwen turned north up Atlantic Avenue, now walking at a brisk pace toward the nearest bus stop. Once there, Gwen caught the first bus north, heading for Merritt Island. She did not notice anyone following, but would take the safe route back, the one Rachel Maris had suggested.

After a short ride, Gwen exited the bus at the Merritt Island Mall off Highway 520. At one point in the drive, Gwen thought she saw the same car from the Hilton parking lot, following the bus, but she could not be sure.

Inside the mall, Gwen felt conspicuously out of place. It was a trendy well kept shopping mall in a nice area of town and a street person was a definite unwelcome oddity. She attracted a lot of attention, and everyone was staring and giving her a wide berth as they passed. That was okay, Gwen thought, it might cause anyone tailing her to get overconfident, let her get way ahead.

Reaching the fast-food court, Gwen turned toward the restrooms. Slipping into a small hallway, she hurried ahead quickly, but instead of going right, into the men's room, she dodged left into the women's restroom. Luckily it was vacant. Her heart thumping rapidly, Gwen hastily discarded her bum's clothing, wig, and beard. Underneath she had on brand new designer jeans and a loud but stylish purple shirt. Gwen splashed water on her face to clean the grime away, straightened her hair, and within seconds was a new person.

Exiting the bathroom, Gwen almost fainted, there he was, the same man who had been following in the car. Gulping, Gwen continued on. Fortunately he gave her only a passing, although appreciative, glance. Once almost out of sight, Gwen stopped to look back. The man appeared bored, waiting for his bum to come out of the restroom. Obviously he thought it a wild goose chase, following the street bum. He would never have dreamed that the dilapidated old man was actually Gwen Hughes, accomplice to the engineer they were all searching for.

Gwen breathed a sigh of relief. She had actually done it. Her heart was still beating very rapidly from the rush of adrenaline. This was exhilarating, Gwen thought, she had actually beaten them.

Heading for the northwest exit of the mall, Gwen walked confidently into the parking lot. She spotted Rachel waiting in a parked car as planned.

"Did you find her?" Rachel asked, glad to see Gwen safe.

"Yes, I sure did," Gwen smiled broadly.

"And you spoke to her?"

"Yes, mission accomplished," Gwen looked totally pleased with herself.

"Good," Rachel complimented her. "I was afraid I might have to go in after you." Rachel could not help being amused by Gwen's obvious excitement.

62

Monday, August 6 at Cape Canaveral AFS, inside the Air Force E&L Building, a clandestine emergency planning meeting was called by Colonel Roe, commander of the 6454th STLG.

As soon as Captain Alexander Hamilton II slipped into the conference room, he knew this was no ordinary meeting. The attendance of several high-ranking base officers was his first indication, the second was the presence of a number of authoritative VIPs whom he did not recognize. This was not the standard planning/status meeting or readiness review, something big was up.

Captain Hamilton took a seat at the back of a long rectangular conference table that ran the length of the room and was surrounded by approximately thirty chairs around its perimeter. His ordinary seat as PE for AFP-775, near the head of the table, and all the other positions near the front, were already occupied by much higher-ranking officials. Sergeant Garcia followed, carrying a stack of vue-foils, and seated himself at one of the side chairs along the wall.

Captain Hamilton and Sergeant Garcia had been asked to bring updated status charts to reflect all the latest activities for AFP-775. They had arrived barely in time, as Colonel Roe stood to commence the meeting at exactly thirteen hundred hours. Captain Hamilton breathed a sigh of relief, it would have been an embarrassment to walk in late and interrupt the meeting in front of so much brass.

"Gentlemen," Colonel Roe began. "Thank you for your support at this meeting. Does everyone have access number 52 on your badges? This is a Program Level 52 meeting. I believe the corresponding number at the factory is 113. I see we are okay. I would like to introduce General Mauvus, the head of Air Force Intelligence Gathering Space Programs and, from the Central Intelligence Agency, Mr. Boruchowitz and Mr. Maxwell. Let me start by announcing we are officially placing the base on Threatcon Charlie and LP-55 on Threatcon Delta."

Captain Hamilton was stunned, he had received no heads-up from the colonel that such a condition was about to be declared. Threatcon stood for a threat condition imposed by base security with Delta being the highest of precautionary levels. Alpha was used as a general terrorist warning alert. Bravo was declared when there was an increased danger, such as during the Desert Storm gulf crises. To impose Charlie meant intelligence had been received that an attack was imminent, and Delta that a specific location had been targeted.

"Before we discuss the nature of the threat and the precautions we shall be implementing," Colonel Roe continued. "I would like to have the status of Program 775 presented for your information, just a brief overview of where we are in the launch flow. Captain Hamilton is my PE for this mission."

Alexander Hamilton breathed another mental sigh of relief, it sure paid to be prepared. Fortunately he was dressed in the more formal air force uniform with a long-sleeve shirt, tie, and alpha uniform jacket. He would look professional, and this opportune exposure to high-ranking officials could be important toward making a name for himself.

Striving to present an image of sharp professional expertise and self-confidence, Captain Hamilton addressed the meeting with enthusiasm. Placing a detailed Tier 2 schedule chart on the vue-foil machine, he stretched out a pointer pen and began his presentation. Starting with yesterday's key events, he briefed them on the current status of standalone and integrated testing. Then, for the benefit of their visitors, and to give himself more to talk about, Captain Hamilton summarized the major launch processing events, beginning with the arrival of the Titan at CCAFS, through the satellite arrival, and up to the current point in the launch flow.

"In conclusion," Captain Hamilton finished with a flourish. "We are on schedule and have only twenty-five days until our ILC launch date of August 31."

"Thank you, captain," Colonel Roe retook the floor. "As you can see, we are marching on schedule toward launch. I have experienced men working the program and have no reason to doubt the August 31 manifest date. Next we shall hear from Mr. Boruchowitz about the nature of our threat, then Major Smith will outline base security measures, and then Mr. Maxwell will profile the individual terrorist involved, and finally we'll throw the meeting open for an informal discussion. If there are no questions, Mr. Boruchowitz."

"Thank you, colonel," Alex Boruchowitz, CIA head of Counter Intelligence Staff, stood and addressed the group. The look upon his face was serious. "We have reliable intelligence that a small party of terrorists are planning an act of sabotage against the SIGS satellite on your Titan IV. There is no hostile foreign government involved, as far as we can ascertain. I repeat, no foreign government is behind the threat. What we have here is a small cell of three to four members, all Americans. They may be considered armed and extremely dangerous.

"The leader is a former aerospace engineer from Krang Enterprises. We have been tracking the group for two months now and have managed to infiltrate them with a CIA undercover operator. Unfortunately, that intelligence officer has apparently joined forces with the terrorist and has been instrumental in aiding the group in eluding all efforts to apprehend them. We feel certain that the group is now in the Brevard County area. Their stated goal is to abort the launch of the SIGS satellite. You shall be given more specific information later. Colonel Roe, I think that about covers what I wanted to say in the way of an introduction."

Next, the Chief of Base Security, Major Samuel Smith, took the floor to explain how Threatcone Charlie and Delta would be implemented and the effects it would have on CCAFS activities and LP-55 operations. Around the launch pad additional security measures included an added contingent of armed security police and rigidly tight access checks. Throughout the base in general, entry points would be reduced and random vehicle searches conducted.

One piece of significant information was the division of responsibilities. The air force would continue to maintain security on the base, with the help of some special forces anti-terrorist units which had been flown in. The local police, CIA, and other government agencies would have jurisdiction outside the base perimeter, concentrating on uncovering the attack before it began.

Henry Maxwell took the floor next to provide further details. He commenced by placing a vue-foil on the projector that showed an enlarged image of John Hughes. Captain Hamilton was shocked, he knew that man, it was one of the KE engineers he had been working with on this very mission. He would never have suspected him of being a terrorist.

"This is John Hughes, an aerospace engineer from Krang Enterprises with ten years experience in launch systems. This picture is an enlargement from his CCAFS badge. As you can infer, he has clearance on the base and is familiar with CCAFS. He was employed by KE in the launch systems integration group for this mission. The man is knowledgeable in Titan IV launch systems and he knows the technical details of the satellite. His expertise and familiarity with this program make this terrorist group extremely dangerous. The threat is very real.

"John Hughes is five feet eleven inches tall, and weighs 180 pounds. He has blue eyes and brown hair. If seen, call security immediately. He will be armed."

Next a photo of Gwen Hughes was presented. "This member of the group is a cousin to John Hughes. She is five feet eight inches tall, weights 110 pounds, and has blond hair and blue eyes. She is a cadet at the Air Force Academy."

Captain Hamilton grimaced at the mention of his alma mater. To think, the enemy was even infiltrating the Academy with spies. That made it personal to Captain Hamilton, it was a disgrace for an Academy cadet to be involved.

Maxwell continued, "We first became aware of some illegal activities in May, when it was discovered that John Hughes and a fellow Krang employee, Bernie Goldsmith, were copying classified documents concerning the SIGS satellite and its integration on the Titan IV launch system.

"We sent an intelligence officer undercover," Maxwell put up a picture of Rachel Maris. "This is Rachel Maris. She has since joined forces with John Hughes and is actively supporting him in the sabotage of this mission. She is five foot six, dark complexion, black hair, brown eyes, and is thirty-three years of age. She is a naturalized citizen of Romanian birth.

"Rachel Maris is a trained CIA intelligence officer with several years of experience in the field. Physical contact must be avoided at all costs. This woman is extremely dangerous, she has killed in the past and probably would not hesitate to do so again. Her expertise in espionage has allowed the Hughes' to elude capture."

Putting up another chart, "This is Randy Ostermann, another CIA intelligence officer. He is six foot three, 210 pounds, brown hair, blue eyes, and is thirty-four years of age. We have lost contact with this officer also. He may have joined the terrorist, he may still be active undercover, he may be working independently, or he may be dead. We simply do not know.

"In conclusion, be aware of these faces. If you encounter any of these individuals, report it immediately. Do not try to interdict them yourselves. I repeat, do not try to interdict them yourselves. We have trained experts on hand, both on and off the base. Let us handle the capture of these dangerous fugitives. Thank you."

"Thank you," Colonel Roe responded. "Now I would like to open this meeting to an informal working discussion. Do we have any comments from the floor?"

Immediately Sergeant Garcia's hand shot up. "Yes, sergeant," the colonel responded.

"Sir, do we have any idea why this John Hughes wants to sabotage the launch?"

Captain Hamilton groaned at his assistant's inappropriate question. What difference did it make why they wanted to attack the satellite? The important thing was how to stop them.

Henry Maxwell rose to field the question. "We do not really know for sure. Who can understand the mind of a deranged man? As near as we can tell, Hughes developed some type of conscientious objection, regretting his own role in the development of a military spy satellite. Why he is going to such extremes, we cannot say. Apparently just quitting the project would not satisfy him, he is openly committed to stopping the launch by force."

"Does he have much of a chance?" Garcia asked.

"We feel confident we can catch him before he gets on base, but yes, he does have a chance. The threat is real! With his knowledge of the satellite, there is plenty he could do should he get close enough."

"But surely we would know," a lieutenant responded.

"You might think we would," First Sergeant Quijano joined the discussion. "If he should tamper with something, we would stand down long enough to fix or undo the damage of course. However, there are things he could mess up that would not be so readily apparent."

"That is true," a verification engineer from KE agreed. "If for instance, he had access to the satellite itself, he could dismantle some key component to the payload, a wire, a command switch, paint over the surface of a sensor, or even just throw a handful of dust into sensitive equipment to degrade performance in space. If careful in replacing the protective bags, we might never know."

"You should all be aware," Captain Hamilton spoke up, he felt it important to make himself a contributor to the discussion. "Standalone testing on the satellite is completed. Now, the principle used for verification at the launch base, is that once you test a requirement, you certify it ready and sign it closed. No further verification checking is performed on those requirements."

Maxwell spoke then, "There are a myriad of things a saboteur might do. That is why we have called you here today. We would like you to explore all the possibilities. Tell us what things he could do, how we might detect it, and what might be done to counter it. Don't limit yourselves to the obvious."

"What is to keep him from simply hiding a small explosive on the satellite somewhere?" Sergeant Garcia asked.

"Nothing, nothing at all, if he gains access past our security team."

Suddenly General Mauvus arose and a hush fell over the room. He glanced around the table with a stern look, causing eyes to be averted.

"General, do you have something you would like to say?" Colonel Roe asked meekly.

"Yes! I want everyone here to understand the importance of this launch. It is important to me and it is important to the nation. The president himself is appraised each morning on our progress. This launch has become a regular line item on the president's morning intelligence briefing. Let me tell you, the president is extremely concerned.

"Our current SIGS constellation is failing. We have one dead bird and another sick one. We need this replacement satellite! It is a matter of top national priority. A lot of time and a lot of money has gone into the preparations for this launch, and even more into the development and building of this satellite, but that means nothing. If we fail now, our national security will be crippled."

Captain Hamilton needed no further words of encouragement, he was psyched. Someone was out to hurt his satellite, and he was not about to let that happen.

63

Eleanor Hughes lay absolutely motionless on her bed in room 530 of the luxury Hilton in Cocoa Beach. She stared listlessly out the window as puffy clouds drifted by, partially obscuring her view of the blue Florida sky. She could hear the sound of surf pounding on the beach. Although it was hot outside, Eleanor's room was purposely cold, providing a haven from the stifling August heat and humidity.

That evening, the air-conditioned cool made her shiver though. Eleanor's relief at speaking with her cousin Gwen had provided only a temporary respite against her worries and troubles. A large brutish man had tried to force Eleanor into his car. He would be waiting for another opportunity, Eleanor knew he would. As if a horrible kidnapper was not enough to worry about, Gwen had also warned that others were watching.

What a dreadful feeling, to think people were watching her again. Perhaps those awful police officers from Tulsa were in Florida—waiting, plotting to bring her back to their awful safe house. Perhaps Officer Blinkerson was in pursuit. No, that was silly, she must not let her fear run rampant, she must not allow herself to become paranoid. Besides, she could handle the situation now. She was a stronger person now.

Eleanor had decided against going out for dinner that evening, the danger was too great. She had stood facing the parking lot for several moments, wanting to be sure it was safe. Unfortunately there was no way to be positive, so she had simply returned to her room and the security of a locked door. If she chose not to, she did not have to go out.

Eleanor glanced at the door to her room, reassuring herself that the deadbolt and chain were both securely in place. Gwen had said to wait three days before trying to come to Jetty Park. That seemed like a long time, but she would do it, even if it meant staying locked up in the hotel for three complete days and nights. Perhaps room service could not be trusted either. If she had to, she could even go without food for three days. It would not hurt her to drop a few pounds anyway.

Eleanor wished she could see John sooner. With an anxious sigh, she switched off the TV and all the lights but one. She left the bathroom light on, not wanting to be in total darkness. Closing her eyes, Eleanor tried not to worry, tried not to think about the strangers who were watching. She knew how to be patient, she could wait them out. She would stay in her room for three days, no one could touch her there.

• • •

A malicious stranger was watching though, not just any stranger, but a trained killer, a renegade, a former CIA intelligence officer, a rogue named Randy Ostermann.

On the second day Ostermann watched the lights in Eleanor Hughes' window go out, and he grinned, fingering the master key card he had stolen from the maids earlier that morning. For a night and a day he had watched. He knew which unit belonged to the wife of the engineer, the one they were all searching for. He knew which window belonged to Mrs. Hughes. He knew Newby was watching too. Although Newby was not learning anything from Mrs. Hughes, he would. He knew how to extract information. No longer bound by the law, he would not feel hampered in his methods, and some of them, although unpleasant, were sure to elicit the needed information.

The lady was going to sleep now, soon he would make his move. He had to be careful. His former associates, Newby's lackeys, had the hotel under tight surveillance. They were in no hurry to act, but Ostermann was. He knew something they did not, he had seen Rachel Maris and John Hughes, he knew they were close. If he didn't grab Mrs. Hughes right away, one of two things would happen. Either she would try to make contact with her husband, leading Newby and his men right to the object of their manhunt, or else her husband would try to reach her and Newby would arrest him. Either way, Newby would reach Hughes first, and consequently, also Rachel Maris.

Ostermann wanted Rachel Maris for himself, and the key to finding her was the engineer's wife. If not for that drunken street bum, Ostermann would have taken her already. No matter, he would kidnap her that night, and if things turned sour again, then he would kill her so she would be of no use to Newby either.

Ostermann had it all figured out. He knew exactly where each of Newby's men was located. They had Eddie Sanders positioned inside at the hotel bar, and two others on backup in a van out in the parking lot. They had Mrs. Hughes' room bugged and kept track of her movements at all times. It was standard operating procedures for their office. Ostermann knew, he used to be one of them.

In the early hours of the night, at closing time for the hotel bar, when Sanders left the hotel to join his partners in the van, Ostermann made his move. He had parked along the back of the Satellite Motel, just next door to the Hilton. The two properties were separated by dense scrub brush. Slipping down a path to the beach, Ostermann cut through the brush and entered Hilton property from the north. Working his way through the dense growth until coming up under the boardwalk, he climbing over the rail and strolled into the pool area as if returning from a nighttime walk on the beach. Posing as a hotel guest, he hoped to not attract attention.

Casually entering the hotel, Ostermann wound his way toward the elevator. He had timed it so Sanders would have long since abandoned his location in the lounge. There would be no spotters monitoring people's comings and goings. Ostermann was right thus far, the lights around the bar were off and the area was dark.

He rode the elevator to the fifth floor of the seven-story highrise and quickly made his way to Mrs. Hughes' room, down the west wing, number 530. All seemed quiet inside her room, and she would be deep asleep by now. The trickiest part of the operation would be breaking into her room. If he made too much noise, or woke the woman and she cried out, Newby's men would be on him in an instant.

First he had to make sure his escape route was clear. Ostermann had done his homework and knew exactly where to go. Returning down the mauve decorated main hallway, he entered through a door marked "Staff Only," across from the vending machines. Inside was a service elevator, stairs, and various supplies for the maids. They kept laundry carts on each floor, conveniently available for Ostermann to borrow. He chose one with a large towel and linen bag, which he would use for Mrs. Hughes instead.

Wheeling his cart back to Mrs. Hughes' door, he confronted the lock. At the Hilton guests received hard cards instead of keys. To enter a room, one slid his card through a slot alongside the handle, deactivating the lock and allowing the handle to open the door. It was normally a good safety measure against thieves, making it hard for anyone to copy a room key and return later. Ostermann had stolen a master though, he could get into any room.

Ever so carefully, Ostermann slid his master through the card reader. Slowly he turned the handle and opened the door. The click of the latch seemed loud, it worried him, but no one stirred inside. As expected, the door chain was on. Ostermann was ready, and reaching in with an extended nose, hand-held, chain cutter, he snipped them apart.

Ostermann froze as the chain halves separated. The scraping sounded loud, but apparently was not bad enough to wake a sleeping woman. Carefully Ostermann slipped his large frame inside and shut the door. Someone had left a light on in the bathroom, how convenient, he need not wait for his eyes to adjust to the dark.

Creeping stealthily forward, Ostermann entered the main room. There was a large bed occupying the majority of the floor space, a color TV on a stand, and a small table with two chairs by the window, which was cracked open. He could hear the ocean outside.

Ostermann knew how to move and breathe without making any noise. He hovered over the sleeping form of Mrs. Hughes. She looked so peaceful, so innocent, so helpless. His intended victim was wearing a flannel shirt. She had the covers pulled up high because of the cold from the air conditioning.

It was absolutely critical to keep things quiet. There was a possibility Mrs. Hughes might cry out in a startled panic when first awakened, and also a risk she might intentionally make noises.

Ostermann had made provisions for both, he had tools with him, and his method would be terror.

Drawing a wickedly large Bowie knife from his belt, Ostermann held the blade wavering in front of the woman's closed eyes. Suddenly he clamped his hand over her mouth.

Eleanor jerked awake in startled surprise, a hand gripping over her mouth, stifling and smothering any noise. Then she saw the glistening Bowie knife in front of her face, and her eyes went wide with horror. Instantly Ostermann's mouth was touching her ear, hissing the universal sound for quiet, "Shhhhh..."

Shocked half to death and terrified that her life was over, Eleanor fought the impulse to sit up. Her heart was beating hard against her ribs as she strained to draw enough oxygen through her widening nostrils and into her heaving lungs.

"Make no sound!" a hissing voice whispered, and slowly the stifling hand was withdrawn.

Eleanor's mouth gaped wide with the freedom, gasping for air, but it was not to last. Immediately her assailant stuffed a rag into her throat, causing her to choke.

"Be still," Ostermann hissed, thrusting the knife at Eleanor's throat again. Eleanor struggled desperately to control the urge to gag. She was having a hard time getting enough air to her lungs, but she feared to move or she would be murdered. Her hands clutched at her face, touching the gag, but she dared not pull it out.

Next Ostermann produced a roll of shiny clear packing tape, the reinforced type used for wrapping packages for postal mailing. He laid his Bowie knife on Eleanor's chest. Before letting go, he pressed the large steel blade hard against her, conveying the message not to move.

After switching on the TV to provide interference noise, Ostermann took hold of Eleanor's hands, roughly forcing them together at the palms, and then wound the tape around her wrists several times, binding her tightly. Next he poked the rag deeper into Eleanor's mouth and throat, stuffing it completely in, and then taped across her mouth and around her head several times.

Eleanor was terrified. She was helpless, totally within the power of this evil man. Suddenly he pulled the covers off her body and she panicked, fearing what was to come.

Ostermann was in a hurry to escape from the hotel. His victim had pulled her knees tight against her chest in fright. Her legs were bare, for all she had on was an oversized plaid flannel shirt. It was probably her husband's. How sweet, Ostermann thought maliciously.

Grabbing her ankles, he wound the tape around her legs, one band at her ankles and another just above the knees. She was his prisoner now, all wrapped up and ready to mail. Ostermann paused, trying to ascertain if anyone had been disturbed by their activity. All seemed quiet except for the TV and the noise of David Letterman doing Stupid Pet Tricks.

Quietly Ostermann returned to the front door and brought his service cart inside the room. He moved very slowly. There was no hurry, his key to success would be the lack of noise.

Returning to Eleanor, he surveyed his handiwork. She was hog-tied as well as any doggie. One more thing was needed, by kicking or reaching out at things, she still had the capability to make unexpected noises and foil his plans.

Cruelly grabbing the terrified woman by her auburn hair, he forced Eleanor into a sitting position. Removing a very fine nylon cord from his pocket, Ostermann dangled it in front of her eyes. Mrs. Hughes was silently crying, with her chest heaving and tears running down her cheeks, wetting the tape around her mouth.

Ostermann snaked the cord around Mrs. Hughes' neck and tied a slip knot. Then he placed his mouth close to her ears, and whispered. "We are going outside. Make a move, or any noise, and I'll kill you." Looking her in the eyes, he demanded, "Understand?"

Eleanor nodded fearfully.

To make his point, Ostermann gave the nylon cord a sharp tug, causing the loop to constrict tightly about her throat, effectively cutting off Eleanor's air supply. As she gagged for air, Ostermann held her about the shoulders to restrain her from writhing. He enjoyed watching her turn red and then purple in the face.

At the last moment possible, Ostermann cut the cord with his Bowie knife, allowing her to breathe once more. He left Eleanor on the bed for a moment while he prepared another noose. Then he slipped the horrible cord around her neck once more, and tied another slip knot.

The rest of his mission was easy. Ostermann carefully lifted the sobbing woman into his arms and placed her down into the white laundry bag of the service cart. Before covering her with towels, he made sure she saw the free end of her choke cord hanging out within his reach.

Ever so slowly, Ostermann pushed the heavy laundry cart, bearing his human cargo, out of the hotel room. Eleanor did not stir. Once in the hall, he moved quickly to the service elevator and rode it to the first floor. Looping around through the service corridors behind the hotel conference rooms, Ostermann came to the side lobby on the north side of the hotel.

Ready to make good his escape, Ostermann removed Eleanor from the cart, pulling her out by the hair and slinging the helpless woman over his shoulder. A short ten-yard sprint and he was into the bushes along the perimeter of the Hilton property. Reaching his car without being seen, Ostermann threw the captive woman on top of the spare tire in his trunk, and shut the trunk door tightly.

All had gone well, he felt like gloating. He had stolen the engineer's wife right out from under Newby's nose. Those fools were incompetent. Ostermann had always known he was better than those idiots. He was the best there was and now he had the means to find that witch, Rachel Maris.

64

"Let me get this straight," Dan Newby questioned one of his intelligence officers, after listening patiently to the man's report. "You are still maintaining the homeless man was a false lead?"

"Yes, sir, it was just a coincidence that Mrs. Hughes spoke with the old man, everything checked out."

"Fine, that will be all." Newby could not shake the suspicion that his man was lying, but what did it matter at this point? Morale was almost as low as it could sink. His intelligence officers knew they were failing, so now they were apparently afraid to admit even small errors. Unfortunately lies and cover-ups would cause morale and self esteem to sink even further.

"What do you make of Ostermann's actions?" Maconey asked, once the junior officer had departed. They were seated in Newby's field office, the spare bedroom of Annette's FCC. At the moment the only other person present in the FCC was Annette herself, in the next room typing up reports.

"Ostermann has kidnapped Mrs. Hughes hoping to get at Rachel Maris, I think that much is apparent." Newby pounded his fist on the table. How could they have let Ostermann abduct Eleanor

Hughes right out from under their surveillance team? Newby opened a bottle of aspirin and gulped down two more.

"Yes, I know what happened, the question is why?" spoke Maconey, "What could Mrs. Hughes tell Ostermann that she could not tell us? If the woman knew where her husband was, she surely would have led us to him by now."

"True," Newby concurred. "It is obvious to us that Mrs. Hughes does not know the location of her husband."

"But Ostermann may not be aware of that?"

"I am sure Ostermann knows too. If he has been watching her for any length of time at all, it would be clear she has been fruitless in her search for her husband."

"Then what is he after?"

"I don't know, but the answer might provide the tip with which to open this dark can of deceit."

"What deceit, sir?" Maconey was mystified by his boss' idiomatic remark.

Newby stood, exhausted with the game. Couldn't Maconey see that nothing made sense? People do not act without a reason, and coincidences can only go so far in explaining odd occurrences. Newby's head was beginning to pound again. Why didn't aspirin help anymore?

Annette appeared at the doorway to Newby's bedroom office. He realized she was wearing a very short and very tight denim miniskirt. She must have had it on all day and he hadn't even noticed, there were too many problems on his mind.

"Mr. Newby," Annette chirped. "I am done for the day, could you watch the phones till Beth arrives?" Beth Lender was their temporary help. She and one other maintained the phone lines and kept the FCC open through the night shift.

"We are busy right now, Annette."

"I have been on duty ten hours and Beth is late again," Annette insisted.

"We are expecting an important call from Dallas at any moment," Newby said in exasperation. Did Annette think it was his fault Beth was late? They were waiting for the home office to call and verify his inquires on the DWARS virus and it was nearing the end of the work day in Dallas.

"I did not plan to leave the phones unattended. That is why I asked if you could listen, since you are going to be here for a while longer anyway," Annette persisted, anxious to be off.

Too weary to argue further, Newby sat down at his desk, softly giving her permission to leave, "Go ahead then."

"Wait a minute, Annette," Maconey interrupted before she could disappear. "I think Mr. Newby would like you to stay until Beth arrives."

"At least until we get the call from Dallas," Newby offered lamely.

Without a word, Annette sulked back to her desk. Maconey shrugged his shoulders at Newby and smiled. "Now, you were saying, Ostermann might be after something else."

Newby's mind begin to clear as thoughts crystallized. "I see a definite turning point in events. Maybe Ostermann is not searching for Maris and Hughes, maybe he is trying to prevent us from finding them."

"Keep us from finding them?" Maconey could not follow the logic.

"Yes, it makes sense if you think about it. Why didn't it occur to me sooner? Look at Maxwell, the head of an entire operations division, he felt so strongly about canceling our investigations into the Baron, which he himself had initially instigated, that he came here personally to call us off."

"Maxwell and Ostermann have joined with the Baron's organization?" Maconey postured incredulously.

"Do not jump to hasty conclusions, Andrew, we are just looking at trends. The turning point seemed to be when Hughes and Maris recovered the stolen documents, with the provocation list we had planted. Before that, Maxwell was the driving force behind this entire investigation."

"True, it was Maxwell that first started us looking into Ellis Hughes, many years ago. Also, he was the one that gave us our one major break, linking Rachel Maris solidly to the organization."

"Yes," Newby felt excited. Rising to his feet once more, he paced to the corner of the bedroom and stood facing the doorway. A few days earlier he had discovered that from the corner of his room, he could see Annette's reflection in a hallway mirror, when she was sitting at the dinette table, her makeshift desk. Annette, knowing she was alone in the room, wasn't even bothering to cross her legs, despite the extreme shortness of her skirt.

"Look at the assassin's actions," Newby continued postulating.

"Originally, he made two incredible blunders in failing to execute John Hughes; after they got the stash, he turned his attention on Rachel Maris and almost succeeded in killing her."

"Yes," Maconey caught the concept, "and once he failed, Ostermann picked up, trying to finish the job. Also, don't forget Rachel Maris claimed to see a definite connection between the two, right from the beginning."

Newby smiled as Annette yawned and stretched, her skirt hiking all the higher. "Then Maxwell cancels Operation Carrier Pigeon," he concluded.

"Why the turnaround though, and how is Maxwell involved?"

"He and the Baron were rivals from the start. It makes sense, he was using us to attack his rival. If the Baron could be implicated with suspicious associations, such as a covert society, even if only a mere suspicion could be aroused, then Maxwell would stand to benefit."

"You cannot mean our studies into the Baron's organization are false, simply an attack by Maxwell on a rival."

"We do not know that for sure, but I am positive that John Hughes' involvement could not be a mere coincidence! Maxwell may have purposely lured him into espionage to cast further doubt upon the loyalties of his uncle the Baron. What if the DWARS virus was simply a fabrication, a means to draw John Hughes into illegal activities with the hopes he would involve his uncle?"

Maconey jumped to his feet, "What fools we are, taken in by one colossal statistical coincidence."

There was that word again, coincidence. Newby did not believe in coincidences anymore.

"I will bet," Maconey exclaimed, seized by the moment, "that if you ran that same statistical study on anyone, it might draw similar parallels. As long as the subject had been in the business long enough and was relatively successful."

Newby felt a little queasy, he was not mentally prepared to give up on the Baron and his imaginary organization just yet. Suppose the Baron was the one setting them up? Suppose the Baron had fed Maxwell false clues implicating Rachel Maris. What if the Baron had purposely involved his own nephew and started the DWARS fairy tale just to discredit Maxwell and derail an investigation that was getting too close to the truth.

Newby turned defendant's advocate on Maconey. "What would make Maxwell suddenly want to kill the operation?" he asked abruptly.

Maconey sat back down to think, and Newby directed his gaze in Annette's direction once more. "Well..." Maconey speculated, "suppose Maxwell did orchestrate this entire bogus scheme from the beginning, and then, people began to see through it. Suppose the DDO was becoming suspicious or maybe was even aware of Maxwell's scheming from the start. Once they were on to him, Operation Carrier Pigeon would become an indictment of his own treachery. The provocation list, with which he hoped to implicate the Baron, could instead be used as proof of his own deceitful treachery, proof of his own guilt." Maconey's voice became very heavy and very low. "So he had to stop Rachel Maris, to destroy the evidence before she turned it over to the Baron. That means...the assassin and Randy Ostermann work for Maxwell...and also that..."

Newby gasped out the awful corollary conclusion, "Rachel Maris was innocent from the beginning!"

At that moment the phone rang. Annette snatched up the receiver before the first ring had died out. "It's your call from Dallas, Mr. Newby," she called into the bedroom promptly.

Newby watched Annette put the call on hold and then stand to leave. His eyes followed as she disappeared into her own bedroom. Presently they heard the noise from the spray of a shower being turned on.

"Aren't you going to answer the phone?" Maconey asked.

Loathe to do so, Newby lifted the receiver and spoke briefly with the people from his office in Dallas, mostly he listened. Newby's countenance seemed to grow paler as he spoke. After a long moment, he turned to Maconey.

"Well?" Maconey begged to know.

With a grim expression, Newby spoke, "There is no DWARS virus. This satellite does not even have a piggyback, the whole affair was one big set-up."

65

On Wednesday, August 8, the dreadful day arrived. The time had come to stop the launch of the top-secret Titan IV with its covert SIGS satellite, purported to carry the awful piggyback DWARS. Their plan was put into execution by Rachel Maris making a phone call from a noisy phone booth outside Denny's Restaurant on Atlantic Avenue, to the Sailors Choice Restaurant. She asked for a waitress called Cindy Ann.

"Hello, Cindy Ann here," Gwen Hughes answered, after being called away from her waitress duties. Gwen's voice was flush with anticipation.

"It is time!" Rachel spoke tersely into the phone.

Gwen felt a tingle run down her spine. She shuddered with excitement. They had planned long and hard for this moment. "You've seen him, you are ready to start?"

"Yes," Rachel responded. "Two hours."

"Good luck," Gwen offered and returned the phone to its receiver. Searching out the senior waitress, Gwen excused herself from work, complaining of a stomachache. The understaffed waitress in charge looked disapprovingly at her, but Gwen did not care.

She had not asked to leave, she had simply told the woman she was going home and then did so, planning never to return.

The drive to Jetty Park Campgrounds was short, back to the Beeline, exit at George J. King Boulevard, and then left on Jetty Park Road. Gwen noticed her hands shaking on the steering wheel. "Get a hold of yourself," she though. Pulling into their campsite she noticed, with an initial moment of anxiety, that her cousin John was nowhere around. He would not have gone far though, not with Rachel out striving to initiate the commencement of their attack upon the Titan IV.

John Hughes stood on the beach watching the seagulls stroll the sand, keeping just beyond the reach of rolling ocean waves. Two Canadian children were feeding them bread crumbs and the hungry birds were beginning to flock about in great numbers. Further down the beach were fishermen with long poles stuck into the sand and barely discernible lines running out into the surf.

The beach was crowded with tourists that day, noisy children playing in the waves, bikini clad girls and slender boys bathing in the sun. A beach game of sand volleyball was underway, and elderly couples walking barefoot along the shallow waves casually collected seashells.

Off to the south the fuzzy outline of highrise condominiums dotted the coast. Out in the ocean was a variety of fishing boats, some small, and some large. John wondered if one of them was the Russian trawler that always managed to appear off the coast whenever NASA or the air force was preparing for a launch. To the north he could faintly see the jutting outline of rocket launch towers.

John noticed his cousin approaching down the beach at a hurried pace. She still wore her waitress uniform from Sailors Choice, black shorts and a T-shirt with a mermaid on the back. Something was up, it was against their practice for Gwen to appear around the campgrounds with her work clothes on. Typically she changed at the restaurant before returning to camp. They were trying to pose as transient tourists on vacation.

"John," Gwen Hughes called to him, and he felt his heart beating faster. He knew what she was going to say. "Rachel called, we have two hours."

"What time did she call?" John glanced at his wristwatch.

"Eleven-thirty."

"Okay, let's hurry."

Taking separate paths back to their campsite, John and Gwen nevertheless arrived at the same time. John had walked at a brisk pace, fighting the urge to break out in a run with each step. Gwen must have felt the same way, for her route was just as long.

Knowing exactly what needed doing, they quickly loaded the necessary supplies into the car, a Pontiac Grand Am, which they had recently acquired in trade for the Celebrity station wagon. Gwen gathered two prearranged changes of clothing for each, one a dark set of clothes for night operations, and the other set composed of loud tourist clothes. Meanwhile John placed a prepacked bag of explosives into the trunk.

Once the car was loaded, John nodded to Gwen and they disappeared into separate tents to change. John reappeared as a typical aerospace engineer, with the same type of clothes he used to wear when at CCAFS on business: black oxford shoes, dress slacks, a nice shortsleeve shirt, and a conservative tie, nothing unusual or flashy.

Gwen Hughes emerged from her tent wearing an air force officer's uniform. Enroute to Florida, they had stopped at Griffith AFB in upstate New York where Gwen had purchased the uniform from the BX. She wore hard black shoes with flat heels, (a requirement at the launch tower, John had said), nylons, a navy blue skirt, a light sky-blue blouse, and a small round cap.

Pinned to the front center of her cap was a silver eagle, and embroidered onto the epaulets on each shoulder, was a gleaming gold bar. Gwen was wearing the rank of a Second Lieutenant, an officer of the United States Air Force. On her chest, one quarter inch above her name tag, was the silver insignia worn by personnel rated on space systems. Just above that was the insignia of a parachute with wings, indicating airborne qualified. Boomerang would have appreciated her wearing that one, even though she was not scheduled for her turn at jump school till later that summer.

The name tag on Gwen's chest had the letters, "HUGHES" in clean white print. She had no way to obtain a false name tag, so she had used one of her own from the Academy, which were identical to those used by the air force.

"Ready to go?" John asked. She was looking at a handful of cherry bombs she had just discovered, long forgotten in the bottom of her black AFA-issue purse.

"Yes, sir," Gwen smiled with excitement and saluted him

sharply. She was in the air force now.

"It's exactly twelve-seventeen, we have just over an hour."

• • •

Rachel Maris stood high up the beach, away from the damp wave-packed sand along the ocean's edge. A hundred yards further down the beach was a man lying in the sun. Rachel studied him meticulously, watching his every move. It was Alfred King from Krang Enterprises, Contamination Engineer for AFP-775.

They had only allowed Rachel two hours, but that was no reason to hurry. Rachel would be late, or even cancel the operation for another day, rather than be careless. It felt exhilarating to be in action again. The same was true with every operation, after painstaking preparation and tension-filled waiting, finally came the moment of action. That was when the nerves calmed and the queasy feelings left. She would execute her assigned task with precision and skill.

Alfred King was lying on a beach towel flat on his stomach. He had a paperback book open, but his eyes were spending more time away from the pages than on them. He was girl watching. King was a tall skinny man, with little muscular development, but not an ounce of fat on his lean body. He wore a sparse black swimsuit. Rachel thought it a bit small and tight for a man, although her own bikini was even scantier.

Moving forward, Rachel approached the man, swooping in like a wild bird for a kill. She felt good, the gyrfalcon was in flight.

Sauntering past Alfred King's line of view, she halted with her back to him, giving the man an easy opportunity to openly stare. Rachel had dressed to attract his attention, and she knew his eyes would surely be on her.

Swaying slightly, Rachel staggered a few steps and then dropped her beach bag. She raised a dainty hand to her forehead, as if faint from the heat, and moaned audibly. Rachel reeled to the side as if nearly falling and then caught herself. So far though, Alfred King had said nothing to her. Okay, she would play him further.

Bending over to retrieve her beach bag, Rachel withdrew a large soft beach towel, careful not to spill her Firestar automatic or any of her knives onto the sand. She spread the towel out on the beach and lay down, stretching out on her back. Rachel had not even so much as glanced in Alfred King's direction, but knew he would be watching her performance since she had halted immediately in front of him.

Perhaps he was shy, she would just lie there and allow his interest to build. Periodically Rachel raised a hand to her head. She kept hoping he would speak to her, but he never did. After approximately twenty minutes, Rachel sat up and gazed up and down the beach, a distressed expression upon her face. When she looked in King's direction, he had his face buried in his dumb book.

"Excuse me," Rachel called. He looked up but did not answer. "Do you have any aspirin?" she asked.

"What...?" he stuttered.

"Do you have any aspirin?" she repeated her question.

"I...ah...no I don't, sorry."

"That's okay," Rachel responded quietly, and lay back down. He was not being too cooperative. What was wrong with the man? Could he spend all day girl watching and then be afraid to talk with a live one? John had said Alfred King was single.

After another few minutes had passed, Rachel sat up again. This time she stood, packed her sandy beach towel into her bag, and then approached Alfred King directly.

"I am sorry to bother you again."

"You have a headache?" King dropped his book, looking up at the beautiful woman standing over him.

"My head is killing me and I simply have to buy some aspirin. Unfortunately, I did not bring any money and I hate to go all the way back home."

Alfred King swung around to a sitting position. Was this gorgeous woman actually paying attention to him? "I could spare enough money to buy you some aspirin," he reached for his billfold.

"Thanks," Rachel smiled pleasantly. "Say, do you know if they sell aspirin somewhere inside the Hilton?"

"Sure, there is a gift shop inside. How much do you need?"

"Well," Rachel looked him in the eye. "I am not actually a guest there. I don't suppose you would go with me?"

"I would be happy to," Alfred King responded, not believing this was happening. He scrambled to his feet.

"My name is Al, Al King," he spoke, as they stepped through the sand toward the Hilton.

"I'm Mary Randall," Rachel lied with fluid ease. She took his arm for assistance when they reached the steps of the boardwalk.

"Say," Al King offered. "I have some aspirin in my room, if you would prefer."

At last, a break, Rachel thought. "That would be most kind," she replied demurely. "Then you can save your money."

She allowed the incredulous man to escort her into the hotel, up the elevator and to his private unit, number 408. Rachel sweetly followed him right on inside the room, but then her demeanor underwent an ominous transformation.

Turning her back to Al King, Rachel locked the door. When she spun around to face him once more, a cruel scowl was now upon her once smiling face. She had a loaded automatic pistol in her hand, pointed threateningly at King's chest.

"What!" Alfred King's jaw dropped open. "Is it money you want? Take my billfold."

"Shut up!" Rachel demanded, and stepped dangerously close. Suddenly she whipped her Firestar at his face in a sharp arc, smacking King across the side of the head. The poor fool did not know what hit him. With a cry he fell to his knees, blood spurting from a foul gash above his eye, caused by the barrel sight.

"On the floor," Rachel shouted. "Spread your legs and put your hands over your head."

Hastily Alfred King complied. Rachel turned on the TV, raising the volume high enough to mask any noises that could be heard if people passed by outside the room. Then she located the phone. Within ten minutes John Hughes joined her in the hotel room.

"Oh my!" Alfred King moaned, when he saw his assailant open the door and admit an accomplice, someone King knew. Back at KE they had been briefed about the Hughes situation, but King had never dreamed to see Hughes in Florida.

"Make another noise and I will kill you," Rachel snarled and kicked the prone man in the side.

John Hughes winced, this was a side of Rachel's character he had not seen before, cold, cruel, merciless. At that moment, John believed she really would kill King, if the need arose.

"Did anyone see you come in?" Rachel asked John.

"I do not think so," John replied. "I was careful." He had parked on the side, entered through the pool patio doors, and then taken the stairs to the fourth floor avoiding the lobby and lounge areas.

"Good," Rachel was in control. "Now, what are we looking for from King?"

"We need his CCAFS badges, and his personal ID card."

"Great Scott!" King moaned, but then shut up quickly when

Rachel moved threateningly close.

In a dresser drawer, among King's ties, pens, and loose change, they found the CCAFS badges. The ID card was in his billfold.

"Take his drivers license too," Rachel advised.

"Good idea," John tucked them all into a pocket. "Let's tie him up and go."

"What about the IAN?" Rachel asked, reminding John about the Individual Access Number they had talked about when planning the operation. All personnel needing regular access to CCAFS had a unique IAN tied by bar code to their CCAFS badge.

"Right," John squatted before King. "Al, we need your IAN."

Alfred King shut his eyes and did not answer. Rachel changed his mind though, by driving the heel of her foot into his kidneys, causing him to cry out in pain. Disgusted at the outburst, Rachel grabbed King by the hair and jerked his head back. Pulling her British F-S stiletto, she pressed it hard under his throat, just drawing a trickle of blood which ran across the black blade of the knife, leaving a sickly red streak.

"The IAN, tell us or I'll kill you," Rachel hissed. Again John was taken back by her cruelty and the deadly seriousness in her voice.

"Twelve thirty-one," Alfred King croaked.

Rachel removed the knife abruptly, allowing his head to fall, "That better be the truth or I will be back to castrate you. Is it, tell me the truth?"

"Yes, yes, I swear."

"What's the significance?" John asked, bending over King. "We both know security recommends picking a number that means something to you, so you won't forget."

"Ahh..." King groped. "It's my daughter's birthday." He looked miserable, and John knew he was lying. Near King's wallet, John had noticed a small pocket planning calendar. Snatching it up, John flipped to the month of December. There it was, marked on the thirteenth, "Tracy's Birthday." King had given them a number with the last two digits reversed.

"Is the number good?" Rachel asked threateningly, eyeing King suspiciously.

"No, but now I know what the true number is," John said grimly. The computer security system at CCAFS was designed with a clever warning mechanism. Should a person desiring access enter his number with the last two digits reversed, it would set off silent computer alarms alerting security. John now knew, without doubt, that King's real IAN was not 1231, but instead 1213, his daughter's true birth date.

"You go on out to the car, Gwen will be waiting," Rachel spoke mechanically. "I will take care of him."

John hesitated, this wasn't according to plan. "You're...you're not going to kill him?"

Rachel looked shocked at the idea, again hurt that John would think her capable of cold blooded murder. "No," she answered, attempting a light hearted smile, as if he was joking. She withdrew a needle and string from her beach bag. "I just thought it prudent we return to the car separately, to avoid attracting attention."

Approaching Alfred King from behind, Rachel jabbed the needle into his neck and injected a serum into his bloodstream. He jerked at the shock, but within moments was calm, and then unconscious.

Rachel glanced at John for approval. He nodded and placed a hand on her shoulder, his other hand clutching their newly obtained badges. "All right then, let's head for Cape Canaveral."

66

Wednesday, August 8 at Cape Canaveral AFS, as John Hughes, Rachel Maris, and Gwen Hughes drove toward the air force installation on that fateful midsummer day in the sweltering summer heat of sun-drenched Florida, a somber spirit descended upon the trio. They realized that they had embarked upon a desperate gamble, an act of sabotage which was legally unjustifiable, and that there was a good chance they would be captured or killed. The risks were unavoidable though, considering the alternatives, for they could not allow the DWARS virus to be deployed. Some things were worth risking one's life for; besides, not one of them truly accepted the possibility that they personally might die that day.

"Over there," John Hughes pointed to a large two-story parking garage, in front of the Cape Winds Condominiums.

Gwen steered their vehicle into the parking lot underneath the condo tennis courts. She drove to the back corner where there were no parked cars, "This will do just fine."

Once the car engine was shut down, Rachel changed into some less conspicuous clothes. She could not be seen on the air force base in a bikini. A business dress, such as a typical secretary might wear, seemed more appropriate.

Pulling out the ID cards they had obtained from Alfred King, they next addressed the matter of John's disguise. His hair had already been dyed black, and with a slight trim across the front, he somewhat resembled the picture on the ID cards of the fallen contamination engineer. It would be good enough for cursory checks they figured, no one looked at the pictures very closely.

Now they felt ready to attempt an entry onto the base. "You first," Rachel gestured to Gwen, as John opened the trunk of the car.

Although their Grand Am had a fairly large and deep trunk, the idea of being restricted in that dark cramped compartment, especially with Rachel Maris, was not an appealing thought to Gwen. She and Rachel did not have any badges though.

"This is going to put some horrendous wrinkles in my uniform," Gwen remarked as she climbed into the trunk.

"Comfy," Rachel joked, trying to make the best of the situation, as she crowded in next to Gwen. "You are not my idea of a fun person to snuggle with."

"Ha, ha," Gwen responded sharply, not at all amused. "Just hurry up and get in before someone sees us."

"Watch your elbows," John called, and then slammed the trunk shut.

Hurrying around to the drivers seat, not wanting to keep the women cramped in the dark trunk any longer than was absolutely necessary, John sped away from the parking garage. Cruising down Highway 528 a short distance, he exited toward CCAFS at North 401, distinguished by a sign reading "Cape Canaveral AFS Closed to Public." Crossing a small drawbridge over the Port Canaveral Canal, there was a three mile drive past the Sailors Choice Restaurant to Gate 1 and the Pass and ID building.

Things were not to go as planned though, approaching the south gate, John ran into unexpected traffic and was forced to a complete halt. Cars were backed up from the guard gate as armed military police assisted the contractor security police in conducting a hands-on ID check. Slowly the line crept along, taking an additional thirty minutes before reaching the south gate. John was beginning to worry about Rachel and Gwen, cramped on top of each other in the trunk, sweltering from the heat, possibly with poor ventilation. There was nothing he could do about it though.

As they inched closer to the guard station, past a turnoff to the navy Trident facilities, John was alarmed to see the reason for the delays, an ominous sign announcing the base had been placed under Threatcon Charlie. John had no idea what that meant, but the thought scared him. He could see they were halting each car, taking CCAFS badge in hand, and visually checking each picture.

John wondered if he would pass for Alfred King? It was fortunate that Rachel had insisted he dye and cut his hair to match the profile in the photo, that would help. At the time he thought Rachel overly cautious, he had never known the guards to pay much attention to detail. Usually cars hardly slowed when driving through the gate, the mere fact that you possessed a badge was enough, but apparently no longer.

As John pulled up next to the guard station for his turn, a uniformed security policeman with white shirt, black pants, and a gold SP badge, stepped up to the window. Under Threatcon Charlie the gate guard was required to physically touch John's ID badge. Luckily it was ninety-five degrees outside, the SP had been checking IDs for hours, and traffic was backing up for miles. In a hurry, he did not notice anything suspicious and let John pass.

Breathing a sigh of relief, John entered CCAFS, past the first hurdle. The main drive into the heart of CCAFS was Cape Road, a modern four-lane highway separated by a broad grassy center meridian. The long straight five miles into the industrial area was a tempting stretch in which to speed. John was careful to keep below fifty mph however, for he could not afford to get stopped for speeding and the security police did have radar guns.

On familiar turf now, John turned right onto Lighthouse Road and drove toward the Air Force Space Museum located at the site of Complex 17, an old Jupiter/Juno launch pad, and Complexes 5 and 6, old Mercury/Redstone facilities. The museum boasted an impressive set of static displays, but had infrequent visitors. It was the secluded spot John was seeking, an out-of-the-way area where he could stop to free the women.

In the far back of the parking lot, John halted the Grand Am and rushed out to open up the trunk. Much to the relief of aching limbs and abused muscles, Gwen and Rachel were finally able to climb out of their dark cramped quarters.

"I thought you said fifteen minutes at the most," Rachel complained, laying her hand on John's shoulder as she arched her back, stretching.

"We've got a problem," John said. "The base has gone on alert, Threatcon Charlie. They were visually checking ID badges at the gate."

"As long as we made it," Gwen brushed at the creases in her skirt. Those air force dresses were dry-clean-only and wrinkled extremely easy. Gwen's skirt looked like she had just taken it out of a washing machine.

"I don't think our plans for entry onto the launch pad are still feasible under these conditions," John elaborated. "My badge may be good, but they probably will not give Gwen a visitor's badge just because she has a badged escort. Security is definitely tighter now."

"What can we do?" Rachel questioned, seeing problems as merely hurdles rather than roadblocks.

"Well," John shook his head. "It appears I'll have to go in alone."

"No," Rachel said flatly. "That's not an acceptable answer. We have been over all possible scenarios. You know the plan will not work without a diversion. *What* can we do?"

John shook his head again. "We need a badge for Gwen, but there is no time, what about our schedule?"

"Forget the schedule! We'll take whatever time we need. I gave King enough juice to keep him under for twenty-four hours."

"So where can I get a set of badges?" Gwen asked earnestly.

"I guess the same way, we shall have to steal them. Let me see, it has to be someone that is on the access list for LP-55 and the UES. I know of two females, there may be others."

"Who are the ones you are thinking of?" Rachel probed.

"A female electrical engineer who works for Martin Marietta and an air force airman who works in safety. I have noticed both of them at several meetings. It is going to be hard to find them though. We might try the E&A Building where Martin Marietta has some of its offices."

"How likely are you to be recognized there?" Rachel asked, worried at the risk.

"You are right, it would be risky."

"Wait a minute," Gwen perked up. "Don't most Airmen live on base?"

John looked at her expectantly, "I don't know, do they?"

"Sure," Gwen said. "All we have to do is find the enlisted quarters, then I could ask at the office for her apartment number."

"That sounds great," John said, "but remember, this is not a full-sized air force base, housing is south at Patrick AFB."

"Continue your thought," said Rachel. "Gwen, you are an air force officer. Now, how would an officer locate someone at work?"

"I could call the base locator for her office number," Gwen suggested.

"Better yet," said John. "I know where her office is located, in the E&L Building with the other 6454th STLG offices. That's where the safety office is."

"All right," Rachel smiled. "Gwen, your job will be to get her out of the building and over to our car. I will take care of things from that point on."

"But what do I say?" Gwen questioned nervously.

"Think of something on the way, let's get moving," Rachel opened the passenger door of their sedan. She naturally fell into the role of leader for their group.

Fifteen minutes later, Gwen marched through the front doors to the CCAFS E&L Building located on Hangar Road. Gwen marveled at how strangely at ease she felt in her disguise as an air force officer, confidently returning the salute of a passing sergeant with perfect protocol.

"Down the main corridor to the left," Gwen mentally reviewed John's instructions, "sounds easy." She was seeking a small woman, probably weighing less than a hundred pounds, a brunette with long straight hair which would be pinned up. Air force regs forbid women's hair from extending past their collar when in uniform. Her quarry's name was Rita Jorgensen.

Gwen located the safety offices without trouble, clearly identified by a sign on the wall just outside the doorway. Entering a small office bay, she found six desks and a door toward the back which led to the private office of the base safety officer.

Approaching the civilian secretary seated at the closest desk, Gwen asked politely, "Excuse me, I'm looking for Airman Jorgensen."

"Over there," the lady directed Gwen to another desk near the far wall. Seated there with piles of papers stacked about, was a petite brunette one-striper. She had to be Rita Jorgensen, fitting John's description exactly. There was a male tech sergeant standing to the side of Rita making small talk, an attractive young man of Mexican descent with a handsome mustache. When he saw an unknown officer approaching, he quickly pulled his hands out of his pockets, but nevertheless remained leaning against the wall in a casual stance.

"Airman Jorgensen?" Gwen questioned authoritatively, as she approached.

"Yes, ma'am."

"You've been assigned to take a no-notice, urine sample, drug test. Purely random you understand."

Rita made a sour face, but did not complain. Working in the air force, she was used to being subjected to unreasonable demands. Gwen noticed the sergeant smirking with amusement.

"Are you familiar with the procedure?" Gwen asked, as if following a base policy.

"No, ma'am."

"I am required to personally escort you to medical. After you provide the sample, I'll bring you back to the office."

"Now?" Rita asked incredulously.

"Sorry," Gwen insisted.

"Be good!" the sergeant next to Rita mocked her.

"Shut up, Garcia," Rita retorted. She had heard that air force policy actually required an officer to escort the unfortunate subject clear into the bathroom and then personally watch them fill the sample cup.

Disillusioned, Rita Jorgensen followed the second lieutenant out of the E&L Building toward her car. She wondered why two civilians were already seated in the vehicle, but climbed into the backseat anyway, as directed by the lieutenant. To her utter astonishment, she found the civilian woman seated in the back holding an automatic pistol. Rita was horrified.

"Make a sound and you're dead!" Rachel threatened, jabbing the cocked Firestar hard against Rita's ribs.

Rita almost fainted as she realized her danger. She had fallen into the hands of those dangerous terrorists Colonel Roe had briefed the launch crews about. It was really them! What did they want with her?

"Put your head between your knees and grab your ankles," Rachel ordered. Terrified for her life, Rita hastily complied.

Returning to the parking lot of the space museum with their hostage, Rita Jorgensen was relieved of her CCAFS badges, her ID card, and her blouse. Gwen changed into the airman's uniform so her name and rank would match her new set of ID cards. The blouse was small, but Gwen managed to squeeze in, although the fit was very tight.

"I guess I have been demoted," Gwen attempted a try at humor. It fell on deaf ears though, the tension at the moment was too high for levity.

"Get out of the car," Rachel ordered their frightened captive, poking at her with the Firestar.

"Aren't you going to put her under?" John asked.

"No, I didn't bring any juice. She will just have to wait in the trunk."

Rachel took the terrified airman around behind the car, forced her inside the trunk, and then paused. Drawing her stiletto, Rachel pressed the honed edge against her cheek. "You listen up Rita, and you listen up good. Do what I say and you will not be hurt. Make a noise and I will have to slit your throat. One way or another, you *are* going to be quiet. Understand?"

Trembling uncontrollably, Rita nodded in the affirmative.

Moments later Rachel was back in the car, tucking her knife into the sheath hanging on her belt.

"Why did you have to be so rough?" John queried.

"Do you want to die?" Rachel defended her actions. "This is deadly serious. Air force guards with loaded M-16s are not going to be so polite. If they discover us, I guarantee you they will shoot to kill."

A heavy silence prevailed upon the group during the twelve mile drive through CCAFS out to LP-55. Rachel's talk of killing had reinforced the dangerousness of the undertaking upon their senses. This was no game, their lives were on the line. Taking Cape Road through the CCAFS industrial area and then down long stretches of highway bounded by dense scrub brush and sand, past several turnoffs for dismantled Apollo/Saturn launch complexes, past the sister Titan Launch Pad LP-54, they arrived at the infamous Titan IV Launch Complex, LP-55.

When the looming launch tower first appeared in view over the scrub bushes, Gwen's heart contracted. There it was, a massive framework of steel girders and metal platforms. Nestled securely inside the tower was the Titan IV rocket, gleaming in the late afternoon sun, a powerful launch vehicle still bound by gravity, but not for long.

Although LP-55 was architecturally ugly, it was both awe inspiring and beautiful to the human eye. An active USAF Titan IV Launch Complex, LP-55 stood 366 feet high at the roof level, the equivalent of a thirty-six-story skyscraper. It was subdivided into twenty-two levels to provide work access to the volatile Titan rocket systems. For all Titan IV Centaur launches, levels Ground through 10 were used for the Titan core, levels 11 through 13 for the Centaur upper-stage, levels 14 through 19 for the satellite vehicles, Level 20 and the attic level 21 for housing the powerful crane, and Level 22 was the roof.

There were two major components to the structure, the UT (Umbilical Tower), and the MST (Mobile Service Tower). The UT remained next to the rocket through launch, whereas the MST was the moveable section of the tower. Shaped like three sides of a square, it would be withdrawn by rail to the north just prior to launch. An AGE (Aerospace Ground Equipment) building on ground level provided a secure area for test equipment.

Once on the turnoff to LP-55, the would-be saboteurs drove past the Ready Building, located just outside the perimeter fence. Along the sides of the building were painted outlines of Titan rockets with the names and dates of successful launches conducted at LP-55. There were several trailers parked nearby, surrounding an overly crowded parking lot.

"This is it," Gwen said nervously, glancing at her cousin as he pulled into a parking slot and switched off the car engine. Rachel was in the back seat priming the explosives and readying her detonating devices.

"Sure you want to go through with it?" John asked, having second thoughts himself. They could see military police at the entry gate, dressed in fatigues and armed with loaded M-16 automatic rifles.

"I'm sure, it has to be done," Gwen responded with conviction. They had to stop this covert Titan IV from placing the SIGS satellite in space with its abominable DWARS virus. The thought of allowing an entire race of the human family to be imperiled was beyond reconciliation, dwarfing personal considerations.

"Get in the back and we'll go over these detonators again," Rachel spoke.

John stepped out of the car and stared up at the launch tower while Rachel briefed Gwen on the explosives. It was impressive.

Even though he had spent his career around Titan IVs, a sense of awe always took hold of John whenever he paused to behold the massive rockets.

Presently Gwen emerged to stand by his side. She had the explosives tucked inconspicuously in the false bottom of a drawings bag. John carried an innocent looking briefcase himself, hidden within were the tools he would need. "Ready?" he asked again.

"Ready," Gwen responded, and they started up the hill toward the tower. Rachel Maris remained behind with the getaway car.

John noticed Gwen was shaking a bit from nervousness. He could not blame her, she was probably scared half to death. He had to admire the young cadet's courage, not a word of complaint or hint of turning back. As for himself, at least he was on familiar ground, having been there many times before.

There was a safety badge exchange at the perimeter guard post on the road up to the tower. John went first so Gwen could observe the procedure. He handed the guard King's driver's license and CCAFS badge, which included the proper access markings for LP-55. The bored SP glanced at the picture on John's badge and then turned to search for the name of Alfred King on an access roster. Finding it, the guard turned to a large rack of badges and exchanged King's base badge with an LP-55 picture badge. The guard then gave John the LP-55 badge and returned his drivers license.

John moved on a few paces and halted to wait for Gwen. He was a fairly good match for Alfred King, but if that guard looked too closely at Gwen, or if he happened to know Rita Jorgensen by sight, she would never get through. Fortunately the man hardly glanced at Gwen's face, his attention distracted by other features of Gwen's anatomy.

"I almost died," Gwen exclaimed, as she caught up with John. She no longer minded the discomfort of having to wear the tight blouse of a smaller woman.

"Nothing to worry about now," John reassured her. "That new badge is all you need to walk around the complex. Put your hard hat on."

Walking slowly so as to not attract attention, they traversed up the incline of a paved road to reach the foot of the launch tower. On the way a young captain crossed their path. He had a serious look on his face, like he was very busy. Gwen saluted crisply and he payed them no further attention. At the base of the tower they paused just outside the AGE Building.

"Okay," John turned toward Gwen. "You saw the liquid oxygen and oxidizer Titan fuel tanks to the left and down the hill. The hydrazine and Aerozine 50 fuel tanks are to the right and further to the right is the liquid hydrogen and gaseous nitrogen facility. The wind is blowing from the southeast, which is perfect, so you head behind the oxidizer fuel tanks to set your explosives. You will see the perimeter fence just beyond that. To find the gate for emergency evacuations, just go straight back till you hit the fence and follow it to the left. There should be an ax at the gate to split the chain with."

"Right," Gwen tried to sound confident. She appreciated John reviewing her instructions again. It would be easy to get confused.

"Give me thirty minutes and then go," John said. He hated to leave his cousin alone, but she was an extremely capable young woman. "Good luck," he offered.

"Where can I wait?" Gwen questioned. "Someone might get suspicious seeing me loitering here for so long."

"Around to the side of this building is a restroom," John responded. "Come on, I'll show you."

They circled the AGE Building to a doorway on the west side. On ground level was a men's restroom, however the only women's facilities were out in a separate building a good distance from the tower. It was planned that someday women's facilities would be constructed within the AGE Building, especially with more and more women working on the launch crews.

"I am supposed to wait in there?" Gwen questioned.

"No, downstairs," John spoke, and led her down the stairway to an abandoned basement storage area. At the base of the stairs was a dusty sink and metal shelves with abandoned janitorial supplies. "You can hide under the stairs should anyone enter the building, and I would be greatly surprised if anyone came down here."

"Okay," Gwen stuttered. Checking her watch, she sighed as John departed.

Alone in the basement of the launch tower, Gwen's nerves started to bother her. She found it hard to take the waiting and had started trembling again, so she paced in the small room to steady her nerves. Her stomach felt like it was tied up in a knot. Gwen noticed a workers utility knife lying on a shelf. She slipped it into her pocket. Looking about the room, she saw several cans of cleanser. On impulse she placed a couple of them in her drawings bag.

Thirty minutes seemed like an eternity. Meticulously waiting till every last moment of the allotted time had expired, Gwen walked bravely out of the AGE Building and onto the pad deck. Heading toward the oxidizer (NTO) fuel tanks, she felt like the whole world was watching. It was now or never though, and John was depending on her.

Glancing nervously over her shoulder, Gwen noticed the same captain again, busily heading back up the road toward the launch tower. He paused to stare at her. Ignoring him, Gwen continued down a grassy slope until she was behind the large white fuel tanks.

Counting off twenty paces further, she halted. Rachel had calculated the distance that would place her just far enough away so that the explosions would not actually rupture or damage the tanks. If that NTO fuel tank developed a real crack, they would all be killed by a cloud of toxic gases. Gwen set her explosives on the grass. Her hands were shaking so badly she could hardly arm the detonator.

Once set, she hurried back to the NTO tanks, taking her remote detonator along. Removing her smoke bombs, Gwen positioned herself on the back side of the white fuel tanks. She lined up her ten smoke bombs on the ground within easy reach. They would produce a nice cloud of brown smoke to simulate a fuel leak. Then Gwen paused, taking a deep breath before activating the detonator.

• • •

Leaving Gwen at the foot of the launch tower was hard for John, she had seemed so vulnerable. Her role was vital though, without a diversion he could never execute his plans.

There were three elevators up LP-55, one on the UT and two on the MST. John checked them all and found the freight elevator was out of order. He decided the stairs would be safer and more discrete anyway. Circling to the southeast corner of the MST, he started the long climb up.

Reaching the Centaur level after considerable exertion, John paused to catch his breath before attempting to enter the UES. Walking along next to a rail, he had an impressive view of the surrounding lands. The twin Titan tower, LP-54, stood off to one side glistening in the sunlight. To the south were the massive VIB and SMAB buildings through which the Titan had recently passed. A short distance away on NASA territory were the squat Space Shuttle towers, 39A and 39B. The Space Shuttle Atlantis was undergoing launch preps at 39A. From his vantage point, John could make out the tips of the Space Shuttle, its external tank, and solid rocket boosters.

Looking down, John felt a slight touch of vertigo. He was practically standing in the open air at a tremendous height. The wind was gusting at that altitude and there was very little separating him from a long drop. John didn't trust the tower railings, they were removable pieces and some sections were even wobbly. He thought perhaps he could understand a bit about how skyscraper construction workers felt.

Scanning the ground below, John searched for some sign of Gwen—nothing yet. That was good, she was waiting as per their plans. He had to hurry though, if he was to be ready when the explosions commenced. Opening his briefcase, John removed the contents and placed them into his pockets and inside his shirt.

Approaching the door to the UES, John attempted the cipher lock, but it didn't work, the combination had been changed. Trying not to panic, John knocked on the solid door. Presently it groaned open to admit him inside.

"Forgot the number," John excused himself to the man who had opened the door. Inside was a small room with a tiny table and two chairs. John was alarmed to see two combat-uniformed SPs on duty there, along with the normal security guard. This was not usual, what were they doing there?

"I need a picture ID along with your badge," the security guard spoke as he resettled himself behind the table. John nervously handed the man Alfred King's LP-55 badge and drivers license. The guard checked a computer printout listing the names of people with access to the UES. Finding Alfred King, he gave John another badge, this one a UES picture badge, again with King's face upon it.

Grateful to have survived, John shuffled on further into the room. Hanging his hard hat on a hat peg, he thrust each foot into a shoe cleaning machine, and then stepped on the tacky mats. John was starting to sweat, it was hot inside that small enclosed room. There were no windows and it was easy to forget he was standing at an elevation of 240 feet in the core of a gigantic metal tower.

The door beyond the tacky mats had an IAN card reader. John slid King's UES badge through the reader and punched in 1-2-...then paused for a moment. If he was wrong about King's IAN number, then he would soon be exposed. Half closing his eyes, he continued...-1-3.

Nothing happened! For a moment John started to panic again. One of the SPs turned to watch, he had a black M-16 slung over one shoulder. John felt the color drain from his face, he could not get in without the right number? Should he reverse the last two digits and try the number King had originally given, and risk dialing in the alarm? No, John decided to try 1-2-1-3 again. He knew from experience these card readers did not always work on the first try.

Slipping King's UES badge through the reader again, John punched the numbers 1-2-1-3. This time he was rewarded with a tiny green light on the reader and the comforting sound of a click in the door handle.

Quickly John pushed through the door and into the change room. There he was met by an attendant waiting to issue sterile white clothing to workers. John was familiar with the procedure and hurried to dress. He could just picture Gwen walking nervously out toward the Titan oxidizer fuel tanks at that very moment. He had to hurry.

Signs outlined the routine to be followed. First John had to remove or tape over watches, rings, etc., then place a white hood over his head and, in John's case, a mask for his beard. Then came a white jumpsuit followed by white cloth boots, attached to the heel of which were static heel straps which grounded out the worker. Last were the clear plastic gloves. All exposed clothing had to be covered to help preserve a clean environment.

Fumbling through the process, John found his fingers strangely uncooperative. He had to slow down, to calm his nerves, to get those clean clothes on. Once dressed, he then stepped onto the static charge tester to check for proper grounding. Receiving a green light, he approached the unlocked door to the UES, stepping on additional tacky mats.

At last John entered the environmentally enclosed area around the sensitive space vehicles. Cooling air blew at a steady pressure, maintaining a constant air flow to keep dust from settling. It felt good against those hot clean-room garments. Carefully John moved about, surveying the technical work in progress.

Up a small interior flight of stairs to the first SV level, John found the SV Test Conductor running through a series of integrated test procedure steps. They were checking electrical mating connections between the upper-stage and the satellite. John gave the workers a wide berth.

The satellite glistened in the light before him, its surfaces shiny new and spotlessly clean from dust. There was that cursed piggyback payload, SPL-551, nestled securely within the adapter, anchored to the bottom of the satellite bus with self-releasing attachment fittings. A temporary facility cooling duct faced the shiny silver box, blowing ground air directly across its exterior. There were electrical wires running from the piggyback down to the upper-stage. It looked so innocent there, just a silver metal box. Who would guess that within that small container lay a deadly genocide virus? John shuddered at the thought.

Higher up on the spacecraft bus he could see the optical Earth sensor. One scratch on the surface of that critical device and the SIGS satellite would be dysfunctional in space. He saw the conic shape of an S-band antenna. Disconnect one wire there and the satellite would be severely crippled in its ability to receive or transmit signals. There were the pyro boxes used for separation. If those failed, the satellite could not properly clear its expended stage vehicle and would never reach final orbit. Other sensitive devices could be seen on all sides of the satellite, including the ultra-sensitive electronic sensors for spying on the Earth.

Checking all levels of the UES, John found workers and spectators everywhere. It was too crowded there with testing in progress, he did not dare touch any part of the satellite.

Returning down the internal stairs to the top Centaur level, John positioned himself just opposite the Centaur Test Conductor, the TC. On each level, platform inserts had been attached and lowered so that a worker could walk right up to, or circle the satellite, and touch it from any angle to perform the desired maintenance or testing. White tape covered all cracks in the floor, completely sealing each level.

On the back side of the Centaur, away from the TC and the UES door, John waited. He had counted fourteen others inside the UES at that level, most simply watching. Spotting a petrie dish, John stooped over the contamination collector as if examining its surface. He was supposed to be Alfred King, the contamination engineer.

Suddenly a series of explosions ripped through the air, startling John, even though he had been expecting it. The tower itself seemed to literally shake and sway.

"What in tarnation was that?" John heard the TC cry out in alarm.

"Was it an earthquake?" someone yelled.

"Not here stupid, this isn't California."

John unzipped his overalls and drew a plastic bag from inside his shirt. The zip-lock bag was filled with ammonia. John yelled with a loud voice, "I see explosions down by the NTO tanks."

There was a moment of startled silence, then alarmed men hurried over to the east wall to see for themselves. Angry brown clouds were billowing around the fuel tanks on the ground below, drifting toward the launch tower with the prevailing winds.

John moved around the Centaur till out of sight again and began sloshing ammonia out into the air and onto the floor. Before being allowed on the launch tower, all crew members received extensive training on emergency accidents and evacuations. The most dangerous of all emergencies was the leaking of toxic gasses, and the most readily recognizable sign was a strong odor like ammonia or rotten eggs.

With great alarm, John cried out in a panicky voice, "I smell gas."

"Great Scott, I smell it too," the TC yelled out, fear gripping his voice.

John raced around the Centaur to face the excited TC, recognizable as the man with a headset on. "Tell them we smell gas!" John yelled. "We have got to evacuate the tower immediately."

The TC touched his hand to his mouth, "We have got gas up here," he yelled over the TOPS voice net.

Almost immediately a siren began to wail over the loud speakers and a voice instructed, "EVACUATE THE LAUNCH TOWER! EVACUATE THE LAUNCH TOWER! THIS IS NOT A DRILL!" The volume was deafening.

Those on the top Centaur level, John included, scrambled toward a large box in one corner of the UES where ELSA (Emergency Life Support Apparatus) gas masks were stored. John grabbed an ELSA unit, lifted the flap, and removed the plastic hood-like bag. Turning on the oxygen valve, he placed the bag over his head. It was a system designed for rapid donning in just such emergencies.

Now John slipped away from the scrambling, frantic, tower workers. Circling around the Centaur, he ducked out of view. His plan was to hang back and hopefully be left alone in the UES to consummate his mission. Then he too would make a hasty exit. Thinking their lives were in danger, no one was paying him any attention, each man seemed totally preoccupied with getting himself out quickly.

For an eerie moment, as the heavy outside doors clanged shut, John seemed surrounded with an unearthly silence. Outside the UES he could hear sirens blasting and the sound of footsteps running down the metal stairs, but inside the UES, he was all alone. John took off his ELSA gas mask. He could no longer smell the ammonia he had spilled. It had been enough to start the initial panic though, it had served its purpose well.

John stepped onto one of the platform inserts and tapped the payload fairing. The bottom tri-sectors of the PLF completely enclosed the stage vehicle. The top tri-sectors were not yet closed out, the junction point being at the ceiling of the level upon which he stood.

Reaching inside one of the PLF access doors, an octangular cut opening, John placed the palm of his hand flat upon the surface of the Centaur upper-stage.

Suddenly, as if in reaction to the unauthorized violation of the intricate spacecraft, the outside door to the UES groaned open and in stepped an armed military SP. John jerked his hand back out of the opening, he had not had time to do anything yet.

"How many possibilities still in there?" a muffled voice called out loudly, speaking through the plastic of an ELSA gas mask.

"Up to thirty," came a response from behind, "and none came out through the main doors for this level."

John retreated further within the UES, circling behind the Titan/Centaur stack until exactly opposite the intruders.

John could hear two, maybe three men, military SPs. "The rest must have taken emergency exits and descended the UT stairs. There is no way to account for them," the voice continued. Apparently the SPs had not yet been allowed to abandon their posts, and were conducting a level by level search for stragglers.

"This is the last level, circle the space vehicle and let's get out of here," one of the SPs ordered.

John could retreat no further. What was he going to do? There was no place to hide. To reach one of the UES emergency exits, he would have to move away from the space vehicle and expose himself to their view. Panicking, he glanced about for a pipe or tool, something to fight with. Who was he fooling? He couldn't fight those men, SPs were armed with fully automatic M-16 rifles.

Footsteps were approaching and he had no place to go. Suddenly John's eyes were attracted to the PLF access openings, easily reachable octangular cut openings at approximately head height. Grabbing the edge of one, John hoisted himself up and scrambled inside the payload fairing. Frantically, he crawled out of sight on a metal catwalk along the side of the Centaur tank. The footsteps were coming closer, John was crouched on an interior catwalk inside the rocket, where GDSS technicians sometimes crawled to make last minute pre-launch checks on their space vehicle.

Holding his breath, John prayed the SP would not notice his presence or think to glance inside the rocket. Why were they still there? Why hadn't they left with the others? Armed SPs had never been posted inside the UES before? The metal of the Centaur tank felt cold against John's side. He could just picture this monstrous firecracker blasting off, blowing him to smithereens and carrying his remains deep into space.

Straining to hear, John listened as the footsteps passed his position. The guard had said it was their last level to check, they had probably started at the top, on level 20, and worked their way down to the current level.

Time was critical, John knew those SPs would not be loitering around, not with a toxic gas leak in progress and emergency evacuation sirens blaring. Deciding to chance it, John swung his feet out of the access hole and dropped onto the metal floor of the UES.

Hastily he peered around the Titan stack. He was alone with the satellite, all levels of the UES had been evacuated and he now had complete freedom to go anywhere. Too much precious time had been wasted though. If he did not act quickly, they would never get off CCAFS alive.

• • •

A micro-instant after pressing her detonator switch, the world seemed to violently erupt behind Gwen Hughes. With nothing shielding the startled cadet from the blast, the shock literally knocked Gwen off her feet. She had no idea there was so much explosive force in those small packages Rachel had given her. Recovering her senses, Gwen scrambled to her feet and began pulling the pins on the smoke grenades. In rapid succession, she tossed all ten canisters under the oxidizer fuel tanks.

She had done her part, now John would have his diversion, and now it was time to get out of there. Thick brown smoke was billowing all about her. Gwen sprinted away from the fuel tanks, racing across the grass toward the outer perimeter fence. When she hit a slight dip, she pitched forward, falling hard onto the grass and sliding forward on her face.

Glancing back at the tower, Gwen saw frightened workers running in all directions. The sirens were making an awful wail and people were pouring down the launch tower stairs like ants fleeing an anthill. Thanks to the prevailing winds, they would be heading for EEAP emergency safe rendezvous points in the opposite direction from Gwen's line of retreat. Their scheme was working.

Then Gwen saw that same captain up on the pad deck. He was still watching her, having seen her emerge from the smoke around the fuel tanks with no gas mask. Although the captain had an ELSA mask on himself, for some reason he was not fleeing to escape the toxic cloud rising at the side of Gwen.

No need to worry, Gwen thought. The man might be curious, but surely he would mistake her for simply another fleeing worker. Leaping to her feet, Gwen grimaced with sudden excruciating discomfort. She had twisted her right ankle. Pain laced angrily up her calf as she applied a small amount of weight to her foot. Hobbling along the best she could, Gwen ran anyway, trying to ignore the piercing nerve-torturing pain. She was too scared not to run, sprained ankle or not.

As Gwen topped a slight hill, and limped toward the fence, the emergency exit came into view, red poles marking the gate. Gwen angled in that direction, Rachel would be bringing the car around and should be visible any moment.

Reaching the first of the double fences, Gwen tugged against the chainlink gate. A padlocked chain held the gate locked, and there were strands of wicked-looking barbed wire all along the top. Removing a fireman's ax, provided there for emergency egress only, Gwen smacked the chain apart, sheering the metal links with one whack. Continuing across a dirt dividing area, she also chopped apart the chains on the gate through the second fence.

She was out. Spinning around, Gwen hoped to see her cousin John running to join her. There was no sign of him though; however, there was a figure running down the slope in her direction. With alarm, Gwen realized it was that captain, and he was yelling for the guards as he ran. Starting to despair, Gwen scanned the road toward the Ready Building, hoping to see Rachel and the car, but they were still not in sight.

As the captain got close, Gwen tried to run. Racing back along the fence, Gwen thought to at least open up John's escape route. She saw the captain rushing straight for her, running hard, and there was no way to outrun him with her injured ankle.

Just as the man was almost upon her, Gwen saw her cousin emerging from the foot of the launch tower. He had descended from the opposite side of LP-55 via the UT stairs. Gwen tried to dodge as the captain lunged, but he caught her around the waist, effectively tackling her and knocking them both to the ground in a tangle of blue uniforms.

Gwen rolled to her knees, but the captain was back on his feet, swinging at her with clenched fists. Screaming, Gwen ducked and buried her head in her arms, taking his fists on her forearms and back. To further escape his blows, she fell to the ground and rolled, covering her head with her hands.

The captain stood over her prone figure, fists still clenched threateningly. "Who are you?" he shouted.

"I give up, I give up, take it easy," Gwen called. She could not believe an officer in the air force was actually beating on an unarmed woman who had not even been hitting back.

Suddenly the captain turned, distracted by the sound of running footsteps. John Hughes was sprinting for the open exit gate, not having noticed them off to the side. Gwen saw the captain start moving to block his path. Lunging out, she grabbed the man about the ankles, tripping him onto the ground.

A sudden burst of gunfire startled them both, automatic M-16 rifle fire. Gwen watched as John, almost to the gate, dove for the ground. They were actually shooting at him. The captain was lying flat in the grass now too, his arms over his head. None of them dared move for fear of being hit by M-16 fire.

Then Gwen spotted Rachel Maris in the Grand Am, squealing to a halt along the two lane road outside the gate. She emerged from the car, Firestar automatic pistol in hand. Stepping just inside the gates, Rachel went to one knee and fired a full clip of powerful .40 S&W bullets in rapid succession, causing the security police to break off and take cover. As the M-16 fire ceased for a moment, John scrambled to his feet and sprinted through the gates toward the car. Rachel reloaded and commenced firing again to provide cover.

In an instant Rachel joined him inside the Grand Am. Stomping on the accelerator, they shot forward with tires screaming. There were sporadic bursts of M-16 fire aimed in their direction, but the car did not slow and soon disappeared down a side road through the scrub brush. As the firing broke off, security police began scrambling for their own vehicles to give pursuit.

There was no way they could have helped me, Gwen thought. She was glad John had escaped. Gwen stood and brushed the grass off her shirt and blouse. There were two SPs approaching down the hill. The captain was still lying flat on the ground with his head buried in the grass.

Gwen knew there was no use trying to run, where would she go? As the SPs drew nearer, she raised her hands above her head so they could see she was unarmed.

"I caught one," the captain called to the security policemen, startling Gwen. She hadn't seen him get up off the ground.

"Is this one of the terrorists?" the SPs drew up before them, eyeing Gwen's uniform questioningly.

"You bet," Captain Hamilton exclaimed. "She set off the explosives trying to blow up the fuel tanks."

Gwen said nothing as an SP politely handcuffed her wrists and led her back to the parking lot outside the Ready Building. The captain seemed so proud of having caught her, he kept going on and on about the fact that her blasts had failed to destroy the fuel tanks. Gwen said nothing to dissuade him of his error.

There were only a few remaining SPs left around the launch complex, most had departed in pursuit of John Hughes and they had taken all available SP vehicles with them. Captain Hamilton seemed anxious to join the chase, for he wanted to be on hand when the arrests were made, but at the same time seemed reluctant to leave his prisoner, as if releasing the captured terrorist from his personal custody would diminish his glory.

"You are the lieutenant who took Rita!" a sergeant exclaimed, startling Gwen as he raced toward them, almost in a panic. His eyes went even wider as he saw the name tag on Gwen's chest "JORGENSEN."

"She is okay," Gwen hastened to reassure him. "We did not hurt the girl."

"Rita, she is okay?" Sergeant Garcia clutched Gwen by the shoulders.

"She is fine, really, we would not hurt her. I just needed..." Gwen was interrupted when Captain Hamilton grabbed her arm and possessively pulled her away from the sergeant.

"Garcia," Captain Hamilton said, "go get the car. I told the SPs we would drive the prisoner back to the Security Police Building on Control Center Road."

After a short explanation as to the whereabouts of Airman Jorgensen, Gwen was unceremoniously taken and thrust into the backseat of a navy blue, government, motorpool car. An armed SP, who had Gwen's document bag for evidence, took the seat next to her, with Captain Hamilton and Sergeant Garcia occupying the front.

As they drove out to Cape Road, Captain Hamilton loudly retold the story of his courageous exploits, for the third time, exaggerating the details with each telling. Gwen sat meekly alongside the young SP. Her head hurt, her ankle ached, and she felt so helpless. Passively she listened to the captain's bravado, her head swimming.

At the junction with ICBM Road, they met a convoy of cars coming in the other direction. It was Colonel Roe and some of his staff, enroute to the launch pad to observe the damage. Captain Hamilton halted in the middle of the road and flashed his lights to flag them over.

Excited beyond compare, Captain Hamilton exited his car, leaving the motor running, and hurried up to the colonel's window. He saluted when the window came down.

Colonel Roe returned the salute impatiently, irritated by the waste of energy, "What the devil is happening out there captain?"

"The terrorists struck at LP-55, sir. They tried to blow up the oxidizer fuel tanks, but I intercepted one of them."

"Blow up the fuel tanks! They attacked the fuel tanks rather than the launch vehicle?"

"Yes, sir," Captain Hamilton exclaimed breathlessly. "I have one of them, a prisoner, right here in the car." He pointed in Gwen's direction. "The SPs are pursuing the others, so we are taking her to the Security Police Building for confinement."

"I want you to come with me back to the launch pad," Colonel Roe ordered. "Let the security police take her in, we need to survey the damage."

"Sir, the fuel tanks are okay."

Gwen looked up as the sergeant in front of her turned to address the SP in the backseat. “Doesn’t Captain Hamilton realize that the smoke around the fuel tanks was just a diversion?”

“I don’t know,” the SP responded. “It’s obvious to everyone else.”

“Sir,” Captain Hamilton argued, “perhaps we should join the chase, the other terrorists have fled and we might be able to catch up and help with the capture.

“No you don’t!” the SP next to Gwen exclaimed loudly and exited the car to join the discussion. Gwen found herself momentarily alone in the back seat, although the sergeant was still in the front.

Gwen reached into her pocket, she still had those old cherry bombs from the Academy. On the floor was her document bag. Quietly Gwen stretched out with her foot and scooted the bag within arms reach. Carefully she pulled it up into her lap.

“Got a cigarette?” Gwen asked the sergeant hopefully. He was so busy trying to follow the conversation outside, that he was paying her no mind. Without thinking, he tossed her a cigarette.

“Matches?” Gwen called. She could not believe her luck when he handed a lighter back to her outstretched handcuffed hands.

Moments later, the SP opened the door to Gwen’s side of the car. “Get out, Captain Hamilton would like the colonel to ask you a few questions.”

“Bring the prisoner over,” Captain Hamilton shouted to the SP, who was not moving fast enough to suit him. The captain was now seated in the driver’s seat of Colonel Roe’s car, having agreed to chauffeur his commander to the launch site.

“See her?” Hamilton remarked happily, as Gwen was brought up to his window.

“I see her, captain, now let’s move on.” Colonel Roe did not appreciate the delay.

His irritation was not evident to Captain Hamilton though. “You should be ashamed of yourself,” Hamilton gloated at Gwen Hughes. “You are a disgrace to the Academy. I cannot believe someone like *you* ever got in. You are a disgrace.”

Gwen stood with her head bowed, taking the verbal abuse quietly. Suddenly she bent over, nearly double, stooping low to the ground, and made a horrible vomiting sound. The SP was standing by sheepishly embarrassed, not looking.

"Let's go, captain!" the colonel said again.

"Wait, Captain Hamilton," Gwen straightened up, speaking for the first time. She looked Hamilton straight in the eye, "I may be a disgrace, but I think *you* need to clean up *your* act." She handed Captain Hamilton a symbolic can of cleanser, one she had picked up at the bottom of the stairs in the AGE Building at the base of the launch tower.

Disgusted, Captain Hamilton threw the cleanser aside. The canister bounced off the seat and onto the floor of the car.

As Captain Hamilton pulled away, Ramon Garcia moved up beside the cadet. She was just a kid and he felt sorry for her. "What a jerk," Garcia said, nodding toward the captain. Glancing toward the female cadet, half-expecting to see her in tears, Garcia was startled to see a smile on the prisoner's face.

Suddenly they heard a popping sound from the direction of the departing automobile. Almost instantly the car containing Captain Hamilton and his colonel was filled with a dense cloud of white powdery smoke. The car swerved erratically down the road, jumped the curb, and slipped off the shoulder into a drainage ditch with two feet of water.

Staggering out of the car, white as ghosts, stepping into water knee high, emerged a furious Captain Alexander Hamilton II and the angry colonel he so wanted to impress.

Gwen was laughing so hard it hurt, but she couldn't help it. She loved tormenting those Dancing Bears.

67

Meanwhile, Rachel Maris sped with wild abandon through the open roads of CCAFS away from the chaos at LP-55.

"You did get in?" Rachel questioned, over the roar of the engine, as she accelerated through an abandoned roadway away from the LP-55 perimeter fence, a direct shortcut back to Cape Road and freedom.

"Yes, yes, I got in," John slammed his fist on the dashboard, worried about his cousin. Twisting to look out the back window, he watched the receding figures dashing for their cars to give chase.

"Then it's done?" Rachel Maris declared with a sigh of relief. She let out a deep breath, adrenaline enlivening her system with exhilaration. They had done it, mission accomplished, the only task remaining was to escape.

"Yes, yes, it's done," John turned back in his seat, facing forward, as they rounded the corner onto Cape Road, tires screeching.

Rachel adjusted her rear view mirror to watch for pursuit as the speedometer climbed steadily toward 100 mph. Now if only she could get John out alive. "So much for quietly slipping off the base," she quipped.

"I cannot believe Gwen didn't make it to the car," John spoke with anguish. "What happened to her?"

"They caught her, John," Rachel was not pleased either.

"We should not have left her," John muttered.

"Don't worry about Gwen," Rachel spoke with compassion. "We had no choice. I saw everything, Gwen allowed them to catch her in order for you to escape. Had she not led them away from the exit through the perimeter fences, you might not have gotten out either. There was nothing we could do for her."

John knew Rachel was right, they could not have waited longer, the guards were already firing at them. "What went wrong?"

Rachel turned to him with shared concern. "She is all right, John. They have her in custody, she is safe now."

John sat back and closed his eyes.

"They may hold her for trial, but you can rest assured Gwen's father will hire the best of lawyers. He will have her out of jail in no time. It is probably better for her this way. Should you and I get out alive, we shall be hunted as fugitives for the rest of our lives."

As if to reaffirm Rachel's words, the wail of sirens sounded to their rear. Looking back, they saw the flashing lights of white, blue-striped, police cars, angry in pursuit.

Actually Rachel had no intention of being caught, or living the life of a fugitive either. She had money stashed in Argentina. If they could just escape CCAFS, she would take John to Argentina. They could assume new identities there, start all over with new lives. She glanced at John and felt a moment of weakness. Rachel just knew she could be happy spending the rest of her life with John.

"We'll never make the South Gate," John lamented. "Not with SPs in pursuit, they will radio ahead and seal off all exterior gates."

"Then we shall have to crash through," Rachel spoke emotionally.

"No, turn right instead, I will show you where, and head for the NASA Causeway. It's a closer gate and perhaps we can make it through onto the NASA side before they seal up the base."

Ten miles down the road they shot into the congested CCAFS industrial area, veering right onto Hangar Road and then making an immediate hard right onto Industry Road toward KSC and NASA. Rachel swerved into the opposite lane, to pass a car stopped at the intersection, and overshot clear onto the sidewalk. As they exited the industrial area out onto the NASA Causeway across the Banana

River, Rachel began to pick up speed again, undaunted by the sight of a closed gate ahead. The small gate between NASA and CCAFS was rarely manned and the guards had not had sufficient time to set up barricades.

Rachel hit the gate at ninety mph, blasting through easily. The car swerved wildly at first, and John thought for sure they were going into the drink, but Rachel regained control and begin to accelerate even faster. "Are we off the base?" she screamed.

"Hardly," John replied. Behind him he could see NASA security police scrambling to join their air force counterparts in pursuit. They were literally flying down the narrow strip of land across the Banana River, the water close on each side of the road's shoulder. Although they had momentarily left their pursuers behind, John knew they were far from being off the facilities. "The main gates exiting NASA will soon be sealed off also," he informed his partner.

"Which way?" Rachel screamed, as they flew over a rounded drawbridge, lifting completely off the ground with all four tires. To the north, up the Banana River, they could see the twin Titan launch towers, a column of smoke faintly discernible at the base of LP-55.

"There is an intersection with Highway 3, which leads toward NASA's south gate, coming up shortly," John directed, as they sped past a set of buildings, including the famous NASA headquarters for KSC. John considered the northern exits off NASA, which would be less heavily guarded, in some cases just a fence separating Merritt Island National Wildlife Refuge, but that would leave them trapped a long way out from the nearest population area, Titusville.

"Which way? This is no time for indecision," Rachel yelled again, as they approached the overpass of Highway 3.

"Straight!" John cried, causing Rachel to speed through the intersection. "Perhaps we can hide among the crowds at the Kennedy Spaceport Visitor Center."

"No," Rachel moaned. "We cannot hide there, they will find us eventually. We have to get off."

"There it is!" John shouted, and Rachel swerved left, passing a tour bus then cutting across the intersection and taking the tourist center turnoff.

Slowing as she drove into the crowded parking lots, Rachel was directed by John to Parking Area 2, directly in front of a blue girder arch, marking the entrance to the front of the tourist buildings. Off to the left was a life-size mockup of the Space Shuttle and a few other space-related static displays. It was a hot summer day and the visitor center was jammed with crowds. They parked illegally near the front entrance.

Rachel jumped out of the car, scooping up a change of clothes from the back seat. John exited also, staring at her in seeming bewilderment. They had traversed the fourteen miles from LP-55 to the NASA Visitor Center in what seemed like scarcely minutes. He wondered how Airman Jorgensen was doing, crammed in the trunk of their Grand Am.

"Come on," Rachel called, and sprinted toward the main entrance.

John caught up with Rachel just as she entered the main doors to the visitor center. Inside was a blue lobby packed with tourists. There were information desks and large digital display boards showing the times for rides and shows.

"The bathrooms?" Rachel clutched at John's arm.

"I don't know."

"Over there," Rachel spotted a dark corridor where stuffed nocturnal animals could be viewed. It was part of a Merritt Island National Wildlife Refuge display, a pitch for saving endangered species. They ran into the dark hallway. There were several tourists inside, only visible when a display periodically lit up to show a natural habitat.

"Quick," Rachel undid the zipper along her back and stepped out of her dress. Pulling down her slip next, she quickly donned a pair of bright yellow shorts and a sheer, almost transparent, yellow blouse.

John gulped in surprise, as did the other tourists present, moving away in shock, amazed at her brazen actions. Rachel had brought John's change of clothes also, a pair of jeans, a brightly flowered tourist shirt, and a pair of tennis shoes. He followed Rachel's lead and quickly changed also.

Once dressed, Rachel disguised herself with a red frizzy wig and large yellow sunglasses. She handed John a pair of sunglasses too, and a Dodgers baseball cap. They abandoned their former clothes on the floor and hastily exited the nocturnal display, pushing past several startled Japanese tourists.

Security Police were just entering the building, scaring Rachel and John out the back door into the Spaceport Square. Passing a character dressed in an astronaut suit, who was shaking hands and posing for pictures with tourists, they circled left through the outdoor static rocket displays and back around to the parking lots. Unfortunately the police had identified their car and were attempting to open the trunk with a crowbar, alarmed by the noises emanating from Rita Jorgensen locked inside.

Retreating back into the crowds thronging Spaceport Square, they hurried to avoid capture. Attracted to the lines waiting for NASA tour buses, they fled the Square toward the east and ran through to the out-of-town bus parking areas. The evening was drawing on and many of those buses were loading up for the journey back home. Rachel was drawn to one Greyhound bus in particular, being boarded by elderly people. The bus was from a retirement home in Miami and was about ready for the journey home.

Hoping not to attract attention, John and Rachel joined the older tourists and boarded. Most of the seats near the front were taken, so they sat quietly in the back. As the last of the real passengers straggled on board, the bus driver, who was also in charge of the group, entered to take a head count.

"We are having a slight delay," the portly driver announced, he was almost as old as most of the passengers. "NASA is going to close down the gates for a routine security exercise. While we are waiting, let's make sure everyone is present. I trust we will be on our way shortly."

Rachel was watching out the window as gray NASA police cars with a gold insignia on the doors, white air force police cars with a thick blue strip and blue insignia, and navy blue pickups containing air force military police in combat uniforms, swarmed the vicinity with increasingly greater and greater numbers.

Swearing softly, she turned to John, "We cannot wait any longer." Slowly rising to her feet, with one hand inside her purse, closing about the handle of her pistol, Rachel stepped into the aisle and walked toward the driver.

"Do I know you?" the man looked at Rachel with puzzlement.

Rachel did not answer, approaching until almost pressed up against the man.

"Shut up," she whispered menacingly, exposing her small Firestar automatic to his view.

The driver felt the color drain from his face. "Whatever you say, whatever you say," he pleaded, falling into his seat behind the wheel.

Rachel turned to a frail older lady in the aisle seat behind the driver, "Might I sit here?" she asked politely.

"Why no, I always sit in the front. In fact, I came back early just to insure I could have this seat."

"Lady!" there was desperation and fear in the driver's voice. "Please move to the rear!"

"Well, I never," the elderly woman complained grudgingly as she vacated the seat.

"Now drive," Rachel sat at the edge of her chair, leaning forward so her breath was hot against the frightened old man's ear.

As the bus lurched forward, John joined them, squatting in the aisle next to Rachel. He directed the driver out to NASA Parkway and then south on Highway 3, toward the southernmost entrance.

They reached Gate 2 without mishap, but there discovered a line of twenty to thirty halted cars, unable to exit. Heavy duty eight-foot gates, reinforced with steel cable, blocked the road with concrete barriers to each side.

"Pull into the oncoming lane and approach the gate," Rachel ordered. Drawing her Firestar, she pressed the barrel into the nape of the driver's neck. A lady to the side screamed at the sight of that handgun. "Everyone quiet," Rachel shouted, suddenly raising her automatic pistol in the air for all to see. "No noise! I don't want to hurt anyone! Now, everyone put your heads down."

The driver shook his head with despair.

"Go," Rachel commanded. "If we don't get through, I'm putting a bullet in the back of your head."

The big bus lurched forward again, out into the opposite lane. Passing the parked cars ahead of it in line, the bus drew forward until alongside the foremost car, a burgundy Corvette convertible. A puzzled NASA security guard approached the bus, perplexed by their rudeness at passing the other cars in line. As the door opened and he stepped into the bus, he was greeted with a loaded gun in the face.

"Get in here," Rachel demanded, stepping up to the startled NASA guard. She could see two other guards out by the gate, staring toward them curiously.

Rachel relieved the man of his revolver, handing John her Firestar. "Keep an eye on the driver," she ordered, her voice husky with excitement. Then she rammed the guard's revolver into his stomach, causing him to double over in surprise, gasping for breath.

"Stand up straight and put your hands in the air. Let's hope your friends cooperate, or you're dead!"

They exited the bus, the guard first with hands held high, Rachel following behind with the gun in his back.

"Sam, Edward, put down you weapons," the guard desperately called out to his comrades.

Caught off guard, they surrendered readily. "Okay," Rachel took charge. "One of you open the gate, the other two lie flat on the ground. Throw your weapons to the side. Move!"

As the trembling guards complied, Rachel's eye was attracted to the Corvette parked alongside the bus. It was a burgundy-colored modified convertible, 1986 L82 model. Rachel had always liked Corvettes. She approached the driver, a fifty-year-old NASA executive dressed in an expensive suit.

Suddenly they were distracted by the wail of police sirens. It was a navy blue air force SP truck coming to reinforce the NASA contingent at that gate. Rachel was not worried yet, she had the element of surprise on her side. Before the startled military SPs could react to the astonishing tableau before their eyes, Rachel fired a well-aimed shot through the truck's windshield, directly between the two sergeants. As the truck screeched to a halt, she was at the driver's window, revolver cocked and pointed at the man's temple.

Disarming the military SPs, Rachel and John each took an automatic M-16 rifle. Under Rachel's direction, the gates were opened, the convertible Corvette driven through, and the bus positioned to block the entrance. Opening the hood of the bus, Rachel placed a bullet into the distributor cap. Then she walked alongside the bus, shooting out the wheels with her M-16. Next she shot out the wheels and the radio on the SP truck. No one raised a hand to stop her. John was amazed at Rachel's mastery over the situation, her indisputable dominance over all those present.

As they sped south down Highway 3 in their stolen Corvette, Rachel smiled at John and laughed. They were actually going to make it. John was slumped in his seat as if totally drained. When he noticed her staring at him, he smiled back. Rachel felt euphoric, she just knew they were free.

As the mighty Corvette accelerated down the road, picking up speed, Rachel's red wig suddenly blew off, allowing her natural hair to blow unrestrained in the wind. "The nearest big city, which way?" she called out cheerfully.

"Orlando, but the Beeline is too open. Just continue straight into Cocoa and we'll take the back roads instead."

Rachel smiled again. Orlando, once they reached the city no one would find them, she would see to that. Perhaps they could even take a day to see Disneyworld. No one would think of looking for them there. It would be fun to visit Disneyworld with John.

"We have to stop by camp," John interrupted her thoughts, speaking loudly over the wind.

"What! Why?" Rachel questioned.

"I need the Goldsmith documents. It's the only way to justify what we just did."

"We can't," Rachel protested. "It's too risky."

"No," John said firmly. "They must be sent to the press. The world must know. If we don't, Gwen will go to jail."

Rachel could see there was no use arguing. She tried to justify the stop in her own mind, but was having a hard time. It did seem important for Gwen's sake. Jetty Park seemed like a fairly safe refuge anyway, and they could change cars while there.

"Besides," John continued, "one direction is just as good as another."

Despite a sinking feeling in her stomach, Rachel turned east on Highway 528 toward the now familiar beach cities. They would have to move quickly. It shouldn't take long though, John had buried the top-secret documents by their tents.

Slowing to a moderately fast speed, they recrossed the Banana River via the Bennett Causeway and turned south on A1A into the narrow strip of land running parallel to the coast. On that bit of thin land were the cities of Cocoa Beach, Cape Canaveral, and also Jetty Park Campgrounds.

As they drove down George J. King Boulevard and then Jetty Park Road, nearing the campground entrance, Rachel spotted a maroon van parked by their tents. Someone had parked pretty close. Taking precautions, Rachel pulled up next to the store and gift shop, just inside the entrance, and parked.

"What's the matter?" John questioned, wondering why she had stopped there.

"Nothing," Rachel remarked. "You get the documents. I'll buy some supplies for the trip and then pull the car up."

John climbed out of the Corvette without another thought and headed for the tents to get his shovel. Rachel watched him go, her fingers closing nervously about the steering wheel. That van was parked awfully close. Feeling too apprehensive to wait, Rachel exited the car and followed John at a distance, trying to keep under cover. She feared for John's safety, a deep swell of emotions that troubled her as much as the ominous van. She had to protect John, nothing could be allowed to hurt him.

As John Hughes approached the familiar dome tents, he was alarmed to hear a muffled noise. Rounding the first tent, John was paralyzed by a startling sight. There was Eleanor, his sweet wife from Tulsa. She had a gag tied over her mouth and was roped to a tree with her hands pulled tight behind her back. All Eleanor had on was one of John's own flannel shirts, she was even barefoot.

With a cry of concern, John raced foolhardily to Eleanor's side. She was shaking her head back and forth, her eyes swollen from crying. She was obviously near hysteria. Frantically John tugged at the nylon rope holding her bound to the tree. He located the knots, but they would not pull loose in his fumbling fingers, he needed a knife. John grasped the gag across his wife's mouth and pulled it down over her chin.

"No, John, no," Eleanor sputtered, gasping and choking for breath.

John heard a mechanical sliding noise behind him, the frightening sound of a shotgun being readied for firing. He spun around to see a large man with a 12 gauge Winchester Model 1200 Defender shotgun, having just emerged from inside the tent where he had been waiting. The man leveled the Winchester at John's chest and Eleanor screamed.

John saw other campers staring in their direction and then running for cover. He felt the blood drain from his face as the man grinned fiendishly and then chuckled at John's dismay.

"Need a knife?" the man tossed a pocket knife at John's feet, the barrel of the shotgun wavering in a tight circular motion. Taking the knife, his hands shaking almost uncontrollably, John cut Eleanor's ropes, freeing her. She fell into his arms and they embraced.

"How touching," Ostermann remarked cruelly. "Where is Rachel Maris?"

John held Eleanor tightly, trying to provide comfort, turning her so that she was behind him. "I don't know, I was alone."

"Don't lie to me," the man raised his shotgun abruptly, pointing it at John and Eleanor's faces, causing them to shrink back against the tree in alarm. John wished he hadn't left his M-16 back in the Corvette.

"I have been listening on the police band," Ostermann challenged. "You and Rachel had a nice little party out at the launch base. They reported the escape of one female and one male. They know you're off the base and they know you have stolen a Corvette."

"Okay," John admitted. "Please don't shoot."

"Stall just a little longer," Rachel Maris pleaded beneath her breath. She was working her way closer from tree to tree. Unfortunately she too had left her M-16 and also her Firestar in the Corvette. Rachel however, always kept knives on hand, and she was already within throwing range. A little closer and she would have a sure throw, then she would bury a Viper in the back of that madman's skull.

Was Ostermann crazy? He wasn't even trying to hide his actions. Frantic people were running all over the campground. The police would surely be notified by someone in the office. Just a little closer. Hold on John, just a little closer.

Suddenly the thump-thump whirl of chopper blades sounded overhead and a military helicopter passed low over the trees, very low. They spotted the Corvette and swung around, then sighted the man with a shotgun leveled at a trembling couple.

"This is the police!" a loudspeaker blared. "Throw down your weapon and surrender." There was a special forces soldier seated behind an open door with an M-16 pointed downward.

Rachel saw the sudden panic on Ostermann's face. "No," she screamed, knowing the look, seeing him raise his Winchester shotgun to fire on John and his wife.

She had no time to hesitate, "Over here Ostermann!" Rachel screamed, and leaped out from behind her cover.

Ostermann spun and saw Rachel Maris, the object of his hate. She was in the act of throwing a knife at him. Not caring enough to dodge for cover, he swung the barrel of his Winchester around and blasted away, firing before she could release one of those lethal blades. He saw Rachel Maris go down, the shot catching her full in the stomach, and he smiled. Then a burst of automatic fire from the helicopter above cut short his glee, knocking Ostermann to the ground in a hail of bullets. In a sudden wave of panic and despair, he died in gruesome agony with shotgun in hand.

"No! Rachel!" John cried out, as he saw Rachel Maris take the shotgun load full on, blood flying as she flew backwards, sprawling onto the ground.

He rushed to her side. She was still alive, but blood was flowing from her profusely. She was dying. No one could live through that. John fell to his knees at Rachel's side, his vision blurred with tears. He lifted her head to provide comfort. In the distance police cars were wailing into the park. He saw Eleanor standing nearby, an awkward expression on her face.

Rachel was dying. John cradled her head, fear contorting his face. She tried to speak, but could not talk. John bent closer and she managed to whisper, "I love you, John." Then her body fell limp.

68

Dan Newby and Andrew Maconey were among the first wave to arrive at Jetty Park Campgrounds, as that normally peaceful tourist site was suddenly flooded with activity: local police cars, air force security police, FBI agents, CIA intelligence officers, and even the United States Coast Guard. Almost instantly the isolated little park became more crowded than Disneyworld on a sunny holiday.

Annette, alert at the FCC, had keyed in on clues that something big was amiss at CCAFS. When the airwaves began broadcasting the immediate closure of all gates, she began contacting her people. Annette worked their communications network like a real professional, announcing each new development with uncharacteristic earnestness.

Annette knew it was Hughes and Maris when an APB hit the police band, alerting the local authorities to set up a dragnet for a man and woman fleeing the south entrance of NASA in a stolen Corvette. The description fit John Hughes and Rachel Maris, it had to be them. Annette relayed the message to her people that an attempt had been made to sabotage the Titan IV.

Newby and Maconey took one of the rental cars and headed north up Atlantic Avenue to aid in the search, along with half the agents in that area and anyone else that could reach a car. Keeping in close touch with Annette at the FCC, they learned with alarm of a terrorist attack out on LP-55, reportedly with explosives, and also of an attempt to unleash a cloud of toxic gasses. One terrorist had been apprehended, but the other two had escaped through a NASA gate.

It did not take long for the dragnet to locate the fugitives though. When the police band broadcast the need for an officer at Jetty Park Campgrounds, to investigate reports of an armed man threatening campers with a shotgun, Newby knew it was them, it had to be. Military helicopters, already sweeping to the east and west, were dispatched to the area, arriving almost immediately.

Driving there without delay, Newby and Maconey joined the growing crowds. Pushing through a gaggle of police officers, Newby surveyed the carnage with dismay. Rachel Maris, his own Rachel Maris, was lying flat on her back in the tall grass near some camping tents. A rookie police officer was desperately trying to administer first aid, but her entire front torso was a mass of blood-soaked, tattered clothes, and he was having trouble finding pressure points to stop the massive hemorrhaging. Rachel was still breathing, and suffering, which made the scene all the more sickening, as she lay limp, moaning, in shock, dying.

Newby turned away, feeling an urge to vomit. He could not watch; the stark reality of the scene was horrifying. Feeling dizzy, he bent over, but then bile filled his mouth, causing him to straighten back up. He felt light-headed, the world was spinning. Beyond Rachel lay Randy Ostermann's body, riddled with M-16 bullet wounds from the helicopter. Ostermann's Winchester shotgun lay in the grass at his side, the one he had used to shoot Rachel. No one was crowding around Ostermann, he was already dead.

Randy Ostermann was one of Newby's men also. He had known and worked with the guy for years. Odd, Newby thought, how he did not mourn Ostermann's passing, he did not feel the same anguish over Ostermann that he felt for Rachel. Still, it seemed obscene the way no one bothered to cover Ostermann's mutilated body, leaving him sprawled in the grass where he had fallen.

Newby felt a twisted moment of satisfaction at Ostermann's violent demise, then became sickened at himself for such morbid, although justified, feelings. Ostermann had been the real traitor, he was the one that had betrayed his fellows, working for Maxwell. Not poor Rachel, Rachel Maris was innocent.

Newby stared at Rachel's prone form, watching in shock as an ambulance arrived and white clothed paramedics bent momentarily over Rachel, and then gingerly placed her on a stretcher to load into their ambulance.

How could Newby ever forgive himself. To think he had sent Rachel to her death. He had betrayed her as surely as Ostermann had betrayed them. Now she lay bleeding her life out onto the grass. She died trying to complete her mission, to serve Newby, and it was nothing but a vain plot against her.

"Good-bye Rachel," Newby cried, knowing he would never see her again. "I'm sorry." He watched the ambulance receding down the road, his eyes burning as he stared without blinking at the flashing emergency lights.

"There goes Hughes," Maconey spoke, nudging his Chief.

Newby had not even been aware of Maconey's presence. They watched the police taking John Hughes into custody. His wrists were handcuffed behind his back and they were forcing him into the rear seat of a police cruiser. Newby watched the engineer's wife, Eleanor Hughes, rushing up to the window. Staring inside, she exchanged looks of care and dismay with her spouse. John Hughes seemed resolved to his fate, a stony look upon frozen facial features, but his poor wife looked scared.

As the police drove away with Hughes, Newby approached Eleanor from behind, "Mrs. Hughes," he spoke to her, feeling utterly sorry for her plight.

Eleanor spun around to face Newby, raw anger in her voice, "YOU! What have you done to my husband?"

Newby cringed at Eleanor's words, her face, stained wet with tears, was contorted with anger and he could not blame her.

"Why did you allow this to happen?" Eleanor shouted. "You could have stopped him!" She had a look of pure hatred on her face, hatred and disgust.

Newby stood before her speechless. She was right, they could have arrested the engineer back in Tulsa. Dan Newby accepted complete blame for this whole ugly horror. It was all his fault for planning and conducting the sick operation.

"Can we take you anywhere?" Maconey offered lamely. "The courthouse? Your hotel?"

Eleanor looked at him spitefully, then turned and stomped away. Once a short distance off, she halted to bury her head in her arms, sobbing with uncontrollable dismay.

Feeling totally numb, Newby turned and walked away too. He felt dead, like his limbs were detached. Noticing Maconey following behind, Newby directed him to take the car back to the condo. Newby just wanted to be alone, to hide.

• • •

Late the next morning, Andrew Maconey trepidly rapped on the door to condo 610 at the Sandcastle. It was already unbearably hot and humid outside, as if he didn't already feel uncomfortable enough. Maconey had no idea if Newby was even in, he had not seen his despondent boss return to the Sandcastle the night before, even after waiting up late into the night watching.

Just as Maconey was about to turn away, the door to Newby's condo creaked open. Maconey was startled by his boss' appearance, Newby looked as if he were still wearing yesterday's clothes, except for his conspicuously bare feet. Although not one to wear expensive tailored suits, Dan Newby had always dressed in a neat, clean, professional manner. Now his clothes were wrinkled, his shirt-tail hung out, he had not shaved, and it was almost eleven o'clock on a paid work day.

"Come in," Newby offered dryly, shuffling out of the doorway.

"You look terrible," Maconey spoke honestly, as he entered the condo unit.

"I don't feel so great either," Newby responded apologetically.

Maconey forced himself to ignore the strong odor of whiskey breath. "When did you get back last night?" he asked Newby with concern.

"Late."

"What did you do, walk all the way from Jetty Park?"

"As a matter of fact, yes," Newby seated himself on a decorative plaid couch in the main room. He had a large sliding glass door overlooking the ocean from the sixth floor. The furnishings and decor were immaculate, contrasting sharply with his slovenly appearance.

Maconey could just picture his friend, walking along the beach through the middle of the night, miles and miles, back to the condominium. "We all have reservations back to Dallas," Maconey informed him.

"Sure, that's fine," Newby shook his head absently.

Maconey wasn't asking permission though. "The home office has been in touch this morning. They have recalled all of us. We have orders to return immediately."

Newby was unresponsive.

"I took the liberty of booking you on the same flight as myself, Delta Airlines at 2:55." Maconey laid a package of travel tickets on the end table next to an ornate lamp. "By the way, they have impounded all our records back in Dallas, at the office. The agency is going to conduct an internal investigation."

"Fine," Newby responded absently.

To Maconey's surprise, the news did not seem to phase Newby. Maconey perceived the catastrophic events of that morning as the end of their world. He spoke to his boss, "The reports are, that Hughes made it to the satellite. The explosions alongside some fuel tanks were merely a distraction. No one knows what damage he has done. The launch is on hold."

Newby was not the least surprised to hear that Hughes got in, he'd had Rachel Maris to run his operation. Rachel had been one of the best, with her aid they had eluded capture from the preventive dragnets of a dozen different agencies, and then penetrated one of the most highly guarded facilities in the free world. Rachel Maris was unbeatable, it was no wonder she got Hughes inside.

"You go on back to Dallas," Newby spoke at last. "I'm going to Langley. Andrew, you are in charge during my absence. See to it that everyone cooperates with the investigation, do not withhold information or try to hide anything."

"You're going to Langley to fight this," Maconey's face brightened. "Take me with you?"

"No, I am going this one alone," Newby's mind was set. "Oh, but, Andrew?"

"Yes?"

"Thanks for your support over the years."

By five o'clock Newby was touching down at Dulles International outside of Washington D.C. Within an hour Newby had rented an Avis car and was driving to the CIA headquarters building in Langley, Virginia, on the banks of the Potomac, via the George Washington Memorial Parkway.

Parking the rental car, Newby approached the concrete building with a sense of anger quickening his steps. Glancing at the statue of

Nathan Hale, he pressed on into the main lobby. The biblical quote carved into the marble wall made Newby all the more angry, "And ye shall know the truth and the truth shall make you free." They had been kept from the truth by Maxwell and it had destroyed them.

Upstairs at the division offices for Western Hemisphere Operations, a state of chaotic pandemonium was in progress. Even after normal quitting time, personnel were scurrying about with great haste, as if a massive evacuation was in progress, somewhat similar to Saigon under the onslaught of the Communist advance.

Newby spotted Maxwell's personal secretary, Joan Moore, a competent middle-aged executive secretary who had been with Maxwell for a decade. She was bent over the bottom drawer of a file cabinet searching for certain files. Approaching from behind, Newby spoke to her back, "I need to see Mr. Maxwell."

"He is not available," Joan replied, not looking in his direction.

"It is important," Newby spoke urgently, causing the woman to turn and glance at him.

"Oh, Mr. Newby," Joan stood up, recognizing him now, appreciative of an old familiar face with which to commensurate their misery.

"What's going on here, Joan?" Newby asked.

"We are being shut down. All operations are suspended. There is the threat of an investigation and we think the records might be impounded at any moment. There is talk Congress is initiating subpoenas."

Newby could picture a similar scene of confusion back at his own offices in Dallas. So, Congress was going to investigate. Well, a Congressional witch-hunt was definitely in order for this one, unfortunately it would turn all of the agency inside out.

"So, where is Maxwell?" Newby tried again.

"I really don't know," Joan answered with exasperation. "He called in this morning and gave orders to close up shop. Rumors have been flying, I really have no idea where he is."

"At a time like this," Newby spoke his thoughts out loud, "one would think he would be here."

"You should talk, why aren't you back at your office?" Joan countered good naturedly, defending her employer.

Newby frowned, she had a point. "Who is leading the investigation?"

"Roland Levasseur," Joan replied.

He was one of Boruchowitz's chief lieutenants. A good company man, but a real ivy leaguer. "Thanks, Joan," Newby said, and took his leave. He had a lot to think about.

Driving to the Jefferson Memorial in downtown Washington D.C., Newby stood in awe of the monument to Thomas Jefferson. Now there was a true hero. Newby had always greatly admired Jefferson, ever since high school when he had first started to develop an interest in history. As Newby had grown older he had found other, real life heroes. Henry Maxwell had been one of those.

The next morning Newby found his way to Roland Levasseur's office back at Langley. An aide led Newby to a small conference room with mahogany paneling on the walls and plush orange carpet on the floor. The table and chairs were solid oak and of colonial design.

Joining him shortly, came Roland Levasseur, appearing fresh and quite chipper. He carried with him a small notebook and a tape recorder. Levasseur was an older man, gray hair, stooped slightly at the shoulders, a capable investigator with a vast experience bank of well-learned lessons from which to draw.

"Good morning, Mr. Newby," he greeted, extending a long-fingered bony hand to shake. Smiling affably, he took a chair next to Newby, rather than across the table.

"Thank you for taking the time to..." Newby stammered.

"No trouble, no trouble at all. What can I do for you, Mr. Newby?"

"Well, I don't know where to start. What is the reason for recalling my people from Florida and impounding our records?"

"Excuse me a minute," Levasseur looked concerned. "Do you mind if I record this conversation?"

"No," Newby responded. He knew their conversation would be secretly recorded anyway, by hidden mikes.

"Now," Levasseur folded his arms, "you ask for the purpose of the investigation. Let me explain by asking you a few questions first. For instance, why was an operation run against a division chief within our own agency, and started well before official approval was even received? Better yet, why was an extensive investigation conducted on that division chief, and continued for years, compiling unauthorized computer data on all aspects of his career and those associated with him? Let me go on," Levasseur was not pausing for answers to his questions.

"Why was *false evidence* compiled on a list to implicate this man, and an intelligence officer in your own section, in a conspiracy? I'm not finished; why was the recovery of secret documents compromised, no, more than that, encouraged? We are now looking at the possible loss of a vital defense satellite, a loss we can ill afford right now. Answer this, why was Bernie Goldsmith's murder covered up? One of your own intelligence officers is also dead now, and another is in a coma, why?"

Newby shut his eyes for a moment to think. It was unbelievable how much they already knew. Obviously Levasseur's investigation had been going on for some time now, perhaps even from before the commencement of Operation Carrier Pigeon.

It dawned on Newby that the only reason the DDO had authorized Operation Carrier Pigeon, was to see just how far Maxwell would go. To think, they were letting the man hang himself, and using Newby and his people to do it.

Newby felt bitter, the way they had manipulated him was unforgivable. People were dead now, careers had been ruined. What was it all for? Office political struggles? Fighting among the upper management for advancement and power? Was this what the agency was turning into without the threat of a worthy enemy like the Soviet Union?

"May I speak freely?" Newby asked.

"Please do, I am here to help."

Newby disliked Levasseur, the man had no idea what they had been through. He did not know Rachel Maris, lying in intensive care at some strange hospital, in a coma, dying. She was just a name to Levasseur.

Levasseur was just doing his job though. Newby commenced his debriefing. He told everything, not just the facts, but his suspicions, his conclusions, everything. He knew his testimony would destroy Henry Maxwell. The traitor deserved it though, Newby felt betrayed. Rachel Maris had lost her life just to further Maxwell's vain power struggle against his rival the Baron.

When he had finished, Newby was drained. His body felt more exhausted than if he had run a mile.

Levasseur seemed satisfied, "We appreciate your cooperation." He switched off the tape recorder.

"I can go now?" Newby asked. He felt as if a burden had been taken off his back.

"Of course, there is no need to waste any more of your time. You realize we will need to speak with you again, in the course of the investigation."

Newby had half-expected to be arrested.

Levasseur continued, "I've been authorized to inform you, that you have been released of your responsibilities as Section Chief of the Southwest U.S. Special Support Office."

The news was crushing, even though Newby had anticipated it. His career with the company was over.

"Go home to Dallas. Get some rest, we'll be in touch."

Newby wondered what Victoria would think. How would he make a living? He didn't have enough years for retirement.

"We appreciate your cooperation," Levasseur said again, extending that bony hand for another handshake. "It speaks well of you."

"I didn't tell you anything you did not already know, did I?" Newby asked, as he shook Levasseur's hand. It felt limp like a dead fish.

"Have a safe flight home," Levasseur smiled, ignoring Newby's question, his face impassive.

Choking back an insane urge to cry like a child, Newby turned to go. It was all over.

69

Friday, August 31 at Cape Canaveral AFS, the final launch countdown had commenced on schedule for a top-secret Titan IV carrying a covert SIGS satellite. Perched high atop the Titan stack, encapsulated by an enormous protective payload fairing, the fragile billion-dollar spy satellite was prepared to fly from its mother's nest.

Anxious air force and civilian aerospace dignitaries watched with breathless anticipation as the countdown clock ticked inexorably closer to L-0. Inside the SCC (Spacecraft Control Center) building, trained technicians monitored vital statistics and last-minute system checks.

No one, regardless of expertise, could ever say without doubt that a risky space launch would be successful. There were too many variables, too many factors to consider, an almost inconceivable number of failure modes. Launches did go on through, risking careers on the successful outcome, and the required go-ahead approvals had been given for this Titan IV.

On this particular launch, tension was acute. After discovering that the fanatical terrorists had indeed penetrated their maximum-security perimeters, panic had initially set in. What had the mad engineer from Krang Enterprises done? His avowed goal was clear, to sabotage the Titan launch.

With awful dread of what might have been done, a meticulous search had commenced. Anxious technicians and engineers carefully pored over every accessible square inch of delicate hardware. His presence was readily evident, the protective wrapping on several boxes had been tampered with, sensors, antennas, the list was quite comprehensive. Although, to the deepening consternation of all, no evidence of destructive maliciousness could be found. Nothing seemed out of place, nothing was damaged, no explosives had been left. If they could only uncover the damage, then it could be fixed. What had John Hughes done?

As the technical experts probed for the end results of the Hughes break-in, experts of another type began their work. Strapped to a polygraph machine, FBI interrogation teams applied the thumbscrews to extract some lead or clue from the man responsible, John Hughes.

The engineer was immovable. He freely discussed the reasons behind his seeming madness, and was quite open concerning the events of the past month, leading up to his entry into the UES and narrow escape from CCAFS and NASA security police. Concerning activities inside the UES though, he invariably shut his mouth and refused to go any further. Normal means of questioning did not prove sufficient to elicit the needed answers.

Unfortunately, political considerations prevented forcing an answer in any sure way, such as drugs, threats, or possibly even torture. Making his influence felt, the father of one of the terrorists was a man of high political standing within the intelligence community. Compounding an already difficult situation, when the deceptions involved in Operation Carrier Pigeon came to light and the threat of public embarrassment became very real, John Hughes was removed from the hands of the unsympathetic FBI agents, the only ones that might have eventually gotten to the truth.

Protected by civil liberties and a skillful set of highly paid lawyers, who disregarded any consequences to national security with negligent impunity, John Hughes was spared any unjust pressure at the hands of FBI interrogators.

Hughes was given an opportunity to tell his story, to try and expose the evil cancer attached to the belly of the SIGS satellite. Of course, all recordings of his testimony had to be impounded, for the benefit of national security.

The captured AFA cadet also talked freely. She had nothing to hide and saw no harm in revealing all she knew about the matter. Unfortunately her role in the attack had been limited to aiding John Hughes reach the SV. She knew nothing about what he had planned to do once on the inside.

Everything hinged upon the engineer, and he was demanding the total public exposure of the SIGS satellite and all its subsystems. He actually wanted a Congressional inquiry to delve into the mission of the satellite and all related piggybacks. Of course the air force could never agree to such a compromise, Congress was notorious for leaks. It was unthinkable. SIGS-4 was a top-secret highly classified project that could never be exposed to the public.

Hughes was equally stubborn. Despite the multitude of documents and technical drawings presented before his face, he would not accept their attempts to prove there was no DWARS virus. Drawings could easily be sanitized, John Hughes knew; he would not be swayed.

"This is it," Colonel Roe remarked to General Mauvus, commander of air force covert satellite programs. It had been a long tedious year preparing for this moment. By their side stood the chairman of the board of Krang Enterprises and various corporate officers of other associated contractors.

"Heaven only knows if this one will work," Colonel Roe spoke ruefully. Their level of confidence was low, especially in light of the terrorist break-in and their inability to find anything wrong.

Colonel Roe had pushed hard to recommence launch processing, but now, with anxious pains of self doubt, he regretted that decision. There was nothing wrong though, every angle had been reviewed a thousand times over. No one could find a reason not to proceed.

A large portion of the standalone SV testing had been repeated, and Titan Centaur functional testing was reapplied, but no anomalies surfaced. Even the integrated testing on the total launch vehicle came up dry. The order could not be delayed; nothing wrong could be found.

Not knowing what else to do, Colonel Roe had given approval to go ahead with RCS tanking operations and final closeout of the forward payload fairing around the seemingly unharmed satellite.

At L-10 days the readiness count commenced and the Centaur LO_2 storage tanks were filled. At L-8 the batteries for the SV were activated. Ordinances power-on checks were performed at L-7 and the Centaur propulsion system was readied. At L-6 the LH_2 storage tanks were filled. At L-5 the airborne instrumentation and telemetry systems were readied. At L-3 the umbilical checks were completed and the electrical systems readied. At L-2 the umbilical and explosive squibs were installed.

Now the final launch countdown commenced, at L-1 day. Flight control checks were performed, IMG (Inertial Measurement Group) calibration, LH_2 and LO_2 system preps, C-band transponder open-look tests, the flight constants loaded, and the guidance aligned. At L-340 minutes, MMC drew back the MST from around the Titan IV. At L-3 hours LP-55 was cleared of all personnel. Fifteen minutes later LO_2 tanking commenced. At L-1.5 hours the LH_2 tanks were filled.

At L-30 minutes, the final count sequence commenced. At L-100 seconds the launch enable was given. At L-75 seconds the terminal countdown started and a multitude of automatic sequences commenced.

At T+0 the fire signal shot up the umbilical, causing the Titan IV SRMs to ignite with fury. Actual liftoff was achieved and the Titan ascent was on its way.

The SRMs ignited first, at T+0 seconds, and at T+0.2 seconds liftoff was achieved. At T+116.4 seconds the Stage 1 liquid rocket engines commenced firing. At T+126.5 seconds SRM separation took place, peeling off from the booster core. At T+229.0 seconds the protective PLF was jettisoned, no longer needed. At T+303.0 seconds Stage 1 was separated and Stage 2 ignited. At T+543.1 seconds Stage 2 separated.

Now it was time for the mighty Centaur to perform its mission. The first burn had an MES (Main Engine Start) at T+556 seconds with MECO (Main Engine Cut-Off) 206.9 seconds later to place the vehicle in park orbit. Second burn lasted five minutes to initiate the transfer orbit, and third burn three minutes to complete the stage vehicle final orbit.

The task was done, the spy satellite had been successfully launched into deep space by the powerful Titan IV launch system, but the SIGS satellite was not safe yet.

The critical acquisition of the satellite by the CSTC MCC had yet to be accomplished. All went according to plan, including the subsequent deployment of the solar arrays and activation, earth and sun capture by the CES and SSS sensors, three-axis stabilization, and finally checkout of the satellite internal subsystems, including the eavesdropping spy sensors.

Now under CSTC control, the satellite had to orbitally maneuver into its highly elliptical, inclined sixty-five degree, final mission orbit. With long dwell times over the Russian continent, and all satellite systems activated and functional, SIGS-4 was ready for mission operations.

Early in the transfer orbit a small piggyback payload separated from the SIGS satellite and moved into a low Earth orbit with a self-contained propulsion system. The tiny SPL-551 space vehicle had a covert mission known only to those who, supposedly in the interest of national security, had the proper security clearances.

Meanwhile the SIGS-4 satellite—Spooky, as it was now known by its CSTC controllers—faithful to her human creators in America, was ready to commence her career of spying on the Russians.

70

Dan Newby sat in his living room, listlessly gazing at the TV. He lived in a comfortable suburban home just off Colt Road on the north side of Dallas. Although nothing extravagant, the house was large enough for Dan Newby and his wife, Victoria. They had four bedrooms, a swimming pool, a large well-equipped kitchen for Victoria, a study for Dan, a nicely furnished living room for entertaining, and a livable well-used family room.

Dan and Victoria Newby had lived in that house for fifteen years now. It was a part of them, their three children had survived their teen years in that home, before moving out to make their own way in the world. Neither Dan nor Victoria could imagine life in a different house. Fortunately the mortgage was clear, for they could never move; Dan Newby used to think his job was permanent too, and now that was gone.

Dan was watching an NFL match-up between the Dallas Cowboys and the Los Angeles Rams. Dallas was hopelessly behind; nevertheless Newby could not bring himself to switch the game off, vainly hoping without faith for some type of miracle. It was not going to happen though, and the minutes just kept counting down. The Cowboys would have to play on through the remainder of the game, even though the contest was lost and the struggle had become futile.

"Daniel," Victoria spoke with concern as she seated herself across the room at her traditional spot upon the couch next to the lamp. She picked up some needlework from off the end table. "Aren't you going out today?"

"Why, Victoria?"

"To look for a job," Victoria was obviously perturbed. "It has been a month now."

"I know, but what can I do? I have mailed out a dozen resumes. It just takes time." Newby tried to be patient, they had been over this so many times before. He really could not blame Victoria though, her security factor had been shattered, just a few years before retirement too. He had let Victoria down.

Sighing, Victoria laid her needlework aside and rose to go in the kitchen. "Dinner will be ready in half an hour," she said.

Dan glanced at his watch. Couldn't she wait till the game was over to serve dinner? He knew better than to ask though. It did not matter anyway, the Cowboys were already finished. They were preparing to punt again even now. He started to switch the TV off but then the cameras focused on the Dallas cheerleaders and Dan left the set on.

When the phone rang, Dan jumped a bit, but then settled back down, ignoring the ringing intrusion upon his thoughts. The call was probably for Victoria anyway. Why did her friends have to call so much, carrying on like his being laid off was such a tragedy?

"Dan, get the phone, I'm trying to cook!" Victoria called from the kitchen.

Stirring as little as possible, Dan picked up the receiver from the phone on the end table. "Hello," he spoke, not revealing his name. Old habits died hard.

"Hello, boss," a pleasantly husky female voice responded on the other line.

Dan almost dropped the phone, it was Rachel Maris, his former employee. "Rachel," he said, the surprise obvious in his voice. "I heard you were released from the hospital."

"Sure," Rachel laughed. "I have been spending so much time in and out of hospitals lately, it has become routine for me."

"I am glad you are okay. How do you feel?" Dan was amazed

that Rachel was calling him. There was no hint of malice or anger in her voice.

"I feel fine, it just hurts when I eat," Rachel joked, "but that does wonders for my figure."

Dan could not imagine Rachel Maris looking any better. She seemed to be in a light-hearted jovial mood. "I guess you heard," he said.

"About your job? Yeah, I heard. Say, boss, I was back in town and thought I would come visit. I am being transferred back to Europe next week. Mind if I stop by this evening?"

Dan was pleased to hear Rachel was back on reassignment, it did a lot to ease his guilt. He was surprised she wanted to come by his house though. The thought was totally unconventional, it just wasn't done. Then Dan remembered, he was not a CIA section chief anymore, just a civilian. "Sure, come on by."

"Great, what time? I could be there in twenty minutes."

"Just a minute," Dan placed the phone down and went searching for Victoria. "Honey, have we got enough dinner for a visitor?"

"Who is it dear?"

"A former employee of mine, from work?"

"Do I know him?"

Dan hated this, why did Victoria have to quiz him before answering his question? Her queries were irrelevant to his original question about how much food she was preparing anyway. "It is not a he," Dan answered, "Rachel Maris, you have met her. Do we have enough food for an extra plate?"

"I'll put in some more spaghetti," Victoria responded. "Tell her, in a half hour." She thought it odd someone from work was coming over, that had never happened before. "Is she the young woman that looks like she came from a communist country?"

"Yes, dear," Dan said with exasperation. "She was born in Romania, but those countries aren't communist anymore."

"Hello, Rachel," Dan hurried back to the phone. "We are having spaghetti, if you want to join us for dinner."

"I would love to," Rachel purred.

"Good, in about a half hour. You have my address? Good, we shall see you then."

As Dan hung up the phone, he suddenly had a dark thought. What if Rachel was only pretending to be friendly? What if she was coming there to mock him and vent her anger? Not in front of

Victoria, not in his own home, hadn't he been humiliated enough? Newby thought about changing his clothes. Rachel always dressed like she was going to a big social event.

When Rachel Maris arrived at the Newby's quaint suburban home, a half hour later than they had expected, Dan was modestly pleased to observe she was wearing a dress of conservative design. She had on an unpretentious, yet fashionable, apron-style dress. There was a hint of gypsy in her jewelry and hairstyle.

The meal evolved into a quite enjoyable time. At first Victoria seemed a bit reserved, but Rachel succeeded in drawing her out and soon had Victoria chatting as if she and Rachel had been friends for years. Dan realized he should have expected that. It made sense, Rachel's social skills were legendary, and of course they would extend to a variety of environments, both humble and grand.

Dan was pleased, he didn't even mind when Victoria told Rachel the story about one of their family camping trips, when a swarm of angry wasps drove Dan out of his shower and chased him clear out of the bathhouse, stark naked. Rachel laughed so hard it gave her the hiccups.

After the meal, Rachel helped Victoria clear the table, much to Dan's astonishment. She did not offer to help with the dishes, but Dan thought just assisting with the clearing was a major accomplishment for Rachel.

Then Rachel asked Dan if they could speak alone. Feeling apprehensive, Dan led Rachel back to his study. They had converted the largest of the spare bedrooms into an office. He had a desk and some furniture, and a PC which he rarely used.

Seating himself behind the desk, Dan watched Rachel shut the door behind her and pull up a chair to face him. It gave him a feeling of old times. "What is on your mind, Rachel?" he questioned, as if she were an employee once more, coming into his office back at work.

Rachel smiled congenially. "Just wanted to talk shop a bit before I left. What have you been occupying your time with, Dan?"

"Oh…well…I am afraid I have not been up to much lately."

"Are you considering any job offers?" Rachel asked.

"Ah…well…yes, there are several possibilities I am pursuing."

"I see," Rachel scooted her chair up to the desk and leaned closer. Dan could almost feel her female presence, she seemed to exude a feminine attraction. He wished she had not shut the door. It was getting stuffy in the room.

"You heard about Mr. Maxwell," Rachel stared into Dan's eyes unrelentingly, probing, feeling him out. "He was suspended from duties also. I think that criminal charges are pending. The Congressional investigation is still underway."

"I knew he was under investigation," Dan squirmed, he felt like he was beginning to sweat. So, old Maxwell got the can too. Dan was glad. He wondered what Rachel was leading up to though.

"There have been a lot of changes," Rachel sat back and crossed her legs, still eyeing Dan intently.

Feeling uncomfortable under her stare, Dan asked, "Hear anything about the Hughes'?"

"What?" Rachel started, thrown off balance by the question.

"I don't get much news anymore," Dan apologized.

"Oh, of course," Rachel smiled. "The cadet is back at the Academy. Her father pulled a few strings, you know the Baron. They dropped all charges against her, and John Hughes too. Considering he didn't really do anything to the satellite, and the launch was successful, it was the least the agency could do for him. We were operating with the best of intentions, you know, having been deceived by that fabricated DWARS hoax. The whole episode had become quite embarrassing for several government agencies. You know the agency, better to forget it ever happened."

"And they realized I was working under orders," Rachel rationalized, excusing her own behavior, causing Dan to flinch nonetheless. Rachel did not seem to notice.

"I am glad," Dan said, feeling guilty once more, although he too had been manipulated. Dan wondered if Rachel had suffered any permanent internal injuries from that shotgun blast. Had she lost a lung, a liver, was she still fertile? She appeared to be fine, but he could not tell for sure.

"So who are you working for?" Dan asked. "Or can you say?" he caught himself.

"No, it's okay," Rachel looked him in the eye again. "I am working for a former boss once more, the Baron!"

The color momentarily drained out of Dan's face. He tried feebly to recover. "I see, that's nice."

Rachel leaned over the desk again, "Actually, with his new assignment as deputy director for operations, the Baron is looking to take on additional personnel, on the side if you know what I mean, from outside the agency."

Dan was speechless, what was Rachel getting at?

"You know," Rachel continued, "John Hughes, he has joined the agency now. The man showed a lot of potential in our little adventure, don't you think? His career as an engineer for aerospace defense companies was destroyed." For a moment, when speaking of John, Rachel's eyes seemed to mist over.

Newby was beginning to understand the implied intent of Rachel's words. She was trying to recruit him. The talk of needing additional personnel, of John Hughes joining the CIA, of Hughes' career being ruined, just like Newby's own.

Newby was flabbergasted. Had he and Maconey been right about the Baron all along? Did his secret organization really exist? Was Rachel in reality a covert member of the Baron's society as they had once believed? How he wished Maconey could hear this now.

"What of Maconey?" Dan whispered to Rachel, wondering what she knew of him.

"Oh, he bought a campground in Florida," Rachel said. "I even heard he got married." Looking serious, Rachel decided to throw all pretense aside. "I'll be frank, Dan, although a moment after I leave this room, I'll deny ever having been here."

"As you probably figured out by now, I was sent here to feel you out. The Baron would like you back in the agency, Dan. It can be arranged. Come join us," she spoke pleadingly, like she was sincerely concerned for his welfare. "I can tell you want to, Dan. Your skills are needed, and if you want Maconey for an assistant, we'll bring him back too."

Dan sat motionless, totally astounded. His eyes took on a slightly vacant look.

Rachel sat watching him expectantly for a moment, then her excitement faded. She stood up suddenly, "I can see you are at a loss for words." She touched his hand with her fingers, "I am staying at the Marriott. If you decide to accept our offer, call by twelve tonight."

Dan did not rise to see Rachel to the door, so she let herself out, thanking Victoria for the wonderful meal and the delightful company. Hearing her leave, Dan struggled to his feet in a daze and returned to his comfortable recliner in the living room. His whole body felt like it was in shock.

Switching on the TV, he saw the Cowboy's football game was

still on. It was fourth down and one yard to go for a first down. They were on their own forty. There wasn't much time left on the clock and they were going to go for it. They were still twenty points behind though, even a touchdown was not going to make any difference in the final outcome of the game. It was all so futile, but the game had to go on.

Acronyms

AFA .... Air Force Academy
AFB .... Air Force Base
AFP .... Air Force Program
AFS .... Air Force Station
AGE .... Aerospace Ground Equipment
APB .... All Points Bulletin
ASP .... Armament Systems and Procedures
ATO .... Automatic Turn-On
BX .... Base Exchange
CCAFS ...... Cape Canaveral Air Force Station
CCET .... Centaur Combined Electrical Test
CCQ .... Cadet in Charge of Quarters
CDR .... Critical Design Review
CEA .... Control Electronics Assembly
CES .... Combined Earth Sensors
CIA .... Central Intelligence Agency
CIC .... Cadet In Charge
CPR .... Cardiopulmonary Resuscitation
CRT .... Cathode Ray Tube

CSD .... Chemical Systems Division
CSTC .... Consolidated Space Test Center
DCD .... Dual Command Decoder
DCI .... Director of Central Intelligence
DCU .... Digital Command Unit
DDO .... Deputy Director of Operations
DGH .... Denver General Hospital
DIA .... Defense Intelligence Agency
DoD .... Department of Defense
DSP .... Defense Support Program
DWARS .... Dormant Womb Activated Reproductive Sterilization
E&A .... Building 1733, CCAFS
E&L .... Building 1704, CCAFS
EEAP .... Emergency Evacuation Assembly Point
ELSA .... Emergency Life Support Apparatus
ETR .... Eastern Test Range
FBI .... Federal Bureau of Investigations
FCC .... Field Command Center
FPL .... Florida Power and Light
F-S .... Fairbairn Sykes
G .... Gravity, 32.1725 ft/sec^2
GDSS .... General Dynamics Space Systems
GHz .... Giga-Hertz
GMT .... Greenwich Mean Time
GN&C .... Guidance Navigation and Control
GRMS .... Gravity Root Mean Square
HP .... Hewlett Packard
IAN .... Individual Access Number
IBM .... International Business Machines
ICBM .... Inter-Continental Ballistic Missile
ICD .... Interface Control Document
ID .... Identification
ILC .... Initial Launch Capability
IMG .... Inertial Measurement Group
IMU .... Inertial Measurement Unit
IUS .... Inertial Upper Stage
JCL .... Jet Control Logic
KE .... Krang Enterprises
KGB .... Committee of State Security
KSC .... Kennedy Space Center

L- .... Launch Minus
LAN .... Longitude of the Ascending Node
LH_2 .... Liquid Hydrogen
LO_2 .... Liquid Oxygen
LP .... Launch Pad
LRE .... Liquid Rocket Engine
LVIC .... Launch Vehicle Integration Contractor
MAC .... Military Airlift Command
MCC .... Mission Control Center
MDAC ...... McDonnell Douglas Astronautics Corporation
MECO .... Main Engine Cut-Off
MES .... Main Engine Start
MIS .... Missile Inspection and Storage
MM .... Millimeter
MMC .... Martin Marietta Corporation
MOL .... Manned Orbiting Laboratory
MPH .... Miles Per Hour
MST .... Mobile Service Tower
N_2H_4 .... Nitrogen Tetrahydride (Hydrazine)
N_2O_4 .... Nitrogen Tetroxide (Oxidizer)
NASA .... National Aeronautics and Space Administration
NFL .... National Football League
NiCad .... Nickel Cadmium
NTH .... Nitrogen Tetrahydride (Hydrazine)
NTO .... Nitrogen Tetroxide (Oxidizer)
NUS .... No Upper Stage
OOH .... Orbital Operations Handbook
OSU .... Oklahoma State University
PC .... Personal Computer
PCA .... Permanent Change of Assignment
PDH .... Presbyterian Denver Hospital
PE .... Project Engineer
PLF .... Payload Fairing
PST .... Pacific Standard Time
RCS .... Reaction Control System
RF .... Radio Frequency
RIS .... Receipt Inspection Shop
RPM .... Revolutions Per Minute
RSO .... Range Safety Officer
RV .... Recreational Vehicle

SCE .... Spin Control Electronics
SCC .... Spacecraft Control Center
SIGS .... Signal Intelligence Gathering System
SMAB .... Solid Motor Assembly Building
SP .... Security Police
SPF .... Sunscreen Protection Factor
SPL............ Secondary Payload
SPO .... System Program Office
SRM .... Solid Rocket Motor
SRS .... Segment Ready Storage
SSD .... Space Systems Division
SSS .... Spin Sun Sensor
STLG .... Space Test and Launch Group
SV .... Satellite Vehicle
SVOD........ Space Vehicle Operations Director
T+ .... Take-Off Plus
TC .... Test Conductor
TCU .... Transitional Care Unit
TOPS .... Transistorized Operational Phone System
TT&C .... Telemetry Tracking and Command
UDMH ...... Unsymetrical Dimethyl-Hydrazine
UES .... Universal Environmental Shelter
USAFA ..... United States Air Force Academy
UT .... Umbilical Tower
VAFB .... Vandenberg Air Force Base
VIB .... Vertical Assembly Building
WCE.......... Wheel Control Electronics